THE
SENATOR'S
WIFE

SUE MILLER is the best-selling author of the novels *Lost in the Forest, The World Below, While I Was Gone, The Distinguished Guest, For Love, Family Pictures,* and *The Good Mother*; the story collection *Inventing the Abbotts*; and the memoir *The Story of My Father*. She lives in Boston, Massachusetts.

THE
SENATOR'S
WIFE

SUE MILLER

BLOOMSBURY

LONDON · BERLIN · NEW YORK

First published in Great Britain 2008
This paperback edition published 2009

Copyright © 2008 by Sue Miller

No part of this book may be used or reproduced in any manner
whatsoever without written permission from the Publisher
except in the case of brief quotations embodied in criticial articles or reviews

Bloomsbury Publishing Plc,
36 Soho Square,
London W1D 3QY

www.bloomsbury.com

A CIP catalogue record for this book
is available from the British Library

ISBN 978 1 4088 0431 5

10 9 8 7 6 5 4 3 2 1

Printed in Great Britain by Clays Ltd, St Ives plc

The paper this book is printed on is certified independently in accordance with the
rules of the FSC. It is ancient-forest friendly. The printer holds chain of custody

FSC
Mixed Sources
Product group from well-managed
forests and other controlled sources
Cert no. SGS-COC-2061
www.fsc.org
© 1996 Forest Stewardship Council

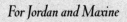

For Jordan and Maxine

The Senator's Wife

CHAPTER ONE

Meri, June 1993

From her perch in the middle of the backseat, Meri surveys the two in front—her husband, Nathan, and Sheila, the real estate agent. There is something generally vulnerable about the back of the head and the neck, she thinks. Nathan, for instance, looks a bit schoolboyish and sad from the back—his ears in particular—probably because of the haircut he had before they started out on this house-hunting trip.

They've been at it for two days. Meri has occupied the backseat the whole time—at first because that's just how it happened when they all got in the car, and then by choice. She finds she likes the sense of distance. She likes the view she gets of their faces as they turn to speak to each other or to her—the profiles, the three-quarter angles. She feels she's learning something new about Nathan, watching him this way, hearing him ask his real estate questions. He has so many! Questions about heating costs, about taxes, about the age of appliances, about insulation and school districts.

Why hasn't she thought about any of this?

Because. Because the other reason she's sitting in back is that she can't bring herself to care very deeply about the house—whatever house it's going to be. The whole thing is Nathan's idea. Meri has sometimes spoken of it to him jokingly as "your big, fat idea," and, as it will turn out, that's apt: the house will cost much more than they'd planned on spending.

3

But even that will have almost nothing to do with her. Nathan's the one with money. Not that he has a lot. But some. He was living penuriously in their midwestern college town when she met him, salting away what he could. He lived penuriously before that in another college town, a saver there too. In the end it has piled up a little bit. But more important, he has a mother willing to give him his "legacy," as she calls it, before her death. She doesn't need it, she has said repeatedly, and he does.

The idea of a parent not only willing, but able, to help you out financially, before or after death, is alien to Meri. A legacy? She will contribute nothing to the purchase of the house—she has nothing, and nothing is coming to her.

None of this means she's unsympathetic to Nathan. She loves him. She understands his impulses and wishes. He was miserable when they met, trapped in the meanest of academic environments, where his brand of scholarship and his popularity with students was looked on with a combination of contempt and envy. To be offered a job at a good college in the East, a job in a department that values the kind of work he does, a tenure-track job, a job with the promise of what might be called *real money* in these circles—this is a coup, an achievement. An escape. They celebrated the news by going out to dinner in the best restaurant in Coleman—the Italian place—and by spending a good deal of the following weekend in bed.

The house they are planning to buy, whatever house it turns out to be, is supposed to be a further celebration of all this—of Nathan's new luck, of his new place in the world. It's supposed to mark, for him anyway, a great change, a beginning.

For Meri, its meaning is less clear. She's sad to be leaving her life in Coleman and her apartment there. She'll miss her job and the people she works with at the alumni magazine. She'll miss their competitive telling of jokes. She'll miss their long meetings, the meandering conversations that would finally and inevitably come around, in some mysterious way that always surprised all of them, to the topics for articles they might do for the magazine.

And she's just a little worried about her marriage. She knows Nathan is planning a life, a life which the house is part of, that she's not sure she wants to live. She doesn't know whether she can be at home in the place he imagines, in the way he imagines her being. She suspects there's trouble coming. But she feels if they can just hold on to the easy camaraderie and sexual heat of their early days, then they can find a way to keep talking about all this, a way of shaping their marriage to suit them both.

THEIR FIRST DAY with Sheila was a waste of time. They had agreed on this in their room at the inn yesterday evening, lying down exhausted and fully clothed on top of the bedspread, not touching. Nathan's hands were folded on his chest, as though he were arranged for viewing at a funeral home. They agreed they would have to raise their upper limit to get anything they really wanted—or Nathan suggested this and Meri went along. To her, everything they'd seen seemed possible. In each cramped little bungalow or shabby row house, while Nathan was getting visibly depressed, she was thinking how, if you just painted the pine paneling white or ripped up the orange carpet, if you took down the heavy layers of curtains and let the light in, the place could be livable. But because she could see Nathan's sorrow, she didn't try to sound hopeful or cheerful about anything. These weren't qualities he seemed to like in her anyway. And back at the inn she didn't even mention any of this. She agreed with him, she bolstered him. She was the one who finally got up from the bed and made the phone call to Sheila—told her they would need to start over with new rules the next day.

Sheila has quickly pulled together a revised list for today's viewings. They've seen three so far. The first one was too far out of town—they both wanted to be able to walk or bike to work. The second one was just ugly, they all agreed over lunch. Fake-brick siding, a tiny dark kitchen. No. The third one, the one they've just come from, was lovely, a Victorian, but also much too big and in need of repairs. The porch actually bounced slightly as they strode across it, and inside Nathan pointed out the water stains on the ceilings and walls, the rotted window frames.

Now Sheila is saying that this next one, the one she's driving them to, is a little out of their range, but she thinks it's so perfect for them that she just wants them to take a peek. She mentions a price that makes Meri flinch in the backseat. She looks quickly at Nathan.

His face is in profile to her as he looks over at Sheila. Meri can see a small, bitter smile move across it. A danger sign, though Sheila doesn't know that. But Meri can sense what's coming. He's about to tell Sheila it's a *lot* out of their range. He's about to ask her not to waste their time. Maybe he's even about to say that they're tired, that they've seen enough for one day.

But Sheila isn't looking at him. Her small, childish voice rolls on, an innocent and unstoppable flow. Meri thinks of clear, shallow water. "It's a double house, actually," she says. "You know, attached. The other side is owned by that old senator who's retired now. Oh, I bet you know him: what's his name? The famous one, more or less the Kennedy era. He even looked kind of like a Kennedy. Oh, shoot!" She smacks the steering wheel.

Meri watches as Nathan's face changes, as the little smile disappears. He says, "Tom Naughton?"

"That's it!" Sheila says. She turns and smiles at him. "They've owned it forever. I've got no idea how long. Since way before my time."

There's a silence. Nathan turns to look at Meri. She can admire the sculpted line of his cheek, his jaw. "It wouldn't hurt to look, I guess," he says.

"You know me," Meri answers. "Real estate *voyeuse.*" She tries to make her voice sound ridiculously sexy, she shimmies her shoulders, and Nathan laughs. That's good. He hasn't laughed, it seems to her, for a few days.

But who's Tom Naughton?

She'll have to look him up.

WHEN SHE MET NATHAN, Meri was living alone, in a place she loved—one vast room in an old brick building whose tall, bare windows looked out over the mostly empty main street of what was euphemistically called downtown Coleman. At one time the building had been a factory—harmoniums had been built there—and, factory-like, it had uselessly high ceilings, of pressed tin. In winter, the warm air rose up and sat just under these ceilings, far above Meri's head. Or at least she assumed that's where the warm air went. There was certainly none down where she lived. There, chilly breezes crisscrossed the room, on a stormy winter day sometimes actually stirring the piles of papers stacked everywhere. Meri wore multiple layers of clothes at home through the coldest months of the year, and huge green down booties all day and well into the night. She wore them to bed. She didn't remove them until she had been under the covers for a while and the heat of her body had begun to tent her safely.

It was for this reason, among others, that she was grateful to have met Nathan in the early summer, when, even though it had no cross-ventilation, the apartment stayed cool and airy with the outsize windows thrown open. When she went barefoot at home, loving the feel of the painted wood under her feet. When she wore skimpy dresses that showed off how tall she was, how strongly built. When you could lie naked in comfort.

They had known each other for only a month, lying naked in comfort for much of that time, when he moved in with her. They had married a month after that. They had been married for ten months when they flew to Williston to spend this long weekend looking at houses they might live in.

WHEN SHEILA pulls up at the curb, Nathan sits quietly for a moment before getting out, looking up the walk. *As though in reverence,* Meri thinks. She follows his gaze. There's a for-sale sign planted in the deep lawn, and behind it rise the two attached brick town houses, built at the turn of the twentieth century, probably, with lots of white carved-stone trim around the windows and doors—curlicues and animal shapes. There's even a small couchant lion at the top of the stone steps up to the porch.

They get out and go up the long walk under a wide oak tree. Moss is growing between the bricks under their feet. Sheila is talking to Nathan about the number of bathrooms, about the kitchen, which they would probably eventually want to renovate. Meri walks behind them, fishing a cigarette—one of the four cigarettes she allows herself daily—from her purse. "I'll come in in a minute," she says as Sheila works the front door with her key.

They don't answer. Nathan disapproves of her smoking. Well, who wouldn't? But the sign of this is that he pretends not to notice it, that he not only ignores her when she's doing it, but any reference to it. It's as though the cigarette is an invisibility device, she thinks. Presto!

Meri watches them step inside the house. She hears Nathan say, "Zowie." She finds her matches. She listens as they talk for a moment—he's asking Sheila about the age of the house; something about the floors—and then their echoing footsteps and voices move back into the house's depths.

She sits down on the stone balustrade that encircles the large, rectangular porch. It's cool and damp under her buttocks. The porch is divided—Senator Naughton's half, their half—by a shorter balustrade projecting out from the wall between the two heavy wooden front doors. The lion rests on top of this, his mouth slightly open, as if he's just seen something that surprises him. She inhales deeply.

She inhales deeply and thinks about sex with Nathan. There's been a drought, the last week or so, and she misses it. She misses him, she thinks. He has gone away from her, into thinking about his future.

Their future, she corrects herself.

From her perch, she can see up the long, broad street where nothing is happening, though somewhere children are yelling. The branches of the trees arch over from each side of the street and meet in the middle. The houses all sit back behind their imposing front yards. The Senator Naughton house is in a series of single and double houses that sit closer together at what must once have been seen as the less-fashionable end of the street. She turns and looks again into the opened doorway. She can see all the way through it, into a room full of light at the back of the house. The kitchen, no doubt. The kitchen they will want to renovate.

Meri thinks about this word: *renovate.* She's not sure she wants to be a person who renovates anything. Renovating is different from painting the paneling or pulling up the orange wall-to-wall carpeting.

Different how?

Different because it takes money. That's the problem, isn't it? She's stepping into a bourgeois life, and she's being a little testy about it. Is it because the money isn't hers? couldn't be hers?

She doesn't know. She inhales again, relishing the acrid taste.

Sex is what did it, of course. They couldn't have been a more unlikely pair, more different. Nathan has what Meri has come to think of as credentials: a distinguished, or at least a solidly reputable, academic for a father—long deceased—a mother who has a silver tea service, inherited from her parents. Who used this tea service on the occasion when she met Meri. A mother who could say, when Meri admired it, "Oh, it's just plate," as though that made it less remarkable.

In spite of herself and the choices she's made in her own life, Meri has a nearly inborn respect for all this, probably as a result of watching too much television in the seventies. When she and her sister played with their Barbies, Meri's Ken doll was always a doctor or a lawyer. Even then, even at eight or nine, she was a sucker for a notion of security derived from prime time. Meri's sister, Lou, was contemptuous. Her Ken was a movie star, or a cowboy, or a guy who raced motorcycles. Meri's Ken, she said, was a dult. This was a word they both used well into their teens. It was born of Meri's childhood misunderstanding of the word *adult,* which she heard as two words, article and noun. Lou had co-opted it to simultaneously point at, and offer judgment on, the world of the grown-ups. *Dults,* almost all of them.

The part of the world of grown-ups that Meri's father came from was very different from Nathan's. He was more like Lou's Ken doll than Meri's—a long-haul trucker, gone on the road for weeks, and then a hard drinker during his restless days at home. And her mother's life had no relation to a life either Meri or her sister was interested in. She altered and made clothes for the ladies in the small Illinois town where they lived. She made all of Meri's clothes, and

Lou's too, until the girls were old enough to babysit and earn a little money. After that they bought their own, mostly jeans and tops as provocative as they could get away with. They'd been wild girls in high school, bad girls, and Meri sees it as a matter of great good luck that somehow she didn't get pregnant, didn't have to drop out, wasn't twice divorced and collecting unemployment, all of which had happened to Lou. Instead Meri took slow, incrementally more ambitious steps—through a community junior college, then the state university, then graduate school in journalism. All this got her to where she was when she met Nathan: a scratched-together life, making most of her money editing the alumni magazine and writing for it—articles on conferences at the college, on faculty projects and publications, on guest lecturers. Occasionally she placed a special-interest piece in the *Des Moines Register,* or even, a few times, in the *Chicago Tribune.*

Meri is short for Meribeth, Lou for Louisa. What was their mother thinking, giving them names like these—feminine, soft, pretty? "I thought you kids would get in the kitchen and help me out once in a while, instead of whatever it is you do all day. Your nails. Your hair."

But that wasn't really what she wanted. Not at all. When they did try to help her, to cook or do the dishes, she stormed into their midst, whacking them with whatever was handy, scolding them for the mess they were making or the insufficiently clean pots and pans. No, what she liked was for them to go away and leave her alone. Fine with them. She liked—at any rate she *seemed* to like—standing at the sink with a cigarette planted in her mouth, the smoke curling up around her squinted eyes, her hands in dishwater, the radio on, her mind far away from them, far away from the tissuey patterns that lay waiting for her on the dining room table, from the women who came and went, talking intimately of their lives while she knelt before them and pinned their clothes to fit.

She had died of breast cancer three years earlier, and Meri had a strange and powerful reaction to losing her, delayed by four or five months and then confusing in its intensity. "It wasn't as though we were close," she said in wonderment to Lou on the phone. She had called her, in tears.

"How could you be?" Lou said. "She never talked."

Was that it? Meri wondered. Was it just a yearning for what hadn't been?

One of the nicest things her mother ever said to her was when she told her she had good teeth. "Smile," she had commanded over coffee one morning, and Meri obeyed. "Straight," her mother said, already turning away. "Not like Lou with her overbite." That was it.

For years in her adulthood, Meri swung between attractions to men like her sister's Ken doll and those like her own. Between danger and safety. When she met Nathan—safety—she was attracted for all her own sorry reasons.

They were both in the audience at a lecture given by a former presidential press secretary on post-Reagan politics. Meri was there because she was going to write about it. Nathan came up to her afterward at the reception and said, "Who are you, taking all those notes? You're too old to be a student."

From across the room, Meri had been watching him talking to the press secretary, taking him in—his wild hair, his tall, shapely body, the quick, slightly vulpine smile that suddenly made his pretty face interesting.

"I'm nineteen," she said in an offended voice. "I've had a hard life, if you must know."

He had flashed the smile. He was at least four inches taller than she was, and she was five eleven. "Would you like to have a drink?" he asked. "There's nothing I like better than a hard-luck tale."

Though Meri was dazzled by him, she consented to go out with him almost reluctantly, knowing she'd be bored—or that she'd get bored, quickly: she always did with the safe ones—and then she'd have the problem of extrication, which she wasn't any good at. Things always dragged on much too long in her life. It was a waste of increasingly precious time. She was, in fact, thirty-six.

But that wasn't how it had turned out, once he touched her, once he kissed her, once they made love—which happened, that first time, in her apartment, in the late afternoon, with the sunlight striping across the painted floor and the sounds of the street drifting up occasionally.

She is thinking about this, her breathing a little irregular, her precious second cigarette of the day neglected, turning to ash between her fingers, when the door opens on the other side of the porch and a woman steps out. She starts, seeing Meri, and then says hello. Meri says, "Hi," and the woman turns away to lock her door behind her. She must be about seventy, Meri thinks. She's tall and erect and somehow compelling.

Meri herself is what she thinks of as an *almost-pretty* woman. A lover had once told her that she looked like an attractive version of Pete Rose. She doesn't think it's that bad, though her features are a little imprecise. *Smudgy* is a word she's used for them more than once. Because of this, she's learned to invent ways of being noticed, of being found appealing without ever being thought beautiful, and this has made her a connoisseur of other women and their beauty. This old woman—she has turned to Meri again—is someone who was a beauty once, Meri would put money on it. A beauty of the handsome, commanding sort. Maybe a little intimidating, actually. She probably still draws attention walking down the street. Her face is deeply lined, but she has strong, regular, lovely features. She's wearing bright red lipstick. Her hair is a mass of curly white, and there's a quality in her expression and carriage of energy, of curiosity and sexual power. She's dressed irregularly for someone her age—a slightly clingy print blouse and flared skirt. Flat hemp-soled shoes, French-looking.

"Are you looking at the house?" she asks. There's something patrician in her pronunciation.

"Yes," Meri says.

"But on the other hand"—she tilts her head—"you're *not* looking."

Meri smiles at her, charmed. "We've had a long day at it. I needed a rest." She waggles what's left of her cigarette. "I needed to be bad for a minute, I've been so damned good all day."

The woman laughs quickly. "Ah, yes. Goodness is so hard to sustain," she says. "Still, when you do finally get around to looking, you'll like it, I think." She smiles. "But I would say that, wouldn't I? It mirrors mine, and I like mine. I've liked it for almost thirty years."

"Thirty years!" Meri says. "Wow. I can't imagine living in any one place for thirty years."

"But I doubt you can imagine living itself for thirty years, can you?"

"That and then some," Meri says, in a stylized, tough-broad voice.

"Which I don't believe for one second," the older woman says.

"Well, you should. I'm thirty-seven."

"Ah, thirty-seven." She nods. "It's a wonderful age, isn't it?"

"It is?" Meri flicks the last of the ash off the cigarette.

"Yes, it is. It's a perfectly balanced age, to my way of thinking. With any luck, you've left foolish youth and vain hopes about your life behind you. You're done with all that kind of pain. But on the other hand, you're still young, you're still strong." She pauses, she looks out over the front yard, then back at Meri. "Ready for real life to begin."

Real life? What does that mean?

"I'm Delia Naughton," the woman says abruptly. She steps toward the lion that separates her from Meri, and Meri steps toward her. Over his head, they shake hands, and Meri tells Delia her own name. She spells it too. She always does.

"Will you be doing something at the college?" Delia asks. Her eyes are a piercing, hard blue.

"Well, I'm not sure about myself," Meri answers. "I've got a job hunt ahead of me. But my husband will. He'll be teaching. In political science and history." She's proud of this, glad to be able to announce it.

"Ah!" Delia says. She nods, several times. "Well," she says, "I hope you *are* interested." She steps back, gesturing at the house. "It would be lovely to have young people on that side of the wall. And if you do buy it, I'll be happy to help you get settled however I can. At the very least direct you to the grocery store and the dry cleaner and that very boring but essential kind of thing."

"Thank you," Meri says. "You're very kind."

"Not at all," Delia answers. She goes down the stairs, a little slowly, gripping the decorative iron rail. She starts walking down the brick path. Meri finds herself wanting to stop her as she moves away, to offer her something. "Mrs. Naughton!" she calls out.

The older woman turns. She takes a step back toward Meri. "Please call me Delia."

"Delia," Meri says. "I just wanted to say that my husband"—she tilts her head back toward the house behind her—"is apparently a great fan of your husband."

Something changes in Delia Naughton's face. She looks a little blank for a few seconds, as though she's forgotten she has a husband, a husband Nathan might have heard of. At any rate, Meri sees that this isn't quite the gift she intended it to be.

But now she smiles. "Ah, well," she says, and looks away, down the block. "He joins a multitude of great fans, I'm afraid. They are my husband's specialty." She waves her hand and continues down the walk. At its end, she turns right, toward the busier street that leads, Meri knows, to the college and the center of town.

Meri watches her until she disappears. Then she puts the filter, which is all that remains of her cigarette, into the little box she carries in her purse for butts. She gets up and goes inside.

She's more interested now. She feels suddenly energetic, a feeling given to her, no doubt, by Delia Naughton. She tries to tell herself that after all, Delia was just being polite, but she can't help her response. The attention of older women always does this to her. Makes her feel, somehow, blessed. *This is what comes of maternal deprivation,* she thinks.

She stands in the living room. She can hear footsteps and doors opening and closing upstairs, and then the low murmur of Sheila's and Nathan's alternating voices. She looks around. The room is large, but in some ways awkwardly arranged. It sits open to the front door—there is no hall—and it features a long curving bench under the six front windows. The bench is made of the same yellowish wood as the wide, ornate mantel. This wood is everywhere. It continues past the mantel as wainscoting, and then as a panel on the side of the landing of the stairs, which projects out into the living room. The next room back, which Meri takes to be the dining room, has three windows that form a bay. She goes through it, her footsteps loud on the bare wood. Just after it there's a closet, then a lavatory, and opposite that, a dark butler's pantry with glass-fronted cupboards. She works the old-fashioned latch on one of the cupboard doors. There's a musty but not unpleasant smell as it swings open. The shelves are lined with a faded, figured paper, splotched and stained here and there. A large refrigerator with chrome trim sits in the pantry too, its door hanging slightly ajar. She hears Nathan laughing somewhere upstairs.

Meri goes into the kitchen itself, which is a long room, full of light. The back of it is almost like a greenhouse, it's so windowed. The yard outside this wall of windows glows radiantly green—a sycamore arches over it, with its beautiful pale, scaling bark and the sun filtering through its leaves. Meri steps over to the glass and looks out. The yard is weedy and overgrown. A weathered stockade fence separates it from the Naughtons' yard next door. Their kitchen doesn't extend as far back as this one, and directly below where Meri is standing, they have a wide fieldstone terrace, rather formal, encircled by a box hedge. Two wooden chairs bleached to a silvery gray sit on it, and Meri thinks of Delia Naughton there, having a drink with someone older and distinguished, someone like Ted Kennedy, only much, much thinner.

She walks away from the windows to explore the cooking area of the room, such as it is. Wedged against the common wall, there's a tiny white enamel stove with four burners and a narrow oven door, and next to it, a wide low porcelain sink on legs, clearly from some earlier era. That's it. There's no counter to speak of. It reminds Meri, actually, of the kitchen area at the back wall of her apartment in Coleman. There she had made a counter and storage out of a solid-core door placed over two bureaus she bought at the funky antique shop in town. Here, of course, Nathan will have a say in all the arrangements, and she realizes that she has no sense of what his inclinations will be, his taste. Will they junk her bureaus? She hopes not. She's fond of them.

Maybe more important, they're hers.

There's a closed door on the wall the pantry backs up to, and Meri opens it. A narrow, steep stairway twists up to the left. She mounts it, using the handrail. On the second floor, she looks quickly through the four bedrooms and two baths that open off the long hall. They are pretty rooms, nicely shaped, especially the largest one at the front, which has the same curved row of windows as the living room. They're all in need of new wallpaper and fresh paint, though. The ghosts of old paintings sit as brighter squares or rectangles on the faded walls, and here and there the edge of the wallpaper is curling back, showing another color or pattern beneath it.

The bathrooms are old-fashioned, with linoleum floors and claw-foot tubs. Meri likes claw-foot tubs. One of the sink faucets has a steady, slow drip that has marked the porcelain with a wide rust stain.

She finds Sheila and Nathan on the third floor in an open, finished room lined with bookcases. Nathan turns to her. He looks happy. The sign of this, besides the grin, is the dishevelment of his hair. When he's excited, he can't keep his hands from running through it, pulling it. Sometimes when she meets him after a class that's gone well, he looks as frazzled as when he first wakes in the morning.

"Be a nice study, wouldn't it?" he asks her, sweeping his arm out.

Clearly he and Sheila have been talking about this. She's primed. She jumps in, pointing out the skylights, the view out into the trees that line the street. She speculates about the logical place for a couch, a desk.

"And tell Meri about the owners," Nathan says to her.

Obediently, Sheila narrates, in her childish, prim voice. The husband was an architect. "A noted architect," she says. The wife was a musician. No children. They lived here all their married life. He died in the sixties, and she lived on alone until her death the year before. He was the one who'd changed the house, Sheila says. This room, for instance, was the attic before he converted it into his office. He'd taken out the walls on the ground floor and expanded the kitchen, all in the late fifties. "After that, nothing. I don't think it's even been painted since then."

"That's why it's so cheap," Nathan says, smiling at her.

She stares at him for just a moment. Cheap?

It's clear that the decision has been made. She gets a breath mint out of her bag, and smiles at Sheila and Nathan as they go on talking.

BACK AT THE INN, as they mount the stairs, as they walk single file down the long, narrow corridor to their room, Nathan is excited, throwing his observations on the merits of the house back to her. Almost as soon as they're inside, he excuses himself to call his mother—he'll need to ask her about the price, which is more than she had counted on. Meri pulls a chair over by the window and peels an orange while he talks. He describes the house lovingly—the crown moldings, the leaded glass windows in the kitchen, the height of the ceilings. "It's beautiful, its bones are right there, but it's also the kind of place where the lights in the bathroom are those overhead fluorescent circles. That's what makes it so great," he says. "It just needs sprucing up, but it's basically very solid, very distinguished."

Their room is on the second floor of the inn. The floor is bare wood. It creaks as Nathan paces back and forth, needing motion as he always does when he's happy. She's seen him teach, and he's always in motion then too.

The window in front of Meri is open. She props her bare feet on the sill. The curtains rise and fall around her, sometimes brushing her legs as she listens to her husband. Oil sparks out from the skin of the orange as she bends it, sparks out and disappears in the air, leaving its scent behind. There's white pith under her fingernail. She eats the sections slowly, carefully peeling off all the threads. Nathan and his mother are talking about money now, about interest rates and monthly payments. Outside, someone passing by is whistling, and across the street, the canopy of leaves on the town common moves slowly in the wind, one mass of green. There were four or five students playing Frisbee on the lawn under these trees when they came in.

Nathan and his mother have agreed on things, it seems. At least Nathan is making agreeing noises, winding-it-up noises. He hangs up, and the room is quiet for a long moment except for the students' faint cries floating in from outside.

Then she feels his hand on her shoulder. "Hey," he says gently. She reaches up and touches him with her own orange-smelling fingers.

"Hey, turn around," he says.

Meri does, gripping the arms of the chair, picking it up and turning it with her. She sits back and looks at him. Nathan is beautiful. You shouldn't love someone for the accident of his beauty, Meri knows this, but it's what drew her to him. How could it not? His eyes are a brown so light as to be nearly gold. He's sitting on the edge of the double bed, facing her. Their knees are almost touching. They would be touching if the bed weren't so high. It's a four-poster, with a white chenille bedspread.

"It's all okay with my mother," he says.

"I gather."

"Are you ready to own a house?" He reaches over and strokes her leg, her jeans. "This is something you want to do, right?"

Meri nods.

He rocks her leg back and forth a little. "Right?" he asks again. He wants more from her.

"Oh, you know me, Nate." Meri makes a face. "I'm always nervous about change. I'd have had us grow old in my apartment."

"I would have had that commute, though. Hard on me."

"Yeah. That would have been the wrinkle." She feels the curtains around her like a quick caress, and then they die back.

"Don't be nervous," he says softly.

"Oh," she says brightly. "Okay."

He laughs. Then his face grows serious and he says, "It's our house, Meri. I wouldn't have wanted a house if we weren't together. It's for us."

She offers him a wedge of orange, and he takes it. They're quiet for a moment, eating.

"Let's celebrate," he says abruptly. "I'll call Sheila and make the offer, and then let's go downstairs and have champagne."

"You think they have champagne downstairs?" The inn's bar is dark and utilitarian. At lunch it was full of people who might have been faculty, having hamburgers and iced tea or beer in heavy mugs.

"We can but try. Put on something hot. Let's be festive."

As she's changing out of her jeans, she calls to Nathan, washing his sticky hands, "Maybe it's because I don't have a job yet. Maybe that makes me feel . . . less *real* about living here."

He's come to stand in the doorway to the bathroom, holding a towel. "You'll find a job."

She opens the closet to get her dress out, smiling at him. "I'm so glad that's settled."

"Well, it is."

Downstairs, the bar is half full. They sit at a square table, its surface a single thick slab of wood, scarred and fissured, with a shiny finish. Nathan goes over to the bar and leans on it. She watches his back and his strong rounded buttocks as he shifts his weight to rest one foot on the rail. The window next to her is open. In the distance, there's the sound of someone running a leaf blower.

Nathan comes back with two champagne glasses, the bubbles coursing frantically upward in each. He hands one to her and sits down. Though it has the weight of glass, Meri's flute feels like plastic to her, and when she touches it to Nathan's to toast the future, there's a dull noise, nothing musical.

But it's good champagne, dry and flavorful. "Yum," she says.

"*You* are yum," he answers, and raises his glass again. "My mistress of the house."

"Now, why does that sound so much more interesting than *wife*?" she asks.

"It doesn't," he says.

She snorts and has another sip of champagne. As she sets her glass down, she says, "I have another question: who's Tom Naughton? Besides being an ex-senator."

"You don't know?"

"I'm asking."

"He's one of the really good guys. He was. I think he had two, but it might have been three terms at the time of all the Great Society stuff in the sixties and seventies. He was part of the whole discussion on poverty, of how it should be dealt with, which *was* the argument for the few seconds they had all that money to throw at it. He was always known to be a straight shooter. Even the guys who disagreed with him respected him."

"And then?"

"Well, basically I think he just retired. Maybe he saw the handwriting on the wall." He frowned. "Or there might have been some personal issues, I'm thinking. I can't quite remember. Anyway, the whole thing died in the seventies, and his heyday was over." Nathan twirls his glass slowly. He shrugs. "He's still around, with some fancy D.C. law firm, part of various commissions. You hear about him every now and then, advising, writing policy papers. Like Hart. Or Rudman." He looks at Meri and grins. "It'll be neat to meet him."

Now they start to talk about the house again, about specific rooms and how they might use them. Meri makes her voice casual as she brings up the solid-core door, the bureaus. When Nathan says, "Yeah, we'll sure need them, won't we?" she feels a rush of something like gratitude. She lifts his hand to her mouth and kisses his fingertips.

But as she releases his hand, then as they sip the last of the champagne, as they leave the bar and head upstairs, she is thinking, as she has at certain moments ever since she married Nathan, of how separate she and he are. She is thinking that she doesn't want to be grateful to him for what he allows her. She doesn't want not to have been consulted about the house.

But she let it happen, didn't she—the situation of her own disenfranchisement about these things? In order to be truly honest with Nathan about all her feelings, she would need to be willing to fight it out, to argue over every small thing. And she hadn't realized, until she got married, just how many small things there were. It makes her feel tired to think of it.

Upstairs they stand on opposite sides of the bed and move quickly out of their clothes. Meri crawls across the coverlet to Nathan. She lies down on her side, looking up at him, opening her knees as he reaches for her.

The air from the open window is cool, but Nathan's body is warm, he radiates heat. He's hard, and she reaches down to help him, to shift him into place. She feels a kind of relief as he enters her. This is what she wants. This is the way she feels honest with him, safe. Here, she thinks. Yes. As he begins to move in her, she whispers it: "Yes. Yes!"

They make love quickly, fueled by his urgency, and when he comes, Nathan cries out so loudly that Meri can imagine someone on the sidewalk below stopping, listening under the darkening trees.

Afterward they lie still, side by side. Meri is looking up at the ceiling, which is low and veined with cracks that have been patched in. She thinks of the ceiling in her apartment, the patterned tin squares. Nathan's stomach rumbles. Meri's mind begins the cartwheels through her life that routinely follow sex. She's remembering how it was to make love with the man she was dating before she met Nathan. Rick was his name. She thinks of his cock versus Nathan's—shorter, fatter. She thinks of the comment he made about the inadequacy of her stereo speakers, a comment that deeply offended her and led directly to their breakup. Then—how? is there any possible connection?—she's off on the article she's in the midst of writing about the research of a young archaeologist at the college. She'll finish this article and one more, a summary of recent faculty publications, and then she will be done, her job will end.

Nathan says, "You like it, don't you?"

She looks over at him. "The house?" she asks. Her voice is croaky. "God! What else?"

She clears her throat. "I don't know." He's silent. "Sex?" She's smiling, but he doesn't look at her. "This room?" She turns on her side to him. "Don't be cranky, Nate. Maybe I just feel less . . . connected to the idea of homeownership than you." She thinks abruptly of Elias, the gay man who works with her at the magazine. When he wants to ask discreetly whether someone else is also gay, he says, "Is he a homeowner?"

She is about to tell Nathan this, but he's moved on, he's started to talk about the house again. This time his angle is the amazement—"I mean, how likely is it?"—of moving in next to Tom Naughton.

"Yes," she answers. She thinks of Delia Naughton's face changing at the mention of her husband's name. She runs her hand over Nathan's belly, smooth and white and hairless. His whole body is long and beautiful this way. He makes her think of an El Greco saint. Her head is propped up on her other hand. "Yeah, I like her, anyway."

"What do you mean, you like her?"

"Oh." Her hand lifts and her fingers make quote marks. "*The wife.* I talked to her for a minute today. When you and Sheila were inside. She was . . . I guess you would say, *welcoming.* Nice."

Nathan is silent for a moment. He gets up abruptly. He goes into the bathroom. She can hear him splashing water around in there. Now he's standing in the doorway, filling it with his long body, wiping his face with a towel.

He's looking at her.

"What?" she says.

"Why didn't you tell me this, earlier?"

He's wounded. As Meri knew he would be. As she had intended, she realizes. Almost as soon as she mentioned Delia Naughton—"the wife"—certainly when he responded with silence, she knew she had wanted this moment, this moment of a kind of revenge. On Nathan. Whom she loves. She can't help it; even now she feels a kind of pleasure.

At what? That she knew something he didn't? Nyah, nyah. Is it that petty? Is *she* that petty?

"I didn't think to, until just now," Meri says. This isn't true and she knows it. There were several moments when she could have offered it to Nathan and she didn't. She didn't because he had made her feel excluded.

Nathan stands watching her for another moment. Then he sits on the foot of the bed. "What did you talk about?" He half smiles. "With *the wife*?" His voice is sarcastic, but he's trying to forgive her, trying to get back to where they were.

"Oh, nothing, really. It was a minute. 'Hi, how are you, let me know if I can help, blah, blah, blah.' Just, she gave it a little more than that. She has serious charm."

He doesn't answer.

"Nathan, I'm sorry. I'm sorry I didn't tell you. I should have told you earlier. But it doesn't matter, does it? We've bought a house. We just made love. I would file this under 'trivial,' this mistake. Not so very wicked, after all."

He reaches down and grips her feet, moves them gently. His hands are warm. "Only a little," he says. "Only a little wicked." He smiles at her in the twilit room. She loves him. That's all that counts. She loves him.

CHAPTER TWO

Delia, August 1993

IT RAINS STEADILY through the night, and Delia wakes from time to time to its heavy racket in the trees outside her open bedroom window. At one point, she gets up and puts another blanket on the bed.

When she wakes for good, though, at about five, light is flooding the room. There's a cool breeze moving the branches of the tree outside, but she imagines she can feel the heat of the day entering the house, rising.

She begins assessing her body—what hurts today, what doesn't— and then flings back the covers in irritation with herself. How tedious can you be? She's up, she goes down the hall to the bathroom, to urinate, to brush her teeth, to lay out her medications and take the morning batch.

The kitchen, at the back of the house, seems cold and dark when she comes down the back stairs, and she's glad for the sweater she pulled on over her bathrobe. She makes her breakfast and sits listening to the news on the local public-radio station. There's much talk, a year later, about the recovery from Hurricane Andrew in Florida. And locally, they've arrested someone who'd been dropping rocks on cars from an overpass on the state highway.

At seven, she goes upstairs and writes a long letter to her older son, Evan. Then she showers and gets dressed in what she thinks of as her work clothes—today a cotton dress and low-heeled sandals. She puts on the makeup she usually wears—mascara, lipstick, a little color on her cheeks—and looks at herself critically in the mirror. Well, she's done what she can, she can do no more.

It's around eight-thirty when she goes back downstairs to make her second cup of coffee at the espresso machine—black this time. She's just sitting down at the table to drink it when she hears a truck pull up outside, and then, in a minute, men's voices yelling at one another. Carrying her coffee, she goes to the living room, to the front windows. The moving van in the driveway on the other side of the double house is huge, red and white, and the men are busy around it, opening doors, pulling out clanking metal ramps. They are young, they are wearing matching T-shirts, though she can't make out what they say. Delia can hear someone next door, inside what she still thinks of as Ilona's house, thudding up the stairs.

As she sits looking out with her coffee, the thudding becomes steady. They have begun to carry furniture in. They shout to one another, they call back and forth from the driveway, from the foot of the stairs up to the top. The new owners, too, have arrived and added their voices to the din. Delia hears the young woman—Mary, her name is. No, *Meri*. She spelled it for Delia, she remembers that now. There was something nervy and tomboyish about her, qualities Delia likes in a girl. In a woman.

So this will be the end of the deep silence on the other side of the wall, then. Delia won't be sorry, though by now she's used to it—the house next door has been empty since Ilona Carter's death eight months or so ago. But even before then, her elderly neighbor's routines weren't the kind that generated much noise. Certainly not noise at a level that could easily penetrate the multiple layers between Delia's house and hers—the solid brick fire wall, the studs and slatted lath on both sides, the two coats of old horsehair plaster, and then all that had been added and attached on top of that over the years—paint and wallpaper and wallpaper and paint again.

The one regular exception to the quiet had been in the late afternoons, when Ilona listened to classical music at a high volume while she had one very strong double martini, consumed with habitual slowness over several hours of listening, of getting up over and over to change the records: Ilona never made the transition to tapes or CDs. And though on Delia's side of the house the music sometimes caused a bothersome light buzzing of the window glass, for the most part she liked it, liked the way it seeped murmurously through the walls. She counted on it, actually. It was like listening to flowing water, she thought. Something as elemental as that.

It was harder occasionally when Ilona invited Delia over for a drink too, and put on a particular piece of music by a particular performer she admired. Then they'd sit together in the overwhelming racket, Ilona smiling, her old head thrown back, her eyes behind the Coke-bottle lenses of her glasses closed in a kind of ecstasy, her large, horsey teeth exposed; Delia waiting with all the impatience of someone under a dentist's drill for the noise and the pain to stop.

Ilona was more than slightly deaf. Thus the volume. She was also arthritic and had macular degeneration. "But I don't complain," she would say, when she'd finished complaining. And it was true that she was by nature a buoyant person. She confirmed Delia's opinion that musicians were usually the happiest people—Ilona had played second violin with a small symphony orchestra in the Midwest earlier in her life. Delia had known her for thirty years and felt an uncritical devotion to her for most of that time.

Ilona's death had been sudden. It was Delia who found her, and it was the silence late one winter afternoon that made her think to telephone over there. That made her go through the hall drawer for Ilona's keys when there was no answer to the ringing and ringing, that made her step across the ice-crusted front porch and let herself in, that propelled her upstairs when Ilona didn't respond to her calls and wasn't anywhere on the first floor.

She'd died in her sleep, apparently. At any rate, she was in bed with the covers pulled up nearly to her chin. Her skin had turned a startling yellow-gray. Her death shocked Delia, though it shouldn't have. The old woman was ninety-two.

Delia herself was seventy-four when Ilona died. Old too, yes. But Ilona's presence, her very existence, had always made Delia feel young and vital—sometimes even girlish. Oh, she knew, of course, that to the mostly truly young families who were her neighbors now, she and Ilona were more like than not. They inhabited a category: old woman. These neighbors might have understood that one was quite a bit older than the other, but what difference really did that make? What they would be focused on was the waste of their both still living alone in those two huge houses. And now Ilona is gone, and her side of the house will be reclaimed, transformed.

But the truth is, Delia is perfectly happy to have young people moving in. More liveliness, more children. There'd been a kind of pause on the street after the last of the previous batch of children had left, vanished into high school or college or life. For a few of those years there'd been hardly anyone playing on the street, there were few trick-or-treaters at Halloween, there were no cries echoing through the early dusk as the children ran through one another's yards.

Delia had missed it. It's good that the silence is over. The childless older couples have moved on. The houses have sold. Some were so large they've been turned into condominiums, so two or three families live where one did in the old days. Once again you saw children, you heard them—their high, light voices, their games, their occasional extravagant public weeping. She's glad for it. She's glad for this young couple moving in next to her. Perhaps they have children, or will have them. She hadn't asked when she met the woman.

When Delia leaves to go to work, there's no one outside. Ilona's front door is propped open though, and she can hear voices in the house.

She takes her car. Usually she walks, but she's decided she'll do some shopping today when her workday is over—she'll buy some little gifts for her new neighbors, something to make them feel welcome.

The air is soft and clear, the roads still black with damp after the heavy rain she heard in the night. The main streets around the town green are already crowded with shoppers, people getting ready for the weekend. Delia likes these days at the beginning and the end of the summer, when the students are gone and the town is suddenly reclaimed by adults. When you can drive from one stoplight to another without dodging the perpetually jaywalking young people, kids who barely glance at the cars before they launch themselves into the road.

Delia drives several blocks past the campus and parks in front of an old white colonial house, set close to the street, a worn rail fence around its shallow front yard. This is the Apthorp house, where Delia works.

This work—her job, as she thinks of it—is not paid. She's a volunteer, a docent, at a house that was the home in the early to mid-nineteenth century of an itinerant preacher and his wife. It's the wife who's made it famous, one hundred years after her death. Her unfinished novel and a group of unpublished stories were discovered in the attic in the late 1950s.

Four days a week, four months a year—June, July, August, September—Delia leads people through the house, answering their questions about the Apthorps. And though Anne Apthorp was admittedly not a figure of any real importance in the New England intellectual scene, there are many questions. About her marriage, about her furniture, about her china, her kitchen equipment, her writing implements, her children. About how she lived and how she died.

Delia had come to her love for all things Apthorpian twenty or so years earlier, shortly after she moved to Williston with Tom and the children. She'd been asked then, as the congressman's wife, to be on a committee whose charge was to raise money to convert the house, which the college had recently bought, to a museum. It was one of many civic obligations she saw as being part of her public life. She said yes, and she did what she was asked to do—she went to the fund-raisers, she worked the rooms, she gave the required spiels.

And then she was asked to read Anne Apthorp's letters aloud at a fund-raising event—perhaps excerpts from three or four. She was free to choose which ones.

She was tempted to say no. She was going through a difficult time in her own life with Tom then, and she was saying no to many things.

But the young woman doing the asking was persuasive, and Delia thought finally that it might be good for her to get out and move around among people. And so, on a winter afternoon, with the sky the even soft gray of a threatening snowfall, she pulled on her boots and hiked over to the college library to go through Anne Apthorp's correspondence, to make her selections.

The letters were still in boxes then, and the librarian put her in a paneled conference room with several of these cartons set out on the enormous table. Delia sat in a comfortable chair next to an old floor lamp and started to read.

Of course, she'd long since read the unfinished novel, about the wife of a sea captain, a man who repeatedly abandons her for a world he's more compelled by, for a life he prefers. But she hadn't known until now about the existence of the letters, and she read them with growing interest.

A small number of them were addressed to Anne's parents—her mother mostly. They still lived in northern Massachusetts, where Anne had grown up. But most were to her husband, and it was clear to Delia as she went through them that this husband, Joshua, had other women—or, more likely, one other woman, who was part of his life, a life of preaching and ardent abolitionism that took him regularly away from home. "I am pleased for you," Anne Apthorp wrote him, "that you have found so congenial a place to stay in Chesterville, for it seems such an excellent center from which to travel to the villages and churches surrounding it in every direction. I would caution you, though, against staying too long or too often with Mrs. Harding when Mr. Harding is himself away. Surely this will unnecessarily provoke comment and perhaps even make more difficult the work you've traveled so far from home and hearth to do."

Mrs. Harding is mentioned three or four times over several years: "Please greet that fortunate woman, who has for her daily companion the person I hold closest to my own heart."

What wasn't in the letters, Delia provided in her imagination, and by the end of the afternoon, walking home in the dark with the expected snow lightly falling, she had the odd sense of having been comforted by Anne Apthorp's story. She felt, somehow, bound to her, linked to her.

SUMMER IS THE busiest time of the year for the house. There are tourists from all over the country, of course, traveling through New England, seeking out historic places, literary landmarks. But there are also the families of the young people looking at the college in these months, trying to fill their time while their children are trooping off to classes or interviews. And then in the early fall, parents stop by, parents who are dropping their children off to start school, or visiting them. The rest of the year the house is open by appointment only, and Delia, in any case, is in her apartment in Paris in the spring and fall, and busy with family visits in December and January.

But for the summer months, she's full of Apthorpian information. She has a desk in the front hallway, where she's available to answer questions as visitors come and go. And three times a day, at eleven, at one-thirty, and at four, she leads groups through the house. Whatever level of knowledge the visitors have, whatever the focus of their attention, it's Delia's job to answer them thoroughly and respectfully, and she's good at it. Once recently a young man with a camcorder hung around his neck and a baseball hat turned backward on his head asked her what she knew about the Apthorps' sexual relationship. Perhaps he was inspired to curiosity by the size of the marital bed (small), or by the two little children's cots wedged into a corner of their bedroom.

But Delia thought there was something teasing in his tone. As he finished his question, he looked around at the little group touring the house with him, smiling, as if to draw them into what Delia suspected he saw as a kind of joke, a joke that perhaps he imagined her as the butt of—the elderly docent who probably didn't even remember what sex *was* being asked to discuss it with someone as young, as sexy, as he was.

Delia treated the question as courteously as she treated any other. She mentioned the nearly annual pregnancies, many of which didn't come to term. She referred to the letters that Anne Apthorp had written to her husband. And she suggested the young man *re*read— she always gave the visitors the benefit of the doubt—the passages in the novel, *Hamilton Harbor,* that referred to the fictional Julia's yearning wait while her husband was at sea, her fevered grief when she thought he was lost to her.

DELIA GETS OUT of her car and goes around to the side entrance of the house. She unlocks the door and turns off the alarm system. She walks through the house and opens the front door from within.

Despite the warmth of the late-summer day outside, the Apthorp house is cool. It's almost always cool. It's also dark—the walls have been repapered in historically accurate patterns that favor deep green or red or brown. Everything smells of old fires and damp. Delia likes this, that the air itself seems to be of another time.

Adele DiRosa comes in, the woman who sells tour tickets and runs the gift shop. Delia calls a greeting to her on her way to the storage closet for more booklets and the little clip-on badges visitors are required to wear.

This is a slow week, the last week of August. Only one couple stops by in the morning, and they turn down Delia's offer to walk them through. They want to explore at their own pace, they say—though they stop and ask her a few questions before they leave.

After they're gone, Delia goes into the gift shop and talks for a while with Adele. The shop is a light space, airy, with large modern windows—completely different from the rest of the house. It was built much later as an addition, a new kitchen, in the years before the college bought the house and reclaimed it for history. Now the cupboards are full of spare copies of the books they sell, and they use the stove and sink to make coffee and tea.

Adele is at least thirty years younger than Delia, but they've known each other for a long time and they're companionable. They talk today about local politics—the closing of a nearby military base, the possibility of establishing a minimum-security prison on its grounds. It's been discussed and debated repeatedly in the local paper. Adele is more in favor of this than Delia, but they both worry about incarceration as a growing American industry.

In the afternoon, there's a little flurry of business. At the one-thirty tour, there are two older couples and a young woman writing a thesis on nineteenth-century New England women. When Delia is done with them, there are several people going through on their own who have questions for her. She barely has time for a cup of tea and a bathroom break before the four o'clock tour.

At just after five, Delia locks the doors again, and she and Adele leave, calling their good-byes to each other at their cars. Delia opens her windows to cool the car off—the day has turned hot, as she thought it would. She drives to the center of town. She parks at a meter there, one of a row installed on Main Street only three years before. In Kitchen Arts she buys two inexpensive champagne flutes and some blue-checked dishcloths. She walks the four doors down to the specialty food shop. There she buys a small circle of goat cheese, several pâtés, a baguette, a box of crackers, a jar of expensive mustard, and some cornichons. From behind the glass doors of the double-wide refrigerator, she takes out a bottle of chilled champagne.

These shops and others like them—a fancy produce store, a wineshop—have arrived in Williston slowly over the last ten years or so, changing the town and the people. Now everyone knows what *confit* means, what *first cold pressing* is, what the difference is between a niçoise and a calamata olive.

It is pleasant to have these amenities, Delia thinks, but they strike her, too, as making this kind of sophistication somehow obligatory. As though to keep up with the times, you have to be more careful about all this, you have to choose just the right cheese, and the right wine to go with it. Delia can remember fondly the parties in their first small apartment, when the children were tiny and she served Wheat Thins and Ritz crackers with a vivid orange cheese streaked with pink—its name lost to time, its dye probably carcinogenic. The booze was all anyone cared about anyway.

The truck is gone when she gets home. She parks in her own driveway by the kitchen door and carries her bags in. She refrigerates the cheese and pâtés, the champagne. Then she pours a glass of wine for herself and goes to the front hall to pick up the mail that has dropped through the slot in the door and scattered on the floor. She carries it to the living room and sits down to go through it.

At about six-thirty, she goes back to the kitchen and arranges the flutes she bought for her neighbors in a wicker basket, nested into the new dishcloths. She puts in the baguette, the pâtés, the cheese, the mustard and cornichons, and the cold bottle of champagne, and carries it outside and across the porch.

The husband answers the door. A tall boy, handsome, with a long face and a strong jaw. Much better-looking in a conventional way than the wife, a disparity Delia always finds interesting. He's wearing work clothes: jeans and a dark T-shirt. Those huge *healthy* sneakers they all have now. When she introduces herself, a wide grin changes his face, and his hand rises as if to straighten his hair, but he more or less yanks it instead. Nathan, he says his name is.

"Please, come in," he says, and steps back, gesturing expansively into Ilona's living room, filled now with enormous boxes.

"No, no," Delia says, though she does, actually, enter the house— just for a minute, she tells herself. "I *won't* stay. My aim here is not to complicate your life, but to make it easier." She holds the basket out. "This is for you. At whatever stage of the evening you're ready for it."

And now the wife, Meri, comes bounding down the stairs, her puggy, somehow sexy round face smutched with dirt. She's in jeans too, but barefoot. Her hair has been pinned up, and long thin strands have escaped around her face.

"Look what Mrs. Naughton has brought us," Nathan says, holding the basket up to her.

"Oh, it's beautiful," she says. "Thank you so much, Delia. It's Delia, right?" She comes through the boxes to the front door, her hand extended, and they shake.

"It is Delia. And you're Meri, Meri with an *e,* I think." The girl nods, and Delia gestures at the basket. "And this is your reward, for such a hard day's work. There is *nothing* as horrible as moving."

Nathan is standing next to her, and he turns to her now. "Won't you join us for just one glass? It looks like great champagne."

"No, no. I'm not staying, not if you tie me down. I know what it is to unpack a house, and the last thing you need tonight is a guest."

Meri looks relieved. "We *are* dead," she says, and then lets her head loll, her tongue hanging out.

Delia watches the little spasm of irritation pass on Nathan's face.

He disapproves of his wife, of her silliness anyway. It makes Delia turn to Meri and smile. "I would think so," she says.

As Delia steps back to Ilona's storm door, reaching for the handle, Nathan moves along with her. He doesn't want to let her go, clearly. He's speaking of his delight in meeting her, in being neighbors, of his admiration for her husband. They look forward to seeing her. "You and the senator, of course."

"Oh, the senator," she says, smiling. "Yes, on one of his ceremonial visits." And waving her hand vaguely, she opens the door. "We will certainly try to arrange that, once you're settled."

They come and stand in the doorway, thanking her again as she goes around the lion to her own front door.

Her side of the house suddenly seems very orderly, in spite of the books piled everywhere and the mail scattered on the coffee table. In the kitchen, she pours herself another glass of wine, the expensive red wine from France she treats herself to. She makes a light dinner. Salad, a few toasted slices of day-old bread, and the smaller pâté she bought for herself when she got the larger ones for Meri and Nathan. She sits at the kitchen table. She has the little brown radio on low, a jazz station she likes at this hour, as much for the soothing deep voice of the host as for the music itself.

Suddenly she hears voices through the kitchen wall, a low, faint alternation of tones. This startles her for a moment; but then she remembers from the earlier days of Ilona's tenure, when the older woman still sometimes entertained, that the sound carries best in here because of the openings made behind the wall for the pipes to pass through. Here, and unfortunately also in the bathrooms. She will have to get used to *that* again. She turns the music up slightly.

But now their voices rise too for a moment—sharp, perhaps angry. She hopes they're not arguing about her. About her or *the senator*.

Probably not, she tells herself. There are many things to argue about when you're tired, when you've labored side by side all day, each of you bossing the other around. She carries what's left of her dinner to the living room.

Later, as she lies in bed reading, there are a few more thumps and thuds. She sets her book down. She's remembering moving in on this side of the wall with Tom, so many years ago. It was 1965, the children all still in college—no, all but Nancy. She'd started law school.

Delia and Tom were still youthful then, youthful and hopeful, in spite of the hard times they'd just come through. Or maybe because of them. This was to have been their new start, this house, though they had pretended, moving in, that they were an ordinary middle-aged couple, excited about an ordinary move. She remembers that after the kids went out for the evening to explore the new neighborhood, they sat in the kitchen together, exhausted by their long day, and drank almost half a bottle of scotch between them. There was a moment when he made her laugh about something or other. About nothing, really. It was a thing he could do effortlessly, unless she was steeled against it.

Her book is lying on the counterpane, her hand resting on top of it. Under the light falling from the bedside lamp, the bluish veins are sharply delineated, the bones and tendons raised. The hand of an old woman. She isn't looking at it though. She's remembering Tom on that night. He was in his forties then, at the height of his attractiveness, his charm—tall and lanky and still somehow boyish, with his long mocking Irish face, his sandy hair. It was after that first flagrant affair. She found out later that there had been others before it, less important, less disruptive, but this was the first big one, the first one she had to know about.

He sat at the table with her, laughing. And then his face sobered and he leaned over suddenly to say, out of the blue, "Thank you."

She knew that he meant *Thank you for taking me back, thank you for forgiving me, thank you for moving with me into this beautiful house, thank you for making things look all right to the world.*

She had raised her hand. She didn't want to talk about it again, to be reminded of what she felt as her humiliation. She didn't want to be thanked for being a person who would consent to such humiliation. She raised her hand to ward all that off, and he let it go. He sat back and began to talk of other things again.

As she lies there, her hand rises now too, involuntarily this time, against the other memories, the later ones—the memories of the second big affair, the other one she had to know about, the one that ended things. Because when Delia gave him an ultimatum that time, he couldn't let go of the woman. He wasn't able not to see her, not to keep meeting her—in other people's empty apartments, in hotels in New York, in their own house in Washington when Delia was out of town. The circle of friends and colleagues who knew about it grew larger. People expressed their concern to her, about her. About him and what he was doing to his career, his future. But in that other world, the world where politicians were still allowed private lives and some protection from the press, it never broke; there was no public scandal.

And then the affair was suddenly over. Or he told her it was over.

They had tried to put that one behind them too. Oh, Delia was good at trying!—a bitter smile changes her face in the light from her bedside lamp. But his sad attentiveness, his kindness to her, his palpable grief, all these defeated her. The memory floods her now, she's helpless against it. She recalls flying to Washington, to Tom and their house there, where he had slept with his lover; from Washington, from Tom, back to this empty house; looking for a place, any place, where she felt whole.

And then, just after a visit he'd made to her here, weeks after he'd promised the affair was over, a friend in Washington—her closest, dearest friend—called to say that she'd seen them together again. She hadn't been sure she should tell Delia, but then thought that someone else might, more cruelly. "I'd rather it was me," she said.

Delia had said thank you, and hung up. She was in the hallway, by the telephone stand. It was an unusually warm day for early April, one of those gifts of a New England spring. The shifting sun through the bare trees made the light move around her. She'd stood there a long time feeling a number of things, which finally coalesced into a sense of relief.

She was relieved. She didn't need anymore to try, to pretend.

She allows herself this memory fully, without resistance: that moment—the front door open, the dirt smell of early spring.

And the relief. It was all over. The lover, Tom, her shame in front of the two younger children, in front of her friends. It was over. It no longer had anything to do with her, it wasn't anymore her job to make things right.

Within a week she'd flown to France, and four days after that, through some friends of friends, she'd found an apartment to rent at the southern edge of the seventh arrondissement in Paris.

Over that long spring and summer apart, she and Tom began slowly to write each other, to try to work out the terms of their life. She would wait until after the elections to divorce him. She agreed, in fact, to campaign with him—it would have been too damaging to him not to. But they wouldn't live with each other again. He would stay in Washington, and she'd keep the Williston house.

And some of these things did, indeed, happen as they had planned. She appeared publicly with him perhaps twenty or thirty times in that campaign—as a favor, and, she told herself, because she truly didn't care anymore.

She surprised herself, though, by enjoying it, tentatively at first, and then fully, truly. But as she told herself, she'd always liked that part of political life with Tom—the long days moving around among people charmed by him, interested in him. The speeches, full of an idealism and passion that were Tom at his best. The late-night sessions with aides, the loose, easy humor, the relaxed public touching—his hand at her elbow, around her shoulders. His claiming her over and over: "My wife . . . ," "My wife . . . ," "My better half . . ." And after all, of course, she believed in him, politically, and believed he was good at what he did. And a part of all this—her pleasure, her sense of *belonging* with him during this time—was that they were lovers again through the months of campaigning. Without really talking about it, without asking each other much about what it meant, they turned to each other this way too, again and again.

Once he was elected they continued to appear together in public occasionally when it was useful to him, but they separated as they'd agreed to. She went to live alone in Williston.

But she missed him, she found. Missed everything. Missed his body. Missed sitting up late with him after a long day of travel.

Confused, miserable, she began to call him from time to time, to see him, to sleep with him. Again and again she postponed starting in on the divorce.

She tried to discipline herself, as she thought of it. She knew Tom had other women, and she told herself that every time she was thinking of him, he was thinking of someone else. Every time she wanted him, he was making love with someone else. But when she was swept with jealous longing for him, none of that mattered. She couldn't help herself. She called him.

And he let her. Whenever she called, he would come. He would stay with her in Williston for a day or two. Or they would meet in New York. She never knew, never asked, what he put aside, what he had to rearrange in his life to make these visits possible, but he'd never hesitated, never failed to come when she wanted him. And he never asked her, either, what in her life triggered the summonses, made her need to have him.

And then, just when he might have been gearing up to run again, there was another young woman, and photographs this time, and he thought it better not to. Or so she'd heard. They didn't speak to each other of such things anymore. He told her only that times had changed so suddenly and dramatically in the political climate of Washington that he couldn't imagine staying on in government. And of course, that was probably true too.

By then, though, things had changed between them, eased. And she had changed. She was stronger, more independent. Once she actually said to her old friend Madeleine Dexter that she felt coming to terms with Tom's infidelity, learning to live without him, had been the making of her. And that was how she thought of it. That she'd made herself, *re*made herself, in the years of her life after he'd wrecked it.

It seemed too that at some point each of them had begun to think of the odd way they were together as the *shape* of their marriage. Years later he wrote to her, "You were right to want to keep things as they are, because much as I love you, I couldn't have been faithful. I know that now, and if I were honest, I'd have to say I probably knew it then too. So you've kept yourself safe from harm. You've made it so I can love you without hurting you. I can't tell you how grateful I am for that gift, though not a day goes by—not a day, I assure you—when I don't miss you."

She hasn't seen him now for almost four months. The last time they were together, he met her for a weekend at an inn in a little coastal village in Rhode Island. She'd arranged it. She usually arranged things.

They'd spent two nights there. Their room looked out over the harbor. They left the windows open, and the noise of halyards clanking against the masts of the boats rang through the dark, waking Delia occasionally. The night air was damp and cool, but the days warmed slowly after the fog burned off. They walked down to the pier, they walked along the empty beach. They made love the first night, after Delia stroked him to a half erection and helped him come into her.

Afterward, lying in bed listening to Tom's breathing and the night noises, she wondered whether this increased need of his for direct stimulation, for being touched—hands, mouth—had changed his life away from her, his sexual life. Were there younger women who would be tolerant of these signs of his age? For herself, she liked it, liked the sense of her own importance in it, her control. "Help me," he had said the first few times he couldn't get hard, and she had turned to him lovingly.

The second night they drank too much, sitting outside with heavy sweaters on at a restaurant whose terrace looked over the grassy dunes to open water. They were both happy just to sleep next to each other, to wake again in the same bed.

On Sunday she had driven him to the airport in Hartford and then come back the long way, on country roads, to the house in Williston, dreading its emptiness as she often did after her times with Tom. And then in the first days home, alone, doubting herself, sensing how much she'd lost by arranging things as she had, by shielding herself so carefully from the pain of daily life with him; only slowly, over some days, coming to feel at home again, at peace, with the decisions they'd made—she'd made—and the life she was living because of them.

IN THE NIGHT, Delia wakes. Something has waked her. What is it? A noise in the house. She looks at the clock, the glowing numbers: 12:03. This amuses her, what suddenly seems absurd in this digital precision. Once you would simply have said, "I woke in the dead of the night." And it *is* dead—black, noiseless.

She lies still, among the familiar shapes and shadows of her bedroom, listening intently. There it is, again, the noise, now repeating and repeating itself.

She's puzzled for only a few seconds, and then she recognizes it. Of course, it's her new neighbors. They're making love—making love in the noisy, passionate way of young people. She hears it as a series of soft structural whumps. The bed, she supposes, against the wall. It slows, it speeds up. It's slow again. It stops. Or diminishes enough that she can't hear it anymore.

But she's been awakened now, she's wide awake, and she knows it will take her a long, long time to fall asleep again.

CHAPTER THREE

Meri, September 1993

WHEN MERI GOT BACK from the job interview, she wove her way through the packing boxes that were stacked two or three high all over the living room, and went up the stairs to their bedroom to change her clothes. Off with the linen slacks, the slouchy silk top, the bra she'd worn as a kind of good-luck charm, she supposed—a rabbit's foot in the form of underwire uplift. From a pile of dirty clothes in the corner of the bedroom—all the work clothes she and Nathan had been wearing the day before—she picked up her blue jeans and pulled them on. Bare-breasted, she went through her suitcases for a clean T-shirt to wear while she got back to work unpacking. Unpacking and then unpacking again. This was her bargain with Nathan, who was spending his first day on campus, mostly at obligatory meetings. If she would keep on unpacking—*keep on untrucking,* she thought—he would make dinner. This was a great bargain, actually, as Nathan was a better cook than she was.

She hadn't said anything to him about the interview. It seemed a bad idea to talk about it ahead of time. She didn't want to jinx it. And she didn't want him to be *involved* in it either, which is what happened when you told Nathan stuff—he made it his own somehow.

She came down the stairs. And stopped, on the landing, looking around her in a way she hadn't the day before, they'd been so flat-out busy. *This is my house,* she said to herself—this big open room below her, that curved bank of windows around the front of the room with the beautiful wooden bench underneath it, the fireplace with a mantel of the same wood.

And of course all those boxes, Meri. Boxes everywhere. All of them to be unpacked. Step one. She came down the last short flight of stairs.

In the kitchen, she spread pâté on three of the crackers that Delia Naughton had brought them last night, and stood eating over the solid-core door, scattering crumbs onto it. She'd have to call Delia today to thank her.

She thought of Delia last night, of how eager Nathan had been around her. It had made him seem like a kid to her, and she didn't like that. But of course, she'd seemed like a flake to him—as he was at pains to tell her afterward—the way she had stuck her tongue out, the face she made. So naturally she'd countered with his doggishness around Delia.

A fight, sort of. A little fight. A little fight after which, she reminded herself, they had made love. But she wasn't used to fighting with Nathan.

She sighed. It was no doubt inevitable. So life begins. They couldn't have stayed sealed up in her apartment forever, showing each other only their shiny, best selves.

She poured water into the coffee machine to make herself another cup. While the machine was percolating, she walked around the first floor reading the labels on the cartons that sat everywhere, and thinking about the interview. It had gone well, she thought. At least she was pretty sure it had gone well. She felt comfortable, anyway, as soon as the receptionist led her into the warren of hallways that comprised the radio station. The people passing said *hi*. She could see groups of two or three talking by their desks in the big open office space. As they walked past one of the rooms off the hall, she saw through a window a bunch of people sitting around a table together, talking, laughing, making notes. She realized that this was exactly how she'd imagined it would be, though she'd never worked in radio before. But what had attracted her to the job description was the sense of familiarity she'd had as she read it. She thought that it might be very like her old job on the alumni magazine, the same combination she'd loved there of schmoozing at the planning stage, and then solitary research. It was reassuring that the schmoozing part, anyway, looked the same.

She'd said as much in her interview with James, the producer of the show she was applying for—an hour-long newsmagazine that aired at noon each day. She said that it seemed to her that the work might be substantially the same, "but faster, of course, and, I don't know, maybe a little shallower?"

He had laughed. "That sounds about right," he said, nodding his head several times in a diminishing motion. He was a short, slightly overweight man perhaps in his late twenties, with a patchy blond beard and shoulder-length hair of a thickness and texture Meri would have killed for.

And she had made him laugh. A good sign.

But enough, enough of that. She didn't want to get her hopes up. She went back to the kitchen and poured some coffee into her chipped blue mug. Moving through the boxes, sipping coffee, she tried to focus on the chores ahead—the things, the endless things, to be unwrapped and put away.

About half of the furniture in the house and at least fifteen of the largest cartons scattered around had come from Nathan's mother—possessions she'd had in storage since her move to an apartment in a retirement community. Possessions she'd held on to to give to her only child when he settled down. Which he'd done now, with Meri. Which she'd done too, she supposed. Settled down.

She said it out loud. "Settled down." And then remembered that this was a favorite phrase of her mother's. "You girls settle down," she'd call up to them at night. "Don't make me come up there, or you'll be sorry."

God, how unbridgeably different her childhood was from Nathan's!

She thought of his mother—so unfailingly soft-spoken. Nathan had once told Meri that he'd never been hit, by either parent. Well, there you had it.

The thing that bothered her most about the gifts from his mother, Meri thought now, was that there had been no discussion between her and Nathan about them. She hadn't even known about them until she discovered that the movers were making a stop in New Jersey to pick them up.

"But what *are* they?" she'd asked.

"What does it matter?" he said. "We need everything."

That was true, of course. Nathan had been living in a furnished apartment in Coleman, with a few of his own things, but mostly with books. Books stacked on the floor, books piled on his desk. They filled dozens of boxes when he packed them up.

Meri had more furniture, but they would leave much of it behind—it was too marginal, too shabby to be worth the expense of moving it. So he was right: it made sense to take whatever his mother had to give them. They could use it, whatever it was. And yes, she said to him, it was generous of his mother.

Still, there was a part of her that was pissed off about this. That felt, again, excluded from decisions that affected her. They had talked about this too, and he pointed out that she had agreed in the end—and that he'd known she *would* agree—so what difference did it really make?

"A big difference," she said. But even to herself that sounded petulant, childish. So she'd said, "Oh, grow up, Meri." And then she said, "Thanks, Meri. I think I will," and he had smiled at her, the hungry smile that made him look dangerous and exciting.

And the truth was that she could hardly complain about the unpacking work involved. To her surprise, it had taken boxes and boxes to contain her own stuff, *her* accumulation of things in this life. Things: her own boxes and boxes of books. A couple more boxes of CDs and tapes. A rusty toy sewing machine that made her think of her mother—she had bought it at a flea market. A large pale pink shell from an old lover, a shell whose two halves fit together in a way he had found sexual. A few old LP records—*Sgt. Pepper,* Bruce Springsteen, Muddy Waters—though she had no way of playing them anymore. A woven-straw cigarette case of her mother's and several pairs of earrings she'd hardly ever worn. Meri had found these in her mother's top dresser drawer when they cleared the house out after her death.

All this, and much, much more. She wasn't quite sure why she'd kept any of it, since the way she felt about her past was that she had somehow come into being who she was without any connection to it. *As if floating in naked and unencumbered on some shell,* she thought now. Her mouth twisted: the only difference being she was not *quite* so beautiful as that.

Oh, of course she remembered the way it had been. Of course she was the person who emerged from that forlorn little house with the dented aluminum siding and the overgrown lawn and the gas station next door. With the dirty screens that crumbled and smelled of rust when you pressed your nose to them. With the sunlight only dimly filtering through the stale curtains that were always pulled closed. She remembered it all—the air inside thick with cigarette smoke, the TV on day and night, the way they would all stop occasionally in the midst of doing other things to watch it for a moment, as if being beckoned by another world. What she, anyway, imagined as the *real* world. She remembered even as a kid wondering how she could *get there*—there seemed no possible connection between her world and that one.

Of course that was part of her, but she was also the person who willed herself away from it. Not because of any focused ambition, any clear sense of direction. Just that at every step when there was a choice, she chose the thing that led away and let go of where she was, of who she was. And somehow that accumulation of forks in the road—all those roads not taken, thank you, Robert Frost—had given her this. This fancy house. This unfamiliar furniture. These boxes full of someone else's past, someone else's beloved *things*.

"But come *on*," she said aloud. "This is enviable." She thought again of the interview, of her ease in talking to James and the others. It was going to work out. She went into the kitchen and rinsed her cup in the old sink. Then she got out a knife and started to slice open the first of the boxes.

When James called from the radio station at three-thirty, she had to ask him to wait a minute while she turned down the stereo—she'd gotten it set up, she'd found some of their CDs, and she had Eric Clapton on at a high volume to give herself energy.

When she picked up the phone again in the sudden silence and said hello, he said, without preamble, "Well, it's yours if you want it."

Her heartbeat felt irregular for a second or two. "Then, yes! It's mine!" she said. "God, this is wonderful!" She jumped lightly in place. "Oh, I'm really happy."

"Yeah, we're all really pleased too," he said. On the phone he sounded even younger than he looked. "The thing is, of course, that we'd like you to start as soon as you can."

Meri looked around her at the room full of boxes. "I think if you give me a couple of days to unpack, I'll be set to go. So, maybe first thing next week?"

They agreed, and then she talked to Jane and Brian, the cohosts of the show, whom she'd met briefly as part of the interview. Just before she hung up, Jane said, "You ought to be told, in all fairness, that it's an insane place to work, but we thought you'd fit right in."

After she'd cradled the phone, she went into the living room and turned Clapton back up. He was singing "Layla." Perfect. She danced, briefly. Her feet were bare, and she could feel grit on the old floor-boards.

When the song ended, she roamed the first floor searching for her purse—it turned out she'd tossed it on the bench under the windows. She extracted her cigarettes and a book of matches and went to sit on the back stoop.

She loved the way the sulfur smelled as she struck the match. She loved the sensation of the first drag on the cigarette. Music floated out from behind her. The sun through the sycamore leaves was warm, and the cigarette shut her off in a little circle of private plea-sure from everything she still had to do. She heard a dog barking somewhere. The breeze pushed at the trees and made the sunlight dance around her. A frenzy of tiny bugs hung like a cloud in the air nearby. She closed her eyes and watched the bloody afterimages slide behind her lids. I am happy, she thought. "As a clam," she said out loud. And then opened her eyes and corrected herself: "As a lark."

SHE DIDN'T HEAR Nathan come in, but suddenly the music was turned down low. Meri was in the kitchen, and she'd gotten almost everything in there put away, into the shelves and drawers in the pantry, into the old bureaus under the solid-core door. The boxes were gone, broken down and stacked flat in a corner of the room. The newsprint that had been wrapped around everything was in many green plastic trash bags, bags she'd tossed with a kind of pleasurable abandon into the backyard for now. She'd put a cotton rag rug down in front of the sink. She'd even hung a few pictures—a Hopperesque painting of the deserted main street in Coleman done by a friend of hers, and a framed reprint Nathan had of a photograph of Lyndon Johnson persuading a much smaller politician of something—the helpless little man bent backward in terror, Johnson looming over him.

"Natey?" she called into the silence.

He appeared in the kitchen doorway, carrying two bags of groceries, one in each arm. He was dressed in his academic uniform—a jacket, a work shirt, and slacks. No tie. His hair was wild. He set the bags down on the door. "Wow!" he said, looking around.

"What do you think?" she said.

"Thank *you,* is what I think." He grabbed her, kissed her. "You must have been at it nonstop, all day." He kept his arm over her shoulders, around her neck.

"It was nothing," she said lightly. She leaned her head against his. His cheek was slightly bristly after his long day. After a moment, she stepped away from him, out of his embrace. "Tell me what you got us for dinner. I am *starving*."

"A big salad." He stopped her and rubbed at something on her cheek. "My, you're a dirty girl."

"Newsprint, I bet," she volunteered, holding her face still for him. "It got all over me."

When he was done, she moved backward, pulling him along with her. She scooted herself up on the door counter, her face level with his. She wrapped her legs around him. She rested her elbows on his shoulders. "How was your day?" she asked. Then she pitched her voice higher and made it singsong. "How was school, honey?"

And so he began—the computer meeting, the library meeting, the departmental meeting. After a few minutes, she got down and began to go through the grocery bags, setting things out. Beer. She held a bottle up.

"Yes, thanks," he said.

She got a church key from one of the bureau drawers and opened two of the bottles. She handed one to him and took a long swig herself of the bitter, fizzy stuff. She was thirsty. She hadn't drunk anything since the coffee that morning.

She was really only half listening to Nathan, thinking more about how surprised he would be when she told him about the job at the radio station. *I've got a secret,* she thought.

He had moved on to an account of lunch with the dean. She made him a cracker with pâté, and had another one herself.

He'd taken her place on the door by now, boosting himself onto it, his legs dangling. His jacket was off and he'd rolled his sleeves up. She loved his arms. His arms, and his hands—so surprisingly long-fingered and delicate for a man his size.

He described the motley collection of furniture in his office. He said he'd gone over to the college gym to check out the pool hours—he was a swimmer, with a swimmer's graceful, strong body. He told her about the colleague across the hall, and the joke this guy had told him.

"A joke already!" Meri said. "What a good sign!" She'd started to eat grapes from the second grocery bag.

"Well, I don't know," he said. "It was a dirty joke. Is that a good sign? I mean, isn't it too soon to tell a guy you don't even know a dirty joke?"

"I don't know either," she said. "But then I've never understood any of the rules for guys." She had another grape. "Was it a good dirty joke?"

"So-so." He slid sideways, closer to the grocery bags. He began to eat the grapes too.

"These aren't washed, you know," Meri said.

"I know."

"Aren't you worried that we'll suddenly break out in some horrible scabrous rash? That we'll develop uncontrollable facial tics?" She blinked one eye rapidly, jerking her head along with it.

"I think there's some danger that our children will," he said.

She had another swallow of beer. "The hell with them," she said. "They're such brats."

"But they're such *interesting* brats. So intelligent. So gifted."

Meri snorted. She tore off a long stem dangling with grapes and handed it to him. "Now it's your turn, buddy," she said.

"My turn for what?"

"Your turn to say, 'How was *your* day, sweetheart?'"

"And? How was it? Aside from being productive." He waved his hand to include all she'd accomplished.

"It was really, really, really productive. In that"—she danced away from him, jumped and landed, spreading her arms wide—"ta da! I got a job."

"What job?" She enjoyed watching his face move from puzzlement to surprise. "The radio job?"

She nodded.

"But I didn't even know you had an interview. Why didn't you tell me?" There was the slightest note of irritation in his voice, but then he said, "That's fantastic!"

He slid down off the door. He kissed her, a beery kiss that was slippery and lasted awhile.

"Let's congratulate me," she said, her mouth only an inch from his. "Let's fuck."

"What? Now? I thought you were starving."

"I've taken the edge off." She stepped back.

"But you're filthy."

"So? Come lick the dirt off me."

She walked with long strides to the back stairwell and started up, peeling her shirt off as she went. She took the steps two at a time, feeling an anticipatory pleasure in using her long muscular legs this way. She could hear Nathan behind her. She tossed her shirt back at him and sprinted down the hall to their room at the front of the house. It was sunny and hot in here—they were sweating almost as soon as they lay down together, grappling with each other to take off the other's clothes. And as they moved against each other, making love, their bodies made slapping noises, squelching noises.

By the time they were done, they were panting and slick with per-spiration. They lay together for a few minutes. Then Nathan unstuck himself from her and fell back. Meri's hand lifted to her chest. She had a little pool of liquid between her breasts. After a few minutes, Nathan propped his head up in one hand, and with the other he began to stroke the sweat there, spreading it out over her nipples.

"Your project," she said.

"I'm doing a very good job at it. A very thorough job."

"Thank you." She picked his hand up and brought it to her mouth. She kissed his salty fingertips.

They talked in a desultory way for a while, each bringing more news of the first day of life here. Meri told him in detail about the interview. The low sun was slanting into the room. After a while, their voices slowed and stopped. The tall wardrobe boxes stood sentinel around them. They slept.

They woke midevening as the air cooled. They got up and put on T-shirts and underwear and went downstairs together to unpack the groceries, most of them still sitting in their bags on the old door-table. Meri found a blue china bowl from Nathan's mother and set the fruit he'd brought home into it—three shiny red apples and what was left of the pale green grapes.

MERI LOVED HER JOB. Even on the first days when she didn't know what she was doing and had to ask for help over and over, she loved it.

The station was based at the college, in half of the ground floor of a building at its edge. The other half held the offices of the campus police. She liked them too—flirty, friendly, middle-aged guys. She liked the long walk or bike ride each day through the center of town and across the campus. She liked the campus itself, with its huge oaks and even a few remaining elms, its beautiful old stone buildings. She liked the little carts selling falafel and wraps that set up in the walk-ways at lunchtime, she liked the students calling to one another across the lush greens, playing lacrosse and soccer and Frisbee on them.

The station did mostly music through the day—classical in the morning, jazz and then rock in the afternoon and evening, and late at night, the blues. There was a short news summary at the beginning of each hour, and four times a day there was a longer break for news.

The noon news show, the one Meri was working for, started with a five-minute feed from National Public Radio, and then covered four or five of its own topics in greater depth. These could be almost anything—peculiar or touching human-interest stories, politics, the arts, whatever the current local or world or national crisis was.

Meri's job was partly helping to generate ideas for these topics, mostly in the afternoon meetings just after the show ended; and partly conjuring and contacting the relevant people to be interviewed about each one—interviewed live at the station, or in another National Public Radio studio somewhere, or by phone. Phone was always the last choice, because the sound quality wasn't as good.

At the afternoon meetings everyone was always relaxed. The show was over and there was a sense of ease and play in the way they tossed ideas around. People brought in newspaper articles, offbeat facts they'd discovered, new books or CDs they'd read or heard or seen reviewed. Burt Hall was the anniversary guy, the birthday guy— he maintained a perpetually updated list of what had happened or who'd been born one hundred years ago tomorrow, or fifty years, or twenty-five—sometimes important anniversaries, sometimes whimsical ones, all of them available to fall back on on a slow day. There was one other person with a job identical to Meri's—Natalie. She'd been there three years, ever since they started the show. She was about Meri's age, small, with wildly frizzing hair. She was patient and generous about explaining things.

By the time Meri had been at the station for ten days, she'd worked on more than a half dozen of the show's segments. The first one was a piece on shaken-baby syndrome. She'd lined up participants for a roundtable discussion with Jane—a couple of pediatricians, a specialist in medical forensics, and a social worker who counseled parents having difficulty with anger. Meri spoke with them all at length by telephone ahead of time to prepare Jane's questions and suggest approaches for her to take in the discussion. This was called, she learned, the *pre-interview,* designed to make Brian or Jane sound intelligent and knowledgeable about whatever they were discussing.

She was so busy learning what the steps were as she worked on this piece, so nervous and distracted about how to frame the questions, how to seek out the appropriate people, that she hardly had the time left to think about the issue under consideration, a topic that had been triggered by the local death of a little girl of five months. Her middle-class father, a cocaine addict, had killed her— accidentally, he said.

As she listened to the program, she was first amazed at how it had come together, at how professional it was; and then she was surprised to find tears welling in her eyes at different points during the discussion. How immediate it was compared to the writing she'd done for the alumni magazine! In this case, how awful: the father's drugged rage, the terrible injuries to the tiny child.

Still, she couldn't help herself, she was pleased. Hearing her words spoken in Jane's melodious, warm, sympathetic voice made them sound so professional.

Radio, she thought, even as she was blowing her nose. *I'm glad I found you.*

Meri was doing research for something else entirely when she found an old photograph of Tom Naughton. He was standing behind the senators on the Watergate committee. He was less conventionally handsome than she had imagined him—tall and skinny—but even in this grainy shot there was a visible kind of relaxation and ease in his carriage that made him attractive. She photocopied the image to take home to Nathan.

They'd speculated several times about his failure to appear next door even once in the three weeks or so they'd lived there. At first they decided he must be traveling. He'd be back at some point soon.

As time went on, though, they conjured other possibilities. Maybe they were divorced, Meri suggested.

But then she had two or three conversations with Delia on the front porch, and Delia didn't indicate anything of the kind. In fact, she always spoke of Tom as her husband; and, as Nathan pointed out to Meri, there was that thing she had said to them the night they moved in—about having them over when Tom was home.

Maybe it was a commuting marriage, he speculated, and she agreed that this was the likeliest explanation. Delia seemed to have been away at least once for several days—that was probably it.

But Meri knew Nathan was disappointed that Tom Naughton seemed not, in any real sense, to be their neighbor, and she couldn't help wondering if in some way he felt he'd been tricked into buying the house. She didn't want to ask him that though—in part because she sensed the question would be connected to something faintly and reasonlessly vindictive in herself, something she didn't quite understand. For why should she take any pleasure in his disappointment?

The Xerox, then, was a gift, a way of commiserating, a way of sharing in his puzzlement.

CHAPTER FOUR

Meri, September and October 1993

THE CONVERSATIONS Meri had had with Delia on the front porch as they came and went were the usual kinds of exchanges, cordial but empty, that people who don't know each other well have. But Delia always brought something extra to them, a certain style.

"Suicidal yet?" she'd asked Meri cheerfully a couple of days after their arrival, when it seemed they'd barely begun to unpack. And told her, in the ensuing conversation, where the best liquor store in town was. "I find that the influence of alcohol makes anything more tolerable," she'd said in a comforting tone.

And on a rainy day, as she and Meri each stood at her own front door, Meri fumbling with the trickiness of the old lock on hers, Delia having trouble collapsing her umbrella, she had turned to Meri and said across the lion, "Don't let them wax rhapsodic to you about autumn in New England. There are about six wonderful days, and then"—she gestured up at the gray sky—"*this*."

These exchanges confirmed for Meri the feeling she'd had when she first met Delia. "She's eccentric," she told Nathan. "But in a warm way."

"As opposed to?"

"Eccentric in an egocentric way, or a chilly way, natch."

They were bicycling home together when they had this conversation, weaving slowly through the wide, untrafficked streets. She had stopped by his office after work to rescue him from office hours. He had them every Wednesday, and every Wednesday he was late getting home. When she'd opened his door—after knocking, after being invited in—he was sitting across the desk from a girl so lovely that Meri had been momentarily stabbed with jealousy. But then she looked at Nathan—Nathan, whose face was lifted in relief and pleasure at seeing her—and she forgave him instantly for the student's beauty.

"Her eccentricity invites you in, that's what it is. It's not self-regarding, the way so much eccentricity is."

"You've got a crush on her, I think." He'd pulled up next to her and they were bicycling side by side. They both had old three-speed bikes they'd bought used in Coleman, and she loved the way he looked, sitting up straight with the wind blowing his hair back.

"I've got a crush on you," she said.

On the third Friday after they'd moved in, there was a message from Delia waiting for her on the answering machine at the end of the day. She was going to drive out into the country tomorrow morning, to a farmstand she liked, and she wondered if Meri would like to come along—it was supposed to be beautiful weather.

When Meri told Nathan about the invitation, he smiled. "Hey. Nice," he said. After a moment though, when he'd gone back to what he was doing—they were in the backyard, and he was grilling fish for supper—he said suddenly, "How come, do you think, she didn't ask us both?"

Meri looked down at him from the stoop where she was sitting. "Natey," she said. "Shame. You're jealous."

"Well, I suppose I am. But I'm the one who'd really like to get to know them, after all."

"What? And I don't?"

"But you know what I mean." He picked up a saucer of olive oil and started to brush some on each fish. "I'm the one who cares more about who they are. Who *he* is, anyway." He replaced the lid on the grill. "Not that he's ever even there." He made a moue.

"Well, maybe that gets tiresome for her, everyone's abiding

interest in 'the senator.' Maybe that's why she asked me—because she knows I'm interested in her, her, and only her."

He came up onto the stoop and sat next to her. Their four bare feet were in a row, and she bent down quickly and touched his.

After a minute, he said, "You know, this is something I just don't get about you."

"What?"

"About you and women. Older women."

"That's because you have a warm, accommodating *enthusiast* of a mother. She's in your corner, always."

They were quiet a long moment. The charcoal smelled wonderful. It was dusky and cool. This would be one of the last times for grilling outside.

Meri said, "The real reason, of course, is that we're the *gals*. She doesn't think you'd be interested in the farmstand. It's not manly enough."

He grunted. "Mmm."

"And you couldn't go anyway, so there's no need for petulance." She had a sip of wine, and set her glass back down next to her on the wooden step. "You'll be working, as usual."

Nathan had gone to his office both days of the last two weekends to work on his book—his second book. The first, which had gotten some attention in his field, had been an expansion of his doctoral thesis on family structure and poverty. This one was more ambitious, more consuming. It was about the Great Society programs. It interspersed an account of the politics that had dictated the shape of those programs with the life stories of five people who were supposed to have benefited from them, bringing their histories up to the present. The research had taken him two years, and he'd been writing it since before Meri met him. He wanted to finish it by the end of the following summer because it would be important in his getting tenure. He'd been working on it every minute he could spare from keeping up with his courses.

"Yeah, you're right," he said. And after a long moment, "I wonder where old Tom *is*, anyway."

· · ·

THE WEATHER was beautiful on Saturday—one of the six fall days Delia had spoken of, cool and dry, with a bright sun.

Meri rang Delia's bell, as arranged, and after a moment, she saw the older woman coming down the hallway toward her.

"Come in! Come in!" she said as she opened the door. "Come in *this* door and then let's go out the back one—the car is in the driveway off the kitchen." She turned back into the house. Meri followed. She was wearing those canvas shoes again, the ones Meri liked. As Meri walked quickly through Delia's rooms, she was startled by how different they were from the ones on their side. She said this to Delia after they were strapped into their seats.

"We owe that to the Carters, who preceded you in your house," she said. She had started toward Main Street.

"Oh, yes," Meri said. "I remember. He was an architect, right? The real estate person said something about that."

"Precisely," Delia said. "Taking out the walls was his notion of the way things ought to be. Open. Airy. And she let him. I don't think she cared a whit about anything to do with the house or any of that kind of thing."

After a moment, Delia said, "Ilona was a musician. Or had been. The violin. It was all she really cared about, music. Besides people, of course."

"Of course," Meri said, though to her mind this did not go without saying.

They were passing through the center of town. The sidewalks were already busy with Saturday-morning shoppers. As she drove, Delia's foot moved on and off the gas pedal whimsically, almost rhythmically. The car speeded up and slowed down, speeded up and slowed down. It was a little like being in a rocking chair, Meri thought.

"In the years right after we moved in, they used to have huge parties quite regularly." She looked over at Meri. "It's a good space for parties, if you're so inclined. That big open area, and then the kitchen. The kitchen that seats *thousands*. We went a few times. They were great fun. All architects and musicians." After a moment she said, "I love architects and musicians, don't you? They're so *healthy*."

"They are?" Meri asked.

"I think so, yes."

"This is something I hadn't realized."

Delia looked over at Meri quickly and smiled. After a moment she said, "Well, I think it's true. Their work connects them so directly to other people, and that makes them happier. Or it seems to."

"Ah," Meri said. She wondered if this was true.

As they drove along, Meri rolled her window down and let the air push her hair back. They were on a closed-in, winding road now. The air smelled of the pinewoods around them. Delia was telling Meri about the history of the town, how it had been centered around a mill on the river built by Gideon Willis; how the center had moved to where it was now years later, after the college was established; how, much later than that, the mill itself was abandoned.

"But it's restored now," she said. "There's a restaurant there. It's quite pretty. Romantic, really. You and Nathan ought to go there sometime."

After a moment, Meri asked, "Have you gone? With your husband?"

"Not for years," Delia said, equably.

They were moving past open fields. Some, here and there, were under cultivation. Some were overgrown. Hay fields, Delia said, waiting to be mown for the last time this year. After about ten more minutes, Delia signaled again and pulled over into a dirt parking lot around a long, low, shedlike building, painted white with dark green trim. Six or seven cars were already parked under the spreading linden next to it, and there were at least that many people at the open front of the building, where bins—wooden boxes, really—were set on two long trestle tables, tilted forward to show their brightly colored contents. Meri got out and followed Delia, walking past the array.

There were tomatoes and peaches and lettuces and apples. There were green grapes, and red ones, and bluish purple ones. There were potatoes in several shapes and colors, and small, fresh-looking carrots with their feathery green tops still attached. There were onions and scallions and heads of garlic and bushels of corn. There were boxes overflowing with basil and mint, tied bunches of thyme. "God, the abundance!" Meri said. "It's overwhelming."

Delia picked up a basket from where two towers of them were stacked at the end of the tables and began to move back along the boxes. "I only do fruit and lettuces," she said. "It makes things simpler. I hardly ever cook anymore."

"I never used to cook," Meri said. "But I'm afraid we do now, every single night. I guess that's what's supposed to happen when you get married."

"They do seem to go hand in hand," Delia said.

"We share it. Nathan's terrific and I'm so-so. But I'm learning."

Delia's old fingers moved quickly over the fruits, gently squeezing. "You'll have to rearrange a few things in that old kitchen if you're going to get very tricky about it."

"Oh, I know," Meri said. She was filling her basket more slowly than Delia, who seemed to know ahead of time exactly what she wanted. Meri chose apples, lettuce. "But Nathan is making plans," she said. "Plans for *renovation.* He loves to roll the word around in his mouth."

"Renovation," Delia pronounced loftily, "is almost as much fun as moving."

Meri laughed, and looked over at her. She was smiling slyly to herself, pleased, it seemed, to have been found amusing.

Meri hesitated by the basket of corn. Should she get some? She and Nathan hadn't discussed what to have for dinner, but it looked so fresh, the tassels still silky and white, the husks tight, that she couldn't resist. Two. No, four. She chose a hard, fat garlic, a sampling of herbs.

They went inside to pay. The shed had a dirt floor and two bare lightbulbs hanging from a wire strung across the ceiling. The plump woman running the cash register knew Delia. She greeted her warmly. She asked about her grandchildren, and Delia inquired about the woman's husband, who wasn't well, apparently.

There was a plate stacked with individually wrapped pieces of fudge on the counter by the cash register. Delia bought two squares as she settled with the woman. "To fortify us on the trip home," she said.

In the car, she unwrapped a corner of her piece. She nibbled on it as she began to drive. Meri imitated her, holding the fudge in the plastic wrap just as Delia did, to avoid getting her hands sticky.

"So. You're pretty much settled in?" Delia asked after a few minutes.

"After a fashion." Meri shrugged. "We don't have curtains, we need a new couch, we need new rugs, we want to paint just about everything, but aside from that, yes, sure, pretty much."

"Agony," Delia said.

"Actually, I think the worst of it is over," Meri said. She let the fudge dissolve in her mouth and watched the fields flash by.

"I hope never to move again," Delia said. "I want to be carried out feetfirst, as Ilona was."

Meri turned back to Delia. "Ilona *was*?"

"Yes."

"You mean she died in the house?"

"Yes." Delia looked at her. "Didn't you know that?"

"No." Meri was startled. It seemed strange to think of. They had been sleeping in the room where someone died. They had been making love in that room.

"Well," Delia said, "she did."

Meri shook her head. "It's just that I didn't know."

After a minute, Delia said, "You'd probably be hard-pressed to find one of the older houses in town that someone hadn't died in. That's where people used to be when they died. Home."

"I just hadn't thought of it," Meri said, almost apologetically.

Delia drove on, speeding up, slowing down. "It was, I think, a happy death."

"I didn't know there was such a thing as *that,* either."

"Well, we can't really know, can we?" Delia laughed a little. "But if you're old enough, I think, you're ready. And Ilona was. She was tired. Her world had shrunk. Her pleasures were fewer." Delia shrugged. "I can certainly imagine it."

She seemed to be doing just that, Meri thought. Her expression was faraway.

Then her face lifted. "She once said to me, 'When you get to be my age, you've had to watch most of your friends die.' Seemingly sad. But *then* she said—after one of her wonderful *judicious* pauses—'But of course you get to watch your enemies die too.'"

Meri laughed. She had the last bite of fudge and crumpled up her plastic wrap. She saw that Delia was almost finished too. "Can I take that?" she asked, pointing to the plastic.

"Oh. Yes. Thank you." Delia popped the last bit of fudge into her mouth and handed over the wrap. Meri crumpled that up too, and put both into her purse.

They drove in silence for a while. Meri was looking out the window. She looked back at Delia, who seemed drawn in somehow. Or maybe just concentrated on driving.

"So, you moved here in the sixties, was it?" Meri asked.

"That's right. The mid-sixties. Before the sixties *were* the sixties."

"And did you love the house right away?" Meri asked, thinking of her own complicated feelings about her side.

"Well, I don't know, really," Delia said. "I suppose a new house often represents something, doesn't it?" Her hand gestured. Her eyes were steady on the road. "Some change in your life, or perhaps, if you're married, a change in your life together. So you feel a kind of hopefulness, usually, with a move, but perhaps you feel a little anxiety too."

"Yes," Meri said. And after a moment, "Was your husband already a senator then? When you bought the house?"

"No, not yet. A congressman. We commuted to Washington. Or he did, mostly. I stayed more in Williston the first few years. Brad, my youngest, was still in high school." She looked at Meri and smiled. "I had the bit part here, the congressman's wife, while he paraded around down there, the hero: the congressman himself."

"But the separation must have been hard," Meri said. She was thinking that she might be able to bring this around to Tom's absence, to unearthing the reasons for it.

"Oh, I got used to it," Delia said. "You can get used to anything." After a moment she said, "It's surprising to discover that, but it's one of the most necessary things life teaches us. Don't you think?"

And Meri, once again, was startled into what felt like confusion by a chance remark of Delia's. She wasn't sure how to answer. "Well, I suppose," she said. "But I . . . haven't discovered that yet, I guess."

"Ah," Delia said, smiling. "*Yet.*"

"Yes," Meri said. "No."

Delia looked quickly at Meri, mischief on her face. "I so love it when people answer a question with, 'Yes, no.'" She turned, in noble profile again, and after a moment she said, "Or 'No, yes,' for that matter."

THAT EVENING when Meri told Nathan about her excursion with Delia, she tried to describe to him the way Delia had affected her several times, in those moments that had startled her. "It's those aperçus, you know."

"I don't know. Tell me."

Meri looked up at him over the table—he was waiting, his eyes, opened wide, on her. She had never met a man before Nathan who said this—"Tell me." Who said it and then sat back to listen.

But just as she was about to explain, she stopped and frowned. "Come to think of it though, maybe they're *my* aperçus, after she says something." She pondered it. "No, that's not the way it works. They're hers. *She* understands what she's saying, what the frame of reference is, but I don't, quite. I don't get the implications, fully, I think, and it stops me in my tracks."

Their knives and forks clinked. They were having a meal cooked by Meri tonight, one of about six dishes she knew how to make. Pork chops with a mustard sauce.

"Give me a *for instance,*" he said.

"For instance," she said. "I was about to ask a direct question about Tom—for *you,* Natey, on your behalf, trying to solve the great mystery of where he is. My angle was sympathy—how hard it must have been when he was in Washington in Congress and she had to stay in Williston for the kids, et cetera. This is what she'd just been talking about. And I was proceeding rapidly down the track, toward the station, really getting close, I thought, when she derailed me. Stopped me dead. With an aperçu."

"Which was?"

"Something about—oh, I can't even remember it, exactly. It had to do with life, as they mostly do. Life with a capital L. How you learn to endure things, or something."

He finished what he was chewing. "Not very remarkable, as aperçus go."

"Maybe not. But it felt remarkable in the moment. It felt like *news*."

THEY HAD TO invite Delia three times before they found an evening she could come over for dinner. The first time she was headed to Maine for the weekend to see her son and his family, and the second time she had a concert she was attending with some friends.

"Why don't we have things to do?" Meri asked Nathan. "Why don't we go to a concert with some friends?"

"Because we're new in town, and we're both out of our minds with work," Nathan said.

This was true, though truer for Nathan than for Meri. On most days, she got to leave her work behind when she came home. Nathan's went on and on, with class preparation in the evenings, with his book on the weekends. And when they did have free time together, the house claimed them. They'd painted two rooms so far, the kitchen and their bedroom. In the bedroom they'd had to strip off the old wallpaper first, with a steamer they rented for one long, muggy day. The air in the room was still damp when they went to bed that night, and it smelled of old wallpaper paste. Meri liked it—the wheaty humidity—but Nathan said it waked him on and off all night.

They *had* gone to a few social events. There'd been an opening tea at the dean's house, and twice different colleagues of Nathan's had

had them over for dinner with others. But generally, unless they were asked or required to do something, they tended to stay home. To stay home by themselves. Delia would be their first guest, and Meri was slightly nervous about the meal—which she was in charge of: Nathan had to work late—and about how things would go.

When Meri answered the door, Delia *sailed* in—for the first time Meri thought she understood that word as it would apply to a human being. She was carrying a huge spray of white lilies. While Nathan opened a bottle of wine in the living room, Meri got out the folding stepladder and looked through the high shelves in the pantry for a vase big enough for the flowers. Nothing. She finally had to put them in a galvanized bucket, they were so tall and full. Even in this homely container, though, they made the living room suddenly more finished-looking when she carried them in to where Delia and Nathan were sitting.

She set them on the curved bench in front of the darkening windows. "They're gorgeous, Delia," she said, stepping back. "Thank you."

"Well, the thing is, lilies *last*," Delia said. Meri looked over at her. Her wineglass was in her hand, her legs were crossed. For a woman in her seventies, she looked absurdly glamorous, Meri thought.

"*And* they're gorgeous," Nathan said.

Meri sat down on the slightly sagging couch, which had come from her apartment in Coleman. Delia was in the wing chair from Nathan's mother, Nathan was in an old armchair of his. None of these things matched, or even began to complement each other.

They talked for a while about how they were settling in, and then Meri had to get up and go to the kitchen. She had to baste the pork roast, being careful not to let the one wobbly rack in the oven tip it onto the floor. Then she had to sauté the shallots for the green beans. She was in and out of the kitchen a good deal, actually, before the meal. It was too fancy, she realized—what she'd planned. It took her away too much.

But she could tell that it was going well between Delia and Nathan. She could hear their voices quickly alternating, and Nathan's big laugh rang out often. Delia was charming him, just as she'd charmed Meri whenever their paths crossed. This was what being a senator's wife would do for you, Meri supposed—turn you into an almost professionally charming person.

When Meri made her last appearance, Nathan was talking about his book. He was expansive under Delia's questioning, and Meri could hear pleasure in his voice. He'd messed his hair up too. *Nate.*

At dinner, Meri had her turn receiving Delia's energetic attention. She found herself explaining her work in almost as full detail as Nathan had his. Delia was a person who could say, "Fascinating!" and make you feel suddenly that your life *was.*

"Why didn't they have jobs like this when I was a young woman?" she asked at one point. Then she smiled. "Not that it would have mattered, since I was not a young woman who ever even had a job. Unless you count summer jobs in college. If that counts, I was a wait-ress, for a combined total of perhaps six or eight months of my life."

They talked about their first jobs. Nathan had been a caddy in high school, Meri had worked as a receptionist at a seedy motel at the edge of her hometown.

"And where was this?" Delia asked.

"Rock Hill, Illinois," Meri said dismissively. "No one's ever heard of it."

"No, you're right. I haven't either," Delia said. "But I don't know the Midwest well. Like so many easterners, I suppose. All of us are really more or less snobs about the Midwest, I think."

"But it works both ways," Nathan said. "Midwesterners don't know the East either," Nathan said. "Meri'd never been east before she met me."

"Not so," Meri said. "I was in New York once for about a week."

"New York is not the East," Nathan said.

"A world unto itself," Delia agreed, nodding. "As Washington is."

"Well, and it was a class trip too," Meri said, remembering. "I was in a *herd* in New York, is what I should have said. A herd of teenagers. And we did things I'd never do again. The Statue of Liberty. City Hall. Though I did like the boat cruise." She had made out through most of it with her boyfriend at the time—she could remember his kisses, which tasted of chewing gum.

Nathan had begun to reminisce about his culture shock on moving to the Midwest—about the food, the flat terrain, about his misery. "In all fairness, though, I was unhappy at the college, and that colored everything. From the day I arrived, I was trying to leave. But it is also true that I didn't find anything physically appealing. Except Meri." His head made a kind of bow to her across the table, and then turned to Delia again. "But my heart never leapt to the countryside. Or to the town either."

"Well, of course, New England is prettier," Meri said. "Greener. *Curvier,* somehow. Perfect, really." She looked from one of them to the other. "I've never lived in as perfect a place," she said. "I can't get used to it. I feel, in a way, *unsuited* to it. It's almost not real to me." She was struck by her own words—she hadn't clearly framed the thought before, but now she did: she didn't feel at home here.

"What do you mean, not real?" Delia asked.

"Oh, I don't know." She couldn't tell them what she felt, could she? That she didn't feel at home?

"Okay," she said. "Okay, for instance, what you call downtown here is so *arranged.* Too prettily arranged. To a midwesterner, it seems . . . not real. Like a stage set." She looked from one of their attentive, polite faces to the other. "Whenever I walk down Main Street, I half expect a chorus of locals to step forward and start singing some happy, civic song." She opened her arms wide, a Broadway gesture.

This made Delia laugh, and Meri felt such a sense of pleasure that she was almost embarrassed for herself. She got up and began to carry plates into the kitchen.

When she came back with the salad, Delia was talking. ". . . the kind of thing a woman of my generation would do, isn't it?" she was saying. "Still, I love it. We have her letters on display in the house, and I love looking at them, the very letters she sat down and wrote to him more than a hundred and fifty years ago."

She looked up at Meri. "I'm telling Nathan about the Apthorp house—have you heard of it?"

Meri was standing by her, holding the salad bowl so Delia could serve herself. She shook her head. "I haven't, no," she said.

"I was explaining that I work there. Volunteer there, actually."

And Delia went on explaining it, about Anne Apthorp's fiction and how it was discovered, about the house and her involvement in its development as a museum.

Meri had sat down opposite Delia now, and was watching her. You lost all sense of her age when she was animated, Meri thought. Of course, the candlelight helped too. Delia's eyes, usually so piercing, seemed softer, gentler in the yellow light. Her wild white hair was an aureole around her face.

"I suppose I'm drawn to her because her life was like mine, in some ways, though of course she did something so different with it. But basically she's someone who stayed at home. She had to stay at home, given the times she lived in and her marital status." She had a sip of wine and set her glass down. Turned it, slowly. "Still, she found a way out, didn't she?"

Delia was looking into the flames of the candle in front of her place. Then she looked up at Meri and Nathan and smiled. "Well, isn't that what marriage is all about?" she said. She lifted her hand. "Staying in it while getting out in some way too?"

Oh! Meri thought. Another aperçu. Another window opening inside her.

Delia was frowning. After a pause she said, "But there's a part of me, I suppose, that more or less regrets the whole Apthorp house thing too."

Nathan asked her what she meant.

"Well, it's perverse, after all, don't you think, to take a life that was so private, so turned inward, and make it a public life, after the fact?" She appealed to each of them, turning from one to the other.

"No." Nathan's voice was absolute. He shook his head. "Nope, I can't *afford* to agree with that. That's precisely how the study of history happens, and I'm an historian."

"Oh yes, I know that. But some lives are *meant* to be public—my husband's, for instance. He can expect no mercy." She pushed her hair back off her face. "Though of course, he's not been in office for so long, people ignore him more than they used to." She smiled. "This is still painful for him, after all these years," she said.

Tom again. Meri and Nathan were assiduously not looking at each other.

"When was it that he left office?" Nathan asked.

"He decided not to run again in '78."

"And that was because . . . ?"

"Oh, all kinds of things." Her hand fluttered in the air. "The point I'm making, I think, is that I spend my days passing on information about the life of someone who had every right to expect that her letters might have been of interest only to the person to whom they were addressed. And yet here I am, here is the whole Apthorp house enterprise, arranging for people to just *poke* through everything, to find out all they can."

"But she was a writer," Nathan said. "A person who wanted her *work,* anyway, to be made public. Isn't that the bargain such a person makes?"

"Oh no. No." Meri was noticing that Delia used her hands almost constantly. "She struck no such bargain. We've no record that she ever tried to publish anything. And the novel was never even finished. So it truly wasn't a public life, not in any way. It was a domestic life. It just happened to have some writing *appended* to it, more or less."

"Still, I think she's fair game," Nathan said. "History is about private people too. About individuals. About the self—maybe you'd call it the soul—and the impress on it of what happens out there. Social change. Political change. Change in cultures, in the world." He'd sat up straighter. He was *on,* his face alive. "We have to look at what you call private people. Like the people I was telling you about in my book. To see what history means. What politics means. How life in a moment, under certain conditions, is *felt,* is taken in." His hands curved in, touched his own chest, his heart. "So we need, really have a need, to find out about people like your Anne Apthorp." He frowned. "What I mean, really, is that someone who recorded her feelings, who can explain them to us across these years, even fictionally, is a resource for everyone else. Everyone else like me, anyway." His hand rose to his hair. "Otherwise we'd just be talking in numbers

—in the abstract—about governments and wars and economics, and not about how they affected *people*. Which is what makes it really interesting." This was Nathan's whole argument with the political-science department in Coleman. They were numbers guys, trends guys. They hadn't much liked his work, and he hadn't liked theirs.

Delia nodded slowly, four or five times. "Well," she said. "I can see that. Of course you're right," she said. "I hate to agree about my Anne, but I can see that." She seemed to be thinking about it. Then she lifted her chin. "But I don't know. It's all Oedipal in the end, isn't it?" Her face suddenly came alive. She leaned forward now, elbows on the table. "Really, isn't that it? That the study of history is Oedipal at its roots? Connected directly to the Oedipus complex?"

"I'm game." Nathan had sat back in his chair, and he was smiling in delight at Delia. "I'll bite. But how, exactly, would that work?"

"Oh," her hand waved, "doesn't it all start—our interest in the past—with our wanting to know more about our own parents? Really, that's what I mean." She smiled. "That drive we all have to get to the root of their attraction to each other. We always want their story, don't we? It's the first history we're really curious about. And the last one. It haunts us. Because it's a history with the most important consequence in the world—us." She turned her hands, palms up. "Us and *our* story. Our history." Her eyes were bright in the candle-light. "*So*," she said. "How did they meet each other? How could they *possibly* have come to love each other? And then sex, the biggest mystery of all. How do they *do* it?" She grinned. "What we'd like is to get right *into* that bedroom and watch them. The primal scene. And if that's not Oedipal, what is?" Her hands rose, dramatically. A silver bracelet on her wrist slid down her arm.

Nathan laughed, and Meri did too. Delia was pleased with herself. Her mouth made a smug little priss. She had finished her wine, and Nathan held the bottle up—an offering. She held her glass out.

Meri looked at him while he reached across the candles with the wine. Did he agree with her? Meri wondered. Had he ever thought about his parents having sex? Meri pictured his mother—her tidy grayish hair, her round, pretty little girl's face. This dining room table had come from her, and these old Windsor chairs, which creaked and complained when you shifted your weight in them. Meri couldn't imagine her moaning in sexual pleasure.

Delia was expanding on her idea. Our interest in history starts with the personal, then enlarges to the political, the global. Nathan made a case for the reverse process. They were enjoying the argument.

But Meri had drifted away. She was thinking of her own parents, subjects of much speculation between Lou and her. *Did* they do it? Ever? Wouldn't it make *some* kind of noise?

This was the sticking point for Lou, especially after she began sleeping with boys. It made a *lot* of noise, she said. You had to hold your hand over the guy's mouth if you didn't want anyone else—at a party, say, or in the front seat of the car—to know what you were doing. And even then, there were the groans. *Those* they could do even with their mouths clamped shut.

Meri looked at Delia. It seemed possible for her, sex, unlike most old people Meri had known.

Why?

The way she dressed, Meri supposed. Tonight, for instance, in a blue sweater and a straight black skirt, a wide silver necklace at her throat, the bangle on her arm—an outfit a woman half her age might have worn.

But no, it was more the way she *was*. Something about her energy, what seemed like her appetite for life.

Nathan got up now and cleared the salad plates. He was going to fetch their dessert, one he'd made. Desserts were his specialty. While he was gone Meri told Delia that when they were courting sometimes one of his desserts would be all they had for dinner. "I can remember sitting at the table in my apartment with him, eating a lemon tart directly from the pan. The whole thing." She didn't mention that they were naked, having made love until so late that there seemed no point to fixing the first part of the meal.

Tonight Nathan brought out a flan and dished it up for them. It was cool and slippery, and Meri slid it around in her mouth, savoring it.

Delia was impressed. She started to talk about French cooking, about Paris.

Paris, where she owned an apartment.

"I'm actually going there in just a few weeks." She set her spoon down. "And this reminds me, I've been meaning to ask, would you mind doing a few house-sitting chores? Just plant watering, the mail, and that sort of thing."

Nathan said quickly, "We'd be glad to." Meri looked over at him. She could see that he meant exactly this, that he was made *happy* by the intimacy implied.

"Think about it before you say yes," Delia commanded. "I'll be gone for two full months. It's more or less my routine at this point—two months in the fall, two months in the spring."

Meri felt a quick pinch of loss, of disappointment. No more Delia this fall, then. She realized she'd seen this dinner as marking the beginning of something. Of her getting to know Delia, of course, but more than that, though she wasn't sure what. That they'd be *pals*? She didn't know. "It's no trouble at all," she told Delia. She had another spoonful of flan.

"You go every year?" Nathan said.

"Yes, twice a year, every year, with the changing of the seasons. I'm like a migratory bird," Delia said. "I think of the apartment as waiting for me when I'm not there. My nest. Though I rent it out occasionally—but only to friends. And of course the children use it often, too."

Now, with her fingers, she drew an elaborate map in the air for Meri and Nathan of where it was in relation to the Seine, to the Luxembourg Gardens.

Meri confessed she'd never been to Paris.

"Ah," Delia said, her eyes fully on Meri. "How wonderful that you have that great pleasure ahead of you!"

"What's the French connection?" Nathan asked. "How did you end up there?"

"Oh, just one of those moments in life when you say, *Let me out.* I needed a getaway. I had a friend in Washington with contacts in Paris, and I spoke a little French." She held her forefinger and thumb about an inch apart. "So I thought, yes. *Oui. Pourquoi pas?* And the rest, as they say, is history. Though not your kind," she said to Nathan.

They talked about France, about its charms. About its economic problems, about unemployment and assimilation. Delia described going on an errand into the exurbs, "and it was like another universe out there—these tall grim projects. And the street life! It could have been a souk in Morocco."

"This is interesting," Nathan said, nodding his head. "When you think of the great contempt all those formerly homogeneous European cultures have for us, for the way we've dealt with the issue of race in America." He smiled. "Now we'll get to see how well they do at it, I guess."

They'd been sitting at the table for a long time. The candles were short and lumpish with wax. Delia's lipstick was gone. She looked tired.

Meri offered coffee or decaf, though she expected to be turned down, and she was. And, as she also expected, this signaled the evening's end. Delia pushed her chair back and got up, unbending slowly into a straight line, as if her body were arguing with each vertebra. Meri was suddenly conscious of her age. It must *hurt* to be that old.

They moved with her back into the living room. Meri inhaled deeply. The lilies had started to open and their smell was thick in the air. Nathan helped Delia into her coat.

At the door, she gripped their hands in turn. "Thank you so much, my dears," she said.

"Oh no," Meri said. "Thank you. Thanks for the flowers. And for making us feel so welcome."

"Not at all," Delia said. "If I have, I'm glad. I wanted to." She turned to go, and then stopped and stepped back. "Now, I'll bring the key over tomorrow, for when I leave," she said. "You should have it anyway. And actually, I suppose I should have told you, I already have yours—from Ilona's day. I hope that's something you're comfortable with."

They both made assenting noises.

"And I'll leave the Paris phone number on the pad on the telephone stand. Plus the children's numbers—there are three of them—ranked in order of who should be called first, second, and third in case something happens at the house and you can't reach me. But not to worry," she said. She'd turned away again, and she was gripping the doorknob. "Nothing happens in October and November."

"When *does* something happen?" Meri asked, thinking mostly of their house, of what they should be expecting.

"September. Rain," Delia pronounced as she stepped outside. "Weep holes clogging up, leaks. And then winter. Ice dams making problems. Pipes freezing."

After they said good night, after the door had closed behind Delia, Meri turned to Nathan. "Okay, what are *ice dams*? What are *weep holes*?"

Nathan knew, of course, even though he'd never owned a house before. He explained them to her.

"How do you always know that stuff?" she asked.

"Are you kidding? Everyone knows that stuff." He went back to the kitchen to start cleaning up.

Meri crossed to the lilies. Bending over them, she breathed in their sweet, almost sexual odor. When she went to the kitchen, Nathan reached to her face—for a moment she thought in love. But no, he was wiping at her nose and cheek with his thumbs. "Lily dust," he explained.

They worked together silently. Meri went back and forth to the dining room, clearing the table. On one of her trips into the kitchen, she said to Nathan, "I used to steal from the motel."

"What motel?"

"My first job. At the motel. I was an embezzler."

He looked over at her, weighing it. She met his gaze. She was interested to see if he'd believe her.

"Come on, Meri. You did not."

"Nah," she said, smiling at him. "Just joking," she said, and left the room again.

She had told Nathan many lies at various stages in their relationship, most of which she had owned up to. She told him when she first met him that her parents had died in an auto accident when she was fourteen. Why? She didn't know. She told him that she'd danced topless in a bar. She was trying to turn him on that time.

But this was not a lie. The manager at the motel had liked the way she looked. He used to hang around after she'd arrived. He'd corner her in the back office. He'd press against her and kiss her, sloppily. This was the worst part of the job, and she thought she ought to get paid for it. She knew that he knew what she was doing, but she knew too that if she kept the amounts small enough, he wouldn't report her.

Nathan had never made such a bargain, it went without saying.

CHAPTER FIVE

Meri, October and November 1993

By EARLY OCTOBER, Meri was fairly certain that she was pregnant. Though she never kept very close track of her periods, she was feeling funny, and she realized she couldn't remember when she'd had her last one. She stopped in the drugstore on Main Street on her way home from work one afternoon and bought a self-testing kit. She was amused to see that it was shelved next to the condoms. Was there some joker on the pharmacy staff? Had he intended the irony?

At home, perched on the edge of the bathtub, she had to read the instructions several times over, but finally she sat on the toilet and held the stick under her while she urinated, as it seemed she was supposed to—though her hand got liberally wet too. And then she waited and watched as a faint blue cross emerged, the vertical line stronger than the horizontal, in the little result window on the stick. She read the instructions once more to be sure this meant what she thought it meant. Then, because she wanted to be certain, she unwrapped another of the little wands and did it all over again, more skillfully this time. Practice makes perfect, she thought, though this seemed a skill she wouldn't need often after this—not for another nine months in any case. She sat on the toilet, her pants down around her ankles, the wand resting on the apron of the rust-stained old sink, and watched as the cross appeared again in the result window.

"Fuck!" she said aloud.

She pulled her pants up and padded barefoot down the hall to their bedroom. She lay down for a while, watching the shadows in the room deepening, going back and forth over it. It was bad timing, yes, but they had talked about wanting a child. It was hard to think of a time in the next few years that would be any better—and the next few years might be the last ones possible for her.

She got up and went downstairs. She was aware of the house around her in a way she hadn't been before—the number of rooms off the hall, the large open spaces below. They'd imagined a family, buying it. Or Nathan had, and she'd agreed. She'd agreed to what he imagined for her. But now that it was upon her she was . . . what? Frightened?

She was. How could they possibly manage this? How could *she*? since Nathan was too busy to manage anything beyond what he had to do right now.

But maybe, she thought, maybe once he was done with his book, his life would be a little more his own. Maybe he could be more involved than it seemed he might be now. She sat in the twilit living room and ran through multiple versions of how it might go. What frightened her the most was how little time they'd had together, alone, to get to know each other, to get used to each other. She'd felt that was just beginning to happen, here, as they started to make a life together in this house. Now they would have to turn out together, away from each other, to a child. To their child.

It was almost completely dark outside when Nathan got home. She watched him come slowly up the stairs outside, the weary warrior from academe. She was glad to see him. She was glad not to be alone with this anymore. She listened to his key in the lock.

He stepped in and stopped halfway across the room, seeing her. "What's up?" he said. "Why are you sitting there in the dark?"

"Hi, sweetie," she said. "Come sit in the dark with me."

He obeyed, still wearing his coat, still holding his briefcase, which he rested on his lap. He was really just a large shape, a bulk in the chair across the room. "What's going on?" he asked.

"Oh, Nate, I'm pregnant," she said. "Or I think I am."

There was what felt to Meri like a long silence. Then he said, softly, "Whoa."

"Actually, honestly, I *know* I am."

"How?" His voice sounded hollowed out. "How do you know?"

"Well, I took a test. A drugstore test. And failed it, twice." She smiled sadly in the dark. "Or else I passed it with flying colors. Blue being the operative color. A little blue cross, which means *yes.*" He didn't say anything. "But also," she shrugged. "I am. I missed my period. I feel strange."

He cleared his throat. "Strange how?"

"Strange *pregnant.*"

He hadn't moved since he sat down, and she couldn't see his face clearly.

"I think it was probably the day I got my job, that first day you went over to the college."

"What makes you think so?" he asked. He reached up to the floor lamp next to his chair and turned it on.

She squinted in the sudden bright light, and put her hand up to her forehead, as though looking off into the deep distance. "I didn't have the diaphragm in. I was cutting it close. It was too close." She dropped her hand and made a rueful face. "I kind of knew it was too close, I think. But I wanted you." She was remembering their sweaty, urgent love, his coming up the stairs after her.

"Ah, no." His voice was gentle. "*I* wanted *you,*" he said.

Suddenly she felt safe.

Neither spoke for a minute. Then Nathan set his briefcase down on the floor and said, "So?"

She looked up. Their eyes met. "So, it would screw a few things up," Meri said.

"But you want to do it? To have it?"

He said this in a tone so open to the possibility that Meri was suddenly sharply aware of loving him, as she hadn't been in a while— they'd both been so distracted by their separate lives. Her Nathan. Her throat tightened.

She cleared it and said in an exaggeratedly shocked voice, "Children are a gift of God, Nate." This was something Nathan's mother had once told them.

He grinned at her. "Yeah, but so, apparently, are pestilence and floods. And the odd boil."

Meri laughed, and went to him. She sat on his lap, straddling his legs. He smelled of chlorine—he'd been swimming today. She held his tilted-up head in her hands, her hair tenting his face. His expression had grown grave. He was beautiful to her.

"So, yes?" he whispered. She nodded, and bent over him.

When they made love that evening, under Meri's old quilt—the night air was chilly now—she welcomed him into her in a way she felt she hadn't ever before. It wasn't just a matter of holding her legs wide apart for him, though she did that; and it wasn't just that they didn't have the diaphragm between them. It was that there seemed some increase of openness deep inside her, though she would have said such a thing was impossible, that she couldn't have felt more open to Nathan than she already did. Yet it seemed almost that some actual barrier of flesh had given way between them as he moved in and back—that he was *of* her, that the child they'd begun to make had, in its turn, made them one. Dizzyingly, overwhelmingly so. This was a sensation so charged for Meri that she was silent and tearful for a moment after they had finished. She didn't have the words to say to Nathan what stirred her.

And then because that was a feeling she was never comfortable with, she made a joke: "Did you hear the angel choir singing when we came, Natey?"

WITHIN TWO WEEKS, none of Meri's jeans fit her. Her waist had thickened, her small breasts were weighted and tender. She was startled by this. She had thought she would have months before she had to accommodate her pregnancy physically. Her sister, Lou, had never showed at all until the fifth or sixth month, and then had only a discrete and increasingly rounded protuberance you couldn't imagine making its way down through her narrow hips.

Meri seemed to be expanding generally. Even her fingers looked fat. The flesh of her face seemed heavier to her when she looked in the mirror. Pete Rose indeed.

Worse, she felt slightly nauseated all the time. She began to carry a large baggie of unsalted crackers in her purse, pulling them out one by one through the day and taking small nibbles, nibbles that she alternated with swigs of water from the bottle she also took with her now wherever she went.

In late October she prepared a segment for the show on a writing program at the prison in Goffstown, which was about twenty miles south of Williston. She made two visits there to sit in on the sessions, both times driving cautiously through heavy rain, clutching the wheel so tightly her hands hurt afterward.

There were strict rules about female visitors at the prison. She couldn't wear open-toed shoes, blue jeans, an underwire bra, or anything tight. No skirts above the knee. Before she was allowed in, she had to put her purse, her raincoat and umbrella into a locker they provided. Then she had to go through a metal detector and several vestibule-like cubicles whose back doors closed behind you before the doors in front of you would open. There were surveillance cameras mounted on the walls everywhere.

She had been given permission to tape the sessions and to interview four of the prisoners afterward. The class met in a large room with a cement-gray linoleum floor and irregular rows of metal desk-chairs, the writing surfaces attached to their right arms. The windows in this room were barred and so dirty you couldn't really see out them. The lights were fluorescent and harsh.

The inmates seemed shockingly young to her, almost all of them. They were mostly Hispanic, a few of them black, two white. The white guys were the oldest in the room—perhaps in their early thirties.

All of the men were writing memoirs under the supervision of a large, soft-spoken woman named Mary Anne, who was in charge of special programs at the prison, and two junior faculty members, both men, from the English Department at the college. The prisoners took turns reading their pieces out loud and then having them discussed by the group.

Most of the writing was about their crimes or about getting caught, though one of the white guys wrote about his grandmother—a completely predictable, sentimental piece. Hallmark card stuff. Everyone loved it.

The most beautiful boy, a Hispanic kid who had the slow beatific smile of an angel, wrote about alcohol—about his love for it, his addiction to it—in an almost erotic and completely compelling way. That one was well written, remarkably so, if with the occasional awkwardness; and there were others that were okay. But Meri could hear that most of them would have been unreadable if you had had to look at the text—if you didn't have the inmates' voices and passionate commitment to help you *get* them.

All the men seemed to care deeply how their work was received. On Meri's second time out, she watched one of them almost give way to tears because of the criticism his reading got. Mary Anne stepped in quickly and softened the tone. She reinterpreted several of the most negative remarks and offered encouragement.

After she'd taped the second session, Meri interviewed the four inmates, with Mary Anne still in the room. The next day she brought her tapes in to be edited. She also turned over her pre-interview notes and suggestions—the instructors and Mary Anne were going to be on the program, the two instructors in the studio, Mary Anne by phone.

The segment ran longer than they usually allowed. Jane and James had done a graceful job piecing together a narrative from the tapes and interviews. At the meeting afterward, everyone was excited about how good it was, almost jubilant. There had already been a record number of phone calls about it. They congratulated Meri. She had the sense of finally having *made* it.

She and Jane were slower than the others in gathering up their things. As Meri was leaving the room, Jane spoke her name. Meri turned around. Jane said quietly, "You're pregnant, aren't you?"

Meri smiled. "You know," she said, "it would be a big embarrassment for you if I wasn't. If I was just getting fat, say."

"Yeah, but you're not. Just fat. You're pregnant."

Meri heaved a fake sigh. "It's so."

"God!" Jane said, making a face. "You know . . ." She stopped, and shook her head.

Meri was taking it in, that Jane might actually be angry. A part of her couldn't believe this. Hoping somehow to make light of it, to make it okay, she said, "I didn't think sex was considered that big a taboo anymore."

"No, but getting pregnant?" Jane said. "Now?"

"It wasn't planned," Meri said defensively.

"Oh! Fine." Jane got up and started toward where Meri was standing, in front of the door.

"Come on, Jane. I'm a grown-up. I know this isn't ideal. . . ."

Jane stopped right in front of her. "Hmmh!" she said. She was a tall, horsey woman, with large black-rimmed glasses. She wasn't homely, but she dressed as though she were, in baggy jeans and men's shirts.

"It's not even good," Meri said quickly. "I know that. I know that, in terms of the job. But I had to make a choice. I'm thirty-seven. I got pregnant. I'll do a maternity leave, and then I'll come back."

Jane took a step back. "Let me just say something, Meri." She looked tired. Meri knew—James had told her—that she'd come to this job after losing one at a big NPR station in Boston. That she was disappointed in her career. Her voice was gentler now, it had that pretty quality again. "I'm happy for you personally, and I promise I won't bring this up again." She opened her hand, palm up. "The thing is, things were easing up around here, which is why we hired you in the first place. This will take us right back to where we were, which none of us liked."

Meri shrugged. Her lips parted for a moment, but she didn't have anything to say.

"And to be quite, quite honest"—Jane's mouth made a sour shape—"if you had said, 'Well, I might get pregnant within a few years'—not to mention two months!—we would have said, Oh, no, no, no, no. No! No thank you."

"I get it," Meri said. Her throat ached. "I got it."

"And now I'll shut up," Jane said, and left the room. The door closed slowly, silently behind her.

Meri cried for only a minute, and then she blew her nose. At least she'd been able to hold it together until Jane left. That, anyway, was good, she told herself.

She sat down and reached into her bag for a cracker. Her fingers brushed against the small cardboard box: cigarettes. That's what she wanted, she thought. A cigarette. As she moistened the dry cracker in her mouth with the bottled water, she lovingly imagined lighting up, inhaling. She hadn't had more than one or two cigarettes since suspecting she was pregnant, but she hadn't thrown this almost-full pack out either; and somehow, over these weeks, it had come to seem emblematic to her of everything she was giving up.

Oh, bullshit. She wouldn't have been smoking here anyway. It was a smoke-free workplace. She blew her nose again.

It was just that she was missing it, her old life. Which she'd given up, she reminded herself, well before she got pregnant.

No, it was more than that. Much more, she thought. It was that several times a day she struggled with a sleepiness so profound that her head felt cottony, her limbs heavy and difficult to move. That she went through every day with a more or less constant sense of nausea. That she often had a sharp headache, centered over her right eye.

She sat for a moment, thinking. No. No, here's what it was, she thought. Here: that she no longer liked the way her body looked and felt—her body, which she'd always taken such pride, such pleasure in. Which was the only beauty she had.

It would pass, she told herself. It will pass.

But she couldn't help it, she hated what was happening to her. She hadn't known it would *feel* so awful. She was frightened.

She didn't want it. She didn't want to do it.

NATHAN WASN'T HOME yet when she got there. It was dusky in the house. She turned the lights on in the kitchen, and suddenly, reflected in the wall of windows, there she was, Meri, in her big sweater and a pair of Nathan's corduroy slacks, moving jumpily across the multiple panes of glass—a herky-jerky version of herself anyway.

She got the plastic-wrapped chicken out of the refrigerator in the pantry and set it on the drainboard. She turned on the tiny stove to preheat. She washed some lettuce, bending over the low sink. Then she took a key from one of the top bureau drawers under the door-table and went outside and into Delia's house. She'd done this six or seven times now, the house-sitting chores they'd agreed to. It had fallen to her, mostly because Nathan got home later, but maybe partly because it seemed to both of them a woman's task.

It was cool in here—Delia had the thermostat set low. Meri picked up the mail from the floor where it lay scattered and carried it back to the kitchen. She separated it—catalogs and magazines into one of the baskets Delia had left out, letters into the other.

Delia had gathered all the houseplants back here onto a plastic tarp in front of the windows. Meri didn't need to be careful watering, Delia had told her. And she shouldn't worry if something died. "I'm fond of the plants, but I'm fickle too," she'd said to Meri. "I've been known to underwater if a plant seems too demanding, just to let it know who's the boss."

Standing in Delia's kitchen, squirting the plants with the special hose Delia had attached to the sink faucet, Meri looked around the room, so much smaller than their expanded version on the other side of the wall. It was square, with two standard-size windows at the back and two along the side, and a glass-paned door opening out onto the driveway. There were sheer white curtains at the windows, pulled back, and paintings on the walls, along with a few family photographs.

Meri realized abruptly that she liked this room better than their vast kitchen. The whole house, actually, with its smaller, enclosed, unrenovated spaces, with all the wood trim painted white and the warm wall colors, was prettier than theirs was.

When she was done with the plants, she walked back into the living room and switched on a lamp on the table just inside the door. The walls in here were a deep yellow. The curved white bench under the windows had seat cushions in pale green and more pillows at each end to lean against. The coffee table in front of the couch had a wide green bowl set on it that had been filled with yellow pears the day Meri came over to learn what her chores would be while Delia was away.

It was cozy, she thought. Welcoming. Something that wasn't true of the open rooms on her side of the wall.

She turned and stepped back into the hall, looking around her there too. On an impulse, she crossed to the stairs and started up.

This was the first time she'd ventured above the first floor. *Probably an inevitability though,* she thought, mounting the stairs. She was insatiably curious about other people's lives, down to the way they arranged their things, down to what those things were. The first time Nathan had left her alone in his place, she had surveyed everything he owned. She looked through his medicine chest, she went to his desk and read several pages from the book he was working on. She'd also read a summary sheet of his student evaluations. All the female students adored him—no surprises there—but the boys too seemed to be dazzled. He was "totally into it," he made everything so real. "He made me care about it because he cares so much, and I *hate* history."

When she quoted this later, he was startled. "You *read* the stuff on my desk?"

"Of course. Wouldn't you? Haven't you?"

"I wouldn't, unless I asked first."

She had shrugged. "To me, all that says is that I'm more deeply curious about you than you are about me."

"You are?"

"It would appear so," she said.

Now she walked slowly down the wide upstairs hallway in Delia's house. The rooms off it were more like hers and Nathan's than the ones downstairs, though the bathrooms had been redone—something that would be their first project, Nathan had told Meri. But like the downstairs, everything up here felt arranged more for comfort than at their house. There were curtains on the windows in each room and old Oriental carpets or rag rugs scattered everywhere. The rug under her feet in the hall was a kilim of many rich colors. Pictures were hung on the hallway walls—old oil paintings or watercolors of the ocean, of fields and woods. There were some family photographs and a few antique maps.

Delia's bedroom was painted a yellow that must have been a just slightly lighter version of the color in the living room. There was a large, deeply cushioned chair, a round gateleg table next to it, a lamp on that. The bed was queen-size, big enough for two, a puffy duvet laid across it. Meri counted five pillows stacked against the white wooden headboard.

She walked back down the hall, looking into the smaller bedrooms. They were guest rooms clearly, set up for Delia's children and grandchildren. One of them had double bunkbeds in it. Photographs of infants, of young people, of mothers and babies, fathers and kids, decorated the walls.

Meri studied them: happy, then happier, then happiest. In one of them, a framed black-and-white shot, Delia—a very young version of Delia—was holding a tiny baby, almost a newborn. She was just as Meri had known she would be, stunningly attractive, every feature strong, well defined. Her dark hair was done in the style of the forties, parted on the side, nearly shoulder length. She was wearing lipstick that looked almost black in the photograph and a strand of glowing pearls around her neck. She was looking directly at the photographer—looking with such powerful intensity, such love, that Meri felt certain that Tom Naughton had taken the picture.

The last room, the one just over the stairs up from the kitchen, the one that would be the nursery in Meri and Nathan's house—though they'd bought nothing for it yet—was clearly Delia's study. There was a wide, old-fashioned desk in front of the window that looked out over the backyard. Meri stepped slowly around the room, examining everything—the books on the shelves, mostly novels, arranged alphabetically. The worn chair with a plaid shawl thrown across its high back. There were very small pictures on the far wall—framed paintings, watercolors—and Meri went close to them to see them better.

She made a little noise, a sharp inhalation.

They were of women, pornographically posed, their legs spread wide or held open in astonishingly gymnastic dancer's positions, their genitals penciled or inked in delicately. There were perhaps a dozen. She looked at each one closely. One was of two naked women in an embrace, their limbs entwined. In another, a greenish nude with red hair was in profile doing a backbend, her long locks nearly touching the ground behind her. There was one of a woman lying down, her legs and sex splayed open for the artist.

This was a surprise. It was a surprise about Delia. It startled Meri.

She went to Delia's desk and sat down in the chair. The light from her own kitchen windows lay on Delia's terrace, on the empty wooden chairs out there. The fallen sycamore leaves were piled on the seats and gathered against the box hedge. The desk was neat, everything in seeming order. She imagined Delia herself sitting here, reading letters, doing paperwork, so private and self-contained.

And that was how she thought of her, she realized. Delia was funny and welcoming, she beckoned you with her charm and seemed very open, very candid and spontaneous, but you got nothing, fundamentally, that she hadn't planned to give you. This was a feeling she couldn't have expressed until this moment, but somehow the pictures on the wall had confirmed it for her: Delia was unknowable. She was private.

She didn't let you in.

Meri switched the desk lamp on. She was facing her reflection, her round, determined face, her straight, limp hair. The desktop was bare, but along the back of the writing surface there was a row of cubbyholes full of papers of one sort or another, and Meri watched her hand reach forward and pull an envelope from one of them.

The name in the upper corner was familiar to her—it was one of the sons, Brad, the second one on the list of emergency contact numbers downstairs.

She took the letter out and started to read it. He addressed Delia as *Dearest Mother.* Her eyes moved down the page. She turned it over and read the back. It was just a note, really, a newsy, chatty letter, the kind of letter no one in Meri's family would ever have written, the kind Nathan often wrote to his mother. It described Delia's grand-children for the most part, their lives as school started up for them.

Imagine it, Meri thought—the wish to convey this, the knowledge that the recipient would actually be interested. It seemed amazing to her. It seemed privileged beyond words.

Meri had just finished it when she heard, and felt, a noise—a structural thump. She started, her heart seemed to slam in her chest. For a half second she thought that it was somewhere in Delia's house, she thought that someone had come in.

And then she relaxed. It was Nathan, of course, Nathan, next door, coming home, shutting the door hard.

After a long moment she turned the desk light off. Slowly, care-fully, she went down the stairs, not wanting to make any noise on her descent that Nathan might hear through the wall. She turned Delia's living room light off too and stepped out onto the cold front porch, hearing the click of the door's lock as she pulled it shut behind her.

THINGS CHANGED. The exaltation Meri had felt the first few nights they made love after she knew she was pregnant disappeared as her body changed, as the sense of thickness and dullness claimed her, as she grew, in her own eyes, fat and ugly—as the project of staving off the faint and then sometimes sharp nausea that threaded through her days absorbed her more and more. Sometimes the very idea of making love exacerbated it. Once she actually recoiled when Nathan reached for her.

"Don't!" she said, too loud. It was escape from her body Meri wanted, not to experience it more intensely.

And there seemed to be a reciprocal withdrawal on Nathan's part, though he masked it as concern, as courtesy. Or Meri felt it as a mask, felt the polite questions as a way of seeming loving while holding himself away from her.

But maybe it was just that their lives too had changed so much from their lazy, sexy days in Coleman. Here, he was up later and later every night in his study, preparing for classes, reading, making notes, grading papers. They didn't have wine with dinner anymore, because she wasn't allowed to, because he needed his head clear to work in the evenings, so their meals were less leisurely, less enjoyable. Once the dishes were cleaned up and put away, he disappeared. When she went to bed, sometimes barely making it till nine or nine-thirty, she could hear him up there, the creak of the floor under his desk chair, the sound of his repeated trips across the room to his bookshelves. When he came to bed, when he slid up against her under the covers, the cool of his long body waking her, beckoning her, as often as not she didn't respond—she would have had to come up from too deep a sleep, she was too stunned with exhaustion, her arms felt too impossibly heavy.

There were two places where Meri could find relief from all this. One was at work, where she was often so absorbed in what she was doing that she actually sometimes forgot, for an hour at a time, how rotten she felt.

The other, increasingly, was at Delia's house.

She had begun to make time to be there, to linger, usually in the late afternoon before Nathan got home, or on the weekends when he was in his office at the college, slaving away on his book. The house was chilly, but Meri came prepared, in extra sweaters. She sat in different rooms, she lay on Delia's bed. *Like Goldilocks,* she thought, sneaking around where she didn't belong, trying everything on for size, for her own comfort.

But she couldn't help it, she liked being in Delia's house. She liked looking closely at the paintings on the wall, at the family photographs. She loved the old maps hung here and there, with their absurd guesses about the shape of the world. She loved walking through the spaces, learning the way the light fell at different times of the day.

And increasingly over these weeks she gravitated to Delia's study—to puzzle at the sexual watercolors there, to sit at Delia's desk, to read through the innocent letters and papers Delia had tucked into the cubbyholes at its back.

It was an appetite—she thought of it that way—this wish to know more, and then more than that, about Delia's life. She felt it as she did the need for the crackers and water that carried her through the day. She thought of it, actually, as being connected to her present state as much as they were.

Her state: her pregnancy. Yes. But something else too. Perhaps her sense of being alone in her state. Her need for something, something she couldn't have named. She remembered what Delia had said the night she was at their house for dinner about her own curiosity about Anne Apthorp's life—about how her wish to know more was connected to something primal in herself. Meri felt she understood that now. That she was living it.

ON A RAINY, cold Saturday morning, Nathan off to the office until late afternoon, she crossed the front porch around the lion, she went through her routine downstairs—the mail, the plants. Then she climbed the stairs and went directly to Delia's study. She sat again at Delia's desk. This time, for the first time, she opened one of its lower drawers.

There they were, more letters, in file folders labeled with the names of her children—Nancy, Brad, Evan. But this wasn't what Meri was looking for—though when she'd mounted the stairs, she hadn't allowed herself to know she was looking for anything. She shut that drawer and opened the one opposite it on the right-hand side of the desk and read the label there—*Tom*. She felt her breath quicken.

After only a moment's hesitation, she pulled a letter out and read it. And then another.

Later she would ask herself how she could have done this. She would feel such a sense of shame as she remembered these hours alone in Delia's house—as she remembered everything that happened after that between her and Delia—that she would think of this time in her life as cut off, separate from who she was before it and who she became afterward. An island of something. Desperation. Need. Occasionally through the years she would wonder about her own mental fragility at this period of her life, about hormones run amok, about depression. She wouldn't know. She won't know. She will never tell Nathan, or anyone else. She will never feel comfortable with this memory.

There were perhaps fifty or sixty letters, some unfolded and filed flat, others still in their envelopes. Over the remaining time Delia was away, Meri read through most of these letters more than once, and slowly, hungrily, she was able to piece together a story, a history of Tom and Delia.

She learned that they hadn't lived together in twenty years, that there was no plan for them ever to live together again. But also that they were still seeing each other at least occasionally, that they still made love. That they had always made love, even through the hardest times between them. That there was still, then, a marriage in some sense—or a love affair—one whose shape Delia seemed to be in charge of.

She learned that Tom had at first begged Delia to forgive him for his infidelities—or for the one infidelity in particular that seemed to have caused their separation. In the early letters, he blamed himself, he described himself as a sinner and beyond help in his weakness. He also never stopped expressing the hope that she would find a way to take him back.

But eventually he recognized that this wasn't going to happen. He conceded Delia's power, even her wisdom. "You were right," he wrote, "to want to keep things as they are, because much as I love you, I couldn't have been faithful. I know that now, and if I were honest, I'd have to say I probably knew it then too."

Only a few years earlier, he'd written, "Wherever you are is home to me, Delia. Lying with you is the deepest and most thrilling comfort I can know. Simply put, I'm myself with you as I am nowhere else in my life, and I'm happy that, clear-sighted as you are about me at other times, you can still love me in those moments."

One note, undated, maybe a note that came with a gift, or flowers, said simply, "Delia. My wife."

Sitting in Delia's house, in Delia's chair, reading Delia's letters from Tom, what Meri was most aware of at the time was a muddled kind of envy. Envy of Delia and Tom together. Envy of their sad, powerful story. Envy of something in it that she would have liked for herself.

Sometimes when she came home and was having a quick meal with Nathan before his evening in his study started, a meal in which they each talked about their work, in which each of them was a little preoccupied—maybe, she thought, even a little bored by the other— she would be aware of the yearning to have, to have had, even the pain that Delia clearly had, if that's what had made it possible for her also to have something as moving, as thrilling, as rich as the love that existed between her and Tom. In what seemed to her like the hollowness of those moments, she felt that the kind of emotion Tom wrote about to Delia wouldn't be like anything Nathan could ever feel for her, or she for him. That there was a way in which she held herself too distant from him—she was too cold a person—to allow such deep feeling, such deep knowledge to live and grow.

CHAPTER SIX

Delia, Christmas, 1971

THE HOUSE WAS COLD, as it always was when they came back after an absence in this season. While Evan unloaded their suitcases and took them upstairs, Delia turned up the thermostat. Then she went out again to the car and carried in the bags of Christmas gifts each of them had brought, four for her, one, half filled, for Evan. She set them in the living room. Still wearing her coat, she walked back into the kitchen and quickly sorted through the mail that had accumulated here and been piled on the table by Marta, the cleaning woman. It was bills, mostly, and dozens of Christmas cards. She looked at the return addresses. Only a few of them were from what Delia thought of as *real people*—the rest just politics.

She'd come up to Williston from Washington five days early to get everything ready for Christmas. Evan, who was on his semester break from business school, had met her at the train station and driven her home. It was five o'clock, the sky completely bled of light by the time they got to the house. The year was 1971, it was the twentieth of December. Snow was predicted for the next day. A white Christmas, then. Delia felt almost a child's delight in the thought.

Tom had stayed on in Washington, but he was pretty sure he'd get home within a day or two. He was a senator now—he had been for five years. Next year he would run again, and though he didn't yet know who his opponent would be, he didn't expect much of a contest. He was widely popular in the state. He'd managed to walk a line between the traditions of old-fashioned liberalism—which were like a religion to him—and the new and ever-shifting demands of the civil-rights movement, the antipoverty movement, the feminists, the advocates of participatory democracy, the antiwar groups. A fancy dancer, he called himself—sometimes despairingly, she thought. He spoke of doing "the new Democratic two-step." It occasionally made his life a difficult balancing act in Washington, but it seemed to work at home with his mixed-up constituency.

When she came into the living room, Evan was crouched at the fireplace, wadding up newspaper to start a fire. "Oh, let's go out, honey," she said.

He turned, still squatting, looking over at her. "Yeah? You don't want to have something here by a fire?"

"No. It'll be cold in here even with the fire, and there's not much in the pantry but canned soup and crackers."

"Canned soup is good by me."

"No. It'll be my treat. Let's go out."

"Your call," he said, and stood up. Unfolded himself, really. Evan, like Tom, was tall, four or five inches taller than her other son, Brad. Several years earlier he had remade himself physically, he'd become more or less a new person. It was after the Peace Corps, which he'd entered as a scruffy kid, his beard always half grown in, his hair hanging down his back—his *costume,* as she thought of it, unvarying and to her mind unflattering: jeans that sagged off his narrow hips, ribbon-like woven belts in solidarity with who knew what tribe of Indians, and T-shirts, half of them torn or stained. Over this, as a concession to the weather and perhaps to some notion of elegance, he sometimes wore a motorcycle jacket—never anything more, even on the coldest days. It hurt her to look at him in winter.

She knew that the Peace Corps had asked for neatness and had insisted on a haircut and general cleanliness, but on his return she was startled at how much further Evan had gone. Tonight, for example, he was wearing slacks, and they were pressed. His hair was short by the standards of the day. He was clean-shaven, though he did have the full sideburns everyone sported now. His long narrow face looked sculpted. He wore rimless glasses and a fitted V-neck sweater over his striped shirt. This was his uniform now, and she preferred it. She told herself that she preferred it because it made him more beautiful, but who knew? Maybe she liked it because it was conventional—the way men had once been expected to look.

He was in his first year of business school, where he'd gone because he was interested in development on a human scale, in small projects that might be of actual help to the people he'd met and loved in South America. For the moment, though, he was learning about plain old raw capitalism, and almost in spite of himself, he was doing well at this.

Evan was the child Delia felt most comfortable with, though she had the tenderest love for Brad, her younger son. But everyone in the family felt that way about Brad—he was their baby. What she felt for Evan—on account of his beauty, his self-containment—moved her with a maternal pride that sometimes felt almost sexual in its intensity.

These feelings had to do also with her sense of something she found touching in what he seemed to feel toward her. It was typical of him to have arranged his schedule to pick her up. Ignoring a few years in adolescence when life with him was as much like hell as she imagined it, he had always been in some way protective of her—even, she would have said, *adult* around her.

Once when he was small, only about two and a half, she and Tom were having a terrible fight—yelling, enraged at each other; and in the midst of it, Evan had come out of his bedroom in his blue sleeper, the plastic bottoms of its feet kissing the floor. He'd walked straight over to her and climbed onto her lap. Of course they had stopped, the moment they heard his approach.

"Evvie," she'd said. "It's way past your bedtime. You need to go back to your room."

"No, Mumma," he said pleasantly. "I'm staying *right* by you." And he had. He was holding on to her arm, smiling across the room at Tom. She could feel the tendons like wires in his compact body.

Later, after he'd been reassured, after he'd been put to bed again and she'd lain down with him until he slept, she and Tom, shamed, took up whatever the issue was between them in reasoned, even hushed tones.

In the car, they decided to go to the Peking Palace—mediocre food, crummy decor, but they both liked the pan-fried ravioli and imported beer. As they settled into one of the booths, Delia looked around at the colored paper lanterns strung from the ceiling, the Formica tabletops, the framed panels on the walls with bucolic scenes of an imaginary Chinese past—scenes that actually looked suspiciously Japanese to her.

"Nothing ever changes at the Peking Palace," she said.

He looked up. "So you say," he answered, and went back to the menu.

For health's sake—vegetables—they split an eggplant dish in addition to the ravioli. This turned out to be so spicy it made Delia's nose run. She had to ask for extra paper napkins. They talked easily, as they always did. Evan told her about a couple of cases he'd studied this quarter, about his exams, which he was pretty sure he'd aced. They talked about movies, and what kind of coffee they liked best. They talked about skiing—Delia was supposed to come up to New Hampshire in January and try to learn how, something she'd attempted several times in the past with no success. But Evan assured her the skis were shorter now than in those days, that the whole way of teaching it was different. He guaranteed her she'd enjoy it.

"When's Nan getting here?" he asked.

Delia was waiting for tea, though she knew it would keep her awake. "Not until midevening Thursday—she has to work that day. Oh! And did I tell you that she's bringing the beauteous Carolee with her? Some family thing means she can't go home for the holiday."

He grinned. "You didn't," he said.

Carolee was Nancy's roommate. They'd met in Boston at a fancy old firm where they both felt incredibly lucky to have been hired directly out of law school. Carolee had gone to Harvard, so she knew the city. She was helpful and generous to Nancy. After only a few months, they'd decided to find an apartment to share. Delia had visited them several times at this apartment, in Cambridge, and she knew that Evan had come down from New Hampshire a couple of times to stay with them too.

"*I* remember." She raised her hand, a finger pointing up. "It's that her parents are living in Turkey now with some engineering project he's doing, and she has so little time off from work she can't possibly get there and back. So we've got her."

"All *right*!" Evan said.

Delia smiled at him. "She is kind of gorgeous, isn't she?" It was true. Carolee was a beautiful young woman, in a richly monochromatic way. She had luxuriant honey-colored hair that fell below her shoulders, and perfect skin that seemed touched with honey too. Her eyes, as though to go with everything else, were a light brown.

"Kind of?" Evan said. "She's preposterously good-looking."

Their waitress came and set Delia's teapot down, and next to it, a little saucer with two fortune cookies on it, wrapped in cellophane. "Which one of these do you suppose is the very one meant for you?" Delia asked, pushing the saucer toward her son.

He chose. "I have a friend who wrote these things for a while," he said.

"It's a job? Writing fortune cookies?" They were both tearing at the wrappers.

"Not a full-time job, but he was a musician, supporting the habit. Anyway, it's left me disinclined to take these things very seriously."

"Which of course you did, before."

He raised his eyebrows at her and unfurled his little paper roll. He snorted. "I hate this," he said. "It's so low risk. It's a maxim, not a fortune. 'The sun shines always in the strong man's path.' Fuck that." He tossed the paper onto the table. He bit into his cookie. "What's yours?"

"Similarly unforthcoming about the future." She flattened the little scroll out and read aloud: "'The dreamer will awake eventually.'"

"Well, it's a *little* about the future," he said. "Assuming you're the dreamer."

"No." Delia poured some tea into her cup. "Assuming I'm the dreamer, it's about the past."

He looked over at her sharply. Then he raised his mug of beer and drank.

TOM WOULD COME UP Wednesday afternoon, he said, by plane and then a taxi. Evan offered to pick him up at the airport, but he insisted on doing it his way.

"He likes that solo, dramatic entrance," Evan said.

"Plus, of course, there's the cabdriver," Delia answered. "One more vote to be gathered in."

When he arrived, Delia didn't hear him come in. She was in the kitchen with the dishwasher running and a pot of sugar water roiling on the stove. His light voice said, "Hello, darling," and she looked up to see him in the doorway, wearing the usual suit, the tie loosened, his face amused and fond.

"Hi," she said. She could feel her smile rise in response. She gestured at the stove. "Hi. I can't come to you." She was waiting for the sugar to caramelize.

"Then I'll have to come to you." He crossed the room and put his arm around her, bent to kiss her neck, then her cheek, then the side of her mouth. In the pot, the sugar was beginning to turn slightly rust-colored under its silvery bubbles. Tom's flesh was cold against her face, his mouth tasted sweet and familiar. He smelled wonderful to her. She leaned against him and was aware of the relief she felt to have him here. To have him home.

At this point in their life together, Delia divided her time almost evenly between Washington and Williston. Tom, of course, was more in Washington, though he came home when he could, on congressional breaks and when something in the state beckoned him.

Delia had liked Washington initially—they had lived there early in their marriage, during the war. There were many young couples flooding the city then. The war gave them all a sense of quick intimacy, of intensity in their friendships. She'd liked it again when they came back, years later, in Tom's first term as a congressman.

But then Kennedy was killed, and in the middle of that public sorrow, she learned that Tom had been having an affair, a serious affair with the wife of another congressman, someone Delia had thought of as a friend. And in the aftermath of that, he confessed that there had been other affairs too, more casual, more fleeting. *Accidental,* Tom had called them, which made her laugh bitterly.

They got through it, but after that life in Washington was more difficult for Delia. She was aware of her discomfort when she moved around socially. She never knew who else might have known about the affair—the affairs—and she never knew what those people who did know about them might be thinking of her. She felt a sense of strain, though nothing changed on the surface, though she was just as publicly charming as ever, was seen as often at the required political-social events. But when they'd bought the house, this house, and Delia began to have a life and friends in Williston, she realized how much more at ease she felt here. She supposed most of it was just getting away with Tom from the sexually charged atmosphere of Washington, where a handsome man with power, a man who talked easily, a man who was charming and chivalric around women, could always find companionship. Or, more accurately, had to actively choose *not* to have companionship, if that's what he wanted. Now, leaning into Tom, she said, "It's so good to have you here."

"Mmm, me too. You can't imagine."

"Sit. This will be done in a second. Do you want a drink?"

"I'll put my stuff away and say hi to Evan. Be back in a minute."

When he came back, in his shirtsleeves, he poured each of them a scotch, and they sat at the kitchen table and talked about the way things had ended in Washington (hectic, with last-minute negotiating about a couple of bills), about the plans for the weekend. About what needed to get done before Christmas Day.

Evan came down too and sat with them, and Delia heard again his report on school, with women embellishing it this time. Inevitable, she thought. There was always this need of Evan's to assert to his father that he was a man too.

After they had gone out to buy a tree and Delia was alone again, she thought about this, about the element of competition between the two of them. Brad was exempt from this. Or perhaps he'd exempted himself with his gentleness, his sweetness—a sweetness that worried her sometimes. Occasionally she had the impulse to grab him, to shake him, to tell him how handsome he was.

She'd brought this up with Tom one night recently, lying in bed—Brad's passivity, his almost deliberate turning away from whatever masculinity was understood to mean. "Or *is* it deliberate?" she asked. "What do you think?"

"Ppph!" Tom said. "Meet the new American male."

"Is that it, you think? It's a cultural phenomenon?"

"Well, it's apparently what the new American *female* wants. Someone she can dominate."

They had both been reading, and now they set their books, opened, facedown, on the blanket that covered them. Delia took her glasses off. "You're just saying that because, a) you dislike the women's movement, and b) you don't want to take responsibility for scaring him."

"*Scaring* him!"

"Yes. Being so . . . male yourself, it's hard for him to make any claims on that territory."

"Evan has no troubles that way," he said. He took his glasses off now too.

"Evan is Evan. And it makes it worse, maybe, that there are two of you floating around here, around Brad, fairly exuding testosterone."

The house was quiet around them. This was in Washington. He said, "I don't dislike the women's movement."

"Hah!" she said.

"I don't. Just some aspects of it."

"Yes." She smiled. "The ones that might apply to your behavior."

But he was frowning now, and when he spoke after a moment, he spoke more slowly. "No, I'm talking about the parts of the movement that so shrilly insist on . . . being *wronged* as a source of identity. I hate what that does to the sense of ourselves as a people. As a polis."

"Oh, how grand!" She put her hand on her heart. "A 'polis.'"

"Well, damn it, Dee, it *is* grand. It was grand, anyway. And it existed for a while, you know it, when we were young—that sense of the state having a responsibility to its people and the people to the state, to each other."

Tom had grown up poor and Irish in Boston. His father was a driver for a small coal-and-ice company. He had a job straight through the Depression, which many people living around them didn't, but there were seven children, and what he earned barely paid for food and rent. Tom and his siblings had all worked too when they could, and Tom and one of his brothers had actually left home for a while in their teens, just to ease the burden. They'd hoboed around the country, working on farms when there was work to be had, fighting fires in Montana and Wyoming one summer.

Roosevelt was his hero. Roosevelt and his own mother, who insisted they tithe despite their poverty, who expected them to give what they could to those in need, who wanted them to hold themselves above no one. All this was part of who he was, and part of why Delia loved him.

"I know the feminists didn't start it," he said, "and I suppose I can't blame them for using it, but what bothers me is that attitude." He shook his head. "'I am *me, the victim,* before I'm a citizen, before I'm one of a multitude, before I have work to do to make this goddam world better for everyone else too.'" He stopped. She could hear from his breathing that he was wound up.

After a moment, he turned to her, smiling the small smile that twisted his mouth. "And I dislike especially the aspects of the women's movement that don't acknowledge that there are major differences between men and women."

"I don't think anyone's saying that." Delia flipped her book up again.

"Well, maybe they're willing to say that women are *better* than men, but that's about it."

She let a little silence gather before she said, "Well? Ain't it the truth?"

Tom had laughed, moving his head back on his pillow, and Delia had smiled at him, but when they put on their glasses and started reading again, she realized that she was feeling a nagging sense of discomfort, as she often did when the women's movement came up.

She had a sense of solidarity, yes, and she knew there were many wrongs to be righted. But she felt that her own life was emblematic in the feminist world of everything that was wrong, that by the light of the women's movement, she'd made bad choices. And having an accomplished daughter had made it worse. She was glad Nancy was a lawyer and proud of her for her ambition, but she felt sometimes that her daughter was sorry for her, occasionally even a little contemptuous of her. That she wondered what her mother *did* all day.

Sometimes Delia herself wondered about it, wondered how she could have filled her life with the kinds of chores and odd jobs that it seemed to consist of now. From time to time she was aware of a pang of something that felt like envy, or perhaps even anger, toward Nancy, toward all the young, striving women they knew, here and in Washington.

While Tom and Evan were gone, Delia fixed dinner—a simple meal: chicken, mashed potatoes, carrots with ginger. They'd have ice cream for dessert, with the caramel sauce she'd just made. She set the table for three in the kitchen, but she used the good china, the crystal glasses.

She heard them come in, talking loudly, laughing, stomping. *They sound just like horses,* she thought. After a minute, she felt the movement of cold air around her legs. She went out to the hallway.

Of course, they'd left the front door open. They were in the living room with the tree, tilting it up into its stand, giving each other advice. She went down the hall, intending to close the door, but instead she stopped, she stood there for a moment, looking out at the night. The predicted snow was falling, dry and light, still just a sheer white transparency on the porch, on the stone rail; still just a filigree where the light fell on the lawn. She shivered. She shut the door and went to look at the tree, a pretty fir so tall it almost touched the ceiling. Its clean wood smell filled the room.

They ate dinner, and afterward, Evan went out to meet friends. She and Tom picked up in the kitchen and loaded the dishwasher. Then he went down to the basement to find the boxes of ornaments they'd accumulated over the years. While Delia prepared a marinade for the beef they were having the next night, he strung the lights on the tree. When she came out, they began to lift the old ornaments carefully out of their boxes and hang them, stepping back often to spot the places that needed filling in. Twice the telephone rang upstairs in Tom's study—he had a separate line for work—but he let the answering service pick it up.

When they were finished, Delia turned off all the lights except those on the tree, and Tom poured them each another glass of scotch. They sat together on the couch in the muted light. Tom's hand was resting on Delia's thigh. He had put some music on earlier—Respighi. He'd turned it up a bit when they sat down, and they listened through to the end of it in silence. The needle whispered in the last grooves, and lifted.

After a minute or two, she said, "Sometimes I wish we'd never have to go back to Washington."

"Ah, Dee. It can't be Christmas all the time."

"I know. And I know you love your work. And I'm glad you do." She put her hand over his. "It's just that life was simpler when you were just plain old Tom. And I was just a frumpy housewife, instead of chair of the fund-raising committee for this and that."

He raised her hand and kissed it. "You were never a frumpy housewife."

She sighed.

He put his arm around her. "And I was never just Citizen Naughton either. You knew me. You knew how ambitious I always was." She didn't answer. "I'm a schemer. I'm a louse." He kissed the top of her head. "It's why you love me."

Was it? she thought. Would she have been interested in Tom if he hadn't been as ambitious, as promising as he was? Hadn't she wanted, hadn't they *all* wanted—all the bright young college women then—men they thought would *take care* of them?

"It's *not,* why I love you," she said.

"But you do love me."

"I do." She turned and smiled at him. "Goddamit."

"You know," he said, reaching up, putting his finger on her lower lip, slightly into her mouth. "When the kids are finally all gone, we'll be able to make love on the couch, right here, right now, if we want to."

"The kids will never be all gone, you know that."

"I do." He laughed. Then his face changed. "Come upstairs with me."

After they'd gone upstairs, after they'd made love and Tom had fallen asleep, Delia lay awake. She was thinking of him as he was when she first knew him, the sense of restless energy in him that made him attractive to her.

He'd been a newly minted lawyer in New York then, and she'd been in her senior year of college, worrying about what came next. She'd majored in English. Could she teach? Should she do something more directly useful? Nursing school? She'd had two intense romances, neither fully consummated, and she felt that they stood for everything in her life: that everything she'd ever done was incomplete, unfulfilled.

Tom, with his certainty, with what she felt was the nearly electric charge he carried, with all that was unfamiliar and exotic to her about his background, made all of that irrelevant.

They met when her older brother brought him to Delia's campus one evening in the early fall, along with another man from the law firm they all worked in. She'd rounded up several friends, and they jammed into her brother's old car and drove to a crowded roadhouse about fifteen miles away from the school.

There was a band on a little stage, elevated just a bit above the dance floor—two horns, a bass, a drummer, and an out-of-tune piano. They danced and drank and smoked. She supposed they talked some too, but she remembered very little of that—and whatever there was was truncated and interrupted in any case, the band was so loud.

Delia had more or less been offered by her brother to the other lawyer, a man named Preston Eccles. But after she had danced with him once, Tom cut in.

From the first steps they took together Delia felt that awkwardness with Tom was inconceivable. He was a wonderful dancer and a sure, graceful leader. All she had to do was let his body tell her what to do.

The air was dense with smoke, alive with music, with shouted bits of talk, with the smell of booze. Delia and Tom barely spoke, but

Delia thought of their bodies as conducting a kind of conversation. Between dances they stood close to each other, waiting for the music to start again, feeling overwhelmingly the wish to be moving against each other; and then when they were, aware of the charge between them, the surprise and thrill of it each time they touched. Once, standing next to him, waiting, she looked at him; their eyes met and they both laughed, knowing what was coming. Before she knew him, she loved him. Her body trusted him.

Now, she supposed, you would be dismissive of those feelings as grounds for marriage, as sufficient reason for joining with someone with the idea that you could live together forever. You would understand them for what they were—desire, hunger. Then, though, the misunderstanding—and the ability to make a decision based on such a misunderstanding—was possible.

Of course, she loved him as she came to know him too, but most of that was after they married, after he swept her up in his sense of who he was, his sense of where he was going. His sense of the adventure he was going to make of his life. His and hers.

And she was swept up. She believed in him, first as a labor lawyer, then when he went to work for less money at the Labor Relations Board in the city, then when they began the jumping around everyone had to do as the war started—to Washington in their case, the War Department, then briefly apart when he went to basic training and she went to Maine to live with her parents, then back to Washington and the War Department again, and later the State Department. She followed him after the war too, when he decided to go back to New England, to try politics at the local level.

She believed in him, and she believed that they were meant, somehow, to be together. That was what was destroyed more than anything else when she learned about his affairs—that sense of destiny.

Thinking about it later, what was most astonishing to her was that she had held on to that idea as long as she did. That was part of the humiliation, she thought now—confronting her own childish notions about love, about what their marriage had meant.

At the time, though, losing that had made her desperate, it had made her wild with grief. She almost literally couldn't believe he had done what he'd done. She wanted more than anything for him to make the affairs go away, make them not have happened. She wept, she hit him, she listened to his promises, to his anguish, she wept again.

But they made it through, and she was older now. She loved him more wisely. She couldn't be hurt that way again.

At 2:10 Evan came in, the front door closed behind him. He went to the kitchen for a while, and then she heard his footsteps on the stairs. Tom stirred and turned over, but didn't wake. Something in her relaxed after that, and in a while she felt it begin—the slow deep dizziness that meant sleep.

DELIA SPENT THURSDAY in preparation. She made the beds in the room where Nancy and Carolee would be sleeping. She sat down and wrote out menus for the long weekend and made a shopping list. She drove to the supermarket at the new mall just outside of town, and went up and down the aisles, filling the shopping cart and even the low basket under it with what she thought of as *largesse*—feeling generous, expansive, as she did so. When she came home, she made two batches of Christmas cookies, and a lamb and barley soup.

She was in the kitchen when Nancy and Carolee arrived with Evan—he'd driven to the train station again to get them. She went into the hallway to greet them just as Tom came down the stairs.

The girls were taking their coats off, talking with Evan. They'd left together straight from work for the train station, and they were both wearing their business outfits—heels and suits, the skirts carefully longer than was the fashion. The jacket of Nancy's suit was boxy, but Carolee's cut in sharply at the waist and then flared out. It made you notice her hips, her shapeliness.

Delia was there first and she hugged them both, first Nancy and then Carolee. She stood back to watch Tom embrace Nancy ("Sweetie!" he said, throwing his arms around her), to watch Nancy in turn introduce him to Carolee, with so much pride that you would have thought she'd *invented* the other young woman.

When the girls went upstairs to change and unpack, Tom followed Delia into the kitchen. "Va va voom," he said in a low voice to her, grinning. He wiggled his eyebrows up and down.

"I know, I know," Delia said. She made a face at him. "But maybe you can calm down for just a minute and open some wine for me."

The girls came back down in blue jeans and sweaters, transformed into kids again, and they all went into the living room and had drinks—beer for Evan; scotch, neat, for Tom; and wine for all three women. Tom, as always when there was a fresh audience for his charm, laid it on, though Delia would have said he was equally flirtatious with everyone.

But Carolee's presence made them all livelier than usual. It seemed to Delia that Evan, especially, was almost jockeying with Tom for position, plying Carolee steadily with questions. And she was expansive under the attention of the two men, explaining her life to them, an explanation Delia had heard piecemeal earlier—the exotic locales she'd lived in as her parents settled in different places with her father's engineering projects. The shock of American culture when she came back for college. "I had an accent," she said, "and everyone thought I was putting it on. A kind of nameless, quasi-British, I don't know, maybe part British-Indian, postcolonial thing." She shook her head, remembering it, and her lovely hair swayed. "Everyone hated me, they thought I was such a fraud. I had to consciously teach myself Americanisms, to say things like *real nice*." She seemed to take their attention for granted, she seemed certain of the fascinating quality of her own life.

Well, it was fascinating, but mostly because she was a lively recounter of it. But she was generous too. She turned to Delia at one point and said, "All this is just so gorgeous." She gestured around her. "I wish I could do what you do—make this home so beautiful, so gracious. It even *smells* good." She laughed. "All these wonderful, female accomplishments I'm just so in *terror* of."

"One succumbs inch by inch," Delia said. She reached over and poured herself another glass of wine.

"Oh, don't say *succumb*. I'd give anything to be able to—I don't know—just have all these things in my life."

Delia smiled across the room at Tom, and was grateful when Nancy took over, talking about the law firm, the kind of fine line the women had to walk between being tough-minded and competent, but also female, nonthreatening to the men.

Delia got up and passed around the crackers and cheese again, the bowl of spiced almonds.

They talked about *Carnal Knowledge,* about what its tone toward women really was. They argued about *Portnoy's Complaint.* They all agreed that part of the reason they liked *The French Connection* was that there was no such problem to consider—women barely existed in it.

At some point later they came inevitably around to politics— Carolee asked Tom about the Pentagon Papers. He was expansive, he had a lot of theories about what he guessed were the complicated motives of Daniel Ellsberg, whom he knew personally; but he said he was glad the papers had come out, that everyone in Washington had known all along that the government had been lying. He said this had been and would be the making of Katharine Graham at the *Washington Post.* He called her Kay.

Carolee seemed happier, more animated than Delia had seen her before. Her cheeks were flushed, though maybe that was from the wine. Delia noticed for the first time that one of her light brown eyes was slightly lazy. When she looked at you, you felt compelled by this, by the intensity of her focus, the sense of something *willed* in it as the slower eye pulled toward you.

She looked at Tom a lot. It was the kind of thing Delia might have been bothered by in another context, but here, now, she wasn't.

Later she asked herself why. It seemed to her it must have been because of Carolee's youth, and because she was Nancy's friend. Or maybe it was because Tom had made her beauty a kind of joke between Delia and himself.

But there were other reasons. Tom had been unusually loving in bed the night before, and she had carried the aftermath of that with her through the day—the image of his long body bent over her in the half dark, the feeling of his hands, his mouth, on her.

And then too, at one point later in the evening when they were all sitting around with empty glasses and he was describing a disastrous camping trip they'd taken years before, he ticked off the afflictions that had struck them, pointing at each of them as he went around the room. "This one had poison oak, this one got food poisoning, and this one"—coming to Delia, smiling that private smile of his across at her—"was so sunburned she couldn't be touched for days afterward." Something in this casual public hint of their married intimacy, and maybe too in the possessive listing of his family members, warmed Delia. Perhaps it reassured her. Perhaps it was intended to do exactly that. In any case, she didn't pick up on the currents that were passing between him and Carolee.

The next day, getting up from the kitchen table, Tom noticed her grocery list, things she'd forgotten or had already run out of—she'd lost the habit of cooking for a crowd. He picked it up and looked at it. "I'd be happy to run out and get this stuff for you," he said.

"Oh, would you?" she said, feeling only grateful. While he went outside to get the car warmed up, she sat down at the table and copied the list over so he could read it.

After he'd left, after she'd straightened up in the living room, after she'd unloaded the clean dishes from the dishwasher and put the dirty ones in, she got out the big cream-colored bowl and the electric mixer and started to assemble what she would need for the cake she planned for dessert tomorrow. As she was sifting the dry ingredients, Nancy came thundering down the uncarpeted back stairs to the kitchen. She was wearing jeans and a sweatshirt and white woolen socks on her feet. She had no makeup on. Her hair was skinned back into a ponytail. She looked like a pretty twelve-year-old. Delia smiled at her.

She asked Delia what there was for lunch. Delia suggested soup, and maybe a sandwich. Nancy went into the pantry. Delia heard the refrigerator door open. "What about Carolee?" she called.

"What about Carolee?"

"Doesn't she want some lunch too?"

"Mmmph," said Nancy. She came around the corner eating something. A carrot, stuck into her mouth. She had a pile of plastic bags heaped awkwardly against her stomach. She set them on the counter, removed the carrot as though it were a cigarette, and holding it between the first and second fingers of her hand, she said, "She went with Daddy. She had a few errands she wanted to do in town."

Delia looked up at her. "Why didn't you go along?" she asked.

"Because *I* didn't have any errands."

"You could have kept her company."

"*Mother,*" she said, rolling her eyes, making fun of the way she'd talked to Delia a few years earlier in her life. "She *has* company. She's with Dad. And it's not like she's ten years old or . . . incapacitated or something, anyway."

"You're right. You're right," Delia said. She poured milk into the flour and sugar mixture and set the mixer going so she wouldn't have to talk anymore.

They were gone for several hours. Delia told herself this meant nothing. He was taking her on a tour of the town. They'd probably had lunch at the funny restaurant he liked at the inn on the campus. He was hosting her. Why not? He was, after all, her host.

After the cake was done and had cooled, after she'd frosted it, she decided to go out. She put on her boots, her coat, a hat, and gloves. She called up to Evan and Nancy that she'd be back in a while.

It was bitterly cold. The sidewalks on Dumbarton Street were covered with ice. Old footprints were frozen in their crusty surface. Half of them hadn't been shoveled of the most recent snow, or even of earlier ones—everyone drove in winter.

Delia stepped over the plowed heap at the edge of the road and walked in the street. It was silent. One car passed her. Her boots crunched on the pellets of salt and gravel in the brown snow. Her breath fogged damply in front of her and bit at her face. She turned onto Main Street and walked the long blocks into town. She passed a young couple going the other way, both of them carrying bags full of gifts. He was wearing a Santa hat. "Merry Christmas!" he said, and the girl echoed him.

Delia made herself smile. "Merry Christmas," she said.

The closer she got to the business district, the busier it was with last-minute shoppers. She had to weave her way down the sidewalk to avoid bumping into people. One of the stores was pumping Christmas music out into the frigid air.

She went into the Five&Ten. Here too Christmas music played, a perky choir doing the more secular songs—about Santa, about Rudolph. The vast store was overheated, and it smelled, as always, of burning coffee. Hardly anyone was there.

She began going through the aisles, pulling things into her basket, things that she hadn't thought about needing. A cardboard placard dotted with small white buttons, for a shirt of Tom's that was missing one. Thread. A new hairbrush. Bobby pins. Notepads to set by the phones. Shoelaces. Manila envelopes, business envelopes. Extra pens. Shoe polish. She took her time. When she was done, when she'd paid for everything, she went with her bag to the lunch counter at the front of the store and had some of their terrible coffee.

On the way home, just as she'd turned onto Dumbarton Street again, she fell on the ice. Nearly until she hit the ground, she made herself believe that it wouldn't happen, that she could right herself. She landed on her side, almost lying down, her purchases scattered on the frozen lawn next to her. She didn't get up for a minute or so, just lay there waiting for the pain and the sense of insult to subside, looking across the crusted snow at the cheap, ugly things she'd bought. As she carefully picked everything up, she felt so sorry for herself that she had to fight back tears.

"Stop it!" she whispered violently.

From halfway down the block, she could see that the car was in the driveway. They were home.

As she came up the front walk, Delia wasn't sure what she felt—maybe relief, pathetically enough. When she opened the door, the house was quiet, and then she heard Tom's voice on the phone in his study upstairs. She dropped her coat and her purchases on the couch in the front hall. In the kitchen, the groceries that didn't need refrigeration were all set out neatly on the table—by Carolee? by Tom? Delia put them away: oatmeal for breakfast, more fruit, English muffins, sugar, jam, bread, baking powder. Everything seemed to be happening in slow motion, even her hands lifting each of these items, carrying it to its rightful place.

When she went upstairs, she could hear Nancy's and Carolee's voices, barely audible over the music playing in Nancy's room. Tom's study door was open and he was still on the phone. He waved at her from behind his desk, he grinned cheerfully, innocently, and then he turned away in his swivel chair to keep talking. Delia went to their bedroom. She shut the door and lay down.

Tom stayed in his study most of the rest of the day, on the phone—Delia could hear his voice when she walked past. When he emerged for a drink before dinner, he was animated and charming, but then he'd been full of charm and blarney all along.

Carolee, though, seemed pitched higher in every way. She talked more, she laughed more, she laughed louder. Her makeup and hair were done carefully. Delia had to will her own voice to sound normal and friendly when she spoke to her.

After dinner, she and Tom left the young people cleaning up and went to the ten o'clock service at the Episcopal church, which had been their compromise between Catholicism and Congregationalism when they married. They were silent in the car on the way over, but she was familiar with this. This was just Tom's sudden collapse after being *on* for a while.

They parked in the lot behind the church and came around to the front. She could feel the stir Tom's arrival caused as they came in, even though they took seats in a pew near the back. Several people close to them greeted him in whispers, and others turned to look, their faces lifted into that embarrassed half smile of recognition of the senator Delia knew so well. It happened all the time to Tom, with Tom, and Delia didn't mind it then. He expanded under it, he absorbed it all. She only had to smile back, to make vague and friendly comments. But when occasionally by herself she would look up and see that someone knew who she was, she always turned away from the eager glance of recognition, she busied herself with whatever she was doing. She felt almost offended to be approached when she wasn't with him. She hated having her solitary privacy invaded.

The service began. They stood for a welcoming prayer, a prayer of thanks, and then, still standing, they sang the first carol of the service—"O Come, All Ye Faithful." For Delia, the carols and scriptures at this time of year were an evocation of her youth, when she had thought of herself as a believer. She didn't anymore, but this service in particular brought those feelings back to her, made her nostalgic for them. She remembered sitting in the church on the Green in the small town in Maine where she'd grown up—sitting with her parents and older brother—growing tearful through certain prayers, certain responsive readings.

It was different for Tom. For him this service—any public gathering actually—was mostly a performance, like so much else in his life. Even as they bowed their heads in prayer, she could feel the energy radiating from him. He was more alive under all these eyes, among all these people.

She felt a sudden wave of tenderness for him. Of pity. How much more he needed than she did! How much harder it was for him to be made happy. That was probably part of the draw of Carolee, part of the reason he'd wanted to linger in her company today. A new audience. A new lovely audience. That's all it was, she thought.

She reminded herself that this was part of his everyday life in Washington—the pretty young secretaries, the female aides, the interns. And just as there was nothing remarkable or threatening to her in any of that, there wasn't in his being charmed by Carolee, in his flirting with her. She reached over and held his hand for a moment, and he looked at her quickly and smiled.

When the service was over, he turned immediately to those around him and began talking and shaking hands. He always kept one hand on Delia too—around her shoulders, at her elbow, her back. She was part of him for now—the senator's wife—and she moved with him the short distance back up the aisle, nodding, greeting people, listening to Tom talk. He told someone how good it was to be out of Washington, and Delia met his eye and made a face at him: *liar*. His mouth tightened in a half smile back at her. He talked about the weather with someone else, about ice hockey. "Merry Christmas!" he said over and over. "Merry Christmas!"

A fortyish man asked him about Vietnam, about the draft. He had sons in their midteens, he said, and naturally . . .

"I'm with you. I'm with you," Tom said. "We're working on it. God willing, it'll be over before they have to go."

They were quiet again in the car on the way home, but as they turned onto Dumbarton Street, as they pulled into the driveway, she could feel him come to a kind of attention. It might have been for Carolee, but it might just as easily have been for his own children. She went with him up the steps, through the door.

The house was silent. On the stand in the front hall, there was a note from Nancy in her round, schoolgirlish script. "We're at the movies. Then maybe a drink. Back late."

"Ah," Tom said, straightening up after he'd read it. "They've left the old fogies behind." He'd made his voice cheerful, but she could hear the disappointment in it.

THEIR ROUTINES FOR Christmas Day were so inflexible as to be ritual. The only thing that had changed over the years was that now Delia and Tom woke well before their children did. This morning they shuffled around the kitchen together in their slippers and bathrobes, making coffee, drinking it, talking in subdued tones. Delia set the dining room table, and Tom put out the ingredients for the breakfast he always made Christmas morning—bacon, French toast, orange juice, coffee.

When they went upstairs to get dressed, Tom went to the closet and brought out a professionally wrapped box, what they called his *real* gift to her. This was ritual too, that he gave her this present in private. It was always something intimate or sentimental, something he didn't want the kids to be embarrassed by, or, in their embarrassment, to make fun of, which they'd done when they were younger. This year it was a jewelry box made of a dark polished wood with ivory inlaid in a floral pattern on its lid.

"Oh, Tom, it's beautiful," she said. She was seated at her dressing table, facing the mirror, the box on her lap. "Thank you so much." She ran her fingers over it. "It's gorgeous."

"Which is why it was the right gift for you." He got up from the chair opposite her. He bent over her from behind and kissed her cheek. She looked at their reflection in the oval mirror—her own watchful face looking back, the top of his head as he bent down next to her, his arms making a frame around her, his hands on her elbows.

Then he stood up and was gone from the glass, off to his closet. All Delia could see behind her was their empty bed. After a moment, she leaned forward and began to fuss with her hair.

No one was stirring by ten, so Tom put on some music—the Christmas portion of the *Messiah*. He turned the volume up high. After a little while, they heard the showers running upstairs. Tom started breakfast—Delia was already fixing the vegetables for dinner, and the lamb was ready to go in the oven.

When the young people came downstairs, everyone gathered in the dining room to eat. The morning sun poured in through the tall windows, glinting off the glasses and silverware. Stars of reflected light danced on the walls and ceiling as they ate. Evan asked Carolee what she thought her parents were doing, and she talked about that, and about the way she'd spent Christmases in her childhood. Her favorite was in Norway, where she'd lived for two years. She got to be Santa Lucia at her parents' Christmas party. She wore a crown—a wreath with lighted candles in it. "I loved that. It was partly the risk, I think. The idea of fire so near your hair, your head."

When they were done, the kids cleared and cleaned up, and Delia reset the table for dinner. As she put the china, then the silverware down in place, she was thinking how much the holidays reminded her of the way her life had been when the children were all small— meal after meal after meal. Why hadn't she gone mad? How had she given over to it as completely as she had? Who had she been then?

As soon as they were through with their chores, they trailed into the living room, one by one. Tom started a fire in the fireplace. Delia had turned the tree lights on, even though their glow seemed anemic with daylight from the windows behind them streaming in through the evergreen branches.

Evan took Brad's usual role this year, moving around under the tree, picking out presents and bringing them to each person, trying to keep the balance even so that everyone would have something in each round. Delia had bought extra gifts for Carolee, small things, to make this possible—a lipstick in a color that looked like the one she wore, a little net bag of foil-wrapped chocolate coins, a pair of mittens, a paperback copy of *The Bluest Eye*.

Evan was businesslike in the distribution at first—an efficient elf, Tom called him. But as he got more into it, he began to make an elaborate show of the presentation to the girls, especially Carolee. He would spin in front of her, bow before her, call her "Your Highness," or "Mademoiselle." She played along with him the first few times, and then pretended irritation. She and Nancy began to throw balls of wrapping paper at him whenever he gave either of them anything. Their voices grew shrill, they were all laughing.

When Delia or Tom opened a present, the game would fade, but it surged again when it was Carolee or, now, Nancy's turn. They seemed like teenagers to Delia, like kids—children playing together.

"You are such a *jerk*," Carolee said, pelting Evan again.

"Ah, the Christmas spirit," Tom said, smiling at Delia. She smiled back.

Dinner was a slow, ceremonial meal, with a different bottle of wine for each course, and a long pause between them. As they moved into dessert, coffee, cordials, the light was fading and then gone from the windows in the dining room.

Once again, the kids offered to clear and clean up. The girls went upstairs to change their clothes first. Tom retreated to his study—the phone had rung several times in the afternoon.

Delia went to sit by the fire and write a letter to Brad. She told him about the weather, about their Christmas Day without him, about her plan to learn to ski with Evan, about what his siblings were doing. She visualized him reading the letter three or four weeks hence—which is when it would arrive in his mountain village in Guatemala. She could imagine his face, so round and boyish. She recalled the way his hair curled down over the nape of his neck. She missed him. She heard the girls in the kitchen, Tom's intermittent voice in his study, Evan's music upstairs.

By the time she finished, everything had quieted. She got up and poked at the fire. The last log crumbled into disparate sparking embers. She put the screen up in front of it.

As she was about to step into the front hall, she saw Carolee halfway up the stairs, just making the turn out of sight. At that moment, Tom walked forward into the hallway too, coming from the kitchen. He saw Delia and smiled. "Darling . . ." he said, in his light, urgent voice; and Delia watched as, invisible to him, Carolee turned back on the stairs, her face lit and expectant.

Delia stepped into her sight line and answered him. "What?"

As Tom began talking—something about business in Washington—Delia could see Carolee in her peripheral vision, quickly vanishing around the corner to the second floor. Even as she heard Tom out, keeping her voice calm, she felt her heart racing. She was seeing again the eagerness—no, the *avidity*—in the girl's face when she heard Tom's endearment, and she knew, she felt it as an undeniable certainty, that something had already begun between them.

Tom was going to have to go back early, the next day, that's what he was saying. There was some trouble with a bill that had passed just before Christmas, some negotiating he needed to be there for.

"I see," she said.

"And so it goes." He lifted his hands, palms up, helpless. His mouth made its small, self-mocking smile. "I'm sorry, really. I thought we'd have a nice long vacation together."

Delia was certain he was lying, but she willed herself to believe him, she willed it to be true. There *was* a meeting, there would be a meeting, he was sad to go. Just as she'd willed it to be true that yesterday Carolee had a big batch of xeroxing to get done in town, that there'd been other work lined up ahead of hers, so that they'd decided to go for lunch while they waited. To go for lunch, to buy the groceries Delia needed, and, yes, to tour the town. And even then they'd had to wait a little longer when they stopped back to pick the xeroxing up.

He packed that night since his flight was so early the next morning. He'd arranged for a car to take him to the airport. She lay in bed and watched him move around the room. The suitcase was open by her feet, and there was a little bounce she could feel each time he added something to it. He was quick and efficient. He'd done this hundreds of times before.

As he was getting into bed beside her, he said, "When will you come back, you think?" There was something too casual, too relaxed in his tone.

"To Washington?" she said. "I don't know. Evan is staying all this coming week, so I'll want to be here for him. And then there were a few invites I said yes to, though that was for both of us. I'll figure it out."

"Will you let me know?"

"Of course. I wouldn't *spring* myself on you."

"Though that sounds kind of interesting, actually." He kissed her lightly.

When he left the next morning, he warned her that he'd be out late at meetings, and "pretty unavailable," he said, by phone. "I'll call you when I can."

Later in the morning Carolee unexpectedly left too, a day earlier than she and Nancy had planned. She had some stuff to prepare for work that she just hadn't gotten done over the weekend because she was having such a good time. She needed to get back and just push through it. An all-nighter, she thought. Evan and Nancy drove her to the train station and put her on.

Delia didn't call Tom that night, or the next, or all that following week. She didn't want to hear the telephone ring and ring in the empty house in Washington.

CHAPTER SEVEN

Delia, Spring Through Fall, 1972

IT WAS NANCY who discovered definitively what had happened. Carolee was embarrassed and nervous around her when she got back a day later. When Nancy pressed her, she said no, no, nothing was wrong, nothing at all. But she was hardly at home after that, and on several occasions, she stayed out all night and was mysterious at work the next day about where she'd been. A few weeks later she moved out. She told Nancy that she'd decided to live alone for a while. She said she thought she needed some space.

But if Carolee wouldn't talk to Nancy, she did talk to various other people—people who were friends of Nancy's too. In fact, in her excitement about the romantic and erotic adventure she was launched into, in her bemused delight with her own charm, she talked and talked and talked. She talked, and then she swore the listener to secrecy, every single one of them.

So Nancy heard, of course, and in her turn she told Delia what Delia had known anyway, the moment she stood in the hall and saw the beautiful young woman on the stairs turn so eagerly to Tom's voice.

And after the winter of trying, after discovering that Tom was still seeing the girl long after he'd sworn it was done; after he told her then that he couldn't, or wouldn't, give Carolee up, Delia had fled, fled to Paris where none of it could touch her for a while, where she could try to think clearly about what it was she wanted to do.

IT WAS MIDAFTERNOON, about a week after she'd moved into the apartment in the seventh, when she decided that she would go to the Rodin museum, one of her favorite public buildings nearby. The day was warm, too warm for late April, and she thought she would sit in the gardens and cool off. Yes, she would walk out and sit on a bench in the shade among the beautiful roses as a way of marking her arrival in the city, her new life—celebrating it.

And she did. She bought her ticket and went around the side of the beautiful old *hôtel particulier* that was the museum, out the long walk under the trees to the fountain. But it was too warm even in the garden, and she began to feel almost groggy sitting there. She got up and slowly walked back up the gravel path to the building. She mounted the stairs to the wide back terrace. She entered the museum through the tall glass-paned doors that opened out onto it.

The crowd inside was thin this late in the day, standing in little shifting circles around one work or another. She joined them, admiring the marble figures, the clay maquettes. But it was even warmer in here than outside—the rooms faced south, and the sun was pouring in. Delia could feel sweat forming at the roots of her hair. A trickle slid down her back, then another.

There was a doorway to a darker space at the end of the last room facing the terrace. She walked over to it and went into a small room with dim lighting. It was cooler instantly, though airless—the room had no windows.

There weren't any sculptures in here, just glass cases of drawings and small pictures hanging on the walls at eye level. Delia leaned over the nearest of the cases. Several quick sketches in it were studies Rodin had done for one or another of the massive sculptures. They were drawn in pencil, or a narrow-nibbed pen—the lines were so light, so quick and thin you had to bend close in this light to make them out. There were paintings too—watercolors. Delia moved from one small, vague sketch or wash of color to another.

And then stopped. She wanted to turn away, but didn't.

It was a woman, lying down, seen from the foot of a bed. Her legs were spread wide, her almost hairless sex open. Her genitals were penciled in, and there was a pale wash of watercolor spread over her—the honey color of her flesh; and another wash, of a deep green, over the bed she was lying on. It was lovingly, attentively done, and intensely erotic. It was impossible to imagine that the person who drew this, who painted this, hadn't stood up when he was finished and crossed the room and fucked this model.

That's what Delia was seeing at any rate, what she felt she had been brought here to see, what she was being punished by having to see. The flesh, the youth, the beauty, the sex, of another woman as Tom would see her, as Tom would respond to her. The inevitability of his desire for someone else made visible.

A couple—young, hippie, with backpacks—began to enter the room. Seeing her there, an older woman alone in the dim light bent over one of the glass cases with tears streaming down her face, they stopped. They whispered something, and then stepped back and disappeared quickly around the corner into the bright light of the room behind them.

IT WAS ONLY a few days after this when Nancy called and wanted to join her for the week's vacation she was taking from her job in early May. Delia's first impulse was to say no. Her visit to the museum was still fresh in her mind—she'd been stunned by how easily she fell apart, by how fragile she was. And she knew it would be hard to be with Nancy—it had been hard all winter. Sometimes her daughter had seemed to be almost physically thrashing around the house in Williston in her powerless anger, in her profound sense of betrayal. Once, yelling at Delia, "How can they do this? How can you let them?" she had risen so abruptly from her seat that she knocked over the glass and plate sitting on the little table next to her. And then, looking at the shards of glass, the pieces of china lying on the floor, she'd reached down and deliberately shoved the table over too. It was as if the betrayal and the end of her parents' marriage had happened fully as much to her as to Delia.

And perhaps, in some sense, they had, Delia thought. Nancy had been an adoring adolescent daughter, caught up in her father's importance. She was always far more likely than Brad or Evan to let her friends know whose child she was—the daughter of the distinguished Senator Naughton. She hung on him when he was home.

For his part, Tom was more flirtatious with her than with the boys, more seductive, as if he didn't know another way to be with a female, even if that female was his daughter. She was the one of the kids he asked to talk to first when he called home. When she went to college, he visited her often, he took her out for expensive dinners, just the two of them. For her birthday, there was usually jewelry.

And so when he fell in love with Carolee, her closest friend, when it seemed that he had left the family for her, Nancy felt shocked in a way Delia wasn't capable of anymore, and Delia had to spend the first few months of the end of her marriage comforting her daughter. It made her aware of how empty, how dried out and exhausted she was. During that period, she sometimes felt that if she thought she could have prevented it, she would have struggled to more for Nancy's sake than for her own.

But once she'd escaped from her family life, from Williston and Washington, escaped to where no one knew her, she thought she was done with that. She thought she could be selfish, think only of herself, of getting better. The idea that Nancy would come into her life again, and bring with her her rage and grief, was almost more than she could bear.

But Nancy was her daughter, after all. She was suffering, and Delia understood and loved her. And so she said yes. Yes. Come.

For the first few days the visit was sweet. A pleasure, Delia would have said. She discovered she had missed her daughter's company— or perhaps just company itself: she'd been too much alone in the month or so she'd been in Paris. It felt good to talk. To have dinner with someone, to say good night before you went to bed. To touch someone you loved.

Delia had told Nancy she would have to continue through the visit with the language classes she'd started at the Alliance Française, and she did, leaving the house early on Monday morning, clutching her notebooks to her chest like a schoolgirl, walking past the Algerian and Moroccan street cleaners pushing rinse water into the drains with their odd arrangement of bits of old carpet—while Nancy, on a different clock, slept heavily on.

After the three-hour class, Delia met her daughter for lunch in a restaurant they'd agreed on. It was a place Delia felt comfortable in, small and of the neighborhood, run by a middle-aged couple who greeted Delia cordially by now. There were half curtains, lace, across the front windows. No one spoke English and the menu was in French—Delia translated for her daughter. Nancy was charmed by all of it.

That first lunch was pleasant. Delia was exhausted by her class as usual, and as usual also, she was lighthearted in the relief of its being over. They split a bottle of wine between them and talked and laughed easily.

But the next day, as the meal ended, Nancy brought the conversation around to it—to Carolee, to Carolee and Tom and the outrage she felt, the outrage she thought Delia ought to feel.

Delia tried to change the subject; she told Nancy it wasn't something she wanted to talk about anymore, that she *couldn't* talk about it anymore; but even back at the apartment Nancy kept on about it. It wasn't enough for Delia to say that she wasn't going to live with Tom again, or that, like Nancy, she found his behavior reprehensible. Nancy wanted him punished, exposed, through a very public divorce, which she argued for. She was incredulous at Delia's apparent lack of venom, at her inability to say what it was she was going to do.

On Wednesday, before she left for class, Delia wrote a note to Nancy, saying that the topic had to be off limits, that she needed to work out the answers to her dilemma herself. She asked Nancy to try to imagine for a moment how painful it was to discuss it with anyone else. She asked her to keep her own sorrow private.

After that, things were easier, though there were occasionally long moments of strain when they both fell silent, full of the awareness of what they weren't talking about. Still, Delia felt she'd taken some necessary step with her daughter, some necessary step for herself. And when Nancy left, she turned back to her solitary life with renewed determination.

She threw herself even more resolutely into mastering French. Her teacher at the Alliance was a racist, she had decided. She brought most of their discussions around inexorably to immigration and its great evils, to the wish of the Africans to live without working on the backs of the industrious French. She harangued, she lectured.

Was this conversation, as it was supposed to be?

In their halting, primitive discussions in the hallways and on the sidewalks after class, she and the other students agreed: it was not. Slowly they began to venture to contradict their teacher, to argue with her. But Delia, anyway, was hampered by her lack of ease with any tense other than the present and the *passé composé,* and by her limited vocabulary. Her French was formal, hesitant, reduced—that of a polite, well-trained child of seven, perhaps. Madame rolled over her, time and time again.

Delia studied longer hours, determined to truly enter the argument by summer's end. It became *what she did,* instead of feeling shame, instead of grieving for Tom and the end of the marriage. It seemed miraculous to her, but she sometimes forgot all that, occasionally for an hour or longer as she labored over an exercise or worked her way slowly through an article in the paper. She started to be able to imagine her life going on, bringing her new pleasures.

The letters from Tom began in late May. The first one was short. It asked if she thought it might be possible for her to "keep the door open" in her life for him.

She didn't know how to answer this. She was overjoyed, momentarily, so happy she could hear the pounding of her heart as she set the letter down. And then almost instantly she felt humiliated by that very joy. She spent the better part of two days listening to music, drinking wine, crying. She didn't write back. She didn't know what to say.

He wrote again, at greater length. He'd made a mistake. Carolee was a lovely girl, but she was, as Delia had pointed out, a girl. He was not now seeing her anymore—in fairness, as much by her choice as his.

In her answering letter she pointed out that he had said it was over before.

He had lied then, he wrote, because he was so terrified of losing her.

When she read that, Delia was incredulous, then amused, then enraged. She wrote him a long letter back in which she spoke of her inability ever to trust him again, of her contempt for him, of her wish to be free of him.

He wrote again. He said he understood her feelings, that he knew he'd done something unforgivable, as he had so many times before; but what he ardently hoped—though he knew he had no right to— was that Delia *could* forgive him again, as *she* had done so many times before.

Then he mentioned the campaign, his campaign for reelection, which had already begun. When she came to this passage, Delia smiled bitterly. So this was what lay under it all—under the wooing, under the regret.

"It isn't going to be a tough one," he wrote, "but my opponent is a good campaigner, and it will surely cut into my advantage if you aren't by my side, if rumors start. I need you, as I've always needed you.

"If you felt that you were able to do this for me, I don't know how I could repay you, but I would look forward to being in your debt, to doing whatever you ask of me. And of course, what I hope most of all is that you can find it in your heart to ask me to come back on whatever terms you set. That would be a request I could comply with gladly."

After thinking about it for several days, Delia wrote back and said she would join him for the campaign.

She wasn't sure, even then, of her deepest reasons for saying yes. She didn't know whether she meant it as a one-time gesture of goodwill, or as the start of a reconciliation. Maybe she just wanted to exercise some power over him, however briefly. This seemed possible to her, as it seemed possible that she really wanted to help him politically in spite of the turmoil in her feelings.

What she knew—what she thought she knew—was that she had no wish to punish him politically because of her personal anguish.

She believed in him, in what he fought for. It was the finest part of who he was, a part she wished to align herself with. She didn't want to see herself as vindictive in this arena.

She tried to lay this all out to him in her letter. She was as honest as she could be, given her own confusion about her intentions.

There was a kind of expansiveness, a joy, in his next letter. He thanked her, he recollected with a perceptible pleasure some episodes from previous campaigns, ones they'd done together.

She wrote back less guardedly too, for the first time describing her life in France, the neighborhood, her lessons.

After this they corresponded until the end of the summer in a more relaxed way. He wrote about their mutual friends in Washington, many of whom weren't speaking to him. She wrote about Nancy, about how deeply he'd wounded her, about how disturbed she was. He told her he'd written to Nancy three or four times, as he had the boys. Brad had written a kind note back, he said, but neither Evan nor Nancy had responded. Eventually he'd called both of them. Nancy had hung up when he announced himself. "Who can blame her?" he'd written. He'd talked briefly to Evan, who was, he wrote, "nothing if not honest about how he feels."

Delia was trying to master the subjunctive tense. And how fitting, she thought, to be struggling here in this foreign city with the subjunctive, when she was going to have to live her life out, for the foreseeable future, in foreignness, in subjunctivity, in the conditional suspension of everything she'd known as real. She imagined herself campaigning with Tom, standing by his side, seeming to be the loving wife. And being, yes, the loving wife. For didn't she love him? Wasn't she still his wife? And yet not allowing herself lovingness, or wifeliness. Was there a verb form that could express this experience?

Intending to amuse him, perhaps also to hurt him, she wrote Tom a letter describing this, her double need for mastery over the subjunctive, in class and in life.

And he wrote back, as she'd known he would—hadn't she invited it, so she could say no once again?—asking her if she couldn't be truly what she'd consented to play at being.

DELIA'S CLASS AT the Alliance was over. She had only four more days in Paris. Already she'd begun to pack. In her apartment there were stacks of neatly folded clothes and books and all the little things she'd purchased.

For weeks there'd been a notice up in the street window of the concierge's living room, announcing an apartment for sale in the building. After Delia had her usual breakfast—coffee and a croissant from the bakery next door—she went down to the concierge's apartment and rang the bell. She asked to see the place for sale. The concierge was busy—Delia could hear that she'd interrupted the family's breakfast. While they were talking, one of the children came to the beaded curtain at the kitchen doorway and stood chewing on a large piece of French bread, watching his mother and Delia, the silly grown-up woman who spoke only baby French. The concierge rummaged through the top drawer in a bureau in the entryway and produced a key. *"Troisième étage, numéro deux,"* she said, and turned away, went back through the clacking curtain.

In the dark hallway, Delia pushed the button for the overhead lights and they came on. The timer began ticking. Slowly she mounted the shallow steps of the curving stone staircase, holding on to the iron railing against the wall. She passed her own doorway on the parlor floor, and went up two more flights. The timer clicked off and the hall went dark again just as she reached the door to number two, but enough light fell from the dirty skylight at the top of the building for Delia to find the keyhole and fit the key into it.

She stepped in and closed the door behind her.

There was a sense of echoing stillness in the empty apartment. The floors were bare, the furniture gone. She was standing in a little entryway, just like the one she had downstairs. As she came into the living room, she saw that it was narrower than hers, and that this was because its windows opened onto a balcony that ate up the space, a balcony that looked out over the interior courtyard of the building. She stepped across the living room and into the tiny, modern kitchen, everything half or even a third the size it would be in America. The floor plan so far was identical to the apartment she was renting, but the ceilings were much lower on this floor of the building, and less ornate. It made the apartment somehow friendlier, Delia thought.

She went down the long hallway, past the WC and the small extra bedroom, the one Nancy had slept in downstairs when she visited. She opened the door to the large bedroom at the back of the apartment. Its windows faced onto the air shaft, as hers did below, but from here you could look up and see the sky. Everything back here was permeated with the sweet, sweet smell of cooking butter from the patisserie on the ground floor next door—a smell that drifted up in the mornings to her lower apartment too.

She came back down the long hall into the living room, admiring the herringbone pattern of the old wooden floors. She opened one of the French doors and stepped out onto the balcony. It was about six feet deep, with an iron rail. There were three double doors from the living room that opened out on it. Their shutters, a peeling faded blue, were folded back against the stone walls. Below Delia, in the courtyard, a man emerged from one of the entryways, carrying a briefcase. His footsteps echoing, he crossed to the doorway that led into the main building and its immense double doors to the street, and disappeared through it.

Delia looked up. The sky was the deep, rinsed blue of late summer. She thought about what she would be doing in a week—the public appearances with Tom, the interviews. She thought about living here, alone, afterward. To ask Tom for it would be a kind of moral blackmail, she knew. She would be exploiting him, using his wish to have her back, his sense of sinfulness, even his Catholicism against him. But she wanted it. She could imagine doing it.

EVAN PICKED HER UP at the international terminal and drove her home to Williston, where he'd been staying by himself in the house since his summer internship ended. She fell asleep in the car on the way. She hadn't wanted to—she'd hoped to stay up until ten or so to get back on U.S. time. She waked as he pulled into the driveway. She was surprised by how happy she was to see the house, to walk into the familiar rooms.

After he'd hauled all her bags upstairs, after she unpacked what she needed for tonight, they decided to go out to eat, to the pub in the inn at the edge of the campus. Delia thought it would help her to stay awake if she were out somewhere, and she'd been yearning for an American hamburger. The pub was famous for its burgers.

There were only a few couples scattered around the large room, couples more her age than Evan's—though it was a Friday, normally a busy night, the students weren't back from summer vacation yet.

They sat down at one of the empty wooden tables. Delia ordered her burger, and Evan a Reuben sandwich. While they waited, the waitress brought her wine and Evan's beer. It was in a frosted mug with a pattern of indentations like thumbprints in its heavy glass.

"Cheers," he said, and drank.

"Here's to you," she said, lifting her glass.

"Why to me?" He thunked his glass down on the plastic-coated wood of the table.

"For getting me, for driving me. For interrupting your life on my account. For being such a good son."

"Yeah, well. The thing is, I'm worried about you."

She raised her hand. "Don't be."

He leaned forward, elbows on the table. "Mom . . ." he began.

"Don't, Evvie." She shook her head.

"Don't what?"

"Don't . . . worry, I guess. I'm all right." She had a sip of wine. It was so cold it was almost tasteless. "I wasn't, before, but I am now."

"But you're not going to *do* this, are you?" His face was pinched.

"You mean the campaign?" She had written each of the children as soon as she said yes to Tom. Evan and Nancy had both announced their opposition, Nancy in a long, difficult transatlantic phone call, with a slight time lag in the line making everything worse. Evan had written a passionate letter.

He sighed wearily, as though she were being disingenuous. "What else?" he said.

After a moment she said, "Yes. I am."

"Well, frankly, I don't get it." He sounded angry. "*Nan* doesn't get it."

"You don't think I should."

"Mom?" He shook his head, his eyes wide in incredulity. "We *know* you shouldn't. I think *you* know you shouldn't."

"I don't. Know that. In fact, I think I should."

He made a face.

"It's not . . . it won't be easy, but the thing is, I want your dad to have that. To win. It's his *life*. I want him to win."

"So? Let him win without you." His fist lightly pounded the table on the last word. Their glasses jumped a little, and a man at a table across the room turned to look at them.

"But he has a much better chance *with* me."

Evan hunched forward suddenly, over the table. He spoke in a lowered voice. "It's a ploy, Mom, don't you see that? To get you involved, to get you back. And when he does get you back, it'll be the same thing all over again. He'll just go on, doing that stuff to you." He shook his head. "This is a chance for you, don't you get it? To start over. You're not so old. You could have a life, another life. You could work. You might even meet somebody else. Someone who . . . who'd be better to you than Dad."

"Evan." Her hand came across the table toward his. "I know . . . it must seem simple to you. I mean, *he did me wrong*." She smiled, but he didn't respond.

"And he *did*," she said. "Do me wrong. And Nancy. And Carolee."

His face changed. "Fuck Carolee," he said.

"Well, yes. I can get behind that." She sat back. "Fuck Carolee." It gave her pleasure to say it.

He smiled back quickly in a kind of delight—though he and the other children, like everyone else their age in America, had become profane over the last years, she never spoke this way.

After a moment, she started again. "The thing is, I love him."

Evan's eyes suddenly wouldn't meet hers.

"I don't imagine I can live with him any longer, but I don't wish him ill, sweetie. I love your father. He's in so many ways an admirable man."

Their food came then, Delia's hamburger smelling wonderfully of fat and blood. She ordered another glass of wine from the student waitress, a girl who didn't look old enough to be serving alcohol. To be working at all, actually. For a while they were busy passing ketchup, mustard, salt and pepper back and forth.

Delia talked about France between bites, between sips. About what American things she'd missed besides burgers and her children. Her wine came.

She pointed to a spot on her own face and said to Evan, "Mustard."

He raised his napkin and wiped at his cheek. Then he sat still, looking at her for a moment. "So is what you're saying that you're *not* going to stay married?" he asked.

She set what was left of her hamburger down. "Not as we were, anyway."

"What does that mean?"

"I don't know. Just . . . things will be different. I don't, I can't, imagine how we'd live together."

"Well, that's a relief, anyway."

"You *want* us to be apart?" She was shocked.

"I don't *want* it, necessarily." He'd set his sandwich down too. He looked down at the table for a moment, then up at her. "But yeah. Okay. I want it."

"But, doesn't our life as a family mean anything to you?"

He snorted. "Get real, Mom. *Our life as a family,* as you put it, didn't much involve Dad anyway, and it's really not going to involve him after this."

Of course, Delia thought. Of course this was how it seemed to them all. She was momentarily startled at the revelation: while for her their family's life consisted in those moments they shared with Tom, Evan and the others thought of their life together as going on all the time, and that meant mostly without Tom.

"I mean, look," he said. He'd pushed his plate away, his sandwich half eaten. "Do you imagine Nancy, do you imagine me, ever being comfortable sitting around with you guys together again? If you got back together? Pretending everything was okay? Pretending Dad wasn't a guy who . . . could do what he did to you."

"He didn't do it *to me*." Delia's hand rose on these words and rested on her bosom.

"Oh, and who did he do it to, then?"

"He just did it. That's all. He did it because he wasn't capable of not doing it. That's part of who he is. And that's regrettable. But I've loved him a long time and—"

"You know, you're an enabler." He'd raised his hand, his index finger. He was almost shaking it at her. "You know that, don't you?"

"Oh, Evan." She made a face. "That's just—"

He interrupted her. "Well, you *are*." He sounded like a child to her, suddenly. A child calling names on a playground.

"That's jargon, Evan. It doesn't have to do with anything."

Then she looked at him. She felt insulted. "Do you think I could have stopped this? Is that what you think? That *I* made it happen somehow? Or I made it possible?"

"I think if you told him you were outta there the first time he even looked at another woman, yes. This wouldn't have happened." He turned sideways in his chair, his face set in self-righteous lines.

"But of course that's what I did say, the first time."

"And did you leave?" His voice had gotten loud again.

She waited a moment before she answered. She said, "I didn't need to. He broke it off, and he asked me to forgive him."

"And you did."

"I loved him. I felt sure it wouldn't happen again, it was so traumatic for both of us."

"But it did, didn't it? Happen again." He seemed almost pleased to be saying this.

Delia looked at him for a moment. Then she said, "What do you know about all this?"

"What Nancy told me. What I hear."

"I'm certain that a great deal of that is exaggerated."

"But he's had other women all along, that part is right, right?"

"He's had several over the years, yes." She drank some wine.

"And you've known about them."

"Never at the time. No. I haven't."

"But you knew later."

"I heard. I heard probably some of what you heard. And he and I talked about it."

"And you agreed to live with it, somehow?"

"No." Suddenly she was angry. "Look, Evan. I don't even think we should be having this conversation. In some sense or another this is simply none of your business. But I will tell you that when I found out about one or another of these things, it was always after the fact. When I learned about the first one, he told me there had been several others. But my sense was not ever . . . that it threatened me. Or us. It wasn't *like* this last thing, with Carolee. It was . . . My sense was of a weakness. One that he succumbed to, from time to time."

"So if you didn't have to know about it, it was okay."

"It *wasn't* 'okay'! Nothing was okay." Now her voice had gotten louder, and she stopped and looked around, but no one seemed to have noticed. She leaned forward, her hands clasped under her chin. "It broke my heart. It broke my heart over and over. We struggled. We fought. But we wanted to stay married. We *both* wanted to stay married."

Evan's face was unreadable. Cold.

"Look, Evvie," she said. She'd made her voice gentle. "I hope that when you marry, I wish for you, that there's only . . . that you both, whoever, are able to be nothing but in love with each other all the time. That neither of you ever wounds or hurts the other. I wish Dad and I, I wish for us, for you, that we had had that."

He met her eyes for a moment, and then looked down at his own hands, encircling his glass.

"We didn't. But we had . . . we had a great deal else. Which kept us together. Which served us well."

"Until now."

"Yes."

They sat quietly. There was a jukebox in the pub, and someone had chosen a series of songs by Frank Sinatra. Now it was "Laura."

He said, "But you're still doing the campaign."

"Yes. I am."

He sighed. "Okay."

"I still love him, Ev."

He shrugged. They finished eating. They talked of other things. When school would start. What courses he was taking. What she'd heard from Brad.

After she paid the bill and they were getting up, he smiled at her—almost sadly, she would have said. "Well, I'll see you in November then."

The next morning, he'd packed his car up and left, early, for school in New Hampshire.

IN THE TRAIN coming down to the city, Delia couldn't imagine how it would be to see Tom, to be with him. She was actually frightened, aware as she watched the dry September landscape and the tired, dusty cities flash by, that her heart was pumping faster from time to time, her breath coming short. She'd brought a book with her, but she didn't even pretend to read. She watched the scenes change out the window—the marshes, then the steely water, then the backside of one little New England town after another—and she felt swarmed by memories.

She remembered Tom promising her he wouldn't see Carolee ever again, his face turned away from her, his shoulders dropped in what seemed like defeat. She remembered his sitting opposite her in the kitchen in Williston after she'd learned that he had been lying, after she'd called him and told him that was it, she was leaving, going away. He'd flown up to see her, to talk, to ask her not to divorce him now, not until the election was over. She sat for what seemed like hours, tears coursing down her face, as he told her he had tried but hadn't been able to give Carolee up. As they talked about when he'd been lying, when he'd been telling the truth. As she announced her disbelief that he could have chosen a woman young enough to be his child; that he didn't see, or wouldn't acknowledge, the lopsidedness of it, its unfairness to Carolee. "Of course the girl adores you. It's in the nature of that difference, that advantage, that she should." Her voice was hoarse, cracked, she'd been crying so long.

"She's not a girl, Delia." He was calm, reasonable. "You and I had been married for more than five years when you were her age, and you were not a *girl*, then."

"But you were not a man thirty years my senior," she shrilled. "You didn't have that advantage to . . . dazzle me with. We were ourselves."

"I am myself with her," he said, and Delia laughed, though she was still also crying.

Delia's tears were for her life, her stupidity, her age, her vanity. She had no control over herself. While they were talking, she had shrieked, she had wailed. How could there be so many tears? She could feel that her eyes, even her lips, were swollen. Once she choked on herself, her pain, and Tom came around the table and patted her back. Her horrid back! Her old, bony shoulders! She shrank from him. She didn't want him touching her, feeling sorry for her.

When she was calmer, when they were sitting opposite each other again, he said to her gently, lovingly, that what he wished for her more than anything was the same happiness he'd found. Delia had thought of this often, with more bitterness than she felt about almost anything else.

And with all this, when she saw him in the lobby of the hotel in New York, what she felt was simply joy. He was Tom. He was so himself, so unchanged. So beautiful to her.

His face was grave when she first spotted him, standing close to the glass lobby doors, looking out at the pedestrians hurrying past under their black umbrellas. He was dressed, as usual, in an expensive suit, a pale shirt. His sandy hair was more silvery than she remembered it. When he turned and saw her, his face lighted with a smile. Or perhaps she was smiling first, and his was a response to that, she couldn't have said. Perhaps they both felt it simultaneously, the sense of all that was familiar and inalterably beloved, no matter what happened between them. She wept then. She wept when he first held her, she wept when they made love.

Afterward they came downstairs and walked for blocks through a fine, misty rain, holding hands, barely speaking. They were both stunned at the ease of their lovemaking, at the power of it. Perhaps, like her, Tom hadn't imagined that they *would* make love, perhaps he too was wondering what it meant.

They saw a bar, which appealed to them with its zinc counter and its twinkling lights. It reminded Delia of Paris, actually. It was quiet at this hour—just after four. They sat at the counter and watched the beautiful young woman in front of them shuck their oysters. Delia felt that something had shifted, had changed. She had control of her own life, she thought. Even, perhaps, of what happened between them.

She said, "It's going to be really almost essential for me to escape all this, to just be far, far away from it all from time to time."

He misunderstood her. "From Washington?" he said.

She laughed. "Once this campaign is over, I doubt I'll ever set foot in Washington again."

He looked hard at her, and then away. She was feeling a kind of joyous recklessness. She had acquired such freedom! He had wounded her so deeply that she could do what she liked, say what she liked.

"No, I mean truly far away," she said. "Where reporters won't call me and invitations won't reach me and I can disappear—from the face of the *American* earth anyway." She put her hand on her bosom and made her voice more dramatic. *"From the margins of your life."*

"Delia." He was turned to her at the bar, and he bent toward her now and gripped her elbow. "You'll always be in my life, Delia. You'll always be at the center of my life."

"Oh Tom, *please*," she said, her voice suddenly impatient. And then she remembered that an hour earlier, making love, she'd been silently weeping. That he had wept too. Her throat tightened. They sat for a moment. Finally she said gently, "Here's what it is: I'd like to go back to Paris. To stay in Paris, at least some of the time. I can speak the language now, more or less, and I can disappear there."

"And that's what you want? To disappear?" His voice was surprised, his face in profile in the mirror behind the bar sad.

She was surprised too, that this could make him sad. That she could. She wanted to cheer him. "Well, as an alternative to *offing* myself, for example, it seems actually appealing. Another kind of *off.*" She waved her hand. "Off to Paris."

"That's not funny, Delia."

She turned and looked directly at him. His face was grim, his mouth a tight line. She lifted her shoulders. "Ah," she said, her voice lowered. "So you can make me want to die, but I'm not allowed to talk about it with you."

"You *don't* want to die," he said fiercely. He gripped her hands, raised them to his mouth, kissed them.

Delia leaned against him, her forehead touching his chin. Then she sat up straight, abruptly. "No. Not anymore. But I do want to disappear."

"What if I don't want you to disappear?" he asked.

She thought for a moment, wanting to be sure she didn't speak from bravado. Then she said, "Well, but you're no longer in charge of that."

The young woman placed the oysters on their bed of ice in front of them. Tom drizzled them with lemon and they ate them slowly, relishing the briny, sweaty, animal flavor. He ordered them another martini. Delia described the apartment in Paris, and Tom said yes, he thought he could find a way to manage that.

FOR THE NEXT three mornings, Delia woke next to Tom in different hotels. They had coffee in their room, they talked, idly and affectionately, as they moved past each other, washing, dressing, packing. Delia was happy in those moments. *Happy in a subjunctive way,* she thought, but in a way she was coming to feel she would not ever be able to give up entirely. On one of those days they made love before they were truly even awake, and Delia lay there afterward in a wash of sensation, the sensation she had when she woke with him already inside her—that they were part of each other, that they were one.

When they were ready, Delia dressed in what she thought of as her costume, they went out and were instantly surrounded by Tom's staff, and then by Tom's public. They became simply the candidate and his wife.

Delia's job was to look as good as she could, to listen with rapt attention to Tom speak, to answer good-naturedly the questions put to her. She had one event on the first day out that she did solo, a lunch with women from across the state who were politically active. Tom's speechwriters had provided her with a text for this, which she changed a little bit here and there before she gave it.

It was only slowly over these days that Delia realized that everyone in the press asking her questions knew that she and Tom had been apart, and that at least some of them probably knew about Carolee. It occurred to her that Tom must have known this would be the case, he'd been so careless in his passion. That he'd understood, that he *must* have understood—as she hadn't—that enduring this was part of what he was asking of her.

She thought of the friends who had spoken to her through the winter of how indiscreet he was being—of how he'd been seen so frequently with Carolee in New York, in Washington. One of them, Madeleine Dexter, had run into them leaving a restaurant in Washington. She said that in spite of every signal she'd sent that she didn't imagine being asked to greet him, he'd brought Carolee over to be introduced, and stood there, clearly expecting cordial conversation from her and her husband. "Is he mad?" she'd asked Delia.

The questions now weren't brutal or aggressive—the time when that would have been the case was yet to come—but they kept being asked. And they were asked with a kind of slightly amused intensity of focus that said to Delia, *We both know what this is really about, don't we?*: "Isn't it hard getting back into the political swing, after being away for so long?" "What do Frenchwomen have to teach American women about glamour?" "How much do you plan to be in Washington if the senator is reelected?"

"*When* he's reelected," she corrected, and they laughed. This was the second day. She was standing in a hotel lobby talking to three or four reporters after a breakfast for local businessmen Tom had spoken at. Tom was standing behind her and just to the side. She could feel his eyes steady on her. "And the answer is that I've always spent more of my time in Williston. I live in this state, as the senator does, as our children do, and I hope never to forget that."

Finally, later that same day, in an interview for the Living section of a local paper, the reporter, a young woman with a skirt so short that when she sat down Delia could see her underpants—could see, in fact, that her underpants were striped—asked the question nearly directly. "We missed seeing you earlier in the campaign, and I know questions have arisen about your absence. Is that something you'd care to respond to?"

They were in the living room of the hotel suite she and Tom were sharing. A photographer had been there before, snapping shots of Delia as she spoke, but he was gone now, off to some other newsworthy event or crisis. Delia looked out the window at the rain for a moment before she spoke. Then she turned and smiled evenly at the young woman.

"Well, of course my instinct is to say that that's a private matter, that it has absolutely nothing to do with my husband's remarkable record, his great. . . . the great strengths he'd bring to a second term. You know—that what we should be talking about is the economic health of the state, is the war, is the cost of the war to social programs." She shrugged. She smiled, kindly she hoped, at the reporter. "But I understand that this is something people are interested in knowing about the senator and me. Part of the package they'd be getting, as it were."

The young woman nodded and kept writing in her notebook. She had a peculiar hairdo, with bangs that reminded Delia of Mamie Eisenhower's. Was this somehow back in fashion among the young?

Delia took a deep breath and went on. "So let me say that I think marriage is a wonderful but a *complicated* institution. I think every long marriage has its difficulties, its ups and downs. I'd ask people to respect that. But I'm campaigning with the senator because I'm committed to him. Because I believe in him. Because I believe that he deserves another term and will be terrific in another term, and because I love him. Because I'm proud to be married to him."

It wasn't until late that evening when she and Tom were alone together that Delia might have talked to him about it. She had planned to. But she didn't. Instead, after everyone working on the campaign had left their suite, after Delia had picked up the glasses and wrappers and plates and called room service to come and take them away, they undressed and showered and got into bed next to each other to watch the eleven o'clock news. There was nice coverage of Tom's dropping in at a diner in a small town they'd stopped in midday, there was a quick clip from his early-morning speech, in which he was funny and charming. The camera panned to her during his remarks, and she was smiling. Good. They waited for the latest poll numbers, which an aide of Tom's had already discussed with them. Then they watched the sports, so Tom could see the baseball scores, and they watched the weather, to find out what it had in store for them the next day. More rain. "Damn," Delia said. When she clicked the TV off, she turned to Tom, but he was already asleep, his face drooped, his mouth slightly open.

At the end of the next long day, they drove with the campaign staff in a kind of cortege of cars back to the house in Williston, and eight or nine people followed her and Tom to the front door. Delia had been home from Paris for only two days before she'd gone to New York to meet Tom, and she wasn't prepared for the house to be campaign headquarters—she hadn't thought about that part of it. Before she took her coat off, she got on the phone and called for pizza from Tony's. She sent one of the aides out for more beer and wine. She had a fair amount of hard liquor on hand, and two bottles of wine she'd bought for herself after she got back. She set all these out with ice and water, and several of the staff helped themselves immediately. She got out the big coffee machine and, while it was percolating, put out mugs and milk and sugar. The pizzas came, and she put them on the dining room table with plates and paper napkins and silverware. She set out a bowl of fruit too, though she knew hardly anyone would touch it.

In the living room, they were going over the week's schedule. Tom was due back in Washington the next day—he'd fly out later tonight. He'd be there for a day and a half in order to be part of a couple of crucial votes. At the end of the second day, she'd meet him for another three-day stint on the road, beginning at a clambake in East Harbor at the summer home of a big contributor who was, as they said, "calling in some chips." Pamela, Delia's staff person, told her she'd met these folks before, and when Delia said she had no memory of that, Pamela made a note to get her some background stuff. Steve Pearson produced her copy of the schedule for those days, and the text for two other short talks she was to give. "Change it at will," he said, "but, you know," grinning, "no changes please." She excused herself and left them talking about the Senate vote, about the slight shift in language they wanted Tom to use when he spoke publicly about it.

Upstairs, she ran a hot bath. She felt let down. She had thought Tom would spend the night, that they would talk then. But perhaps it was for the best. She was exhausted.

When she slid between the cold sheets, she could still hear their voices downstairs, and spikes of laughter now and then. The smell of cigarette smoke was in the house and at least one person was working on a cigar, she was pretty sure. It might be Tom, who liked a cigar from time to time.

It was all so familiar, and yet different. In the past the children had taken time off from school to be part of the campaigns. They'd enlisted their friends. Often there were three or four kids as well as the younger aides sleeping in every bed in the house, on the couch, on the floor on air mattresses. They had run the campaign from home as well as from local offices all around the state, and a hum of activity enveloped you every time you walked in the door. Posters and flyers were stacked up everywhere, mail was arranged in piles on the dining room table waiting to be answered, the phone rang continually. Delia had big picnic coolers set up in the kitchen, and she kept them stocked with Coke and beer. The coffeepot was always on.

She had loved all of that, the sense of their whole lives, and the children's too, being given over to this.

This time neither she nor Tom had mentioned the children's absence, but for her it stood for everything that was lost. She thought of Brad's carefully worded letter to her, saying that no matter what they decided, they would both still be his parents. She thought of

Nancy, lashing out however she could in her grief, sometimes seeming to blame Delia for the loss of her father. She thought of Evan when she'd talked to him only this past weekend, of how angry he'd been at what she was about to do.

Before Tom left for the airport, he came upstairs to say good night to Delia. She was still awake, with the door open and the light from the hallway falling into the room. Tom sat on the edge of the bed. He was happy, she could tell. She didn't speak to him of the reporter's questions, of how exposed she'd felt. She let him think that her quiet was because she was exhausted, maybe even still a little jet-lagged. After he kissed her, after he'd gotten up to go, he stood in the doorway a moment, looking back. She couldn't see his face, but his voice was full of tenderness, of gladness, when he said, "This is fun, isn't it?" He tapped the door frame lightly and she heard the clunk of his wedding band on the wood. "Thank you."

CHAPTER EIGHT

Meri, December 1993

You're pregnant," Delia said as soon as Meri started to take off her coat.

"I am?" Meri said. Her mouth and eyes opened wide in mock surprise and she looked down at herself, at her abdomen's rounding curve under Nathan's stretchy wool sweater.

"Aren't you?" Delia's smile faltered. "Oh! I'm so sorry! I thought—"

"No, no, of course I am, Delia. I was just kidding."

"But I *am* sorry. How rude of me."

"Delia. Come on. I'm virtually a tank." She gestured around the rise of her belly with both hands.

"Oh, you look wonderful, dear."

Meri snorted and rolled her eyes.

"No, truly. And of course, congratulations! This is *thrilling.*"

"Well, thank you. Thanks." Meri laid her coat on the little striped couch in Delia's hall. Its sole function seemed to be this, the receiving of outerwear.

"I'd bought some wine for us, but maybe you'd like cider? Or tea?" Delia looked tired, her eyes pouchy. She was just back from her two months in Paris—she'd arrived home sometime late in the afternoon the previous day. The phone message with her invitation had been waiting for Meri when she got back from work. She wanted to have Meri and Nathan over for a drink the next day—today—to thank them for "minding the house," as she put it.

Meri had come over at the appointed time alone, crossing the porch in a slushy rain. Nathan was late, still on campus. He was often late, by a wider and wider margin as the semester progressed.

She had been nervous all day about this, about seeing Delia again. The moment after she pushed the button on the blinking machine and heard Delia's voice, she was aware of a sense of shame, a feeling of being caught out. She knew that Delia couldn't know what she had done in her absence—it was likely that she would have been incapable, actually, even of imagining the possibility; and Meri had always been careful to put things back exactly as they were. Even so she felt, almost superstitiously, that she would be unable not to betray herself, that it would show somehow—in her face, in how she behaved.

But nearly the instant she saw Delia, she knew that she was safe. Delia was *herself*, and Meri had the same comforting sense she always did of being swept along by her, of being nearly *absorbed*, as she felt it, by Delia's buoyancy, her energy. In her gratitude that this was the case, she was feeling an instant deep affection toward the old woman.

"Yeah, I'd better have some cider," she said. "Otherwise the pregnancy police will get after me."

"Oh yes, I know how ubiquitous they are nowadays. And so strict." Delia started back to the kitchen, and Meri followed. She looked around. The house felt different now with Delia in it. It was hers once again, a private realm.

"I drank through all three of my pregnancies," Delia was saying. "Probably a drink or two nearly every day, actually. And it was hard liquor at that. We'd practically never *heard* of wine then. I count it as a great retroactive blessing to have been so ignorant."

The lamp was on over the wooden kitchen table, the light pooling on its surface. The plants still sat clustered on their tarp. The baskets of mail, though, were gone.

Delia looked up at Meri, smiling. "I smoked too," Delia said. "We knew *nothing*." She'd gotten Meri's cider out of the refrigerator and was pouring it into a wineglass. Her own glass of wine, half full, sat on the table next to a tray with crackers and cheese on it.

"And there were no pregnancy police in those days either, praise the Lord." She set the glasses next to the crackers on the tray, picked it up, and started back out into the hall. Meri trailed her. "When are you due?" Delia asked.

"May."

"Oh, a heavenly time of year," Delia said. "Perfect for having a little baby around. Winter is so hard, you're all cooped up. And summer is just too *sweaty* to be pregnant." Delia had a fire going in the living room, and the shutters were closed against the dark and wet. They sat down, Delia in the rocking chair by the fireplace. She passed Meri's glass over to her.

"Are you jet-lagged?" Meri asked Delia. She had a sip of the cold cider.

"I don't know what I am." Delia had rocked forward. She bent over the tray and began to spread the crackers with cheese. "I feel oddly peppy right now, but I'm sure I'll just collapse quite suddenly sometime this evening."

Meri was looking around the room. She said, "This house is so lovely, Delia. Every time I came in while you were away, I admired it." She blushed, unexpectedly, thinking of being alone in here. She said quickly, "We still haven't done anything with ours."

This was true, and of course, Meri did feel crummy about it; but when Delia said, "Well, you're busy. It'll come. You can't expect to get it done overnight," she felt comforted, and realized she had wanted this comfort. She'd been asking for it.

She said, "Yes, but we've been here more than three months."

"And you have a job, and you've gotten pregnant. That must have taken some time." She widened her eyes in mischief, and then barreled on. "And you've taken care of my house, for which I'm forever in your debt." She lifted the plate with the four or five crackers spread with cheese, and passed it to Meri. "And the job?" she said after a moment. "It's going well?"

Meri laughed. "I love it," she said. "It's just the most varied, the most *various* job, I guess you'd say, that I've ever had. Completely different, from day to day." She had a bite of cracker, of rich cheese. "For instance, I did this one at the end of October on Halloween, on how commercialized it's getting."

"Oh yes, I've been aware of that—all those hideous store-bought costumes."

"Well, that's true too, but in this case my focus was dogs."

"Dogs! What have they to do with Halloween?" She had gotten up with a poker in her hand to tend the fire, but she turned to Meri now.

"You'd be surprised. Turns out costumes for dogs are a big market. I went to a dog parade in town, and it was amazing. There was a dog dressed as a firefighter, there was one who was supposed to be a Frenchman, with a beret and a striped shirt. He had a rubber baguette tied to his back." It had looked like an enormous dildo to Meri, but she didn't mention this to Delia.

Delia laughed. She turned back to the fire and poked at it, and the logs rearranged themselves with an explosion of white sparks.

"Maybe it's because I've been out of the country, but I find this completely ridiculous," Delia said. She sat back down and picked up her glass, sipped at the wine. She said, "Still, it's wonderful to have a job that's silly sometimes. Hardly any jobs are, are they?"

"None that I've had," Meri said.

They talked for ten or fifteen minutes about the last few months—Delia's time in Paris, the weather in Williston—and then the doorbell rang, and Delia went to answer it.

"But you're soaked!" Delia's voice said.

"Yeah, it's really pouring now," Nathan said. "I ran the last bit."

Meri came out into the hall just as Nathan was taking his coat off at the foot of the stairs. He draped it on the newel post, and they kissed. It was perfunctory—Nathan didn't like kissing in public.

Delia started back to the kitchen, to get him some scotch, she said. "Just the thing to warm your innards." And then she called back, "Go in and sit in that chair right by the fire. You need it more than I."

Meri and Nathan sat down together in the living room, Nathan in the rocker. He rubbed his hands together, looking at the fire for a moment, and they talked about their respective days, how they'd gone.

Delia came back in and handed Nathan his drink.

"Thank you," he said. He sipped and set his glass down. "You're back," he said to her. "How was it?"

Delia sat down next to Meri on the couch and started again to talk about Paris, about the weather there, the darkness, the politics, the pattern of her days. She still took French lessons, "at a very high level, I want you to know," so that absorbed a good deal of her energy. And she was actually more sociable there than here, she told them, though it was more a matter of meeting people in cafés and wine bars and restaurants. "I think that's why I love having people over when I'm home," she said. "It's so familiar and sweetly *American*, don't you think?"

They talked for a while about the college, which was conducting a search for a new president. Delia asked Nathan about how his semester had gone, and got his story. When he was done, she seemed to pause for a moment, and then she said, "My husband will be here briefly sometime over the holidays. I want to be sure to have you both over then, especially as you've heard of him—always a selling point with our Tom. He'll like you."

Meri watched as Nathan's face opened in pleasure. She smiled too, she echoed him—it would be great to meet Tom at last. But the mention of Tom's name made her think again of the letters she'd read, made her think of all that she knew about Delia's life, about Tom and Delia's life, that she had no right to know. As the other two talked together—Delia so animated, Nathan so quickly responsive to her— there was a part of Meri that sensed her secret as something she had done to each of them. To both of them. She looked from one of them to the other, from Delia's lined face, her liveliness fighting off what must have been fatigue; to Nathan, his hair ringleted and dark from the rain, and she felt an unbridgeable distance from them both that made her sad. But she had done this. She had done this to herself.

What if she just blurted it out now? what she'd done, what she'd read, what she knew.

Nathan laughed at something Delia had said, and her blue eyes widened in pleasure. Of course it wasn't possible. And it wasn't ever going to be possible. She would never be able to cross back over to where they were, to where she'd been before.

CLASSES WERE ALMOST OVER at the college. Suddenly everyone was having a Christmas party. The invitations arrived, by phone, by mail. They were supposed to go to a potluck at the home of one of Nathan's colleagues—they'd been assigned a salad for twelve. Jane was having an open house the day after Christmas. There was a departmental carol sing. The dean sent a stiff, printed card announcing her holiday reception. It said that dress was informal.

Informal or not, Meri had nothing to wear to any of these events. She'd managed so far buying only two items of maternity clothing, both pants with ugly little aprons of stretch fabric stitched in over where the belly bulge was. One was a pair of corduroys, for when she was being fancy, and the other a pair of blue jeans for everything else. If she hadn't been married to Nathan, this wouldn't have worked, but he'd let her borrow any of his sweaters or shirts she liked. She'd been rotating a group of the loosest, the bulkiest of these over one or the other of her pants.

Her only other concession to her altered state was brassieres, something she hardly ever wore normally. Now suddenly she had breasts, actually fairly large breasts, and she'd purchased what Nathan called "industrial-strength" brassieres to accompany them. *To keep them out of her way,* was how she thought of it.

She'd bought the pants at an outlet shop in one of the malls that lay in all directions on the outskirts of town, but there was a small, much fancier maternity shop in Williston itself, and she'd looked in its window from time to time, walking or cycling past.

On the way home from work the second Friday in December, she walked almost the length of Main Street in a light rain, the sidewalks glistening. Many of the store windows were decorated with strings of little white lights. All the lampposts along the sidewalks had wreaths. The town was gearing up for the holidays.

As she got close to the maternity store, she became aware that she was hearing the sound of a child, a child wailing in some epic sorrow. She came to the cross street, and saw that a little boy of perhaps three or so was coming toward her, trailing his mother down the sidewalk, sobbing and calling out as he came, "I *can't,* I can't walk anymore. Please. Please carry me. I'm too tired. Why won't you carry me? I can't walk. I *am* trying. I'm trying, but I can't."

The mother was lugging a heavy-looking grocery bag, and she looked grim. When she turned around and spoke to the boy in a low voice, it changed nothing. He was not to be corrected, or consoled. Meri had stopped on the corner to watch, pretending to wait for the light to change. The noise the little boy was making diminished only as he and his mother slowly moved away, down Main Street.

How does she stand it? Meri thought. Why doesn't she just slap him?

And then Meri remembered her mother's voice: "What you're asking for, missy, is a good slap." "When your father gets home, you're gonna get a good slap." She remembered hating that term—*a good slap.* It seemed *mean* in a way she couldn't have explained then. And she remembered being a child waiting for that slap—how that had felt. She turned away and crossed the street.

The maternity shop was called MaDonna. Meri stopped in front of it. In the window, there was a mannequin wearing a little black dress and very high do-me heels, with smoky black stockings. She was virtually anorexic. The only sign that she might have been a few minutes pregnant was the slightest curve to her belly. The fantasy of glamorous maternity, Meri thought. And the woman with the boy the hard reality thereof.

She would save this for Nathan—the accident of this contrast. It was funny. It was sad.

The bell on the shop door jingled as Meri entered. A small woman in her early fifties, Meri guessed, emerged from the back. She was wearing a loose wool dress, gray, austere. Her hair was pulled back cleanly into a bun, the kind of bun ballet dancers wore, and she had that toes-out, rolling dancer's smoothness to her walk. She was thin. She didn't look as if she'd ever been pregnant. She greeted Meri warmly.

"I'm just going to look for a bit," Meri said.

"Lovely," the woman said. "Let me know if I can help." She went to sit behind the counter. As soon as Meri began to take things out of

the racks, though, she was there, offering to put them in the dressing room.

She was so gracious Meri actually got into it. She picked out four possible dresses and several blouses, plus a pair of black velvet slacks with the familiar unattractive panel in front. She followed the dancer to the back of the store, where the dressings rooms, two of them, were. The woman had hung Meri's choices on a hook, and now she slid an ample curtain across the open doorway. "Let me know if you need any more help," her drifting-away voice said.

Meri was alone with her brightly lighted reflection.

She and Nathan had no full-length mirrors at home. The closest Meri had come to seeing how her whole body actually looked in this new incarnation—pregnant woman—was in the wall of kitchen windows, clothed, as she made supper or cleaned up, usually moving around in front of her reflection with Nathan as they shared these chores.

But *this* was appalling, she thought, as she stood in front of the mirror in her underwear. Industrial strength, indeed. She was huge. Not so much the belly, which, yes, was large, but not ridiculously so. It was everything else. Her hips, which up to now had always been narrow and well muscled. Her upper arms. These gigantic breasts, smashed together in the bra. She had cleavage, something she'd never remotely wanted, and which she saw now only as a place for sweat and crumbs to collect.

Feeling hopeless, she started to try on one of the dresses she'd picked out. She could barely get it on over her head—it was too tight around the back and the arms. Standing there in her socks with the fabric of the skirt stuck around her chin and chest, Meri realized that there probably was such a thing as maternity panty hose, a thing she would have to buy if she was going to wear this or any other dress. No.

No. She took the dress off and returned it to its hanger.

The pants fit. They were fine. The black blouse she'd brought in to wear with them was too small, though. She sent it out, and the dancer came back with a larger size in fuchsia, the only other color choice. Meri could hardly stand to look at herself, but it was better, much better than the dress at any rate. You could see that she had long legs, which was really all there was to recommend her body at this point.

Carrying her bag on the way home in the misty rain, she was thinking of her reflection under the lights in the dressing room—her pale, stippled flesh. Flesh that looked *corrupt,* she thought.

Corruption, that was the word for what was happening to her. She'd entered the biological procession, the one that ends in total corruption. She'd been claimed, by time. By birth and death. She'd been changed.

But this was what happened. This was what women *did.* She thought of the mothers she'd known. Her own. Nathan's. Lou. Delia. Several of her friends. They'd all had to give up some sense of themselves as inviolably *who they were,* physically. They'd all had to learn to watch their bodies change in ways they had no control over. To learn to share their bodies with the stranger taking shape inside them. Why should she be any different? If her mother—mute, incapacitated before the complications of life—could manage this, surely she could.

She tried to imagine her mother, pregnant. Had she been afraid? Had she been as reluctant as Meri was? Certainly she had said, more than once, "I wish I never had you kids."

Meri thought of the crying little boy, of the anger she had expected his mother to feel. Maybe her difficulty with all this was her own history, her past reaching into her present to claim her. Her life becoming in this way like her mother's too.

She couldn't let that happen. She would do better than that. She absolutely had to do better.

AT THE OFFICE PARTY, of course, everyone was dressed as usual. Only Shirley, one of the producers, had any sense of style anyway, and this usually consisted in some scarf draped around her neck, or long, dangly earrings. In early September, it's true, she'd often sported strappy little high-heeled sandals, but now, like everyone else, she wore boots—boots and jeans and big sweaters. They all looked like those *New Yorker* cartoons by Koren, Meri thought, hairy and fuzzy and funky. Of course, she reminded herself, she did too.

To call it a party, as Brian had pointed out when they divided up preparation chores the day before, might have been an exaggeration. "It's going to be, like, a regular meeting, but with alcohol." And as the afternoon meeting was coming to an end, James carried in a large cardboard box with three cold bottles of champagne and a bag of plastic glasses. He popped open one of the bottles and started around the table with it.

Should she have a glass?

Here, among her coworkers, she wanted to be in the party, of the party. She thought of Delia, of Delia telling her how she drank through her pregnancies. She'd take that as her permission for tonight, she decided. She held up her glass as James passed behind her. But she was still self-conscious enough to feel a need to explain herself. "This will be my fourth drink since I got pregnant," she confided to Burt Hall, who was sitting next to her at the conference table. And then, remembering, "Oh wait, maybe my fifth. Or sixth. Or tenth. But that was because I had some before I knew I was pregnant."

"Is that a big deal?" he asked. Burt was a geek, tall and much too skinny. Nerdy. Sometimes he forgot and wore his bicycle clips around his ankles all day. Now, sitting next to her, he was concentrating so hard on unwrapping a tube of goat cheese that he didn't look at her when he spoke. He'd pierced the outer layer of plastic with a ball-point pen, and he was trying to pull this covering back. The cheese was blue where the pen had gone in, and his fingers were covered with white goo.

"Well, the doctor was dire about it," Meri said. "But I think the rule was constructed for people who drink like fish." The champagne fumed in her glass, tasted sour and sweet at once.

"Who are breathing, actually," Brian said above them. He reached over their heads to set down a paper plate with crackers arranged carefully around the rim.

"Did you do that?" Natalie asked. "So *pretty*."

"Who?" Burt asked, looking around. "*Who* are breathing?"

"We're all breathing, Burt," Shirley said. "You too."

"Fish," Brian answered, taking his seat at the table. "When fish are drinking, they're actually breathing."

"Well, thus the metaphor, I suppose," Meri said. The champagne was so cold her nose ached with each sip.

Meri had had two stories on the show today, both holiday related. One was on unsafe toys, the other on a lawsuit brought by a local atheist who objected to the town crèche and menorah. He was a phoner, as they called them. Both pieces had gone well, and she felt lighthearted. She loved her work. She loved her colleagues. This was the best party of the season, she decided preemptively.

Jane had started in on suicide by drowning—which famous people had done it. Meri pointed out its delicious ambiguity, since you couldn't ever know for sure whether it was intentional or not. They all speculated on Natalie Wood.

"I bet it isn't as bad as you'd think," Jane said. "The only really hard part is that first long inhalation of water."

"How would you know anything at all about this?" Meri asked.

"I read it."

Brian laughed, and Shirley smiled at him and said, "Oh, well, then it *must* be so."

"You know," he said, "*I* read somewhere that there are more suicides at Christmas or around the holidays than any other time of year. If that's true, that might be a story we could check out." The cork exploded from the second bottle.

"This is not cheerful talk for our party," Shirley said. "It's Christmas. Let's have some Christmas cheer."

"Christmas. Big deal," James said. "I'll be sitting home with my roomie."

They talked about plans for Christmas. They talked about the day's show. Brian told several Jesus jokes. "How *sea*sonal," Jane said, inflecting it oddly. They started to talk again about tomorrow's show, but James made them stop. "The meeting is over, folks. No more planning."

Someone poured Meri another glass, and she drank it, more

quickly this time, while the conversation meandered. She felt a little dizzy, actually. How could she be? How could she be tipsy?

She leaned over and said to Jane, "How could I be tipsy?"

"Easy. You're unacclimated to drink." Jane said this so slowly and incorrectly—nun-acclimated—that it struck Meri that she might be tipsy too.

"What have you eaten today?" Jane asked.

Meri pondered it. Not much. Since she'd stopped feeling nauseated all the time, she'd stopped eating crackers all the time too. And though in her joy at beginning to be able to eat normally again she had sometimes put away vast quantities at meals, she also sometimes forgot to eat at all when she was busy, and she'd been busy today. She took a cracker and asked Shirley to pass the plate of inky cheese.

At a point slightly later, the first person got up to leave. Meri began to help Natalie and James pick up glasses and debris. Then they were all putting on coats, wishing one another a good weekend. Meri had a sense of munificence, blessing. How kind they were, these friends of hers.

Outside, they called good-bye into the chilly night. James offered Meri a ride, but she said no, she wanted to walk.

She started across the dark campus, her breath pluming in front of her. She strode rapidly down the walkways, then across the road and past all the shop windows on Main Street, and finally, down the shadowy length of Dumbarton Street. She felt better, stronger, as she went along. By the time she got home, she had warmed up and she was sober.

Nathan wasn't back from work yet. She went upstairs to brush her teeth, to find her polar-fleece socks. She came back down to the kitchen. When she turned on the light and saw herself in the glass, she was startled for a second or two by her reflection—for the last few hours, she realized with surprise, she hadn't thought of herself as pregnant.

"DON'T YOU HAVE something that makes you look less like . . . Barney?"

Meri paused, putting the coat on over her fuchsia blouse. This didn't seem to be an attempt at a joke, which she could perhaps have rolled with. She looked at Nathan, so perfect, so beautiful in his tweed winter coat—so very unpregnant—and felt a pinch of anger. "The short answer is no," she said.

As they were getting into the car, Nathan said, "What's the long answer?"

"It's a little more ad hominem. I don't think you want to hear it."

They sat silently as he drove. Meri was waiting for him to apologize. Maybe he was waiting for her to apologize. They were going to the dean's party, held in her house, one of the nineteenth-century frame mansions lined up across the street from the campus.

When the door opened, they were assaulted by the sound, the general hubbub. A student wearing a white shirt and black slacks pointed them to the back of the room-size entrance hall, where their coats were taken from them by another student, also wearing a white shirt and black slacks; and Nathan was given a numbered chip, which he pocketed.

They headed to the bar, in one of the two facing parlors on opposite sides of the hall. As they hitched their way through the clots of people, Meri put her hands on her belly so it wouldn't get bumped. All around them, people were greeting one another with pleasure, standing in little groups, catching up, gossiping. Nathan knew some of them—people spoke to him, and from time to time they paused to talk and he introduced Meri. As she stood, smiling and nodding, Meri took in the spacious, comfortable room. The lamps gave off a gentle light, and in its glow everyone looked pretty and well. There were groupings of large, soft chairs and couches everywhere, and paintings—modern, vivid, well lighted—hung on the walls. It was impossible to imagine this as a home, the scale of everything was so immense, the taste so impeccable and impersonal.

Meri got her Perrier and slipped away from Nathan, who was talking to a colleague of his who looked just like Danny DeVito, but bigger. She moved her immense blouse around, standing at the edges of groups, waiting to be recognized as a stranger, to introduce herself. And people were kind. They turned to her, they asked her about herself. Mostly, though, Meri listened. She listened to the jokes they were in the middle of telling, to the long stories—about trying to get on a bus in New York City with a cello, about waiting in Ecuador for months to adopt a child.

She was waylaid several times by Nathan, who had forgotten she was supposed to be angry at him and wanted to introduce her to someone or other; and twice more by women she'd met at earlier parties. One of them, a young colleague of Nathan's, tried to recruit Meri for a departmental baseball team in the late spring. "You'll have the kid before the season starts, right?" she asked.

Meri crossed the hall to the parlor on the other side of it. She moved around, offering her opinion on various things she'd never thought about before. A man no younger than she was got up and gave his seat to her, and she took it and was suddenly part of a group of people discussing Bill Clinton and his sex life. At a certain point in this discussion, just after the woman next to her said, "I hear that the man is in *thrall* to his own prick," Meri realized that she needed to pee. As usual. And, abruptly, that she was tired too. She wanted to go home. They'd been here for almost two hours, and Nathan had promised they'd stay for only one. She got up to find him.

The crowd had thinned a little now—others had also counted on less than two hours—and she walked more easily through the room she'd been in and out into the hall—and there he was, his back to her, leaned against the arched opening to the opposite parlor, easy to spot because of his height, because of his wild hair.

The hall was crowded, though—people out here were getting coats and taking their leave—so Meri had to thread her way across it. She could see that the woman facing Nathan, talking to him, an older woman in a green dress, was a person from the department—she'd met her before, but she couldn't remember her name. She had a drink and a napkin in one hand, and she was looking up at Nathan and listening intently to what he was saying.

It was something—Meri was so close she could hear him now—about rolling with the punches.

What punches?

"It's no one's fault, of course," he said. "Or it's both of our faults."

He gestured with his drink. "But it's a disaster for me with this book. The timing couldn't have been worse. It's due at the end of the summer, and of course the baby's coming at the beginning."

The woman started to ask him some question about his progress, but Meri was turning away, moving back toward the other room. She could feel her throat tightening. She willed her face to be normal.

In the opposite parlor, she stood silently, her back to the noisy room, facing out the dean's windows toward the white wooden chapel across the street, gleaming in the spotlights trained on it. Its steeple pierced the black sky. She was telling herself that this was not news, that she'd known that Nathan felt this way. He'd as much as said this very thing to her, and she'd as much as said it to others—that it was bad timing. For him. For her too. Maybe she had actually said this *exact* thing.

Why shouldn't he be allowed to say it? Why shouldn't he be allowed to speak to a friend about his reluctance, his ambivalence?

He should, she thought.

But another, more lost part of her was thinking, *He shouldn't. He just shouldn't.*

OCCASIONALLY, mostly in the evenings when she was making dinner, Meri had heard a noise from the other side of the wall, from Delia's life now that she was back—the sound of something dropped on the floor. The running of water, and then the little *thump!* in the pipes that happened when the water was turned off. The almost inaudible murmur of a radio voice, inhumanly steady.

Tonight as she was standing at the sink, she was startled to immobility for a moment by the faint sound of a deep voice, a male voice, talking, and then, a few seconds later, the softer female response. These were the first voices that she'd ever heard from that side of the wall, Delia had been so solitary when she was home.

It had to be Tom Naughton—Delia had said he was coming "for a quick visit," and she'd invited them for drinks the next night to meet him. Meri had somehow assumed—hadn't Delia even suggested it?— that Tom wouldn't arrive until then. But here he was, apparently.

The voices alternated lazily, almost inaudibly, on the other side of the wall, and Meri turned the radio on—doom and gloom from NPR—so she couldn't hear them. As she moved around the kitchen getting supper ready, it dawned on her that their own lives, hers and Nathan's, must always have been audible to Delia in her kitchen at this same dim, distanced level.

When Nathan came home, she turned the radio off before she kissed him, before she held her finger to his lips. Before she said, "Shhh. Listen." They stood there in a loose embrace, Nathan frowning in concentration, and then they could just hear a man's laugh.

"That's your senator, I'm pretty sure," Meri said. "Tom Naughton, in the flesh at last."

Throughout the meal they continued to hear from time to time a voice, a laugh on the other side of the wall.

"You know what it means that we hear them as much as we do?" Meri said. They were doing the dishes. She was drying. Because she was pregnant, she always got to dry. Nathan was the one washing, the one bent uncomfortably over the low sink.

"I'm afraid I do." He looked up at her sideways and made a face. "It means she's had the odd earful ever since we moved in."

"It means that, unbeknownst to us, we've been leading a rather public life, wouldn't you say?"

"One little old lady is hardly the public." He handed her a dripping plate. "But maybe we should learn to live our life more quietly anyway. It'd be a good exercise for us to learn restraint."

"Never my forte," she said as she wiped the plate.

"Do tell."

"Hey!" She swatted him with her damp towel.

He smiled up at her from under the thatch of hair hanging over his forehead. "Mine either, I know."

They began to speculate about what Delia might have had to listen to, calling up the possibilities as they remembered them. The one or two loud arguments they'd had. The night Meri came down to the kitchen in despair about something or other and wept loudly until Nathan came down too, to talk to her, to bring her back to bed.

"But that was really late. Delia was probably in bed already."

"Sound asleep, we can hope."

Both of them were quiet at their tasks for a moment. Then Meri said, "You know, actually, I think she might have been gone then. She was gone for a lot of all of this, when you think about it. I think she was in Paris then."

They remembered the night they'd put on music, loud, and danced barefoot in the living room until they were both damp with sweat. It was before they knew Meri was pregnant, when there were still unpacked boxes in the living room—boxes they moved around, incorporating them into the dance. That one Delia had definitely heard.

THE SENATOR himself opened the door and announced to them that they must be Nathan and Meri. His voice was strangely light for a man his size, Meri thought, light and dry, a little parched-sounding. He was taller than Nathan, though slightly stooped. He had a strong nose, a little flattened at the bridge—it had been broken at some time in his life. Meri liked that. His mouth was small and amused, almost smirky, his hair was as white as Delia's. He had tangled white eyebrows over deep-set pale eyes—grayish, greenish. He was wearing a suit and tie, a very expensive suit and tie. Meri felt both dazzled by the warmth he brought to simply saying hello—he gripped her hand in both of his when he greeted her, he stared deeply into her eyes— and embarrassed for her frumpy self. She was back to one of her uniforms: the corduroy maternity pants and a big wool sweater of Nathan's.

Tom Naughton turned to Nathan and gripped his hand in the same way. Nathan said, "I would have known you anywhere, sir."

She might not have, Meri thought, though he did look like the man in the Watergate photo, only older, thinner, a little frailer, maybe. But she would have known he was someone important no matter what—he had that air.

"Don't you *sir* me," he said, smiling. "It's Tom. Tom to both of you."

He led them down the hall and took their coats, headed back to the closet with them; unlike Delia, who just let you drop them on the little striped couch.

And here she came, out from the kitchen, carrying her tray. "Come in! Come into my parlor," she cried, and they obediently followed her into the living room. She was wearing a red dress with a fitted top and a loose skirt that swirled around her as she moved. She set the tray down on the low, square coffee table, and stood up to kiss Meri's cheek. Meri felt enveloped by the rush of perfume. Delia stepped up to Nathan and kissed him too.

Then Tom was back. Nathan began talking to him about some paper or editorial of his that he'd read recently.

"Sit, sit," Delia commanded, and when Meri obeyed but not the talking men, she touched Tom's elbow. "Darling, make your admirer sit down and have a drink."

Nathan turned to her, grinning his wolfish grin. "More than an admirer." He turned back to Tom. "I'm a fan, I'm afraid."

"Nothing to be *afraid* of," Delia said. "In the old days, Tom loved anyone as long as he was registered to vote. But now he's going to be your servant. You'll do the drinks, dear?"

She turned to Meri. "What will you have? We have to work fast. I've wedged you in, I'm afraid. It's why I asked you to come a little early. My younger son arrives, with his *entire family*," she exaggerated this, waving her hand dramatically in the air, "at about seven. A Christmas visit. A *week*'s Christmas visit." She raised her eyebrows. "So I'm so glad you were able to make it."

While Tom went back to the kitchen to get their drinks—scotch for Nathan, sparkling water for Meri—Delia passed around the little dishes of nuts and olives she'd brought out. She was talking about the son who was about to visit—where he lived, how long it had been since she'd seen him, the ages of his children.

Nathan asked what he did.

She smiled. "Oh, he's kind of a dropout, I think you'd say. He builds sailboats—beautiful, old-fashioned, handmade, wooden boats. One at a time. Much in demand, and very costly, but it's so labor intensive that there's no money in it at all for him." She was flushed,

Meri noted, and she seemed wound up. But she looked prettier—less severe, less grand—than Meri had seen her look before. "His wife teaches high school, and I suspect makes twice what he does. But he is, I would say, our sweetest child. Don't you agree, Tom?" she said to her husband as he came back with the drinks. "Is Brad not the sweetest of our children?"

Tom turned to his wife. Meri watched his expression shift, his face open, warmly. His eyes, which had seemed cool and keenly observant earlier, did something when they looked at Delia that she'd read of but never seen: they *lit up*. "Whatever you say. I defer to you," he said.

"Oh, who on earth wants to be deferred to?" Delia said, looking over at Meri and Nathan, inviting them in. "I want you at least to *seem* to consider this question. And *then*, of course, I want you to defer to me." She smiled up at him, the dazzling smile that lifted Delia's face into agelessness from time to time.

They were *flirting* with each other, Meri thought.

"Well, he is. You know he is," Tom said. He turned to Meri and Nathan. "Have you met any of the children? Which is what we still call them, though they are all older than you by some years."

Meri shook her head.

"No. Well." He sat down. "In a nutshell, then, Nancy is formidable and fearsomely well organized. Fearsomely." He pretended to shudder. "Evan is easy, I would say. And funny. And Brad is, always has been, the gentle one. The good one. Which is sometimes a burden, I'm sure. The sweetest, yes."

Delia thanked him.

Meri watched them as the conversation began, and meandered. They talked about Clinton, and Tom said that once he got this Whitewater thing off his back he was going to do interesting things.

"Now that's worrisome," Delia said. She made a face. "A president who does interesting things."

Nathan and Meri laughed, and Tom's face lifted in a wry smile. But he went on. He said, "If there's anyone who can pull the Democrats back to a path less . . . driven by political correctness, I think it might be him. And that's what we're going to need to get anything done around here." He shook his head. He smiled again, that small, charming smile. "And he's a political animal. He really lights up a room. That helps."

Meri thought this must have been true of Tom too, when he was in politics.

"A bit of an animal generally, maybe," Nathan said. When Tom looked up, a question on his face, Nathan said, "The Gennifer Flowers thing."

"Which, by the way, he handled well," Tom said. "Though he could have pushed that public-private distinction harder. It'd be a gift to the political life of this country if that line got more clearly drawn." He swirled his drink, and sipped. "Still, it's clear he enjoys women. But I don't think it'll hurt him. It's pretty much a Washington disease, I'm afraid I must say. People are used to it."

Meri had been looking at Delia, and now she noted a shift in her expression.

"Do you remember when everyone thought Bush had a mistress too?" Tom asked. "But she was rumored to be someone wealthy and WASPy, of course." He set his glass down. "The problem here is the goddam Democrats, who sleep *down,* you see. They love that white trash." He barked, a short laugh. "And white trash loves publicity, so the Democrats are the ones who get into all the trouble. As opposed to the Republicans. They sleep *up.*" He gestured. "Up, where all is Episcopalian and quiet as death itself, and no one ever has to hear a thing about it."

"Surely that's not the only problem," Delia said. Her smile seemed tight to Meri.

Tom looked at his wife, his jokiness abruptly vanished. "No," he said. "No, of course it's not. But it's the political part of the problem anyway, Dee."

A little later, Meri mentioned the photograph she'd found of Tom at work, the Watergate photo. They talked about the Senate hearings, about that period of time generally. About where they were, what they were doing then.

Tom shook his head. "My God, what a terrific cast of characters they were," he said.

"*My* favorite of the entire group was Martha Mitchell," Delia announced. "Old Martha, who critiqued the whole thing from home by the telephone. Do you remember? She'd call someone up and announce one loony event after another with her big wide mouth. Remember, Tom, when she said she'd been kidnapped by the FBI? And it was *true*?"

Tom was watching her, smiling.

Delia turned to Nathan and Meri, her face open in delight. "They were *all true*, all these things that people assumed were dipsomaniacal."

"Yes," Meri said. "And they named a psychiatric liability after her. The Mitchell effect."

"Meri," Nathan said, shaking his head. "A 'psychiatric liability'? 'The Mitchell effect'? Please."

"I will explain the Mitchell effect, and why it's called a psychiatric liability." Meri curtsied her upper body to him, to the room. "It's more or less when a shrink makes the assumption that a statement which is true, but strange and unverifiable—when he assumes that it emerges from mental illness. Like, ta da! the FBI drugging you and kidnapping you: *Oh, you must be a paranoid schizophrenic!*"

"Poor Martha," Tom said. He stood up, holding his empty glass, and offered to get another round of drinks. Only Nathan said yes, and they went together to the kitchen this time. As she and Delia started to talk about what her other children were doing for Christmas this year, Meri could hear their voices, back and forth.

When they came out, Nathan was talking about his students, their romantic passion for the sixties, or for what they imagined the sixties to have been.

Tom said he'd encountered that in young people too, especially when he visited college campuses. "It's all they want to hear all about, as though it were some golden age. The sixties, the sixties, the sixties."

"I was glad when they were over," Delia said. "It was just so complicated, threading through all that in Washington. And then I moved back here more or less full-time, and that was that, for me. A private life."

"Do you miss it?" Meri asked. "Washington?"

Tom's gaze was steady on his wife as she answered. "There are things I miss about it," Delia said. "I had dear friends there. I miss them." The animation that had lit her face earlier was gone now. "But we see each other now and then, and call. And write." She lifted her wineglass. "It's true my life is narrower now. But so is everyone's at my age." And then something livened in her again. "Except, of course, for Tom."

Tom gave a little snort. After a moment, he turned to Meri. "You haven't said what you're up to in Williston, and I want to know."

Meri answered quickly, dismissively, describing the program and the kinds of topics it covered. "I'm in charge of the culture beat, mostly," she said. "The arts, somebody's latest book, but also 'the culture,'" her hands made quotation marks. "Sort of whatever the latest new *thing* is."

She stopped. She'd had the sudden thought that Tom might be useful to her, a good connection, a resource. She said, "But sometimes they let me do something political. So maybe I'll end up calling you, eventually. If you'd consent to be called."

"Of course, I'd be delighted. Remind me to give you my card."

Meri could hear the perfunctory note in his response. Using a tough moll's voice, she said immediately, "Gimme your card."

He looked at her sharply, and then he laughed. He had a wonderful laugh, Meri thought. It was like his voice, light and dry, and his head tilted back a little, giving over to it. Meri felt she'd *accomplished* something, provoking his laughter.

He stood up, and reached into his back pocket for his wallet. She had the sense that he was really looking at her for the first time tonight, that she'd moved from invisibility to . . . what? Personhood, anyway. She wondered fleetingly what it would be like to be attractive, sexually, to Tom Naughton, something she clearly wasn't in her present state.

He had come over in front of her now, and he was almost bowing as he handed her the card. She took it, looking up at him. There was a smile playing over his small mouth. He was conceding the point, she thought: he wouldn't have "remembered" to give her the card if she hadn't insisted.

"Thanks," she said, smiling back. "I'll use it sparingly, if at all."

"Anytime," he answered.

She took it in only as Tom moved back to his chair, that Nathan was talking, had been talking, and now she heard him: he was talking about her. He was revising her description of her job, talking about the prison writing program. ". . . you know, some of these guys were in for murder. And she went out there to Goffstown and sat with them and taped these extraordinary interviews. . . ." Meri watched him, his face so earnest as he went on, about the response the radio station had had, the people wanting to donate funds to the writing program.

She saw what he was doing. He didn't want to be seen as having a wife who wasn't smart, who wasn't important in some way. She was *his,* after all. She was part of who he was. She couldn't be *frivolous,* which is how she'd presented herself—because that was how she'd been flirting with Tom.

This, now, was how Nathan did it.

So they were *all* flirting with Tom, she thought. How strange. How funny. She wondered how it would feel to be a person whose attention everyone wanted to have.

Nathan caught her eye, saw something in her gaze, and stopped abruptly.

Delia broke the short silence. She was worried about Brad, about his being a little late.

"It's fine, Dee," Tom said. His tone was reassuring. "There's no weather. It's just traffic." He got up and put another log on the fire.

"Are you folks traveling for Christmas?" Delia asked.

Meri gestured at Nathan. "We're going to his mother's house. New Jersey. It's our first joint Christmas with her." She made a little face. "Nervous-making."

Nathan looked at her. "Come on, you're not nervous."

She waited a beat. "Oh, that's right." She turned to Delia and Tom. "Apparently *not* nervous-making," she said.

Tom said to Delia, "Remember our first Christmas at your parents' house?"

Delia smiled at him. "I'd rather not."

"Were *you* nervous?" Meri asked.

"I wasn't smart enough to be nervous," he said. "I had no idea."

"My parents disapproved," Delia said. "We had just told them we were engaged, and they couldn't have been less pleased."

"On what grounds?" Nathan asked.

"Mother of God, what wasn't there?" Tom said. "Every prejudice of the day. I was poor, I was Irish, I was Catholic, I was déclassé." He had a swallow of scotch. "Now, I'd known all that, you couldn't be those things in that day and age without knowing how others thought of you, but I hadn't fully taken in what an unattractive package I was until I arrived to stay at Delia's for two long, long days."

"I should say that they were not unkind people," Delia said. "They were just frightened for me."

"The papist, the lowlife, was taking their lovely girl away," Tom said.

Delia rolled her eyes.

"Would *ruin* her." He smiled. "Conversion, God help us, was a possibility." And he went on, talking about Delia's parents, the impossible stiffness of the visit, the long silent meals, his early departure.

Meri watched them both, their pleasure in passing the subject back and forth, their ease with what must have been this hard part of their history. She was wondering whether she and Nathan would ever be able to be as playful about the differences between them. The parallel differences, actually—she, the Tom character, the lowlife, the outsider. Nathan was as patrician as Delia really, as completely comfortable with himself.

Suddenly there were voices outside, and before they could get up, they heard the door open and a young voice calling, "Grandma?"

Delia was up instantly. Moving quickly as a girl, she disappeared around the corner to the hall. Tom stood too, and went more slowly around the corner. Then Meri saw the kids in the wide doorway to the hall—three kids, the oldest in her early teens, Meri thought, the youngest maybe eight or so. They were shimmying out of their coats and talking rapidly, mostly to Delia, who was still out of sight behind them. One of them, the youngest, sat on the little couch and began to heel off his boots. Now a man's voice, a woman's, could be heard in the mix.

Nathan and Meri were standing up in the living room. Nathan said, "We should go, no?"

"Absolutely." But they stood awkwardly a minute longer, listening to the family assembling in the hall, not wanting to interrupt the moment of reunion.

Delia came back, leading the others in to introduce them all. Nathan and Meri said hello to everyone and almost simultaneously began to make their excuses. Tom went to get their coats. The kids in their stocking feet had come into the living room and were unloading the bags of presents they'd carried in with them, arranging the bright-colored packages under the tree.

While Meri talked to Brad's wife—Susan—asking her about the drive down, Tom reappeared, holding her coat. Meri turned and let him help her into it. Awkwardly, bumpily, they moved into the hall. The kids made no show of sociability, but the four adults trailed out with Meri and Nathan, Delia in the lead.

"I'm so glad you could get over while Tom was here," she said. "He's leaving after dinner tonight, so it really was right now or never. It's wonderful you were free at *exactly* the time that would work."

"We wouldn't have missed it," Nathan said.

"Same for us," Brad said. "It's a miracle when we get to see him at all, so this is really great, short as it is." He was smiling, almost shyly, at his father.

"Where are you headed now?" Nathan asked Tom.

"Oh, I've got to get to New York for some business first thing in the morning. I've got a car coming, after dinner. Poor guy's probably sitting in some bar watching sports till it's time." He turned to Brad. "He brought me down from Boston this afternoon."

"Hey, he's getting paid to watch those sports," Brad said. "Not a bad gig at all."

As they left, stepping out into the cold night air, Meri looked back for a moment through the glass pane of the closed door. Brad and his mother had turned back into the house behind Tom, and Brad had his arm around Delia. Their heads were bent down, almost touching each other.

"I need food!" Nathan said as soon as they opened their own door.

They both headed back for the kitchen, Nathan dropping his coat on a dining room chair on the way. "Too much booze on an empty stomach."

Meri stopped in the pantry. "We've got pasta," she called out. "Fusilli and penne."

"Let's do penne." He was already clattering pots and pans. "Fast and easy. We can have oil and olives and herbs."

"We've got lemons too," Meri said. "I'll zest one, if you like."

When she came into the kitchen with the box of pasta, the lemon, the herbs, he was already carrying a pot full of water from the sink to the tiny stovetop. He turned the flame on under it, and they worked in silence for a few minutes at the door-table.

Nathan said, "Big lie there, did you notice?" He had started to pit the olives.

"What? That he came down this afternoon?"

"Yep." He looked up, frowning. "When we know for a fact he was there last night." His hands stopped moving. "What would be the point of that, you think?"

Meri knew that this was the moment when she could confess what she knew. When she could tell the sad story of how Delia and Tom had separated so painfully years ago, how they'd painfully come back together and created a new way of being married, which was private, just for themselves. When she could say, "They're supposed to be just friends. That's what the kids think."

This was the moment when she could speak also of what she'd done, of how she'd come to know all this. When she could tell him how sorry she was, how ashamed.

But she didn't say any of it, of course. She couldn't. Nathan would never understand how she could have done what she did or why she felt so compelled by Delia, by her life. Why she let herself open the drawer, take the letters out, read them. She could never explain it, because she wasn't sure herself. And if she said something like, "I was lonely, Nathan. I *am* lonely. I'm lonely and scared," he would think that she was only trying to excuse herself for what he would see as a reprehensible act. For what she saw as a reprehensible act too.

And was it that she was lonely? Was it that she was scared? She wasn't really sure that either was the reason, that either was true. For how could she be lonely or scared? She was married, married to someone she loved. She was going to have his child. She lived with him in a beautiful house, they were making a delicious supper together. They would sit down and eat it and talk, and perhaps, later on tonight, make love. She looked over at him. He was bent over the table again now, his long, delicate fingers working carefully with the olives, his face sober at his task.

"Maybe there's no point," she said. "Maybe some people just like to keep things private. *Secret,* I guess you'd say."

CHAPTER NINE

Delia, Early May 1994

Is THIS MRS. NAUGHTON?" The voice at the other end of the line was female, distinctly American, older.

Delia had just come in. She was standing at the desk in the entryway to her apartment in Paris. It was raining out, and she was damp—she hadn't had time to change her clothes. "It is," she said.

"Ah. This is . . . well, you don't know me, but I'm a friend of Tom's, of your husband. I'm Alison Miller."

Delia didn't know the name. Her throat seemed to have dried up. She heard her voice as a croak. "Yes?"

"It's about Tom. I'm afraid . . ." And then she said in a rush, "Oh, he's *alive*. I'm sorry. I should have started with that. He *is* alive."

Delia sat down, hard, so hard that she nearly dropped the phone.

"But he's had a stroke," the woman was saying, this Alison person. "He's here, in Washington, in the hospital."

Delia was supposed to talk, she was supposed to say something. "But he's . . . he is, all right?"

"Well, no. He's in intensive care. They don't know, I guess, no one seems to know, if he's all right. I guess . . . it seems that it's not easy to tell right away how bad these things are."

"He's had a stroke?" It was as though Delia's brain was catching up, a half minute behind what this woman was saying.

"Yes. They're doing all they can, but they can't say, yet, how he'll be."

"But, is he conscious?" She was seeing Tom, or she was trying to see him, and this seemed important to her, to know this, as a way of imagining what had happened to him.

"Sort of. He seems, almost not conscious. Perhaps, I don't know, he's in a kind of shock." Her voice rose at the end of the sentence. When Delia didn't say anything, she said again, "I don't know."

Delia was too confused for the moment to respond. She could hear the drumming of the rain on the balcony, the hum of the refrigerator from her kitchen. Her umbrella was dripping slowly onto the floor next to her in the foyer. She'd need to wipe that up.

After a few seconds, Alison Miller's voice continued. "I think—well, they think too—that someone needs to be here who can . . . someone from the family. With the power to make decisions."

"Well, yes. One of the children would . . . do the children know?"

"No. I . . . No, I didn't. That would be . . . I just thought to call you."

Delia cleared her throat. "I'm sorry," she said. "Would you tell me your name once more?"

"I'm Alison Miller. I'm a friend of Tom's."

"And you took him to the hospital?"

"I called the ambulance, yes, and came in with him."

Delia was beginning to make sense, a kind of sense, of all this, though she wasn't certain what was being asked of her. "Do you know . . . I mean, had Tom made any arrangement? In case of such an event?"

"Arrangement?" Now Alison Miller sounded confused.

"Yes. What . . . ?"

Alison Miller's voice was dry, suddenly: "I think the *arrangement,* as you put it, was immortality."

Delia was silent.

And now the woman said, more gently, "There was no arrangement, as far as I can tell." There was a silence. "Mrs. Naughton," she said, "you need to come home."

"Home?"

"You need to come to Washington. Tom needs you."

"But Tom and I, we are not—"

"I know that. I know. But there is no one else."

"But are you . . . ?" The rulelessness of her life with Tom had left her unable to be certain of anything in this moment.

"No," she said. "No. Not me." And then she said again, "There is no one else."

Delia had to buy a first-class ticket, the only space available on the next morning's flight out. She was seated next to someone famous, someone whose face she knew, she knew very well, but couldn't place. He drank three glasses of champagne quickly, and once the plane was in the air, put a mask over his eyes, tilted his seat back, and went to sleep. After a while he began to snore, to snore in what Delia thought of as a feminine way—little fluttery spurts, as though each breath were a great surprise to him, something to exclaim over. *Gasps* of snoring, nothing like the steady, deep rasps Tom produced.

Sleep wasn't possible for Delia, although to her surprise, she'd slept well last night. And now, sitting on the plane, she remembered that she'd had a dream. She'd dreamed of Tom. She began retrieving it bit by bit. An odd dream. Well, weren't they all? She was with him in a clearing in a wood—a kind of glade. She saw it suddenly. It had been like a scene from Bergman, struck with a kind of holy celluloid light, the way his dream sequences often were—full of yearning and nostalgia. She couldn't have said what she and Tom were doing there, but when she'd waked, it was with a feeling of joy. Within seconds, though, lying in her dark bedroom, listening to the rain outside, she'd remembered the reality: that he was ruined, he was dying.

Or not. She didn't know. That was the problem, wasn't it?

Immediately after she got off the phone with Alison Miller, she'd called the doctor—a man named Ballantyne, whose number Alison Miller had given her. She'd had to wait a long time while he was paged. Twice someone clicked onto the phone to ask if he could call her back, but Delia said no, she'd hold.

When he finally came on the line he was noncommittal. For now it was better not to speculate. "The next few days," he said, "will tell the tale." This phrase struck Delia, it seemed so old-fashioned and familiar. It was something her mother had said to her, something she herself had said occasionally to one of the children when she didn't know how to answer a question.

After Delia had hung up, she sat for a long time in the hallway in her wet shoes. It was too much, too much to take in. The woman—a friend? a lover? Tom, in some kind of limbo, where no one could tell how he would be, who he would be, when he emerged.

She'd called the hospital again this morning before she'd left for the airport, but it was still night in Washington and there was no further news. The nurse or receptionist answering the phone had sounded irritated with her, as though she should have known better than to call asking for information at such an hour. She spoke to Delia as you would speak to a child, and in response Delia had felt like a child—shamed, but angry too.

She'd calmed herself by carefully setting the table on the balcony for her usual breakfast. She'd had to wipe the table and chair dry with a towel. Then she brought out a tray with the croissant, the seedless raspberry jam, the rich dark coffee with steamed milk. She sat down and laid her napkin across her lap. *The consolation of the daily,* she thought.

There were children playing in the courtyard below, their shrill voices rising. The sky was a pale blue above her, with smears of thin high clouds moving fast across it. She was aware of actually enjoying the musical ticking of the spoon stirring the little lump of brown sugar into her coffee, the sound of the china cup clinking lightly against its saucer as she set it down.

That world, so fresh, so perfect, washed so clean by the rain, seemed unconnected to this one—this plane with its stale air, with this unkind person sleeping next to her.

And this world in turn seemed not possibly to be leading to the one she would arrive in later today. To Tom, lying damaged in a bed in a hospital. To the hospital itself and its terrible life—the routines, the boredom, the anxiety. To the questions she would be in charge of finding the answers to.

Tom. Tom, whose face stayed blank when she tried to think of him as he might be now. She could only remember him in motion—talking, laughing.

Oh! In the dream—Delia's lips parted, thinking of it—they'd been practicing cartwheels. How silly! But she remembered the sensation of it, the wild physical abandon of throwing yourself forward in space, of flipping upside down—as wild as sex, really. She remembered too that it was understood between them that they had come to the woods to do this in private so that they wouldn't embarrass the children, who didn't know they had this skill, who wouldn't have liked seeing them do it in any case.

She leaned forward to look out the window at the cottony fields of sunstruck clouds below her.

TOM WAS LYING propped up in bed, his eyes open, conscious.

Conscious, but absent, Delia thought: he seemed not to notice her as she approached, he seemed not to hear her voice when she spoke. Or perhaps to hear it from some great distance he'd traveled. He turned now to its sound, turned slowly, his eyes not homing in on her, but moving around. It made her think of the way children follow sound in their infancy, vague as to its purpose or its source. Tom had just that blank, swimming gaze.

She spoke again. "Tom. Dear. It's me. It's Delia."

He frowned. That was all.

He was wearing a patterned hospital johnny. His arms appeared skinny and flaccid, emerging from its wide sleeves. His hands lay curved and useless-looking on the sheet pulled up to his belly. His hair was in disarray, spiky, and Delia, unable to stand this, smoothed it. She stroked his face. His eyes closed. He leaned his face to her hand. "Unnnnh," he said.

"Sweetheart," she answered.

But when his eyes opened, they still didn't quite fix on her. He looked only puzzled. The blankness of his stare, the way his face drooped, his apparent inability to understand anything going on around him—all these made him seem animal to Delia. Like a large, sad, frightened animal.

It was better not to speak at all, she thought. She knew something about strokes. Several friends had had them, and her father had died of one, lying speechless and motionless in a hospital bed for more than a week. Delia knew that it was conceivable that nothing made sense to Tom right now. Her appearance here, her words. The very *here* of it, in fact—the hospital itself. Did he have any understanding of where he was? of how he got here? Possibly not. That must be more frightening than anything.

She decided that she wouldn't speak again. She'd just be here, a presence. A reassuring presence, she hoped. But silent. She'd save her speaking for the doctors.

She pulled a chair close to the bed and leaned over Tom, holding his hand, stroking his head, as that had seemed to comfort him. And it did again. He turned into her hand, his mouth resting on her palm like a kiss. She thought of his kissing her hand like this at various times. Seizing it, opening it, pressing his lips to her palm in passion, in sorrow—and over and over through the years, in apology.

But his face was dead now—no emotion—and there was nothing at all to read in his lips' touch. His eyes closed again. After a few minutes, saliva started to pool in her palm. She pulled her hand away, wiped it on the sheet.

DELIA HAD CALLED Madeleine Dexter from Paris. She knew she didn't want to stay in a hotel, or in Tom's house. Madeleine lived in Georgetown, near the hospital. She was an old friend, one of the earliest friends Delia had made in Washington, way back when Tom was first a congressman. For the last few decades, Delia had seen her only once a year or so, usually in New York, where they met to see a play they were both interested in, or a show at the Metropolitan Museum. They always stayed at the same hotel and had dinner together. Between them as they talked they usually drank at least a bottle of wine, and then a smaller bottle of dessert wine. They caught each other up on the children, on their marriages, on the shape of their lives and their feelings about that.

Madeleine had known Tom and had loved him too, though more than once she had said to Delia—and reported that she'd said to him—that she could "skin him alive" for what he'd done to his marriage. She was one of the few people Delia could talk to about the complexities of what Madeleine called "your arrangement."

She was alone now. Her husband, who had worked in the State Department, had died a few years earlier. Dan.

She opened the door and held her arms wide for Delia to step into. She was a short, plump woman with one of those enormous bosoms that occupy the entire space between the shoulders and the waist. Delia felt it like a large soft pillow pushing against her own more meager front.

"Ah, Delia," she said as they stepped back from each other. Her face was round and full, prettier now than it had been in her youth, when it had been her figure that had attracted men. "Let's face it," she had said more than once. "I was stacked."

Now she held her head tilted up to see Delia through the lower lenses of her bifocals. "Here you are, darling. Here you are, and with a chicken—actually, a *rooster*, I guess I should say—come home at last to roost." She smiled. "Yes, of all things."

Delia smiled back. "It's true, I'm afraid. And I'm Henny Penny. Or maybe Chicken Little. And it seems the sky *is* falling."

"Was it awful?"

"It seemed so to me. He just seemed . . . ruined."

"Oh, Dee."

"But the nurses say you can't tell yet. That there are good signs, that he has good responsiveness. He's moving everything, though not perfectly. And I haven't talked to the doctor yet. So I don't know. I truly, truly don't know a thing."

"That must be harder than anything."

"Well, not than anything, but it's hard."

"But is he . . . alert?" Madeleine asked.

Delia laughed dryly. "Not so's you'd notice, I guess. Anyway, I need to change. I need to shower. I'm exhausted."

"Of course, of course," Madeleine said. "You know the way. I'll be in the kitchen, fixing us supper for whenever you're ready. Just take your time, my darling."

Delia carried her suitcase down the long hallway. The apartment, deeply carpeted everywhere, curtained in multiple layers at all the windows, swallowed every noise. As she unpacked in the chintzy, plush guest bedroom, Delia could smell garlic, herbs—maybe tarragon. She was hungry, she realized. And so tired. Several times she had to stop and sit at the edge of the bed for a moment, feeling a yearning as strong as her hunger just to lie down. But as soon as she stopped, the image that rose in her mind was Tom—the new Tom—and she didn't like thinking of him.

The shower wakened her. Wearing her robe, she went to the kitchen doorway. Madeleine's face opened again when she saw her, and she offered Delia wine. There was a bottle, uncorked, on the kitchen counter next to the sink, a glass set next to it. Madeleine's glass, half empty, was on the island by the salad bowl where she was tearing lettuce.

"I'll take a glass, and then retire for a minute," Delia said. "I'm going to call the kids. They haven't heard yet."

"Ah!" Madeleine was pouring. "Well, you'll need the wine then." She lifted the glass to Delia.

"I'll be quick," Delia said. "Since there's not much to report to them. Just the event itself, I guess."

Madeleine sighed. "It's so hard to imagine the dashing Tom, brought so low." She shook her head. "I would have thought he was exempt from the universal fate, somehow."

"I think he thought so, too." She remembered what the woman's voice had said on the phone—that the arrangement was immortality. It occurred to her that Madeleine might know Alison Miller, or know who she was. "I'll be right back," she said.

Brad was out. She left a message with Ellie, his oldest child, just saying Tom had had a stroke, but was going to live, that she was with him, staying at the Dexters'.

Evan was solicitous, quick with questions, questions she couldn't answer. She told him she'd call him back as soon as she really knew anything. Yes, she said, maybe he *could* come, but for the moment she didn't think there was much point.

Nancy was still at work. Maybe because of that, her tone was businesslike and efficient. Once she had the basic information about her father's condition, there was a pause. Then she said, "You're *not* managing this." It wasn't quite a question.

This is why I called her last, Delia thought. She had a sip of wine. "I'm afraid I am."

"That's completely inappropriate, Mother," she said flatly.

This was so Nancy-like, so predictable, that Delia laughed. "That's the least of my concerns at the moment, dear."

"It is not *possible* that you should become his . . . caregiver. Whatever."

"Nan." Delia set her glass down on the bedside table. "I don't know what's possible or impossible right now. Let's not get ahead of ourselves."

"It's not 'getting ahead of ourselves' to start thinking of ways to manage this without your direct involvement."

"I am involved, I'm afraid. I'm the one empowered to make decisions."

"But surely you can pass that power to one of us."

Delia didn't answer her. Even though she'd thought of this herself, thought of it instantly on the phone with Alison Miller, now, with Nancy, she was aware of the notion as encroachment, as threat. A *no* rose in her.

"Have you explained your situation with Dad to anyone?"

"I haven't had time to do anything, Nan. I just got here. I'm exhausted."

"Well, that's part of it. You're seventy-five years old, you haven't been Dad's wife in decades except legally, and you should *not* be doing this."

"Well, I am." Delia's voice sounded childishly defiant to her own ears.

Nancy didn't answer for a moment. Then she said, "Have you talked to Evan about this?"

"I have."

"And what does he say?"

"He says, he'll wait for me to call him when I know more."

Nancy must have heard in Delia's voice the suggestion that Evan was behaving better than she was, that he was being the good child, and she the difficult one. She didn't say anything for a few seconds. Then: "And this will be tomorrow, you think?"

"Yes. In the morning, they said. They do rounds or something."

"And you'll call me then also?"

"Of course, dear. As soon as I know what the prognosis is. Or the general picture anyway."

"Then I'll wait too." This sounded reluctant, a concession.

They said their good-byes. Delia said at least once more that she'd call as soon as she knew anything, and then Nancy said, "You know, Mother, I'm only thinking of you."

Her voice had changed, and Delia felt guilty about her own anger, her resistance to her daughter.

"I know," she said.

Madeleine had set the table in the kitchen. She had lit two candles, and when Delia came in, she turned out the overhead light.

They talked as they always did, easily, intimately. After Delia had explained what she could of how Tom was, after they'd speculated and commiserated, Madeleine spoke for a while of Dan's death, spoke at greater length than she had before about how hard the adjustment to widowhood had been for her.

They sat silent for a moment, and Delia reached over to touch Madeleine's hand. Two old hands, she thought. Hers looked gnarled on top of Madeleine's. Even Maddy's fingers were plump.

Madeleine looked up at her. "At least you won't have that adjustment if Tom dies—you've lived apart from each other for so long."

Delia moved her hand. "Don't say that, Maddy. He's not going to die."

"Well, but it's the beginning, isn't it? Even if he recovers completely, there's a process that's begun. It's like the dreaded hip fracture for women."

Delia shifted in her chair. Her back hurt—the long plane ride, and then of course lugging her suitcase all over creation. "I suppose you're right," she said, making a face. "The famous slippery slope."

Madeleine smiled. "Which we're all sliding down, aren't we? from birth on." She lifted the bottle. "A splash?" she asked.

"Oh, why not?" Delia said. Madeleine poured, and Delia drank. It was a good French pinot noir. Maddy must have gone out and gotten it especially for her. She set the glass down and sighed. "Who knows?" she said. "Maybe, if he should die, maybe I'd miss him more deeply for *not* having had him all this time."

"Now that would be foolish, dear, which is something I don't think you are."

"Well, but when I am foolish—when I have been—it's always been in connection with Tom, hasn't it?"

Their old faces mirrored each other across the table, in rue, in affection. A little while later, they got up and Madeleine turned the light on. They cleared the table and loaded the dishwasher. As she was standing with her back to Madeleine, wiping the table, Delia asked, "Do you know someone here in Washington named Alison Miller?"

"I don't think so," Madeleine said. "Why?"

"She's the person who called to tell me about Tom. She was with him when he had the stroke."

"Ah!" Madeleine said.

Delia turned around. Madeleine had turned too, and was facing her. She was wearing yellow rubber gloves so big they reached nearly to her elbows. She still had her apron on. She looked like a charwoman, Delia thought. Not that Delia had ever seen one.

"Yes, 'ah,'" Delia said.

"She could be anyone, Dee. A friend, someone he knows from work or politics. Tom has a thousand friends, and at least half of them are women."

"I know. I just thought you might . . . know."

Madeleine shook her head. "I can't help you with that one, sweetie."

Later they said good night and went to their bedrooms at opposite ends of the apartment. When Delia shut the guest room door, there was only silence. She could have been alone in the world.

She lay in bed, looking at the unfamiliar greenish shapes in the room, dimly lighted by the glow from the electric clock. She was remembering what she'd said about Tom, feeling ashamed of herself for having been glib about the possibility of his dying while he was lying so confused and lost in the hospital.

But the problem, she thought now, was that she'd been as blink-ered about the possibility of Tom's falling ill or dying as he had. She'd thought he was immortal, that he'd always be there. Or at least as long as she was. She'd always thought that there was time, ample time ahead, to work things out, to find a way to be together again at some point.

She would have said she'd made her peace with their situation years earlier. She would have said—indeed, she had said—that their solution worked for them, that they both liked it just as it was. But it seemed she'd been waiting all along. Waiting for something to change, to bring them together. Because, after all this, it must still be that she thought of them as *belonging together*. That he was her *destiny*.

Foolishness. Her head swung back and forth on the pillow, she made a little noise.

EVERYTHING ABOUT Dr. Ballantyne was large, most of all his head, which was completely bald, though he couldn't have been more than fifty or so. His teeth were large too, with wide gaps between them—the kind of teeth, Delia thought, which, if he were a child now, would be fixed, at great expense to his parents.

They talked in the hallway, with nurses and patients passing around them. He towered over her. His voice was big too, loud, and Delia kept having the impulse to shush him. It felt wrong to her to broadcast Tom's fate this way to anyone who'd care to listen. She had to force herself to attend to what he was saying, rather than how he was saying it.

He told Delia that Tom's stroke was treated quickly enough that there was a good chance of substantial recovery. It had occurred on the left side of the brain, though, which meant that language skills and speech were likely to be affected to a greater or lesser degree. And for now, he was having trouble moving the right side of his body. Improvement was likely, and radical improvement was possible, he said—though it was harder for older people. The important thing was that therapy begin quickly and continue as long as it was helping. He said the hospital did rehab for only two weeks. They would plan on keeping him here for that long. After that there were excellent facilities nearby, right here in Washington. She should talk about this with Tom's physical therapist and his discharge planner, and, of course, with Tom when he could take it in. In the meantime they were doing a sort of baby-step rehab in his room, and he'd been put on medication to reduce the chances of another stroke.

"So nothing is really clear," she said.

"That's not true." His voice, though loud, was kind. And he had an unhurried air, which Delia was grateful for. "A great deal is clear. He's doing well, at this point. And he'll do better. We just don't know how much better."

After a moment, Delia said, "And is that just luck—how much better he'll do?"

"It's luck, some, and then willpower, the desire to get well. But yes, luck probably controls more than half of it."

Delia was standing with her back against the wall for support. She shifted her weight a little.

"I'll tell you what else was luck for him: his friend," the doctor said.

She made a quizzical face.

"I guess whoever was with him got him here more or less instantly."

"Alison. Miller."

"Is that her name? I met her so briefly. A nice woman. She was terribly concerned. Anyway, they were only a couple of blocks away, at some restaurant, having lunch. That was luck too."

Lunch then, Delia thought. It could have been just friendly, or even business. "Yes," she said. "Yes, well, thanks." She pushed off from the wall.

He told her anytime, that she was to call with any questions—call him, or the physical therapist. "She may be more in charge of how things go with him from now on than I am, actually." He showed her his wide array of teeth one last time, and then he lumbered down the hall, around the corner.

Delia went to Tom's room. He was gone, his bed freshly made up. The flowers had begun to arrive, she saw. There were five or six arrangements of funereal size set around the room, and the heady, slightly rotted aroma of hyacinths was in the air. She would be the one writing the thank-you's for these, she supposed. For now she didn't want to think about it. She left without looking at the cards and went down the hall to the nurses' station.

The woman on duty there told her Tom was having some tests done. Delia asked her where she could find Tom's discharge manager, and the nurse told her that social work was downstairs, on the third floor. As Delia turned to go, the nurse called her back. She'd remembered Tom's things, which they'd kept for him in a locker. "You should take them," she said. "There's his clothes, and then a bunch of stuff from his pockets—his keys and his wallet, things like that that he can't be in charge of right now. I'll get them." She disappeared into a room behind the open station.

When she came back, she handed Delia Tom's keys and his wallet. His clothes were in a clear plastic bag.

She was talking again. She said they were going to move Tom to rehab in a day or two. "And it'll be better for him to have some of his own clothes to wear over there. You know, it helps them, psychologically, to be dressed each day."

Delia said she'd get some things to bring in for him.

She took the elevator downstairs to the department of social work, riding with a group of nurses who were laughing about how good-looking one of the interns was. The receptionist in that area said that the social worker who managed patient after-care was busy just then, but she scheduled Delia for an appointment with her in the afternoon.

After she'd taken the little card, Delia rode the elevator down all the way to the lobby, crossed it, and stepped out into the humid Washington air. Almost instantly she started to perspire. There were no cabs around and no cabstand visible in the flow of people, so she went back inside. The young man at the information desk pointed out to her the taxi telephone on the wall by the glass doors. When the dispatcher asked her "Where to?" she gave him Tom's address— her old address, the apartment they had lived in together in a town house on Capitol Hill.

When she drove up in the cab it looked the same, except that the white paint on the brick had eroded here and there and a faint sandy pink was bleeding through. But the front yard, which had been mostly crabgrass and packed dirt in their day, was different. It was flourishing, full of crowded perennials coming in green and lush, with pastel tulips thrusting up through their foliage. Tom must have hired a gardener.

Delia opened the low iron gate and went up the walk. She had a sense of being conspicuous, as though she could be seen—the ex-wife, arriving where she didn't belong. She had to try three keys on Tom's ring before one fit in the lock on the shiny black door.

When it opened and Delia stepped in, she felt the familiarity of it like a wash, a smell. There *was* a smell, in fact—the scent of Tom and how he'd lived here: cooking odors, the faint tang of cigar smoke, his aftershave, and others, unnamable. Just *Tom*.

She shut the door behind her and walked slowly through the rooms on the first floor—the living room on one side of the hall, the back room Tom had used as a study, the dining room, the small kitchen. They were unchanged, except that one chair in the living room had been reupholstered, and the framed family pictures that had once crowded the round table next to the couch were gone. And he never used the dining room for entertaining, that was clear: the enormous table was stacked with papers, the chairs pushed back against the walls.

They had lived together in this house at least part-time for almost ten years, renting it from the owner, who had a small apartment on the third floor. It was in what was then a dangerous part of town, but it was what they could afford. Sometime after they separated, Tom had bought it, and now he was the landlord, with a tenant above him. She hadn't been in these rooms for nearly twenty years.

She had exiled herself, in effect. Tom had been only welcoming, only eager when she came here the first couple of times after Carolee, during the campaign for the Senate in 1972, the campaign she'd agreed to help him with in spite of the affair. He'd been hopeful that the house itself—which she'd loved, she thought now, moving through the spacious rooms—would call her back. It was what they'd planned, after all—that after Brad, the youngest, left to go to college, they would sell the house in Williston and Delia would come to Washington full-time.

But Delia had known, even as she lived through those days, that the campaign and the way they were together through it were a reprieve from reality. A reality that gripped her once he'd won, once she'd stood beside him at the podium for the last time, smiling and waving and fighting back tears. Once the party in Williston to celebrate was over, once he'd made love to her in their bed there, once he'd left the house in the morning to go back to Washington.

That was when what Delia thought of as *the crazy time* began for her, a time when she didn't know what she wanted; or when she wanted conflicting things in rapid succession.

Or not so rapid. Sometimes she was sure she'd chosen the right thing. She would stay in Williston, alone, for four or five months, feeling certain that she was getting over him. Once she didn't see him for an entire year. But then something would happen and she'd want him. Or perhaps what she wanted was evidence that he wanted her, that she still had some power over him. She didn't know. She didn't ask herself to know. She'd beckon him to Williston or New York, and they'd fall into each other's arms, they'd make love over and over, and when they parted, Delia would leave feeling sore and well used, her face chafed, her sex swollen.

Throughout these years, Tom, sensing her anguish, was kind. He was also steady in his sense of what he wanted—to live together again. Not to divorce, ever. He said that he loved her, that he would always love her, that she was the love of his life, in spite of his unfaithfulness. He described that as his own weakness, having nothing to do with failures on her part.

But he had other women. He was discreet, much more discreet than he'd been with Carolee. But he had lovers. She knew this. She knew it because he told her that unless she came back to him, he would. She knew it because she could occasionally sense, when she called him in the evening, or at night, that he was with someone.

They argued about this. He said that if she were coming back, of course he would stop, he would be faithful to her. But that she couldn't have it both ways. If she was never coming back, as she insisted she wasn't, then he needed to have a life.

Their arguments during this time were sometimes ugly, sometimes fierce. Delia was worse than Tom—she felt freed by what he'd done to be so. She called him names. She called his lovers names: his cunts, his sluts. She accused him of trying to hold on to her because of his career—she said he had *used* her in the campaign.

Even years later—when Delia had come to believe that Tom really had loved her in some way through everything, that he had wanted to stay married on account of those very real feelings—even then she thought in her most cynical moments that she'd probably been useful to him more than once in warding off one or another of his lovers. She could imagine the scene: his oh!-so-regretful calling up of the older, now solitary wife who wouldn't, couldn't, give him up. *Religion, you know.* Though of course it was *his* religion—and then too the religion of politics at that time—which prohibited divorce. But his lovers wouldn't have known that. She could imagine the younger women pressing, threatening, and Tom coming back with his impeccable excuse, about Delia's sad absolutism, about their resulting arrangement and her prior claim.

This period, the crazy time, lasted for six or seven years. Then slowly things got easier for her. She had several affairs of her own, and that helped. It made her feel less desperate, less as though Tom were the only man she could ever love—not that she loved either man she became involved with, just that they made love seem a possibility.

She had grown very close to one of them, a widower, a composer she met through Ilona. She felt that she might have loved him, but she could never adjust to the way he made love. It was always impassioned, always *hard,* she would have said. Quick. There was none of that lazy playfulness that she and Tom had learned together, none of the loving attentiveness to her body that meant release for her. Finally they stopped being lovers and became friends, for a while anyway.

But even more important for Delia in coming to some kind of

peace about Tom was her sense of enjoying her solitude. Her new life in France was part of that, but in Williston too she found she felt a new ease moving around socially by herself. That need of Tom's to occupy center stage, which had always kept her in a supporting role— or maybe even relegated to the audience—that wasn't there to limit her anymore, to hem her in. She formed friendships differently, she took greater pleasure in them. She could feel that people liked her, something she'd never been sure of in the past, so focused had everyone always been on Tom.

More and more Delia let go of Tom, of his life away from her, his life in Washington. At one point she made a list of things she wanted from the house in Washington, and he had movers come and truck everything up to her.

She climbed the stairs to the bedrooms. She went first to what had been their room. It had been painted and redecorated—it was dark and modern now. Where before the walls had been a soft gray and the bedding and furniture white, now things were brown, brown, brown. The curtains and bedspread were a rich, dark paisley.

She sat on Tom's bed and called each of her children again—at home, so she wouldn't interrupt their work; but also so that she wouldn't have to talk to them, Nancy in particular—she'd be dealing with answering machines. In the messages she left, she repeated as accurately and carefully as she could what Dr. Ballantyne had said to her in the hospital.

When she finished, she sat still a moment, looking around her. Then she got up and went down the hall to what had been their rooms—the children's—to see what had become of them. The doors were closed. She opened one, then the other, and stood there, taking them in.

In terms of furniture they were unchanged from the time she and Tom had separated—the four-poster with the frilly canopy in Nancy's room, the two matching beds in the boys' room. Even the pictures on the walls were the same. Posters of the Andes, of Machu Picchu in Brad and Evan's room; in Nancy's, framed paintings and reproductions chosen by Delia—they'd used this as a guest room after Nancy went to law school.

But in both rooms there were also odd collections of objects, clearly deposited there over time—lamps, framed pictures leaned against the walls, rolled-up rugs and pads, an upright vacuum cleaner, some cardboard cartons. Clearly no one had stayed in them for years.

Delia knew that the children didn't visit Tom. They saw him when they came to Washington, but they saw him in neutral territory—at their hotels, or in restaurants. And on Tom's visits to them, his infrequent visits, he stayed in hotels too.

She and Tom had talked once about this—she had wanted him to know that she hadn't encouraged their distance, that she hadn't asked any of them to be her ally against him. And he in turn had told her that he didn't hold her responsible.

It had seemed to her as they talked about it that he was almost welcoming of the distance from the children. Perhaps he saw it as a kind of penance for what he'd done, for being who he was. What he said was that the children had made their choices clear early on, and that he understood the bases for those choices.

But the fact was that all of them, except for Nancy, had yielded and drawn closer to him over the years. Delia thought now of this past Christmas, of the dinner with Brad and his family in Williston. Of course, Brad was the easiest one, but still, everyone had seemed happy and relaxed.

She went back down the hall to Tom's room. She opened the closet. She chose clothes quickly and set them out on the bed—just shirts and slacks. None of the expensive suits, of which there were perhaps eight or ten hanging up. She sighed, looking at them. Even when they had no money, Tom had been profligate with clothes. It was a weakness—another weakness. And she was left there too to deal with the problems, the marshaling of their limited resources that resulted.

But the truth was that she too had loved the way he looked in his fancy suits, in his expensive shirts and suspenders and shoes. And she had been sympathetic to what they meant to him—the entrée he felt they offered him into a life he wanted. He had told her once that he'd practiced standing casually, his hands in his pockets, that he'd imitated the gestures, the expressions of people he met in college and law school and early in his practice. And finally, he'd been success-ful—he'd truly become what he played at being. The clothes were the least of it, actually.

From his bureau she got out underwear, socks. She went down the hall to the storage closet, and there, on a shelf above the linens, were the suitcases, as they had been in the past. There were even a few she recognized. She brought one back and opened it on the bed. She folded the clothes carefully—professionally, she thought, with a little prideful pleasure—and laid them in.

She went to the bathroom for Tom's toiletries—a hairbrush, a razor and shaving cream, aftershave, toothpaste and a toothbrush. Even if the hospital provided some of these, she thought, he would probably like his own better. She put them into his dopp kit and wedged it into a corner of the suitcase, on top of the clothes. She zipped the suitcase shut and set it at the top of the stairs.

Then she came back into the room and crossed to the bed. She lay down heavily on it. It was the warmth in here, the stuffiness, she thought. And of course, it was the jet lag hitting her too—she'd waked several times in the night in Madeleine's apartment, confused in that silent darkness about the hour, about where she was. The last time had been about four-thirty, and she'd been awake ever since, though she'd lain in bed until almost seven, when she heard Madeleine in the kitchen.

I'll just sleep for a few minutes, she thought now, as her eyes closed.

SHE WAS ALMOST late for the meeting with Tom's social worker. When she got back to Tom's room afterward, it was around four. He was in bed. There was a wheelchair pushed back into a corner of the room, though, a sign of some recent activity.

His eyes opened and followed her as she approached. His hand rose as if to greet her, his lips parted. He made a noise, a noise that might have had a *B* or a *D* at its beginning; producing this noise, his open mouth had to labor, his tongue had to work.

Delia willed herself not to look away. She greeted him in return, saying her own name, saying she was glad to see him looking better. She spoke slowly, telling him she'd brought some of his things.

He didn't seem to understand her, so she set the suitcase across the chair and opened it. She took out a shirt, one of his beautiful, expensive shirts of a cotton so fine it felt like silk, and held it up. He cried out, seeing it, as though he recognized some part of his lost self.

She spent the rest of the afternoon with him. First she asked for a basin, got some hot water, and shaved him. Then she found a nurse to help her dress him. In his own clothes, clean-shaven, his hair combed, he seemed suddenly almost whole again, a *person* instead of a patient. Delia thought she could actually feel a difference in the way the nurses and aides treated him when they came into the room. She helped to feed him too, spooning the mush he was allowed into his mouth.

Mostly, though, she just sat by him, sometimes saying a few words, more often humming or singing. The time seemed to pass with a glacial slowness. When Tom dozed and she could relax—she could walk in the hallway for a bit, or go into the bathroom and splash water on her face—Delia felt a gratitude so profound it was almost physical.

She was grateful too for the news she'd gotten earlier from the social worker, and the physical therapist who'd come in briefly to Delia's conference. Tom's ability to eat was a good sign, she'd learned—some people couldn't control their mouths after a stroke and had to relearn this. And he was trying to name things, the social worker said. Both of these were indications of the potential for a strong recovery. They'd already started working with him in his room, moving his weak side, trying to get him to stand, to walk by himself. They would start taking him over to the rehabilitation unit in a day or two; and pretty soon after that, she'd have to make some decisions about where to have him treated, and for how long.

When Delia called the taxi to go to Madeleine's, it was almost eight, and she was exhausted again. She must have looked it too, because the driver got out from behind the wheel and opened the door for her, helped her in, holding her elbow. Or perhaps it was just that southern courtesy. Watching the congestion on M Street, listening to the car horns, she started thinking about Washington, about the southern quality of the city, which always struck her when she came back after an absence—particularly as it connected to race. There was an omnipresent country graciousness on the part of the blacks who were in serving positions everywhere in the city. The hospital staff, the waiters in restaurants, the cabdrivers—all, all smiling and polite. And now, getting out of the cab, here was Madeleine's doorman in his fancy uniform, greeting her by name, smiling too, opening the door for her.

All this politeness, this graciousness, contrasted to the abject, angry poverty of so much of the city. She had often wondered how this struck visiting foreign dignitaries—but of course they were used to this divide in other countries too. Maybe it was strangest to someone raised here, she thought, where equality was the supposed norm, or desideratum anyway. She and Tom had talked about it sometimes, about all the failed promises of the civil-rights movement, the poverty initiatives that he'd been so passionate about in the early days. About how ironic it was that Washington itself was emblematic of this, if only those in power cared to look around.

And now, getting into the elevator, she was thinking about how they used to talk—about everything, it seemed to her. And everywhere. In bed, at the kitchen table when the children were asleep, in the bathroom where he'd sometimes come and sit while she was in the tub. A confusion of images, images of Tom, alert, argumentative, of his mouth moving in that tight wry smile of private amusement after he'd made a point. She thought of his mouth as it had moved today, working to say her name. She thought of its kissing her, caressing her body. Her mind was full of all of this as she rode slowly up in the antique elevator, as she pushed its flexible cage door open, as she got out, as she rang Madeleine's bell.

Perhaps this was why for a long foolish moment she didn't recognize the person who opened the door—though later she would think maybe it was also in sympathy with Tom, with his inability to assimilate all that was incongruous and out of place in his life. But then things righted themselves, and she said, she hoped with more pleasure in her voice than she felt, "Why, *Nancy*!"

CHAPTER TEN

Delia, May 1994

IT WAS NANCY who insisted that they go home to Williston for the weekend. She said Delia needed the rest, she said they could talk better at home. Delia hadn't resisted. The truth was, the thought of home was welcome to her; and she sensed that she could make it through Nancy's visit better there than at Madeleine's or in the hospital, around Tom.

They flew up Friday afternoon. Their plan was to go back to Washington together Monday morning. After her second quick visit with Tom, Nancy would fly back to Denver that evening—she'd already left work for longer than she should have, she told Delia.

At home, in Williston, Delia unpacked. She unhooked the hose from the kitchen faucet and carried the plants from the tarp in the kitchen to their permanent locations—the jade to the living room, the fern to its stand in the dining room. The hibiscus stayed where it was. She went through the mail that Meri had sorted and took some of it up to her study, where she wrote a few notes in response. She drove to the grocery store in the mall and bought food, ticking the items off her list.

She tried to stay as busy as she could, because whenever she stopped—or even slowed down—Nancy was there, wanting to talk, insisting that Delia should leave Tom in Washington in a rehab place Nancy had found, where he would have, as she said now, "the best of care, Mother. And where his various Washington *friends*," she emphasized this word unpleasantly, "can visit him. Let's not forget, Washington is his home. It makes no sense, none, for you to bring him here. And we all know that that would involve you in his care in a way that's completely inappropriate."

Who is this *we*? Delia thought. Who is this *us*?

"But what would be the point of keeping him in Washington if it just meant I worried more?" she said. "That I'd have to keep flying down there because of that? That would be far more inconvenient for me."

"If that's what you did, yes. But you need to avoid doing that. You need to extricate yourself from this . . . web that's catching at you."

This time they were talking in the Peking Palace in Williston, but they'd had earlier versions of this conversation on the plane up from Washington and at the house. Nancy had even stood in the door to Delia's bedroom last night and kept at it, *though surely she could see,* Delia thought, *how exhausted I was.* Even after Delia turned out the light, she'd gone on talking, her silhouette dark in the doorway. Delia had had to tell her, finally, that she desperately needed to sleep.

Desperate or not, after Nancy left, Delia had lain awake for a long time in her bed, feeling a kind of terror envelope her. What frightened her was that she wasn't sure she could resist her daughter's power. She thought this might be the moment, actually, the moment she'd heard about from a friend or two—recollected sadly, ruefully— when the grown children swept in and irresistibly took over your life. When you could no longer say no, because it was so clear that all the things you thought of as *belonging to you* were in the process of becoming theirs—their possessions, and, of course, their heavy burdens, too: your life, your spouse's life, your illness, his illness, your death. The moment when you *owed* them something, when you *had* to give way, out of a kind of fairness to them; and then also because you just didn't have the strength left anymore to fight.

"It's not a web, dear," Delia said now. "It's life. It's life that catches you. Life changes. And we change in response to it."

"Mother. This is your decision."

How narrow her lips were, Delia thought. How tight her mouth. Like Tom's, but without the playfulness.

"You aren't *caught*," she said. "You do not *have* to do anything about Dad. I will handle it. I've spoken to the best place for brain damage in Washington. I've made the arrangements. You won't have to do anything more about it. You're not obligated to him. It would be absurd to think that, after what he did to you."

Suddenly, watching her daughter's face, Delia was taken back to the memory of those weeks just after Tom had launched himself into his affair with Carolee, when, even in the midst of her own grief, she'd had over and over to try to ease Nancy's, to comfort her. To *apologize* to her, it sometimes seemed.

This, now—this insistence that her father had no right to Delia's attention or love—this sprang from the same place in Nancy's psyche, Delia thought. It was the little girl in Nancy, pleading that he needed to pay for wounding her, for betraying her.

Delia could feel the truth of this instantly, and oddly, it helped her, seeing things this way. It let her dismiss the notion of Nancy's power, the notion that had made her heart pound in her ears as she lay awake in bed last night. It let her feel the same loving pity for Nancy she'd felt so long ago when her daughter couldn't let go of her rage and confusion, couldn't stop herself.

Delia sighed. "Nor are you, dear. Obligated." And then because she thought it might help Nancy to hear it, she said, "After what he did to *you*. To you, and Evan, and Brad."

Nancy looked startled, and Delia felt she'd gotten it right. She felt, for the first time, that she might have the better hand in this situation. "Look, Nan," she said, leaning forward across the table toward her daughter. "Given that, given that he's an old man who long ago disobligated all of us—*disobliged* us, I guess you'd say—shouldn't it be the person who's least . . . offended by that, least disturbed by it, who steps forward now? I *want* to do this and you don't. I . . . I've forgiven your father for what he did, in a way, it seems to me, you haven't."

Nancy made a face, but she lifted her hand too, in a gesture that seemed to be an acknowledgment of the truth in what Delia had said.

"I suppose . . ." Delia said, and stopped. She wanted to be careful.

She wanted not to push too hard. She knew Nancy was capable of resisting her just out of stubbornness.

"What? You suppose what?"

"I suppose, come to think of it, that the kind of hurt he offered me was so much more . . . predictable. It was really banal, in a way. Whereas the way he hurt you was *not* banal at all." This was true, wasn't it? He had done a terrible thing to Nancy at that vulnerable stage of her life. He and Carolee had, together. "It was worse."

But Nancy wasn't biting. "Both hurts were awful, to me and to you," she said. "Both of them were unforgivable."

After a moment Delia shook her head. "You can't speak for me, Nan. About what I find forgivable or unforgivable. I'm different from you, and my understanding of your father is different from yours."

She watched as her daughter played with her chopsticks, lining them up precisely next to each other.

Nancy looked up. "What is it you'd like to do, then?"

Delia felt a relief so deep it was as though the breath she drew now were the first full breath she'd drawn since she heard the news about Tom. "There's a good place near Williston, too. For the brain-injured. The discharge worker told me about it. I'd like him there. It would make my life easier to have him there. Why don't I see about that?" she said. And then quickly went on, "And if it doesn't work out, we'll have all the legwork you've done in Washington to fall back on."

There was something reluctant in Nancy's face, something petulant, Delia thought, but she capitulated, she agreed, more or less. What she said was, "Well, I suppose I can't stop you, if this is something you're determined to do."

"I think I am determined. That's a good word for it. And I want to. I'm not exaggerating in any way when I say that: I *want* to."

They talked for a while of logistics, of how Delia would manage it. Nancy wanted Delia to check in with her about everything as she went along, as she made decisions. She would expect regular calls.

Delia agreed. She agreed to everything. Yes, that all made sense, everything made sense. She kept her voice conciliatory.

As they drove to the house, Nancy said, "You have to promise me, Mother, that if it gets to be too much, you'll let me know. We'll figure something else out."

"Of course."

"There may be good places near me too. Or one of the boys."

Delia didn't answer. To leave him to Nancy's tender mercies . . . well, such a thing would not be possible.

"And I want you to go to Paris, too, in the fall. No giving up the things you enjoy because you're Dad's . . . case manager or something."

Paris. Delia hadn't thought of it once through all this. It seemed another universe. She remembered her last morning there, her breakfast on the balcony, the light in the sky around her. She remembered the call from Alison Miller the afternoon before.

"Maybe we could take turns coming to stay in the house and visiting him while you're away—to make sure everything was going well."

"Yes," Delia said.

Nancy parked in the driveway, and they walked to the side steps, the ones that led into the kitchen. It was dark, they'd forgotten to leave the outside light on, and Delia stumbled over something. Nancy caught her elbow and continued to hold it as they came up the back stairs to the door. When they went in, Delia reached over in the black kitchen and switched on the lamp over the table. Blinking in the light, Nancy looked exhausted.

Why, she's *old*, Delia thought, looking at the deep, bitter grooves around her daughter's mouth, the lines in her forehead. She spoke gently to her. "Well, we seem to have made a plan then."

THE REHAB CENTER was about forty minutes from Williston. Delia drove slowly along the two-lane highway, watching anxiously for the signposts and turns she'd written down when she called for directions. She'd just come past the rotary and the yellow farmhouse when she saw it, as described, on a hill to the right.

"Rather imposing," the woman on the phone had said, and it was—a grand old mansion, Georgian. On either side of it, low two-story brick buildings stretched out, back into the woods that pushed up toward the top of the hill.

She drove under a bright blue canopy by the front door and parked in the asphalt lot marked for visitors. Inside, there was a wide entrance hallway. Just visible behind a blond wood counter, a receptionist smiled up at her. She had flyaway gray hair. Delia told her the name she'd been given, and then sat down to wait, looking around her.

Everything was of a fine quality for what it was, and what it was was deliberately bland, painstakingly inoffensive. The color scheme was gray and a deep green—restful to the eye, she supposed. The pictures on the walls were anonymous pastoral scenes or framed posters from shows at art museums. Haystacks by Monet. Out in the hallway, flowers by O'Keeffe.

Walking with Mrs. Davidson minutes later, Delia was both impressed and oppressed by the place. The doors stood open to many of the little apartments off the long corridors, and Mrs. Davidson called out hello to various residents who seemed to be just sitting there idly, waiting for an invitation to talk. She was a pretty woman, perhaps in her fifties, slightly overdressed for her job—a purple suit, a big scarf knotted at her shoulder. She looked like a high-school principal, Delia thought.

She pointed out to Delia that the residents had their own furniture, their own pictures on the walls and mementoes set out. And Delia could see these as they passed slowly by—the figurines arranged on a table, the Victorian chair, the family photos cluttering a wall, the Persian rug spread over the institutional floor covering. The remnants of a full life led elsewhere.

This was where they would hope Tom could be moved in due time, Mrs. Davidson said.

Delia took all this in, commenting politely. As they moved around, she looked at the residents, old, like Tom, but ambulatory for the most part. Once they saw a young man walking the corridor ahead of them with an aide who was holding his hand. Delia asked Mrs. Davidson about him.

"He's one of our *boys*," she said. "They're the other part of our population. When you're talking about neurological damage, there are two main culprits, and those are a stroke, and trauma. A few other illnesses, a few other possibilities. But mostly stroke and some violent event. And the population most likely to invite a violent event—to have a motorcycle accident with no helmet, to dive into a quarry without knowing where the rocks are, to drive too fast, to pass on a hill—those are, of course, young men. We try to offer them more discipline, more physical activity. And we actually house them in a different wing—they can be disruptive to the older population. I can show you if you wish."

"No, no. It's not necessary," Delia said.

They went next to the rehab and nursing-care wing, where Tom would be, at least at first. Delia saw the elaborate equipment he would work out on to build his strength, the rooms where his speech therapy would take place.

In the open main room here, a birthday party was in full swing. There was a speechless old woman slouched off center in a wheelchair at the head of the table, her mouth open as if in permanent shock at what had become of her, a little pointed hat held to the top of her head by an elastic band running under her chin. Ten or twelve other residents sat around the table with nurses or helpers next to most of them, a few being fed, more helping themselves—some competently, some as awkwardly as little children. Many of them too wore hats. A young woman wearing a flowered smock was chattering as she cut the cake, explaining, as you do with small children: "We're having ice cream. It's vanilla, vanilla ice cream. And look! Here's some cake! Two cakes. This cake has chocolate, and that one doesn't. So if you don't like chocolate . . ."

There was a kind of din under this, the noise of the patients' conversation in response, taking place in a different rhythm, a different style.

Delia's main thought as they left the ward, as she walked back with Mrs. Davidson down the enclosed corridors with their slightly floral smell, as she sat listening to her talk about finances in her office, was that Tom would be appalled. And then, sitting there, nodding at Mrs. Davidson as she spoke, she realized that she was thinking of another Tom, one who would have walked with her through this place in one of his suits, a beautiful tie at his neck, his hand at her back, at her elbow, looking at her from time to time, commenting privately on things to her with the slightest wry twist to his mouth, an almost invisible lift of his eyebrows.

The Tom who existed now was used to this, to his compatriots in the new country he lived in. He probably wouldn't notice any of the things that so disturbed her. He would be in them. Of them. He would be one of them. It seemed almost unbearable. She didn't want to think of him this way. She *wouldn't* think of him this way. She couldn't.

And then she remembered something from the literature they'd sent her. She interrupted Mrs. Davidson in the middle of what she was saying. "You have a day-care program too, don't you?"

OVER THE NEXT week or so, Mrs. Davidson and the staff at Putnam managed the details. They coordinated with the hospital in Washington, where Tom was still doing his poststroke rehab. Together they agreed on another ten days of work there. Then he'd come to Putnam for at least a week as an inpatient. Then, if he was progressing as well as he had seemed to be, he could come home, home to Delia. He could live with her and continue to use the rehabilitation facility, but as an outpatient.

Delia mentioned none of this to Nancy when they talked. She just spoke of the quality of the place, of the programs, of the various levels of care. She couldn't face another struggle with her daughter right now. She let Nancy believe she was implementing the plan they'd agreed on, which was, of course, already a compromise on Nancy's part, as Nancy saw it. The time to tell her, Delia thought, would be when it was a fait accompli, when Nancy could see how well it was going.

In the meantime, Delia was busy with her own arrangements. She hired a driving service to take Tom over and back to his five days at Putnam each week once he'd come to stay with her. She called the student employment agency at the college and listed a caregiver's job

for the afternoons starting in mid-June—she wanted to go on working at the Apthorp house this summer, so she'd need someone to
come and stay with Tom then—there was a gap of about an hour and
a half between the time he would come home from Putnam and the
time she'd get back from her docent's job. Also she'd need help getting Tom upstairs for a shower a few times a week at the minimum,
and there might be odd tasks around the house she could think of.

She decided to conduct interviews for the job—it seemed important the person be someone that Tom might like. There were three
young men who called her in response to the ad. She arranged to
have them come seriatim on a Wednesday afternoon.

She was nervous ahead of time. She dressed carefully—a white
linen shirt and black slacks, sandals. She chose bangle-y jewelry for
her wrists—youthful jewelry, as she thought of it. She knew this was
ridiculous, but she felt she ought to try. She didn't want them
discouraged too much by her in advance of what was bound to be dis-
couraging about Tom. She spiffed the room up a bit, and bought
Coke and chips, which not one of them touched.

She had decided beforehand that she would choose on the basis of
two qualities, physical strength and the degree of relaxation the
young men had around her.

But they were all enormous, and they all said they did one sport or
another. All strong then, she assumed. Two of them, though, were
formal and embarrassed in her company, each in a different way—
one too polite and ingratiating, the other too distant, as though a
person as old as she was somehow a different species, not amenable
to idle conversation or laughter. Talking with them was exhausting to
Delia, since she had to do all the work.

The third one, Matthew, seemed unafraid and curious, and he'd
heard of Tom. Tom would like that. And though he was shy, though
he kept calling her Mrs. Naughton even after she'd asked him several
times to call her Delia, he was, in his youthful fashion, interesting. He
also didn't know what he wanted to be or do as an adult, and Delia
liked that. Young people ought to be more indecisive, she thought,
since they knew so little.

She told him a bit about Tom, about how he hadn't known either what he wanted when he was Matthew's age, how he'd traveled around the country as a young man, doing pickup work. How he'd fought fires and worked briefly as a boxer in a border town in Texas. As she was describing this, she had a momentary vision of the young Tom, that tall brave boy, off on his own.

"That is so cool," Matthew said. He had a big square head and a face that might be handsome in a few years if what gave it thickness now was just baby fat—you couldn't tell about that.

"Hardly," Delia said. "It always sounded to me a bit like a cock-fight. They just threw them into the ring together for the pleasure of betting on it. The bloodier the better. He got five dollars if he won, and nothing if he didn't. Of course five dollars was a great deal in the Depression."

"But nothing was nothing then too," he answered.

Delia laughed, and he looked so pleased—he blushed!—that that was it for her. They made their arrangements, they talked about a salary.

A few days later, Matthew and a friend of his came to rearrange things in the house for her. They carried the dining room table and chairs to the basement, and they moved a double bed into the dining room from one of the guest rooms. They brought a bureau down too, and the rocker from the living room, replacing it with a wing chair from Delia's bedroom. There were a few extra lamps in the basement that Delia had them cart up, and two bedside tables. They put a little chest in the first-floor lavatory so Tom would have a place to keep his toiletries, and Delia cleared all the old coats out of the hall closet so she could hang his clothes there.

In addition, she had bought what she thought of as a booster chair for the toilet from a medical supply house, and a tray with fold-down legs on it so he could eat in bed if he was tired.

And every fourth or fifth day through all this she flew to Washington to see Tom, to arrange with her lawyer and Tom's for her to take over the decision making, the finances, to talk to his doctors and his therapists about how he was doing.

What she heard about his state, and what she could see for herself, was that his progress was steady. He was walking, with a cane on good days, with his walker when he was tired. He was eating well, and swallowing real food, which was important. If he went very slowly, he was able to read simple texts. He could print with his right hand, though it looked like the work of a child. His speech lagged behind, but he knew what he wanted to say and understood what others were saying to him if they spoke slowly and simply. The focus of his ongoing rehab would be speech therapy and increasing his strength.

But what was most important to Delia in all of this was that he seemed to be *there* again, in his gestures, in his face. That he could signal to her his pleasure when she came into his room, that his mouth tightened sometimes in the old way—ruefully, wryly. That he reached to push her hair off her face when she bent to help him. He was himself. He was becoming himself.

ON MAY 31, four weeks to the day after his stroke, Delia flew back to New England with Tom. A driver met them at the airport and took them directly to Putnam. When they pulled up under the blue canopy and the driver came around to help Tom out of the car, he was confused. He seemed suddenly lost. He grabbed her arm.

"Hoooom," he said to Delia insistently. She had told him she was bringing him home, but she'd also told him about Putnam.

"In a week or so," she said. "In a week or so I'll take you home."

"Hoomm, nao." Home now. It was like lowing, the noise he made, and Delia felt on the edge of tears.

But he fell silent once he was in the wheelchair, and he said nothing as Mrs. Davidson greeted him, as they rolled him down to the rehab ward, as the driver settled him into a chair in his room. Delia was talking to him off and on through this, explaining over and over that he wouldn't be long here, that it would be only days, really, until he could be in Williston.

He wouldn't, or couldn't, answer. When she left him, he was sitting in the dark green armchair in his room, his face haggard with exhaustion. He didn't meet her eye when she said good-bye.

Even so, Delia was excited, full of the same fierce energy that had carried her through these weeks, these days, the trips back and forth, the work of making the house ready for Tom. She had felt—she felt now—that she was living in the past, the present, and the future all at once, a sense of elation at returning to a happy time in her life. She knew she was wound up, she knew she should try to tame it, but she didn't want to.

On the way home, she asked the driver to stop and wait for her at the gourmet shop. Inside, she bought some triple crème cheese, some olives, and the crackers she liked best.

At home, after she'd prepared her plate and poured a glass of wine, she started to carry them to the living room, where she often sat to eat her minimal supper, but changed her mind as she passed the open door to the transformed dining room. She went in and set the plate down on the tray table by the rocker. She turned on the radio. On the jazz show she liked, someone was playing boogie-woogie piano. She sat in her rocker in the half-light. Slowly, enjoying the ritual of it, she spread a cracker with the buttery cheese and bit into it. Self-indulgence, Delia knew, the cheese so rich you could imagine it clogging your arteries even as you swallowed it. She sipped the wine and tilted back in the rocker.

The sky outside was pinkish through the black leaves of the oak tree. She looked slowly around the room. The sheets were neatly tucked in on the bed, the pillows stacked just so. Her father's antique maps, those other versions of the world, were dimly visible on the walls, strange organic shapes, like amoebas. In a week she would have Tom here. He would be home, truly home, for the first time in more than twenty years.

CHAPTER ELEVEN

Meri, May 1994

THE OUTSIZE, flat cardboard box was leaned against the curve of the windows next to the front door when Meri arrived home from the grocery store. It was the morning after her last half day of work—a half day, for what would have been the point of staying for the planning meeting when she wasn't planning anything?

She read the return address. It was the crib. Meri had ordered it from one of the many baby catalogs that had been arriving in the mail, unbeckoned, unsolicited, for months now. She had said to Nathan that it was as though the U.S. government had wiretapped her uterus and notified the postal service of its condition before she had even the slightest idea that she was knocked up.

He had laughed and told her how his father, in his last illness, had thought his catheter had been implanted by the IRS and was the means by which they were accessing all his money.

"Citizenship," she'd said. "It isn't all it's cracked up to be."

But how timely this arrival was, she thought now, leaving the box on the porch as she went inside. The due date was just ten days off, and they hadn't even really started organizing anything having to do with this baby. Nathan was still finishing up his semester at school, and she had just gotten through her most intensive month at work yet. In addition to her regular load, she'd tried to set up a dozen or so pieces ahead of time—mostly in the arts, since these didn't have to be so tightly connected to the news cycle.

After she'd taken the groceries to the pantry and put them away, she went back out onto the front porch and tilted the box, testing it. It was heavy, but she thought she could manage to get it through the door if she slid it. Bracing her legs apart, she lifted one edge of it up onto the doorsill; and felt a liquid spurt wet her pants.

Meri was immense. Last week, as she'd come into the room where everyone had their cubicles, Jane had looked up at her and said in a tone of mock surprise, "Gosh, Meri, just when I think you couldn't possibly *get* any bigger, what do you go and do?" And several people standing around chimed in: "You. Get. Bigger!"

Meri had given them all the finger. But the truth was that even she was surprised by how huge she was. And by everything else about her that had changed. Her belly button had popped out and was clearly visible under the four maternity dresses she'd bought early this spring—she'd finally had to give up on Nathan's shirts and sweaters. In these last weeks, her ankles and feet had swollen so much that all she could wear were rubber thong sandals. Her immense breasts rested on her huge belly, and she actually had a rash where they all touched each other constantly. She treated this with cornstarch, which gathered unattractively in her flesh's creases, like some exuded grayish matter. Like *smegma,* the all-time ugliest word in the world. In the grocery store just now she'd had to ask someone to lift the cereal down from a not-very-high shelf—her arms couldn't reach that far past her stomach.

And for the last month there had been incontinence, this added blow to her sense of herself as an adult human in charge of her own body. Every time she sneezed or laughed hard, or even sometimes just moved too suddenly, her body released a little trickle of urine.

She went inside now and up the stairs to the bathroom. She rinsed herself off. She got a clean hand towel from the cupboard and went into the bedroom. There, she tossed her panties and the old towel into the laundry basket, and put on a clean pair of panties. She slung the towel across her crotch, then pulled the panties back up, the towel held loosely in place by them, a kind of diaper. She'd gotten used to treating her body this way—casually, scornfully.

She went back down to the front door and finished sliding the box into the house. She shut the door. She got a sharp knife from the kitchen and cut the many places where tape was holding the box together. When she was done, the front flap of the box unfolded slowly away and wafted to the floor, revealing one of the side panels of the slatted white crib, its frame wrapped in a plastic covering.

She cut through the string holding this plastic on, as well as the string holding the side panel to other pieces of the crib behind it in the box. She lifted the panel out. It wasn't bad. She could probably do this, get the crib upstairs and assemble it, the whole thing, if she did it one piece at a time. It seemed a good project for this first empty day alone, a way of definitively turning from her life at work to her new life, with this baby.

She lifted the side panel against her hip, her left hand gripping the bottom rail through the opening between the slats, her right hand steadying things. She carried it upstairs, stopping for a long moment to rest on the landing. She took it down the hall to the littlest bedroom, which Nathan had painted a sunny yellow over the semester break after Christmas. They'd bought a bureau, and Nathan had painted that too—white, like the crib they'd ordered. The baby clothes and bedding they'd been given were stacked in its drawers. Some were from Nathan's mother, and some were from a shower Jane had organized at work—true to her word, she'd never mentioned her anger at Meri again, and the shower had been a kind and conciliatory gesture on her part. Meri and Nathan had yet to tally any of this stuff, yet to figure out what else they might need. In fact, most of the presents were still tied in ribbon or encased in plastic.

Before she went downstairs for the next piece, Meri looked around, appraising. It was fresh and pretty, but it also did look a little eggy in here, with these colors. But maybe that was just the mood she was in.

When she'd got everything into the baby's room, including the screwdriver and wrenches the instructions for assembly told her she would need, she went to the linen closet and got a fresh hand towel for between her legs. She could feel that the effort of doing all this had fairly soaked the towel she'd been wearing.

Just as she came back into the baby's room with the dry towel snugged into her panties, there was a motion out the window that caught her eye. Ah, it was Delia! settling into one of the Adirondack chairs in her yard in the weak sunlight. Meri stepped back into what she assumed was the black of the window from the old woman's perspective, and watched her.

She was reading a letter—its envelope lay on her lap and she was wearing her glasses, holding the white paper close to her face. After a moment, she set the pages down in her lap too and leaned back in the chair. She took her glasses off. She held her hand up to the bridge of her nose and massaged it gently. Then her hand fell and she sat utterly still, eyes closed, her face slack, the sunlight glinting off the glasses in her lap.

She'd been home for several weeks. Or back from France, anyway. Not exactly home. Tom's stroke had kept her in Washington most of the time. Meri had hardly seen her, and though she knew it was childish, she couldn't help feeling neglected, cast aside.

MERI HAD WALKED slowly back from work the afternoon that Delia unexpectedly arrived home, looking at the pale green of the tight leaves of the trees overhead, of the shrubs. Here and there a magnolia flared in bloom, and Meri could catch its beery smell as she passed. The first tulips were up.

In her dreamy mood, she came inside. It took her a moment after she started to pry her shoes off to realize that she was hearing voices from Delia's side of the house. Women's voices, rising, falling.

She was confused. Could it be Delia so early? Perhaps something had happened—she'd fallen ill and had to return ahead of schedule. But Delia and who else?

Meri had done the house-sitting chores at Delia's again this spring, though she'd spent less time there than she had in the fall. She'd been busier at work and staying later for one thing, but mostly she was ashamed of her earlier behavior.

Still, she had thought of the letters often, particularly after she met Tom at Christmas. She had thought of their language—the language of deep desire, of yearning and loss—and tried to put it together with the image she had of Tom and Delia from the hour or so she and Nathan had spent with them, the gracious, amusing, poised elderly couple, flirting with each other, flirting with their guests, even as they skillfully managed their visit and then the arrival of their son and his family.

And she always felt a sense of something like hunger every time she walked through the door of Delia's house, though she couldn't have said what for. She'd actually spent a few minutes just the day before sitting in Delia's living room, watching the light fade from the late-afternoon sky through the mostly bare branches of the oak tree in the front yard, her hands on her belly where the baby was restive, elbowing and kicking.

Over dinner that night, she and Nathan had speculated on the voices she'd heard. The next morning Meri had gone across the porch and rung Delia's bell.

A tall, slim woman about fifty answered the door. Her voice was chilly, with a jittery, impatient quality to it. "Yes?" she said. She held the door only partially open, as though she thought Meri was a salesperson, or a Jehovah's Witness. She wore an expensive silk blouse, and her hairdo was expensive too, with carefully frosted high-lights.

Meri introduced herself as Delia's neighbor, gesturing at her own side of the house. She asked if Delia was home.

"No," the woman said. "She's out, doing errands. I'm Nancy Naughton. I'm her daughter. Maybe I can help you?"

Meri explained that she'd been taking care of things while Delia was away, that she'd noticed Delia was back, early, that she hoped everything was all right. Also she wondered whether she should stop her chores.

"Ah," Nancy said. She looked more like her father than like Delia, Meri thought. She was tall, with his long face. But she had neither of her parents' charm.

Though now she said, "Come in for a few minutes, why don't you?"

She stepped back and gestured into the hall. Meri came across the threshold and followed her into the living room.

"Mother's fine," she began as they were sitting down. "It's my father, Tom Naughton . . ." She stopped, looking hard at Meri. "Do you know anything about him?"

Meri nodded. "I actually met him once."

"Oh," she said, eyebrows raised, as though surprised by this. But she went right on. "Yes. Well. My father's had a stroke, so she came back from France ahead of time." She paused. "To *take care of him,"* she said with heavy irony, as though Meri could easily see the absurdity of this.

"Oh!" Meri said. She was thinking of him as he'd been the night she met him, she was remembering him in the photo. "I'm so sorry to hear that."

Nancy nodded.

"Will he be all right?" Meri asked.

"Oh, who knows?" Nancy Naughton said. "No one can say yet. It's possible that he may be able in the end to manage on his own. But he'll need care for quite a while certainly, and my mother imagines that because technically they're still married, that she's somehow . . . obligated to give him that care."

"I see," Meri said, taking it in slowly—the news about Tom, the news about Delia, and then Nancy's attitude toward all of it too. "So she's been with him—Delia—in Washington, then?"

"Yes. She went there straight from France before telling any of us a thing about it. This was Wednesday, three days ago. Stepped off the plane, completely jet-lagged, and started in." At the end of almost each sentence, Nancy's lips pressed together, a kind of physical punctuation mark. "When I heard, I came out immediately, and I've persuaded her to come home for at least a few days."

"Ah-ha. To rest."

"Well, yes. And, I hope, to see the folly of this notion that she's going to be in charge. I mean . . ." She paused and looked hard at Meri. "How well do you know my mother?" she asked abruptly.

Meri lifted her shoulders. "We're neighbors. My husband and I moved in last September. I enjoy Delia. I can't claim to know her well."

"But you know about her and my father."

"Well . . . I've surmised a bit. I mean, he doesn't live here with her, obviously." Meri was blushing.

Nancy's hand moved a little, dismissing any of Meri's conclusions. "My mother is a very loyal person," she said. "Which is too bad, as my father isn't. He left her years ago, left her for a completely inappropriate choice—a very much younger woman. Which didn't work out, of course. And since then there have been many others." Her eyebrows rose. "*Many* others. Who also, as it happened, didn't work out. But my mother—and here's the loyalty thing. I mean, they've always stayed friends. She's helped him politically."

She drew her chin in, doubling it. "Anyway, you can see, I think, how disastrous it would be for her to get sucked into this unattractive proposition—being his caretaker or nurse or whatever, now that he's incapacitated."

"Yes, of course. Well." What to say? "Well, I can see that of course that would be . . . upsetting, to you."

"No, it's *not* upsetting, because it's just unthinkable." She breathed deeply. "I shouldn't be boring you with all this. Just, that's the story, for the moment."

"Well, it's not boring, of course," Meri said. There was an awkward silence. "So Delia's home . . . for a while, then?" she asked finally.

"No, no. Just a few days. Then she insists on going back to Washington. Meanwhile, I'm on the phone, madly trying to make arrangements behind her back, that's how crazy this is. Good enough arrangements that she'll feel comfortable leaving him there."

"In Washington."

"Yes."

"But, in a nursing home?" Meri was thinking of the VA hospital her father had been in at the end of his life. When you came in, you were assaulted by the smell of urine and the braying of men in wheelchairs in the hallways, next to the nurses' stations, crying out for help—to be changed, to be fed. To go home, now.

"Well, or a retirement community with some nursing care. But a place that will have a rehabilitation center for people like him."

"But is Delia . . . ? I mean, is that what she wants? I can't imagine . . ."

Nancy's hand dismissed Meri again. "I'm good at persuasion. And it's so clearly the only reasonable choice."

"Well." Meri got up. Nancy got up too, and they started out of the living room, down the front hall. "Good luck, I guess," Meri said. "Maybe I'll see Delia before you go back. But please, if you could tell her I stopped by. And to let me know when and if she wants me to take up my chores again."

As they said good-bye at the door, Meri was struck again by something hard, something embittered in Nancy's face. But maybe, she told herself, it was just the presence of the fierce, deep lines around Nancy's mouth that unfairly made her look that way.

As she talked with Nathan about it that night—talked about what Nancy had told her of Tom's stroke, what Nancy had said about Delia and Tom and their marriage—Meri was gradually conscious that she was feeling relief. Relief in being able to discuss with Nathan the things she'd known all along from reading Tom's letters; relief that she could be honest, with him at last about all of that.

Or partially honest, anyway.

WHEN MERI STOPPED working on the crib for a minute and looked out the window again, Delia was gone from her backyard. The chair was empty. She resolved to ask Nathan about a time they could have her over for drinks or dinner, if she was going to be around for longer than a day or two.

It took her more than an hour to get the crib set up. When it was ready, she put the mattress in it. In the bureau drawer she found a stack of rubber-coated pads covered in flannel and she laid one on the mattress. She unwrapped the plastic from around a crib sheet. It had little figures printed on it, animals—rabbits, kangaroos, sheep. All the sweet ones, she thought. None of the killers.

She made the bed, and stepped back. It looked nice, actually. It looked as if they were people who'd planned for this baby, organized themselves around it, instead of the slackers they were. She went downstairs to start supper.

When Nathan came home, she took him upstairs. He was

impressed, but he was also worried about her having done it by herself. "Should you be doing this stuff? Working so hard this late in the pregnancy?"

"Oh, sure," she said. "It was like mild exercise. It was probably good for me."

Over dinner, they talked about what else they had to do—Nathan was taking the weekend off, just to focus on baby-related chores at last. Meri had a pen and pad by her place at the dining room table, and while they talked, she jotted down what they'd need to buy, what had to get done.

As they were clearing their places, she said, "I saw Delia today."

"And what's happening with her?"

"I don't know. I just saw her. We didn't talk. She was out in the backyard when I was up in the baby's room." She set her dishes on the drainboard. "She looked tired."

"I'm sure she is," Nathan said. "We should have her over."

"My thought exactly," Meri said. And then she said, "I wonder how *he* is."

When she came to bed with Nathan, late, she'd slung another towel between her legs. She'd explained to him earlier the genius of this arrangement. Now she wondered aloud why she hadn't thought of it earlier.

"Because, of course, it's so attractive too," he said.

They laughed, and Nathan switched the lamp off. He touched her face, he kissed her quickly, bringing her his swimming pool smell—and then he fell back away from her and both of them turned on their sides. They hadn't made love in almost a month, it seemed by mutual consent. Certainly Meri had no interest.

Maybe it was the exertion of the previous day, but Meri slept through until almost five in the morning. This was unprecedented in her life of late. Usually the pressure on her bladder got her up several times in the night.

When she woke, it was with the first easy contraction of her labor. Even as she realized this, even as she was taking it in, she was also taking in the fact that the bed was soaked. Nathan was snoring lightly. The wet towel between her legs and the sheet under her were clammy and cold. What a disgrace, she thought. What a disgrace I am.

She eased out of bed and stood, feeling liquid gush out of her. In the bathroom, she removed the towel. It was soaked and there was a faint, pink smear of blood on it. For a moment she was startled, and then she realized: this had to be her waters. Not urine, then. Perhaps not urine yesterday either, though she wasn't sure of that. She stood, looking at herself in the mirror for a minute. What came now? What was the next step here? She put the bloody towel into the hamper. She washed her legs, her crotch. She got a clean towel and put it between her legs. She brushed her teeth, and her hair. She washed her face. Bending over the sink to rinse the soap off, she felt another tightening of her body.

She was frightened, suddenly. She wasn't ready for this. They'd been to only a few birthing classes, they'd both been so busy. She hadn't packed a bag with any of the things you were supposed to pack a bag with. She didn't even remember what those things were. Somewhere in the house was the book they'd bought that told them all that, she could see it in her mind's eye—a fat yellow book with a happily pregnant woman on the front cover, her hands resting lovingly on her belly. *Now* was when they'd been planning to read it carefully, now that they were done with work. Now was when they'd been going to do everything.

She went downstairs. She searched the shelves in the living room for the book, the book that would tell her what to do next. It wasn't there. She went back upstairs, to her study. It wasn't there, either.

She sat down in her desk chair for the next contraction. It was almost five-thirty. She noted the time, and went downstairs again. She would time the contractions, time the intervals between them— she remembered that this was important information, information the doctor would need. She made coffee for herself and she had some toast. She ate a banana too. She had another contraction, like a terrible cramp, while she was doing all this. The interval had been twelve minutes.

At a little before seven, when the intervals were still about ten or twelve minutes, she called the doctor and got her answering service.

She gave the woman at the other end of the line the timing, and told her she thought that her waters had broken too.

Ten minutes later, as she was stopped with another contraction, her coffee cup set down on the counter, the doctor called back. She asked Meri about the contractions, about the blood, about exactly when her waters had broken. Meri said this morning sometime, while she was asleep. That she woke to a wet bed.

And then she said she wasn't sure, but she thought they might have been leaking since yesterday morning, actually. The doctor's voice sharpened. She asked Meri what made her think so, and Meri described it, the liquid leaving her body, the damp towels through the day and overnight.

The doctor told her to come in to the birthing center now. "I think we may need to get that labor going," she said. "I don't like a baby to be high and dry for too long in there." Meri said she'd be there within a half hour and hung up.

Nathan was coming down the back stairs—she heard his footsteps. She turned to see him step into the kitchen barefoot, wearing his pajama bottoms and a T-shirt. His hair was scrambled, his eyes puffy. "Who called?" he asked, frowning. "What's going on?"

IN THE BIRTHING CENTER, everything happened quickly, too quickly for Meri. There was the ugly hospital johnny she had to put on, and the exam with Nathan standing right there while the doctor's hand went inside her. There was the frowning, serious, pretty doctor, peeling the glove from her hand, wanting to know why Meri hadn't called her yesterday. Meri felt in the wrong, as though she hadn't lived up to her part of some bargain.

The doctor said they were going to start her on a drip of Pitocin to speed things up. She was sorry to do it, it was likely to make the labor harder, she said, but she felt it was necessary. The concern seemed to be the possibility of infection after the waters were broken—but for whom? For the baby? for her? Meri wasn't sure. The doctor hadn't said, and Meri had felt too rushed, too confused to ask.

They stuck a needle in her hand, and hooked her up to a bag of fluid on a pole. And then suddenly she and Nathan were alone in the birthing room.

"Hey," he said. He sat down next to her at the edge of the bed.

"Hi," she answered.

"It's exciting, isn't it?" he said.

She smiled at him, and nodded. "It is." It was. She was excited. And scared.

She looked around the room, only now really taking it in. Everything seemed to her like the adult equivalent of the crib sheet she'd put on the baby's mattress yesterday: everything was prettied up, everything was *nice*—the bed with flowered sheets, the La-Z-Boy reclining chair with its striped slipcover. Even the curtains.

"What's *dimity*, Nathan?" she asked.

"Where is *this* coming from?" He looked incredulous, and then amused too. He'd pulled on a T-shirt and some jeans, and his jogging shoes. His hair was still a mess.

She lifted her hand toward the window. "Just that I have a sneaking suspicion those curtains are dimity," she said.

"Look, if you say the curtains are dimity at this particular point in time, I'm going to say they are too. But if I were you, I wouldn't waste my advantage on the *curtains*."

She laughed. And then a contraction started. "Here we go," she said to him.

It was harder, fiercer than any so far, and Meri wasn't able not to make noise through it. Nathan held her hand through it. As her noises eased, so did his grip, and only then did she realize how hard he'd been squeezing her.

"Too tight," she said, when she could speak. She was rubbing her hand.

"I'm sorry," he said. "Just, you scared me."

"Imagine how much I scared myself," she said. "It really hurt, Nate." He kissed the top of her head. "I'm so unbrave," she said.

"You are not."

"Am too."

After a minute she pointed to the pole, the bag of liquid dripping into her arm. "Did you get exactly why I'm on this?"

"Because your waters broke a while ago? Because that's not good?"

"But why?"

"I guess you and the baby are sort of . . . open to the air, as it were. To germs. That's what I gathered anyway. And I guess the labor wasn't going much of anyplace on its own at this point."

She sighed. "How can it be that I'm a fuckup already?"

"The kid will never know. We'll never tell him."

"Or her."

"Or her."

After a minute, Meri said, "But Nate, don't you have to tell the truth once you have a kid?"

"Was that in the pregnancy book?" he asked.

She smiled. "Neither of us has the least idea whether it was or not."

"Well, we're both fuckups," Nathan said.

Over the next half hour the contractions gradually intensified and the intervals between them shortened, and then suddenly Meri was swept by a wave of pain in her back and belly that grew so extreme that she cried out in a guttural deep roar of agony, of insult, a voice she hardly recognized as her own. The nurse, who had come in to check on the baby's heartbeat just before the contraction started, stood still and watched her.

Even after the pain subsided, Meri was panting—grunting really, each breath coming out angry and deep. And it seemed to her that she barely had time to breathe normally again before the next contraction came and she was making her noise again, her mouth open wide now in shock. The nurse left to get the doctor.

When she came in, she took one look at Meri, hunched over the end of the bed, roaring, and she grabbed the drip, she made some adjustment to it.

After that the intervals between contractions grew gradually longer again, but the overwhelming force of them didn't change. Meri waited, dreading each one, grunting much of the time between them now. Each time she was seized, her knees bent, on their own it seemed. She squatted, holding whatever was closest—Nathan, the bed, the La-Z-Boy recliner. She felt as though her spine would crack, her body rip open. She couldn't believe there could be such pain without permanent damage, without death. She was terrified.

She knew she was making too much noise—Nathan's frightened face showed it, and the nurse spoke gently to her over and over, trying to calm her: "Meri. Can you stop now, and just breathe? Just breathe. Just use your panting."

But it seemed Meri couldn't, though in the intervals between blows she was sometimes quieter. But then the brute pain would seize her again, would hold her in its vise, and she would roar, she was so scared, she was so angry, she was so beside herself.

The hours went by, though each time the pain came she couldn't imagine how she would bear the next minute. Her throat grew sore and dry from crying out, and they gave her ice chips to suck on. Sometimes she walked in the intervals, sometimes Nathan rubbed her back as she stood braced against the wall. For a while she found that she could endure the seizures better if she was on all fours, kneeling on the bed. She felt like an animal, a beast, braying in terror.

At some point she noticed that the light in the window had faded, and then later, that it was gone. The nurse stayed in the room, checking the baby's heartbeat often, and the doctor came in frequently; and then, when the window had gone black, there was another, different doctor, one who had apparently taken over.

By now, though, Meri had stopped caring who was there, whose hand was going up her. She was limp, lost, between contractions, and then helpless and lost too in their grip. It seemed impossible to her that it could go on, but it did. It went on and on.

When she began to weep at the end of one long seizure, Nathan turned to the nurse. "Can't you help her? Can't you give her something?"

Nathan. Nathan was her husband. Nathan would make them stop this. Meri felt such love for him in that moment, such hope lift her.

The nurse said, "I hate to do that, when she's getting so close." She turned to Meri. "Meri?" She spoke louder, as though Meri were deaf. "Meri, just a little longer, honey. You can do it. I bet you can."

"No, no," she said, shaking her head. And then she bellowed

through another long convulsion that seemed unending, unbearable. When she was done, she sat slumped on the edge of the bed. Mucus ran from her nose, tears from her eyes. She was panting. The nurse was holding her hand, her arm around the back of what had once been Meri's waist.

"I want it to stop," Meri croaked. "I want an epidural."

"You're sure?" the nurse said, disappointment in her voice.

"Yes, yes, I'm fucking sure!" Meri said.

The nurse went out. The doctor came in and checked Meri once more. She too asked Meri if she was sure, and Meri, weeping openly now at the start of another contraction, cried out, "Yes! Yes, yes."

When the anesthesiologist came, Meri had to lie down for a swab of something cold on her back, for the needle. Just afterward, just as she was curling tight on the bed through another hard seizure, she felt it—her body's easing. It seemed the most wonderful thing that had ever happened to her, it seemed a miracle. And in a few more minutes—so fast!—she was truly numb.

She was still lying curled up on the bed, crying harder now in the gratitude that had swept her. Nathan, misunderstanding, held on to her hands, tight, trying to give her courage. "I love you," he whispered. "I love you."

"No, no, it's all right," she told him. But then she realized that her voice wasn't doing that, wasn't saying that. That she was still just making noise. She shut her mouth. She put her hands over it. After a minute of silence, Nathan brushed the hair off her face. She took her hand from her mouth. With the tears still streaming down her face, she said, "It's working, Nate. It's better," and he bent over her in the bed in relief.

AFTER THAT IT was bearable, the pain more a feeling of intense tightening, of great pressure, only her back still splitting, so that she moaned, sometimes she even cried out. But she was not, as she felt she had been before, reduced to some monstrous creature. And she was so exhausted by now that she actually dropped off into a dizzy short nap in the brief intervals between pains.

Thirteen hours had passed in an eternity. She was barely aware of the next three as she drifted in and out of sleep.

They stopped the epidural before the delivery so she could push. Meri heard her voice start up again, but there was some relief in the pushing, in feeling she was making something happen. She was sitting up now at the end of the bed, her legs spread wide, her feet planted in the stirrups she had asked for in order to brace herself. Nathan sat behind her, holding her up. She could feel him bearing down against her back, bending with her as she pushed, as she willed this baby—this horror that wanted to tear her apart—out. She yelled at it. She screamed. "Out! Out! Out!" This was the enemy. Never had she had such an enemy. "Out!" she screamed. She was full of fury.

The doctor called back to her, "Yes! That's good, that's good!"

They'd set a mirror up so Meri could see herself, the impossibly distended version of her sex, made meat now, bloody and purple, unrecognizable as it gaped open. And now a flat *thing*, the whitish, blood-streaked top of the head appeared inside it, and Meri bellowed and pushed. It paused. It went back. It seemed stuck. Beside herself, enraged, Meri pushed and yelled again. She pushed so hard her eyes hurt, and Nathan pushed against her. And then it was out, the head was out! It was a creature down there, bloody, crusted with gunk. Her panting slowed. Her body wanted nothing but to rest.

"Just a little more now," the doctor said. "One more, one more for the shoulders. Ah, it's easy now, it's easy."

Meri pushed again as hard as she could and felt the baby, the pain, slip away. It was gone. It was over.

She sagged back against Nathan, and he held her. He was kissing her hair, her ear, he was laughing lightly in relief.

"It's a boy," he said. He swept the hair off her face. "Look, sweetheart, it's a boy."

But it didn't matter to her. She had turned to rest against Nathan's chest and she wanted only to stay here, to sleep, to be without pain. She didn't turn. She didn't look. Her eyes were shut. It just didn't matter to her.

CHAPTER TWELVE

Meri, May and June 1994

THE MEMORY OF the labor was like a nightmare whose ugliness ran through the days afterward. Meri felt it as a kind of displacement from herself, a displacement that fed her sense of distance from Asa.

Everything she did for him—and when was she not doing something for him?—she did with a sense of belatedness, of absence, of exhaustion and incapacity. He cried. He cried because he was hungry, or because even though he was hungry, he didn't seem to be able to fix on her breast. He cried because as soon as he fixed on her breast and sucked for a few minutes, he fell asleep again, and then, within twenty minutes or so, woke, famished. He cried because no sooner had he nursed than he threw it all up, white curdish stuff with a sharp, sour smell.

He cried because he was sleepy and wasn't yet asleep, because he was waking up, because he was wet, because he'd shat in his diaper, because he was about to vomit, because, it seemed to her, he didn't want to be here. How could this be her life, this sleepless, exhausted stumble from one failed activity to another?

She was unable not to watch him. She sat by him as he slept, observing the puckering and smoothing of his face, the little convulsive starts of his body. He seemed so unhappy. Sometimes he stiffened and straightened out. Sometimes he lay with everything curled up, his legs and his pathetic arms folded in. He had oddly too-large hands—hands that were at the same time so tiny they frightened her. His hair was patchy, dry and black, unattractive. His head was elongated from the pressure of the labor and birth. His navel and penis were still bandaged. His open mouth, when he shrieked, was all tongue and naked gums. When she picked him up, he felt boneless, limp. His limpness itself felt like a rebuke to her.

She wished she had had a girl. She wished she'd said no to Nathan, that she wasn't ready, that she couldn't do it. She thought of the shock of the labor and the way it had changed her, taken her over. Asa seemed almost as unreal, as impossible as that.

The second weekend Meri and Asa were home, Nathan's mother, Elizabeth, came up from New Jersey. Meri felt so exhausted that she wasn't sure she wanted her, but once Elizabeth arrived, she was grateful. She was as undemanding as ever, and she took over Asa's care almost completely in the daytime. Meri napped twice in the two days Elizabeth was there, hours-long naps that felt like small, restorative deaths.

Waking, lying in their bed, she could hear the peace Elizabeth had brought to the house, the noises of kitchen work below her, sometimes Asa crying briefly in a way that didn't seem connected to her. She could hear Nathan talking, his voice alive and buoyant as it wasn't with her now, maybe because he was so shocked at what she'd gone through, at the state of fatigue she was in, at her bloodshot eyes.

Cooking smells floated up, food appeared, Elizabeth brought Asa in to nurse, and then whisked him away.

Nathan and Elizabeth went shopping, they got the things Meri and Nathan should have bought long ago. They showed her—the baby carriage on the front porch, the straw basket with handles for Asa to lie in, the little pack to carry him in. In the spare bathroom sat several enormous boxes of Pampers, and in Meri and Nathan's bathroom, a box of maxipads for her almost as big.

Elizabeth was small, plump, energetic. She made Meri even more aware of her own huge body, still sore, still so swollen she looked four months gone. And she made Meri feel inept—she seemed so utterly at ease with Asa. She picked him up unhesitatingly and walked around the house with him tucked back along her bent arm, his head resting on her hand. She popped him in the Snugli while she did the dishes.

Inspired by Asa, she spoke of Nathan as an infant. He too had regularly fallen asleep at the breast. He too had cried when he was in the process of falling asleep. "You can't pick him up," she said to Meri. "It just makes it take longer. Just leave, you'll see. Leave, walk right out, and in five minutes' time he'll be sound asleep."

Meri was more dubious about some other things she said. That babies *ought* to cry sometimes, that you couldn't let them have their way or they'd be spoiled. That she should start bottle-feeding within a month or so, so Nathan could take some responsibility too. That it wasn't healthy for them to have him in bed with them at night, which they did.

Coming to bed a few nights after Elizabeth had left, carrying Asa—newly Pampered, powdered, and fed—Meri mentioned this to Nathan.

He looked at her—at her and Asa. "You know you don't have to do everything the way my mother did it. You don't have to do *anything* the way she did."

"Yeah, but do you think she's right?"

"Right, wrong, I don't think those apply."

After a moment, she said, "You sound so *wise,* Nate."

He smiled, sheepishly. "I don't mean to," he said. "What do I know?" He shrugged. "I just mean whatever you do is probably okay. Is probably just fine. As fine as whatever my mother does."

"She was a big help."

"I know. Just, she's not the source of absolute wisdom of any kind."

Asa wuffled and snuffled, then turned a little to the side and slept again. Nathan was reading. Meri was doing nothing. She was often doing nothing now, when she wasn't tending to Asa. After a while, she said, "The thing is, Nate, she's relaxed around him. She's not scared."

He put his book down. "And you are."

She nodded.

"You're scared of Asa?" He sounded incredulous.

She fought down the tears that threatened. "I'm terrified," she said.

IN THE DAYS after Elizabeth left, Meri tried some of her tricks. She put him in the Snugli while she did the dishes, while she picked up. She even ventured out on a walk with him. But she was still waiting to feel what she'd thought she would feel. What she was supposed to feel. This was what she said to the pediatrician on the first visit.

"Oh, don't worry about *supposed-to* feelings." The pediatrician was another pretty young woman. All the prettiest ones must specialize in obstetrics or pediatrics, Meri thought.

"But I feel so guilty. He's like . . . an alien, to me."

The doctor was bent over the baby, smiling at him, pulling her finger away from Asa's tiny grip. She looked over at Meri for a moment. "What's your model here?" she asked.

"Model?" Meri said.

"For mothering. Yes." She stood up. She tilted her pretty head, smiled, and said, "What was *your* mom like?"

Meri laughed sharply. Sadly. "Brain-dead?" she offered.

MERI GOT ALMOST nothing done in the course of a day except tending to Asa. When Nathan came home—early now, and reliably, as he had no classes and was just trying to finish his book—he was astonished. Astonished at the dishes still on the counter and in the old sink. At the food left out, the bed unmade, the diapers heaped in the baby's room and the bathroom.

She tried. Sometimes she started the day by tidying up, by doing a load of wash, by cleaning the kitchen. But usually by the end of the day, everything had gotten away from her. The only thing she did reliably was to listen to the radio every day from twelve to one, sometimes through Asa's wails. She listened to Jane's voice, to Brian's, and thought about how much she wished she were back there. How differently she would have done this piece, on girls' sports; this other one on the building of a controversial dam. But mostly she just pictured it, imagined how it felt—the long dark corridor with posters on the walls, the glass windows between the engineers and the broadcast rooms, the coffee mugs everywhere. She thought of the afternoon meetings, the jokes, the excitement over some story idea or another. She thought of herself there, that other version of herself, unbruised, uncut—that whole, independent Meri—with a yearning that once or twice brought tears to her eyes.

DELIA WAS HOME. Meri heard her one evening in the kitchen—the pipes thumping and a distant clatter. The next morning the phone rang. It was she, wondering if this was a good time to come over "for a viewing," she called it.

Meri was wearing Nathan's jeans and a T-shirt with milk stains where her breasts had leaked through it. She was standing in bare, dirty feet in the kitchen. She had just buttered some toast to have for breakfast. Asa was upstairs, beginning to stir, to make the little scratchy noises that signaled the onset of waking, of hunger.

Nathan had cleaned the kitchen carefully before he left for work, so things didn't look too bad, but Meri was not ready, she felt, for Delia. It wasn't just that she needed to clean up, to wash her hair, to change clothes. It was also that she needed to change *herself* somehow to meet Delia, with her lively presence. With the way in which that presence demanded your energy in return.

"I'm just about to go through the cycle with the baby," she said. "You know, changing, feeding, changing, et cetera. So it's not so good right now. Could you come this afternoon? About two or so?"

"Two is *perfect*," Delia said.

And at two promptly she rang the bell. Meri opened the door, and Delia stepped in. Meri was holding Asa curled up against her shoulder and neck. He smelled of Pampers and baby talc. She smelled clean too—her hair, her body. She'd put on an old sundress that was still snug, but not as bad as it had been last week. As usual, she had a towel slung over one shoulder.

"Here you are," Delia said, her arm sweeping the air grandly in Meri's direction. "The one, miraculously become two."

"Some miracle," Meri said.

"Oh, I know!" Delia said in instant sympathy. "No one has ever truly conveyed the scope of it. *Labor* is finally such an . . . *inadequate* word."

She was holding a basket again—she must have a closetful of empties, Meri thought. It was full of things tied with gold ribbon. They sat down in the living room, and Delia asked to hold Asa. "We'll trade," she said, and held up the basket. Meri passed him over to the old woman, as an afterthought passing the towel from her shoulder too. And then it occurred to her: "But don't you want some coffee, Delia? Or water?" She realized abruptly how little there was in the kitchen to offer. "A beer?"

"I don't want a thing, dear. Just to gape at this darling boy. What have you named him?"

Meri told her.

"Asa," she repeated. "How lovely he is." Delia laid him on her lap, his head in her hands at her knees, her arms resting on her legs along his sides. His face was looking up at her, he was frowning. "Hello, beautiful boy," she said, smiling down. "He*llo*, beautiful boy." She lifted him gently, up and down, rocking her whole body. "What are you like, you lovely new person?" She looked up at Meri. "Is he what they call 'a good baby'?"

Meri shrugged. "I wouldn't know. He's sort of . . . not *there* yet, as far as I can tell."

Delia's gaze sharpened. "Ah, you're having a hard time with it all."

"Yes. Well, no. I'm doing okay. I'm just . . ." Tears suddenly sprang to her eyes. "It's okay, really. It's just that I guess I'm not by nature very maternal."

"You will be. You will be fine."

"Well," she nodded, "thanks for your vote."

"It's very hard, I think, caring for someone so . . . utterly dependent, especially when you haven't before. But it will ease, very soon, really, and *you* will be easier, and at some point you'll realize that

you've passed through this, that everything is just as it should be."
Delia's voice was warm and gentle. Her body was still moving slightly
as she rocked the baby, but her attention seemed to be focused
entirely on Meri, and Meri felt it as another kind of gift. Maybe this
was what she had wanted from Delia all along. She was afraid she
might cry.

"Open those presents, dear," Delia said abruptly.

Meri looked down and took the first of the presents out. None
of them was wrapped, just tied with the ribbon. There was a striped
T-shirt and matching shorts for Asa, and a book, *The Shipping News.*

"To read while you're nursing," Delia said. "It's supposed to be
quite good."

There were several pacifiers in different shapes, one with a
straight short nipple, one with a longer one, one whose nipple was
wide and curled. "Apparently there's some disagreement about the
way a baby's mouth is formed," Delia said. "But if you don't believe in
pacifiers, you can just chuck them all."

"*Do* I believe in pacifiers?" Meri asked. "This is not something I
know about myself, I'm afraid."

Delia smiled and said, "You'll make lots of discoveries about what
you believe in and what you don't as this one grows up. Children: if
nothing else they force you to take a stand. On practically everything."

"Like what?"

"Well, for now, pacifiers or not. Then there's the question of
breast-feeding versus bottles. Later it will get even more complicated. Later come sex and booze, and maybe drugs. 'Are any of these
okay for my darling child? And if they're okay, how much? at what
age?' And on and on and on." She smiled and shook her head. "It's
endless, really."

Meri reached into the basket again. There was a rattle, a simple
picture book, and a short nightgown for Meri. Black. Sexy.

Meri held it up. "It's gorgeous, Delia." Delia had the baby against
her shoulder now. "And maybe in a year or two, I'll find a use for it."

"Nonsense. That will come back too, sooner than you think."

"It seems unlikely. I just feel so exhausted. So *mired.*"

"We're both mired, dear. Perhaps we can help each other out."

"You're mired?"

"With Tom. He's to come home in a few weeks."

"Home. To you? Here? To the house?"

"Yes. He's in a rehabilitation place in Putnam for a bit, but then I'll have him, until he can manage on his own. Assuming he'll be able to. We'll see. But I think it's going to work just fine."

"But I thought he was going to stay in Washington."

"Oh, no." She shook her head. "That was never the plan."

"But when I spoke to Nancy . . . to your daughter . . ."

Delia smiled, a worn smile. "Nancy would have chosen that, but it wasn't her choice to make, you see."

"But, isn't he . . .? She said he was, pretty . . ."

"Damaged. Yes. He is, that's true. But he's already made progress. Good progress. And they think there's a chance for a reasonable recovery. And he's *himself*, which is what's important to me."

"So, he can talk?"

"Well, some." Delia smiled. "You might not call it talking. But he can . . . communicate. He knows me, he has wishes and wants that he signals me. Like our little friend here." She patted Asa. His head was tucked under her chin.

Meri was surprised, surprised and then impressed with Delia, that she'd won, that she could be so stubborn, so powerful. Meri would have bet on Nancy.

"And more," Delia said now, her face lifting. "He's funny, sometimes. He's happy every now and then. He's there, you can see it in his eyes. Behind his eyes." Delia shrugged. "It makes it all seem eminently doable."

"But, by yourself, Delia?" she said.

"Oh, I'll have help. Tom, in case you hadn't noticed, is loaded." She raised her eyebrows significantly. "And *I* have access to that. That part will be the easy part."

"And the hard part?"

"This," Delia said, holding the baby out a little, looking at him. His head lolled. "This dependence. This helplessness." She smiled at Meri. "Only instead of sustaining myself, as you must do, by dreaming of who he'll *become*, your fine boy, I'll dream of who Tom was, once upon a time."

They talked a while more. Delia said she was still working at the Apthorp house, that she was going to continue to work. Meri told her a little of the labor and birth, and about Elizabeth's visit. Delia offered to babysit too, and insisted that they set a time. Meri said she'd check with Nathan. Maybe they could have a quick dinner out somewhere in a couple of weeks.

"Or not so quick," Delia said. "Think about that."

It wasn't until Delia was gone, until the house was suddenly silent but for Asa's little rooting noises against her shoulder, that she thought about what Delia had said about Asa and Tom, that she realized, almost startling herself with it, that she hadn't once dreamed of Asa as becoming anyone other than who he was. She hadn't imagined a life, a future for him beyond this, beyond here, where she was stuck, with him.

MERI HAD READ that when babies were troubled sleepers, riding in the car could be helpful. They'd been given a car seat by one of Nathan's colleagues, and Nathan had installed it, but it hadn't occurred to Meri until now to do anything other than errands with Asa; and in truth, Nathan had been the main shopper, the errand runner, since Asa was born.

One day, though, when Asa seemed inconsolably tired and yet couldn't stop crying long enough to drop off, she took him to the car, strapped him into his seat in the back, and drove to the highway at the edge of town. He was asleep before she got there.

Once she pulled into the rushing traffic, though, she was frightened by its speed, and also by her inability to turn and monitor Asa at all. She took the second exit she came to, to Route 43 North and Correy. It seemed to her she'd heard of it. Someone she'd met in the past year must live there.

She got on a two-lane road, winding through fields and little villages where she had to slow down to twenty-five. As she came into Correy, she remembered: it was a colleague of Nathan's who lived here. She and Nathan had gone to her house in the winter sometime, driving here through the dark one evening. The whole night seemed years ago.

The hills, which looked blue and distant from Williston, were closer here. They loomed over the town. The fields she passed through were small, prettier than the vast squared acreage of the Midwest—wedged in odd, organic shapes, their boundaries ending at streams, hills, the edges of towns, tree lines. She passed several men out on large, rusty red tractors, mowing hay. Asa, tilted awkwardly in his car seat, seemed happily silent.

And then he'd been silent for so long that she leaned back to look at his face, and saw that he was awake, that he was staring out the window above him. At what? She leaned forward and looked up out the windshield as she drove. The shapes of the trees and the clouds, she supposed. Or more likely, the way the darkness of the trees alternated with the blue light of the open sky.

He didn't fuss for almost two hours. By then they were in a village almost at the state line. Meri pulled off in a turnout overlooking what was called a scenic vista, and nursed him. He was so hungry that he sucked for almost twenty minutes on each breast.

She was hungry too, she realized. When he was finished, when she'd burped him and changed him, she turned the car around, back the way she'd come. She stopped in the first village they passed through and went into the country store. Asa was on her shoulder. She picked out two candy bars, ones she had liked in her youth, a Butterfinger and an Almond Joy. There was a young girl of maybe fourteen or fifteen at the cash register, apparently manning the store alone. She was a pale redhead, with freckles and white eyebrows and lashes. As Meri was paying for the candy, she asked, "How old's your baby?"

"Almost a month," Meri said. And then realized. "A little over a month, actually."

"He's *so cute*," the girl said, leaning over to smile at Asa. She had braces on her teeth, and Meri felt a tug of sympathy for her, for her homeliness.

"Thank you," Meri answered.

As she bent over Asa putting him back in his car seat, she looked closely at him, trying to be objective. Was he cute?

He was better than he'd been at first. He'd fattened and filled out. The patchy dark hair was mostly gone and thin, paler hair glinted blond on his scalp. His slate-blue eyes staring up at her seemed to be taking something in, or trying to. His limbs had the beginning of real flesh, rounded flesh, on them. "Asa," she said, and he frowned and opened his mouth.

So now she drove almost every day, unless it was raining or she had things she had to get done in the house. She liked to go slowly, to look around her at the lazy town greens, at the sudden, shocking abject poverty that presented itself—rusted cars and appliances in a yard, clothes hung to dry on a porch slowly listing sideways away from a house with almost no paint left. Cars piled up behind her, and she pulled over when she could to let them pass. Then she started out again, looking, trying to imagine the lives, the way they might play out in places like the ones she saw.

Asa rode silently, sleeping or looking, his eyes perhaps trying to make sense of all this. She saw them moving, saw his hands and feet lift and move in what must have been his version of excitement—or interest, anyway. She felt a sense of companionship with him in those moments: he'd been feeling trapped too. She'd been able at last to offer him something he liked.

Sometimes Meri brought food with her. Sometimes she stopped in a store and bought something—fruit, if she was feeling virtuous and they had it. More often chips or a candy bar or a can of cashew nuts. Occasionally she stopped at a little coffee shop or an inn for a sandwich and something to drink.

She was at such a shop one afternoon, a rectangular box of a room with a few booths along one long wall and a counter along the other and three square tables pushed up next to the plate-glass window at the front. She was sitting at one of these. She'd ordered some tea and half a tuna sandwich, which came with a pickle and potato chips. Asa had been asleep when she came in, and he slept long enough to let her eat part of the sandwich. But then his nickering complaint in the Snugli began. Quickly, so he wouldn't start shrieking, she slipped him out of the little pack, laid him back across her left arm, and with her right hand, lifted up her shirt by his head.

He turned to her and immediately found her nipple—he was getting better at this, at least some of the time. Meri turned her body away from the window. She was able to reach over Asa with her free hand and have a sip of tea, grab a chip from time to time. But mostly she held him, watching him intently as she often did, as though she could somehow discover who he was and how to love him by looking at the way he performed his small repertoire of behaviors.

She had just had the thought—which made her smile, a little sadly—that to an observer she would be a picture of maternal devotion, nursing as she was, turned to watch her tiny child, when the door opened and an elderly couple entered. They were overdressed for the hot day, for the shop. They paused just inside the door. Tourists, Meri thought. They had the air of surveying the narrow room, likely making a decision about where to sit, something a local wouldn't have had to do. They murmured to each other, and started toward one of the two other little tables by the window.

Meri was still watching them, so she saw the quick recoil on the old woman's part, how her fat placid face was made suddenly ugly when she realized what Meri was doing, when she took in the bit of exposed flesh of Meri's breast, the way the baby's face was pushed into her. Meri saw how she turned, how her husband bumped into her from behind, how they awkwardly moved back from the tables, their bodies almost tangling—the woman's voice lowered, trying to urge him away, far enough away so that she could explain to him the impossibility of sitting where they'd planned to sit.

It would have been comical, Meri thought, if . . . if what?

If it weren't also shocking to her that she, that she and Asa, could be the cause of such revulsion. She felt a sudden sense, the first sense she'd had, of being somehow *in it together*. Asa included in the old lady's disgust. Asa, wronged.

Asa, asleep now, his full lips open, her body's milk a watery white in his mouth.

That night at about ten, she was nursing Asa again, in bed. She'd waked him up to do this, actually, in hopes that she would only have to get up once more before his day started at five or so. But this meant that he kept falling away from her breast, nodding off. She picked him up and burped him vigorously against her shoulder, in part to wake him again. Then she cradled him. "Come on, baby," she said. "Let's do a little *work* here."

At one of the moments when his head had fallen heavily back once more from her wet nipple, she looked up and saw Nathan watching them. Something in his face made her think of the old woman earlier, in the coffee shop. The idea frightened her.

She set Asa down in the little bassinet by the bedside and crawled back over to Nathan. She curled against him. He put his arm around her in what felt like a comradely, comforting way, nothing more. His book lay facedown across his lap. They hadn't made love since well before Asa's birth, though the doctor had told Meri several weeks ago that it would be all right now. Suddenly it seemed urgent to Meri that they should, that Nathan should want her.

She opened her nightgown, she began to stroke her breasts, her body. "Nathan," she whispered.

But he didn't respond. Or rather, he responded by setting his free hand over her moving ones, stilling them. They sat there for a moment, and then Meri turned away. She sat up straight.

"Meri," he said.

She looked at him. *Let him,* she thought. Let him explain this.

"I want you. I do," he said. "It's just that it's so . . . Your whole body is so much, for the baby now. So . . . *functional.* And I'm just feeling it might be easier for me to wait. Just for a while. Just to wait for a while."

She began to cry, silently at first, and then sobbing loudly. She knew what her face looked like, doing this, and she simply didn't care. There was nothing left, nothing to think of as connected to what had once made her pleased with herself physically, to what had made her feel she owned herself, was in charge of herself, could use herself as she wished. To what had made her feel safe, with Nathan. Why not weep if that's what she felt like? Nathan was right—she lived for the baby now, a baby she couldn't know, in spite of her best efforts, and who couldn't know her, except as she failed him.

Nathan had his arms around her again, he'd pushed his book aside. His breath, his voice were in her ear. "Shhh, love. Shhh, Meri. Please. Please."

But Meri was beyond consolation. Her voice soared in its grief. In his bassinet by the bed, Asa woke and added his song to hers.

CHAPTER THIRTEEN

Delia, June 1994

Dᴇʟɪᴀ ʜᴀᴅ ʙᴇᴇɴ in a state of controlled excitement since the moment she woke, around five this morning—woke, thinking *this is the day,* the day he comes home. Now in the car, he'd fallen asleep. She looked over at him from time to time as they drove along. His mouth sagged open. He looked like an old, old man, hardly recognizable as her Tom, the Tom who had always appeared to be years younger than he was, so that sometimes in Washington, people had been confused about what her relationship to him might be: "You're his *wife?*" She'd occasionally been prickly in response.

How strange life was, she thought, that she should be the strong one now, the young one, and he the old man. She pulled into the driveway. She turned off the ignition and looked over at him once more. He was white, his face was sunken. It was so suddenly silent without the noise of the engine. Didn't he hear the difference?

It seemed not.

She got out and opened the back door, pulled the walker out from the backseat and unfolded it. She came around to Tom's door and opened it. She leaned in, she gently pulled on his arm, saying his name, and then she was frightened for a moment. Was he *there?* Had he had another stroke?

But he opened his eyes and saw her, standing above him, holding his walker. "Deeehl," he croaked.

"Yes," she said. "When you're ready."

He moaned, and sat still for a full minute, breathing heavily, regularly, as though to locate himself, as though to gather strength. Then in one long effort, he hurled his body back against the seat and turned it, swinging his bad leg along with his hands.

He was sitting sideways now, facing out of the car, his feet on the ground. He looked around him, at the oak tree, at the lawn, at the old brick house. "Home," he said.

"Yes," she answered. "Finally."

Delia waited a minute or two for him to catch his breath, and then she pushed the walker up to him, around his legs. He leaned forward and put his hands on the top bar. He sat like that for a moment.

"You're tired today," she said.

"Mmmmh." He nodded his head. He tilted it a little to look up at her.

"There's no rush," she said. "We can take forever, if we like. We've *got* forever, you know."

He smiled at her. They waited, not talking. The breeze shook the trees, a door banged somewhere, and she thought she could hear the baby next door cry in that creaky, halfhearted newborn way, but it stopped quickly.

His grip tightened and he started to pull himself up. His body moved, his arms tensed, he came forward, but he seemed unable to get beyond the halfway point. Delia reached for his upper arms and pulled too, pulled him toward her. He was heavy. For a moment it seemed they would fall back into the car, both of them and the walker between them—they were in a ridiculous state of equipoise, their startled eyes looking fully at each other: can we make it?

But then the balance shifted, they teetered slightly Delia's way, and he was up, resting his weight heavily on the walker. They were nearly embracing. He was panting a little, and Delia realized she was too.

She laughed then, in relief, and at the comedy of it. "Graceful, aren't we?" she asked.

He nodded. He was smiling. "Dhans," he blurted. Dance.

"*You* say it's a dance," she answered. "Thousands wouldn't."

When they had recovered, he rolled slowly up the walk, and then she helped him carefully ascend the stone steps. She was grateful for their wasteful width and depth.

Inside the house he moved down the front hall and then paused, as though awaiting instructions.

Delia pointed the way: to the lavatory. "You need to pee, and then you can lie down for a bit. I'll show you your room."

He stopped and looked at her, as though startled, or offended. At what? Perhaps he didn't like her playing the nurse.

Too bad, she thought. Too bad for both of us. "Those are the rules, I'm afraid," she said firmly. "You pee on a schedule now. And it's time."

He turned away. He wheeled slowly to the lav and went in. This was a triumph, she'd been told, that he was continent, that he could manage this on his own—though they'd also told her that some of this was keeping to a regular schedule. That would be part of her job, and Matt's.

When he came out, she was standing in the doorway to the dining room.

"Come see," she said. She couldn't keep the excitement out of her voice.

She stood aside as he rolled in. "We set it all up for you," she said.

He sat down at the edge of the bed, resting his arms on the walker, while she moved slowly around the room, pointing everything out. He watched her steadily. She wasn't sure how much he was taking in. She talked slowly, keeping her vocabulary simple, gesturing—at the bed, the bureau, the rocker, the pictures she'd hung on the wall, the radio on the bedside table. She tapped it. "This is a very fancy number, I'll have you know," she said. "Much more expensive, and, we hope, much better than the one I have in the kitchen."

He nodded, a kind of thanks.

"Do you like it?" she asked. She was nervous about this, she realized.

"Unnh," he said. "Yessh."

"Good. I had two young men as my slaves for hours getting it just so. I enjoyed it, actually."

He smiled at her, but he looked tired. Exhausted, really.

"Do you want to eat in here?" she asked. "I've got a tray I can bring things in on if you want to stay here. Or we can eat in the kitchen."

"Here," he said.

Delia helped him swing his legs up on the bed, and propped him up with pillows. She took his shoes off.

"Do you want the radio on?" she asked.

He nodded.

"Music? Or the news?" she asked.

"Nhooos," he said.

She turned it on, adjusted the volume down, and found the news station. Before she left the room, she kissed him. He reached up and touched her face. "Stay," he said clearly.

"I'll be right back," she said. "I'm going to get us something to eat."

In the kitchen Delia moved around rapidly. She'd boiled eggs early this morning and made egg salad. She'd brewed tea and put it in the refrigerator. She'd mashed strawberries and sprinkled sugar on them. Now it took her only a few minutes to assemble sandwiches and pour iced tea for them both. She set out the ice cream to soften.

After she'd served him, she brought the tray table for herself into the room so she could eat with him. The radio was still on, and she and Tom talked only occasionally. He commented on the news with grunts, with monosyllables. The Clintons had been questioned at the White House about Vincent Foster's death, about Whitewater. The wife of O. J. Simpson had been murdered, and he was a suspect. Two more candidates had announced they would run in the Virginia primary along with Chuck Robb and Ollie North. His head swung in apparent disbelief, and she laughed.

The news was over, and the jazz program came on. When they'd finished eating, she moved his tray to the bureau, and he lay back again. He fell asleep nearly instantly.

She sat for a while in the rocker, watching him. Slowly the room got fully dark. She knew she should wake him, that she needed to get him into his pajamas, to have him go to the bathroom one last time. Then she would go upstairs to her own bathroom, to wash her face and brush her teeth, to change out of her dress.

But just let me sit here for a while longer, she thought.

There was no danger of her falling asleep. She was excited and alert. She was thinking about waking up tomorrow and coming downstairs to find Tom, to greet him, to have breakfast with him. She was thinking about Matt, who would be coming over to meet Tom in the afternoon. She was thinking about the days spooling out from now on, with Tom always at their center.

Finally she got up, she turned the lamp on, she reached over and gently moved his shoulder, said his name.

He turned to her, and his voice was surprised and tender. "Delia!" he said.

"Yes. You're home, darling. And we need to get you ready for bed."

Slowly, laboriously, he stood up. He let her do the work of removing his clothes—he seemed more incapacitated than usual in his fatigue. She wouldn't again let him fall asleep without getting him ready, she thought.

She was moved to see him naked—his skinny old body with the drooping dusky genitals, the pouches at his breasts. She kept whispering slow encouragement, explaining each step. His damaged limbs were heavy and awkward, and he seemed unable to help lift them as she pulled his pajamas on. She minded none of this, though she supposed there would be times to come when she would.

After he'd used the bathroom, after she'd helped him brush his teeth and lie down again, after she'd pulled the sheet and light blanket over him and kissed him just as she used to do for the children each night—after all this, she went upstairs. She wandered the rooms on the second floor as though she were a stranger in her own house, seeing everything for the first time. She looked at her own bedroom, made so comfortable for one person to live in, to grow old in. She went into the guest rooms, peering closely at the pictures of her grandchildren at various stages, at the wedding photos of the kids, all of them so happy to be recklessly hurtling forward into their versions of marriage. She went into her own study and examined the pictures there. The little framed prints of Rodin's erotic watercolors which she'd bought in Paris to discipline herself about Tom's affair with Carolee and the ones after it. The photo on her desk of herself at a family reunion with the kids and their families, as though Tom, the old progenitor, didn't exist.

From next door she heard the faint catlike mewling of the baby, and she thought of Meri. How strange that their lives should be so seemingly parallel in this moment. She remembered calling it *mired*, but she hadn't meant that, not really. Neither of them was mired, though surely it would feel that way every now and then. But Meri would fall in love with her little boy in her own time; and she, of course, had never stopped loving Tom.

After she'd gotten ready for bed, she still felt wakeful. She tried to read, but she was too excited. She looked at the clock. It was only ten-thirty. Perhaps not too late. She dialed Madeleine Dexter's number.

Madeleine said she was in bed, but not asleep yet, which Delia knew was likely a lie. But she needed to talk. She told Madeleine about Tom's arrival home. She summarized his progress, the therapies to come, "among them what they call 'alternate forms of communication,' whatever that may mean."

"But what *does* it mean?" Madeleine asked.

"Oh, who knows?" Delia said. "I just feel—I guess I need to feel, that he will talk normally again." She could imagine it, that they would one day sit again at the kitchen table and talk as they had in the past. He would make her laugh, he would laugh at himself.

"But perhaps what they're saying is that maybe that's not going to happen."

Delia didn't answer.

"Am I right, do you think?" Madeleine's voice was gentle, careful.

"I suppose," Delia said. "I suppose that's what they mean. But what could they be talking about? Notes?"

"I like notes," Madeleine said. "I have notes from Dan and sometimes when I'm lonely, I read through them. It's comforting."

"That's different."

"Of course it's different. But it's real. It's real too."

"But Tom is alive."

"But he's been changed, Delia. It's not going to be as it was."

"They say he's making great strides," Delia said. "His progress is very, very good."

"But there may be some limits on that. It sounds like they're saying that too." Delia was silent, and Madeleine waited for a long moment before she went on. "Sweetie," she said. "I think you feel as though you've waited all these years, and now it's somehow going to *have* to work. He's safe, you're getting him back, so it has to be as it was. But the *reason* it's safe, my darling, the reason you're getting him back, is that it's not as it was."

Delia was silent. She knew Maddy was right. She wanted her not to be.

Maddy's voice was soft, loving, when she spoke again. "You're just a little crazy right now, I think."

CRAZY INDEED.

The next day at the Apthorp house, which was at its busiest time of year right now—the alumni in town for reunions, the tourist season just starting—Delia came into the gift shop to gather the small crowd waiting for the four o'clock tour. It was her second week back at work.

As Delia introduced herself, they turned to her from the books for sale, from the case of Anne Apthorp's letters, from the postcard racks. It was a mixed group of ten or twelve people, including two men her own age wearing straw boaters, striped blazers, and badges that said "Class of 44." They looked like elderly twins, carefully dressed by some demented mother, Delia thought. There were also a family with teenage kids, a couple of women who seemed to be together, and—her breath stopped for a moment—there was Billy Gustafson, Delia would have known him anywhere, her first true love in high school.

"Oh!" she cried, delighted, and crossed the room to him. He was the same—the same silky black hair, the dark eyebrows that almost met over his nose, the same wide, amused mouth—though as she approached him eagerly she could see a look of increasing perplexity, almost fear, cross his face.

And then, just as she was reaching out to touch his sleeve, to claim him, she remembered: of course this wasn't Billy! Billy was her age, gray or white, transformed, withered—if he was alive at all. Her hand flew up, her mouth opened. This young man—this boy, really—was too young by fifty years, sixty years.

"Oh, I'm so *sorry*," Delia said.

Her quickened breath was audible to everyone, she was sure. She needed to talk, to say something to make him more comfortable, to make them all more comfortable. "I thought you were someone else, but now, up close, I see you're not." She laughed, carelessly, she hoped, though her heart seemed to be pounding. "You're *you*, of course! Please forgive me."

She turned away from him to the group, which was watching her curiously. "I'm Delia Naughton," she said, trying to calm her own voice. "I'm here to lead you through the Apthorp house and to answer any questions you have about it. Please," she gestured at the doorway, "let's begin."

She could feel herself settling down as she led them through. She started, as always, in the living room, with the family portraits, talking about their provenance and the questions about their accuracy.

As the tour went on, she monitored herself. She thought she was performing adequately, if not well. As soon as they left, she felt swept with exhaustion. She was grateful they'd been the last group of the day, so that she could go home. Though she remembered now that she had to stop at the supermarket on the way.

The accident was entirely her fault, which is what she said to the woman driving the other car, and to the policeman when he arrived. It occurred at that stretch of mall outside Williston where all the signs and ads made the traffic lights on the side of the road a little hard to spot, though Delia had successfully managed to stop at them hundreds of times before. No, she was inattentive today, lost in thought when she went through the red; and the truth was that if the other driver—Heidi Rosenberg was her name—hadn't been as quick to swerve and brake as she was, it could have been even worse. As it was, Heidi had damage to her fender and right front headlight. Delia's car was worse off—the back door and rear panel were stove in, crumpled.

Both cars were drivable, though, and so after the young policeman had given Delia a ticket, after the little crowd that collected had dispersed, after Delia had sat for a while and *gathered herself,* as she thought of it, she drove very slowly and carefully home, going over it again and again, the feeling of the moment it happened—that everything had suddenly exploded, become senseless and unreal. Each time she thought of it, it made her breathless again.

Matt and Tom, the wide and the skinny, were walking down the sidewalk—she could see them almost all the way to the Sternes' house as she turned in the driveway. When they got back, she didn't mention the accident to either of them. She and Matt helped Tom make his way upstairs. While Tom showered, Delia waited, resting on her bed, and Matt went outside to mow the front lawn. When Tom was done, he called Delia and she helped him dress; and then she called Matt and they got him back downstairs and settled in his room to watch the Red Sox.

Matt left. Delia made a pasta salad for supper. She set up tray tables and they ate in the living room. They didn't talk much, but the silence felt companionable to Delia. It wasn't until Tom was in bed and she was upstairs that she let herself think about the accident again.

She had been absolutely in dreamland. She was paying *no* attention. She shook her head, and her lips tightened. What would become of them if she couldn't drive safely anymore? She realized that this was what had frightened her most, the notion of their joint helplessness, what that would do to this thing she'd made of their lives. She wouldn't let it happen. She couldn't.

THE SUN WAS still high, slanting through the moving leaves, strobing Delia's face as she walked slowly over the uneven brick sidewalks. They had heaved and cracked here and there under pressure from the root systems of the old trees, whose branches arched out and met in the middle of the wide street. It was July 1, the night of the party her neighbors, the Sternes, threw every year before they went away to their summer house on Cape Cod. They were careful to invite everyone on the street, and Delia always looked forward to this gathering as a way to continue to know the younger and younger families who had laid claim to its houses.

From halfway down the block she could hear the hubbub of voices, the high lift of a throwaway female laugh. She was thinking that she would have a gin and tonic to celebrate. Yes, that's what she'd do.

To celebrate what? Oh, summer, let's say. The end of the week. Tom, resting on his bed in the dining room, waiting for her return.

They'd talked yesterday about the possibility of his coming along with her. They could have used the wheelchair or driven down with the walker in the car, or his cane.

But Tom had said no, he didn't want to spoil her fun. Though what he'd actually said was, "Shpa! Phnn!" He'd shaken his head, hard, his lips pressing together, and said it again, a little more clearly.

She got it, as she did more and more now. She told him he couldn't spoil her fun, her fun was in being with him.

Bullshit, he said, ("Buh! Shi!"), and then his mouth tightened into the familiar small smile that almost always made her smile back.

It was just as well, as it turned out. When he came home from rehab this afternoon it was clear that he wouldn't have been able to do it even if he'd wanted to. He was just too tired. He'd had a snack, and then he'd lain down. When she'd gone in to say good-bye, he was asleep.

She wondered who would be at the party this year. She saw as she turned up the walk that there were at least a few young couples she didn't know. She came up the steps onto the crowded front porch and introduced herself to the young woman standing at the top.

She was in an interesting conversation with her about Hillary Clinton and feminism when Gail Sterne saw her and came over, drifting up in one of the gauzy caftans she wore to hide her bulk. She wanted to know how Tom was—they'd heard about his stroke. She took Delia to the bar, set up at the end of the porch, and Delia ordered her gin and tonic. While she waited, she described Tom's progress. Then she told Gail that he was home, with her.

"Well!" Gail said. "My! Well, I won't say I'm surprised, but . . . Yes, I will! I am surprised."

Delia had her first bitter sip of the gin and smiled at Gail. "You're not the only one. Nancy says I'm trying for sainthood."

This was only one of the many things Nancy had said to Delia on the phone when Delia had finally told her what she'd done.

"You've definitely got my vote," Gail said.

"Nonsense. It's mostly just a matter of arranging things. He has plenty of money. All I'll do is spend it on him."

"But you're so used to your privacy, Delia, to your own life." Her hand came up and rested on her bosom. She had large, glittery rings on almost every finger.

"Oh, I've had too much of that," Delia said. "It will do me good to be caring for someone besides myself." She'd made this argument to Nancy too, and Nancy had said, "So? Go work in an orphanage. Get a dog. You owe Daddy *nothing*, Mother."

"I don't do it because I feel I owe it to him," Delia had said.

"Then why? Why do you do it?" Nancy's voice was shrill, as it had been throughout this conversation.

"Because I want to. Because this is what I want to do."

And though she had answered every argument Nancy mounted with equal assurance, equal conviction, Delia had been aware that this was only the beginning of the discussion. That Nancy would come back to it again and again, particularly if Tom stopped making progress. That everyone who learned of Tom's arrival at her house, of her decision, would wonder at it, and those who were close to her would ask her openly about it, would argue with her. The only ones who hadn't so far were Madeleine Dexter and Brad. Though Brad had assumed it was only temporary, his father's stay with her in Williston, and she didn't correct him. Because maybe it was. And a few times when she was feeling a little overwhelmed, she had comforted herself by saying that nothing was permanent. "We'll see how it goes," she said to herself from time to time.

And now she said it to Gail, too. "Anyway, we'll see how it goes. How I stand up to it. Intestinal fortitude, as it were." She had another swallow of gin and made a face. "What a revolting idiom that is when you think about it!"

But Gail was preoccupied, frowning. "Yes, it's all improvisation from here on in," she said, her voice slowed. She started talking about Bob's open-heart surgery last fall. How they spoke together of each annual event now—this party, their summer on the Cape—as though it might be their last. "The point is to do everything you can as long as you can, isn't it?"

"Yes," Delia said. "To use yourself up." And suddenly she had the image of herself having her solitary dinners, in the living room here, in her apartment in Paris. How wasteful that seemed to her now. How selfish.

Now Delia looked up and saw her neighbors, Meri and Nathan, just turning into the Sternes' walk. He had one of those kangaroo pouches slung around his belly—the baby. Asa. She felt bad that she'd seen so little of them, but she had a proposition for them, an exchange she wanted to work out. She excused herself to Gail, who was turning to talk to someone else anyway. She stepped to the railing and called over to them.

Meri's face, which always had that slightly sullen look, bore the stamp of her fatigue—Delia had heard the baby in the night from time to time. It lifted now when she spotted Delia on the porch.

Delia beckoned them. "The booze is this way, my dears," she called, and several of the young couples turned and smiled at her.

Meri and Nathan threaded their way through the clusters of people on the porch. Delia hugged each of them, leaning carefully over the baby in Nathan's case. As she stepped back, she peered in at him in the pouch. He was ridiculously small, curled in almost a half circle, his little hands at his face, his head flopped over sideways onto one shoulder, eyes closed.

"Now if you or I did that," Delia said, pointing, "we'd have a stiff neck for a week."

Meri said, "I wouldn't mind the stiff neck if Nathan would just *carry* me everywhere I went."

Nathan grinned his toothy, boyish grin. "I would if I could, it goes without saying." His big hands cupped the little shape at his front, just the way you did when you were pregnant, Delia thought. Maybe that's why they had these little pouches, so men could have the tiniest sense of the experience.

Now he announced that he was going to get a beer for himself—did Meri want anything? She asked him to bring her some sparkling water.

When he was gone, Delia turned to the younger woman. "How are you getting on? Do you need anything? Does the baby need anything?"

Meri shook her head. "Nothing. We don't use half of the stuff we've got. All he wears are little T-shirts and diapers. Or just diapers, it's been so warm." She sounded hoarse and exhausted.

"And you? How are you? Any better?" Delia asked.

Meri shrugged.

"It's a trying time," Delia said. "When they're so little and feeding and being changed all the time."

"I sometimes feel I'm living in a big cotton ball. In a fog." She tipped her head from side to side, almost shaking it.

"I wish I could be of more help. Once I get Tom settled in, I will. I'm actually quite fond of infants. Some people aren't."

"Do tell," Meri said. "And how is that coming, Tom's being here?"

"Early days," Delia said. "We haven't sunk into a routine yet, though I suppose we will. We really have to. I want to keep on at the Apthorp house. It's a busy year—the sesquicentennial of Anne Apthorp's death. The college is publishing a new edition of the letters. Many celebrations."

"A sesquicentennial? What, pray tell, is that?"

"The one-hundred-fiftieth year. But there's always something. Two hundred years from her birthday. Two hundred years from the building of the house, and on and on. And all of it's just about raising money, of course."

Nathan came back with the drinks—Meri's silvery water and his beer, which was almost black.

Delia gestured at it. "A murky brew," she said.

"Murky, but fantastic." Nathan lifted it and drank.

"Our host is peculiar about beer," Delia said. "Or so it has always seemed to me. He specializes in the opaque."

"I like opaque," Nathan said. "In a beer anyway." Nathan offered Meri a taste.

She tried it and made a little face. "I'm not even jealous of you. Though Delia's lovely drink with lime," she lifted her chin toward Delia's glass, "is another story."

"I'd hate to tell you how good it is," Delia said. "It's very good." She had another sip.

"Delia's still doing her volunteer work," Meri told Nathan. "Even with Tom living with her."

"Impressive," Nathan said. He had a little mustache of brown foam.

"Yes, I am," Delia said. "And this brings up something I wanted to propose." She set her glass on the wide porch railing. "You know I've hired this wonderful young man, Matthew, to take care of Tom for about an hour or so each day when he gets home from rehab and I'm still at work." Meri nodded. "Well, it turns out he can't be there two days a week. Tuesdays and Thursdays. A class he needs to take this summer, which turned out to be held later in the day than he'd originally thought." They were both waiting, attentive. "If one of you could possibly come over for about an hour and a half on those two afternoons for the duration of summer school, I would be *eternally* grateful. And I will insist on taking the babe for at least one evening a week in exchange. I'd been meaning to offer this anyway." She turned to Meri. "Don't you remember I told you I would sit for you?"

"I do," Meri said. "It's a lovely offer."

"It wouldn't be any real work," Delia said. "Tom, I mean. He'll likely just sleep, he comes home so thoroughly worn out from his day. There will almost certainly be nothing for either of you to do except perhaps get him something to eat or drink if he wants it. It's just that I'm not comfortable yet leaving him by himself. I suppose in six months I'll look back at all this elaborate hoo-hah I've arranged and think I was silly, but for now I seem to require it."

Meri said she understood, absolutely. "I'd be nervous about leaving Asa, too," she said.

"Not *would be* nervous, because I'm absolutely going to take him."
She smiled, she picked up her glass again. "You *will* be nervous, I'm
afraid. Those are the terms. I will take him."

They agreed on it. Meri and the baby would come over and stay
with Tom, starting the following Tuesday.

Nathan said, "And if you ever need anything in the evenings, I
could help too. It's just I'm trying to finish this book. But I'm free
then, and if I can be of service . . ." He bowed slightly, his hand
reaching up to support the curve of the baby.

"Wait a sec," Meri said. "I get first dibs on any extra time."

Nathan laughed, but Delia, looking at the younger woman,
thought it was possible she wasn't joking at all.

"Let me take you to meet your hosts," she said, and turned to try
to spot Gail or Bob. The crowd on the porch had thinned a bit, so
they went inside, and yes, there was Bob, only slightly less fat than
Gail, in front of a painting.

In his rushing voice, Bob was explaining the artist's technique to
two seemingly interested guests—the layers, the sanding down, the
layers again. When he paused for air, Delia interrupted and introduced Meri and Nathan. Nathan immediately began to ask more
questions about the work.

Delia took the opportunity to move away. Though she liked
Bob, she'd heard the lecture, about this painting and many of the
others, about the beers, about his garden, more than once. He loved
his life, he loved to talk about every aspect of it. Admirable, but often
hard to take, she thought. She stopped to talk to a few more old
friends and then got into a long conversation with a woman she'd
never met before, about O. J. Simpson and race relations.

When she looked around again a little while later, she saw the
party was thinning out, that most of the younger couples had left,
and now even the old ones were gathering purses and shawls. The
student helpers were moving through the rooms clearing, carrying
trays of glasses, some still half filled.

Delia found Gail in the kitchen and said good-bye, wished her a
wonderful summer. They embraced, and when they stepped back,

Delia saw that Gail's eyes were full of tears. But then, Gail's eyes were often full of tears. It didn't mean much of anything.

Delia walked slowly back down Dumbarton, savoring the anticipation of her arrival home, of Tom's voice welcoming her. The lights were coming on in the houses up and down the street. The moon was low to the east, low and orange and fat through the trees, though there was still an astonishing, almost navy blue high in the sky. *Summer,* she thought.

Her own windows were dark, though Meri and Nathan had turned the porch light on. Inside, it was silent, and she assumed Tom must still be napping, but when she opened the door to his room, he called to her, a soft sound.

"You're awake?" she asked.

"Uh. Ah pee." I peed.

"You remembered! Good. Do you want anything from the kitchen?"

"Nhaa. Khaah." Come. He patted the bed next to him. He'd left room for her, Delia saw. She went over to that side of the bed and sat, then swung her legs up and leaned back against the pillows.

"Tahk," he said. Talk.

"What about? The party?" she asked.

"Uh."

"Well. The party," she said. "Would you like the list of who's still extant, among those you used to know?"

"Unh!" he said. She could see his smile.

"Let's see. Well, Stan and Petra were there. She still wears those Marimekko dresses. The tent effect." He laughed, a light, hoarse sound. "I wonder where she gets them anymore? Remember them? You used to say they made you dizzy, those wild prints. She's shriveled up to nothing now, though. She's more or less the tent *pole*. Remember how fat and jolly she used to be?" Delia sighed. And she went on, calling up the names: Peggy Williams, whose husband Rudy had died. Ed and Bettie Friedman, whom they always called Bed and Ettie, after a slip of the tongue Delia had committed a few times. "They've signed up for that retirement community."

She talked about the new people she'd met, the array of Bob's beers, "everything either brown or black, and simply not potable, it seems to me. Like drinking mud."

He had his good arm around her shoulders and she was leaned against him. She could feel his heart, its sturdy beat, under her head. Now his weak hand reached up and rested on her breast—her old drooping breast.

Delia shuddered with longing, and turned to him. They lay back, she curled along his side, and held each other. After a while, she could hear that he was asleep again. Even then she lay by him for a long time. The moon had risen above the roofline of the house next door, and its light lay across Delia's and Tom's legs, their stick legs, she thought. It crept higher and higher.

When it reached her chest, she got up. She stepped quietly into the hallway, leaving the door open behind her. As she was climbing the stairs she could feel her heart thudding slowly. This is it, she was thinking. The new adventure of her life, which would be, too, its final chapter. She had thought there would be no such event, that she'd have to hold on to life by charm, by effort. And she could have done that. It was her understanding, after all, that life was a matter of effort, renewed every day. She stopped on the landing of the stairs where the side window showed her again the moon, the enchanted summer night.

But now, she thought, now to have this unexpected, almost last-minute gift, this unlooked-for return to her of all that she had loved most—it was almost too much. A cloud skiddered across the golden moon. The crickets called to one another. She turned away, and continued up the stairs in the dark.

CHAPTER FOURTEEN

Meri, July 3, 1994

MERI GOT TO pick the restaurant, and at breakfast she told Nathan she'd meet him at Tony's, the pizza place.

"Tony's?" Nathan had asked. "Are you sure? Not someplace fancier, to celebrate?" He picked up his briefcase. He was about to leave for his office.

"It's the lowlife I miss," she said, which was true. The ordinary times, the smallest freedoms, without Asa. Tony's was dark, it smelled of beer. The TV over the bar always had a game on. She and Nathan had met there a few times before she knew she was pregnant, and the thought of its cheesy darkness appealed to her now.

As the day progressed, though, she grew more anxious. No surprises there—she was full of anxiety about everything to do with Asa, and this would be her first time leaving him with anyone else. She nursed him as long as she could beforehand, jiggling him awake every time he fell back from her.

She had to make several trips across the porch to Delia's house with stuff she thought it would be possible Asa would need in her absence. She brought over what she knew was a ridiculous number of Pampers and a bottle of milk she'd expressed. She'd brought over the Snugli, the bassinet—which he was sleeping in—towels to mop up spit-ups, a music box that sometimes seemed to soothe him if he was upset. She'd written a page of notes on various aspects of his routines that she handed over to Delia.

After she'd sat in the car a minute, she abruptly turned the engine off and went back to knock on Delia's door, to tell her that sometimes Asa seemed to be waking when he wasn't, and that she should wait, maybe one or two minutes, if he fussed lightly, to see if he'd drop back off.

Delia had been patient and apparently receptive to all this, for which Meri was grateful.

And now she sat having a beer. The occasional beer or glass of wine was okay, the doctor had said, so she was sipping this one slowly, making it last. Nathan was, as ever, a little late. The TV over the bar was tuned to the brilliant green of a baseball game. It was the Red Sox, Meri noted. Nathan would want to check the score, and then he'd want to sit on the side of the booth with its back to the screen so his attention wouldn't drift that way.

When Nathan came in, he looked for a moment like a tall, pretty stranger. She hadn't seen him outside of the house for weeks, she realized. He was *new* to her suddenly in this place. New, and attractive. She waved.

He took long strides over to her, his briefcase, which hung by a strap from his shoulder, bouncing against his side. "Sorry, sorry, sorry. Jerry caught me just as I was closing my office door to leave." He kissed her, bringing a pocket of warm air down around her—he'd ridden his bike here—and then he slid into the booth opposite her.

"He had pressing world news, no doubt."

"Yep, more about Sarajevo. It's as if he doesn't believe anyone else knows how to read the paper. He has to catch you up on everything. I was rude."

He waved to Tony, behind the bar, and pointed to Meri's glass. Then he turned to Meri and sat back. "*So,*" he said. "Asa's settled in with the surrogate grandparents?"

"It seems so."

"This is a milestone, Meri." He leaned forward and took her hands.

"Believe me, I know."

"And you look beautiful."

She shrugged.

"I mean it."

"Thank you," she said. She slipped her hand out from under his and lifted her beer mug. "This is a milestone too." She held it up. "My first."

He congratulated her. Tony came over with Nathan's beer and took their pizza order while he was there—sausage and onion.

"How was the writing today?" she asked after Tony had left.

"Good, I think. I've started on Mayleen's kids, the way things fell apart for them." Mayleen was one of the people he'd interviewed many times over for his book. She was a single mother who'd been part of several federal poverty projects in Chicago in the sixties, none of which had been able to improve her life in any lasting way.

They talked about the chapter, what he hoped to show with it, what details he would need to include. DeShawn's conviction for assault, Aaron's slide into addiction and his hope for the methadone program he was in.

"It's such a sad story," she said. "Doesn't it depress you?"

"Well, sure." He shrugged. "But it's odd. Writing about it is so interesting to me that, in another way, it doesn't. When I think of it humanly, of course, God, I feel horrible. For her. For them. For this country. But when I'm writing about it, I feel like I'm making *use* of it somehow. Do you know what I mean? Redeeming their lives, a little."

"I think I do, yes."

"So it's pleasurable." He shrugged. "That's a rotten thing to say, but true."

"No, I understand." They sat for a moment.

He reached over and cupped her elbow where it sat on the table. "And your day? How?"

"More of the same. Eat. Sleep. Cry. Poop. Throw up. Oh! But I expressed milk for the first time today—*that* was exciting. Kind of like being a Holstein, I suppose."

He laughed. "That was for our esteemed sitters to use?"

"If they have to, yep. I nursed him right before I left, too, so I'm not sure they will." Even talking about it, Meri could feel her breasts get heavy, and she thought, abruptly, of the night when Nathan hadn't wanted her, the last time she'd nursed Asa in front of him.

"Was Tom there when you dropped him off?" They'd seen Tom only briefly, as he came and went with the driver Delia had hired to take him to the rehab center. Nathan had tried to talk to him once. He'd been shocked at Tom's limitations.

"Yes."

"How did he seem?"

"No different." She thought about it. "Well, that's not true. He was interested in the baby. That was sweet, really." He had gotten up when she brought Asa in, and bent over his bassinet to look at him.

They sat for a moment. Nathan turned to watch the game. Tony came with the pizza and their plates, and each of them took a piece and started to eat.

"Do you think Delia should have taken him in?" Meri asked when her mouth was a little less full.

"Who? Asa?"

"No." She made a face: don't be silly. "Tom."

"Tom? How could she not?"

"Oh, I don't know. Maybe just what the daughter said. What's-hername. Nancy. That it wasn't her duty to. Her obligation."

"But Delia feels it was, so that's that." He took another bite.

"But maybe it's more insidious than that," she said.

"How 'insidious'?"

She set her pizza down. "Do I mean invidious?"

"I don't know. Do you?"

She thought a moment, and shrugged. She said, "What I mean is just, maybe there's something Delia likes about having him in her clutches. Weakened, as he is."

"Christ, Meri. What an ugly thought."

"But perhaps true. The truth is ugly sometimes."

"And sometimes not." He took another slice of pizza, the mozzarella pulling into long threads as he picked it up. Just before he bit into it, he said, "You're just jealous."

"Jealous! Of what?"

She had to wait for a moment until he swallowed. "You wanted her all to yourself," he said.

Could that be true? She had wanted something from Delia, she knew that, but she wasn't sure Nathan was right. He was nodding his head emphatically, though.

Meri chose to ignore him. "Anyway, I don't mean she wanted this consciously," Meri said. "But look." She leaned forward, her elbows on the table. "Look: he leaves her, years ago, for another woman. Other women. She still loves him. Throughout."

"According to you."

Meri sat back, silent for a few seconds, feeling the pinch of shame, of anxiety she always felt when she thought of how she'd learned the elements of Delia and Tom's story. Then she said, "No, remember? That's what Nancy thought too."

He waved his hand. Okay.

"Anyway, now she has him back, under her wing, in her house, in her charge, and he can go no more a roving."

"This would be, I think, so unconscious as to be irrelevant."

"I don't know." Meri picked up her pizza slice again. "Haven't you read *Jane Eyre*?"

"Nope. I saw the movie though. But I don't remember much. Just, George C. Scott seemed like he was playing Patton all over again."

"This is a pathetic answer from a supposedly educated person."

Nathan chewed and lifted his eyebrows.

"See, in *Jane Eyre,* the *book,*" she said, "our heroine, madly in love with the difficult, the inaccessible—because, in this case, *married*—Rochester, is finally able to live happily ever after with him once he's maimed. Once he's brought low. In the same fire which conveniently kills his wife."

"So?"

"So, it's a theme, in literature about women."

"That they like their men *maimed*?"

"Well, I think it's about equality, actually. That is to say," she raised her finger, "in an era when women's lives were terribly constricted, maybe a man whose life was constricted too was more a soul mate, or something like that."

"So I should be watching my back, is that the message?"

"Nah. It's different times for us. We have different ways of being a couple. We're more on an equal footing. We're *pals*." This was true, she thought. "I suppose that's the good news and the bad news. The 'for better or worse.'"

"How could it be bad? How could it be 'worse'?"

"Well, it's not bad, I guess. But it is different."

"Different from . . . ?"

"Well, from Delia, and Tom, for instance. Their sort of old-fashioned and kind of unequal *romance* of a marriage."

"Is that how you see it?" he asked. He seemed genuinely curious.

"Yes. That's *their* good news and bad news."

"Bad because unequal?"

"Right. And good, or maybe good, because more romantic. I don't know." She looked at Nathan. "Though to be quite old-fashioned myself, I *do* feel the odd pang now when you walk out the door to go to real life. The wish to maim." She grinned.

He snorted. "It's not very *real,* holed up in my office all day every day."

"You bump into people. You bump into Jerry. I even envy you that. You talk about the world."

"I have to get this done this summer, hon." There was apology in his voice, but a little edginess too.

"I know. But we need to figure things out for the fall better. Because I need to go back to work then or a) I'll lose this job, this job that I really, really like, and b) I'll go crazy. And then you really will need to watch your back."

And so they started to speak again of Asa, and of his care and Nathan's fall schedule and their options, something they'd danced around before. This time, though, they divided up chores. Nathan would call the day-care office at the college and see if faculty kids had any preference. If so, she would do the research on day-care places by phone and schedule a visit to each.

They finished the pizza. Nathan turned around again to watch the game for a few minutes. "Shit," he said, and turned back.

Meri had another infinitesimal sip of her beer and set her mug down. "It's the ruination of a perfectly good love affair," she announced.

"What? Asa?"

"No!" She stared at him. "No. Delia, Tom. You thought I meant *us*?"

"I thought maybe you were teasing about us."

"No. We're still having our affair. Sort of." She looked at him. "Aren't we?"

"I'd like to resume it, anyway."

"Would you?" she said.

"I've been thinking about you all day." His face had changed, sobered.

"Between thinking about Mayleen and the boys. And Sarajevo."

"All day." He smiled. "Dirty thoughts."

"Because we were going out for pizza tonight?"

"Because I miss you. I miss us. I miss making love to you."

She looked away. This was fraught for her. It made her sad.

After a few seconds he reached over and took her hands again. "I'm sorry for whatever was hurtful to you when I didn't want to."

She didn't answer for a moment. For a moment she didn't know how she wanted to answer. Then she looked up at him and said, "So how did you get over that?"

He visibly relaxed. He grinned. "I got just a *little* more desperate."

"Ah, I like a desperate man," she said, smiling back.

"I'll get the check."

They came out together into the dark parking lot. Nathan had his arm around Meri's shoulders. His body pressed against her side. They walked back to the car, and he let her in—he would come home on his bike. He tossed his briefcase into the backseat.

Leaning over the open window as she started the engine, he said, "This was fun. May I call you?"

"I'll think about it," she said as haughtily as she could, and drove away, out of the lot.

The streets in this part of town were hardly lighted at all, so she could barely see Nathan when he appeared in the rearview mirror. He was only a vague shape on his bicycle.

He pulled up beside her at the second light, breathing hard. "Hey," he said. "Hey baby. Hey mama."

She pretended disdain. The light turned green and she gunned the car. She could see him in the mirror better now, his white shirt rocking back and forth as his body moved, standing on the pedals. *Nathan.*

He caught up to her at the next light just as it turned green. "I'm coming for you," he called. Meri felt as excited, as free as she had when she and Nathan were first sleeping together, in Coleman.

She laughed and hit the gas so hard the tires squealed as she pulled away.

They teased each other this way through three more traffic lights. And then there was a long stretch of road that didn't have any. She watched the white shirt grow smaller in the mirror.

She had to go slowly again on Main Street, stopping at the signs and the one long light, and as she turned onto the dark of Dumbarton Street, she thought she saw Nathan a block or two back, catching up. She turned into their driveway and cut the engine by the house. She got out of the car and leaned against it, waiting for him. And after a moment there he was, turning into the driveway too.

He pedaled up next to the car and stopped. He stepped away from the bike, letting it fall. He came toward her. He was panting. He pinned her against the car and she felt the entire length of his strong body push against her, damp, hot. His mouth tasted of beer and of his own sweet saliva. He grabbed her buttocks and lifted her, pressed into her.

"Natey," she whispered to him. She put her fingers into his hair and pulled his head back. "Nate, we have to get Asa."

"No. No, we don't. We can get him after," he said. She let go of him and he bent to her neck again.

"You think?" she said.

He moved his mouth up her neck to her cheek, her ear. "We've only been gone an hour and a half or so," he whispered. "Come on, come on, let's go in."

He was right behind her on the kitchen steps, his hand between her legs. They stumbled across the dark kitchen together and into the main room. He pulled her by the hand over to the hulking shape that was the couch. They fell onto it and he pushed her skirt up, even as she was fumbling at his belt, then at the multiple steel buttons of his fly. Together they pulled his jeans below his hips. Meri got her panties off one of her legs. He lay on top of her, kissing her neck, settling himself, and then he pushed into her.

She cried out in pain, and he froze.

"What?" he breathed. He rose up on his elbows above her. "What, what is it, Meri?"

"Oh, Jesus, it's the scar!" she whispered. "The tear, where the stitches were." It had felt like a knife cutting her again.

He cocked his hips and pulled slowly out of her.

"God, God," she whispered, and curled slightly away from him, pulling her legs up.

"I'm so sorry," he said. His head was buried in her hair.

She could feel his wet penis, getting soft against her thigh. "Oh, *I'm* sorry," she said. "I'm sorry." She turned and lifted his head. She held his face. Her eyes were used to the dark now and she could see him, but his expression was unreadable. He lay down again, wedged against the back of the couch. They lay spooned together for a few minutes, his arm around her.

He whispered, "If I licked you? If I made you wetter?"

"But I *am* wet, Nate. Feel."

Their hands met, his fingers slid slightly in her, and she inhaled sharply again, flinching away.

"Jesus," he said.

After a moment, Meri said, "She said it might hurt a little."

He was silent. Then he said, "This seems like more than a little."

"It is. Yes."

They weren't touching now. After a long moment, he said, "I can't stand this, Meri. I can't stand how hard this has all been." His voice was hoarse, anguished. "How awful the labor was, and now, to hurt you with sex . . . I can't. I just can't. I can't stand it."

"I know," she said.

They lay next to each other on the couch for a while, not speaking. Then Meri sat up and pulled her skirt down.

Nathan was still lying with his jeans around his shins, his arm thrown up over his face. She could see the white length of his body, his penis a dark shadow across his thigh.

"I'd better get Asa," she said.

CHAPTER FIFTEEN

Delia, July 5, 1994

"So Tom has just been asleep the whole time?" Delia asked. She and Meri had just sat down at the kitchen table to have some iced tea. It was Meri's third time sitting with Tom while Delia was at the Apthorp house.

"So far as I know," Meri said. She had the sleeping baby perched on one curved arm, his head turned sideways on her shoulder. Delia could see the bottoms of his feet, smooth flat little pads, silky and unused. "At any rate, he went into his room and shut the door, and I've heard nothing since. Just like last time."

"Well, they work him hard at rehab," Delia said. "It exhausts him."

"He's walking so much better though," Meri said.

"He is." He was. Everything seemed better to Delia, even just these few weeks along. He could almost completely dress himself—though it was true that she still had to help him with buttons and zippers. He'd graduated from the walker to a cane, one of those peculiar metal canes with multiple prongs fanning out at the tip. His right leg dragged, his right arm dangled and flopped, but they could be made to work when he concentrated on them. Even his pronunciation was clearer.

It was only the sentence structure that wasn't there. The nouns came, and the verbs, but no pronouns, no prepositions, few adverbs, few adjectives. It was like the speech of a two-year-old. *Go hospital. Eat supper. Want radio.* They had told her this was one form the aphasia could take, and that it was one of the more difficult to work with.

And yet he got her jokes, he got her stories if she went slowly enough and more or less acted things out as she spoke. He was himself, responding, thinking—yet still unable to convey any complexity to her, except through his eyes, his gestures. But when she looked at him, everything seemed to be there, in his face. Everything she loved.

"It must be strange to have him home all the time after all these years of living apart."

Delia looked at the younger woman. Her eyes were steady, looking back. This moment had happened before, a moment when Meri seemed to be probing, trying to get Delia to be more open, more explicit about Tom or the history of her marriage. Delia wasn't sure what that impulse was, what it was that Meri wanted to know, exactly, but she didn't welcome it.

But Delia was good—she *felt* she was good anyway—at the honest answer that still didn't reveal much. "Do you know," she said confidentially, smiling, "it truly feels as though he'd always been here."

"Really?" Meri said. The baby stirred now, turning his little face against her neck.

"Oh, he's changed, of course, and then he's not changed. In some ways he's still the same old charming, imperious Tom. While being the complete Democrat, of course." She smiled.

Meri picked up her glass with her free hand and drank. The ice cubes made a light noise as she set it down.

"How are you doing with *your* charge?" Delia gestured at the baby.

"Oh," Meri said. "All right, I suppose. He's still up two or three times a night, so I feel as if I more or less stagger through the days."

"But your husband is a help, is he not?"

"Oh, Nathan's been wonderful. He does the shopping and the dinner. He even sort of cleans." She made a face. "But that's mostly because he can't stand the way things look if he doesn't."

"Well, this too shall pass."

"Actually, that part of it probably won't. I've always been a slob. It's just that in the olden days, I had only myself to care for."

"Well, yes, I know how that is." She shifted in her chair. "One more or less loves one's own messes."

Meri looked up and smiled in what looked like surprise. "We do, don't we?" She nodded, and then turned to the window. She frowned, looking at something, and then she turned quickly back to Delia. "My God, Delia, what happened to your car?"

"Oh." Delia felt a pulse of shame, of embarrassment for herself. "I had an accident."

"Well, *yes*," Meri said. "But what happened?"

"It was my fault," Delia said. "I was lost in a dream and I ran a red light. The other car plowed right into me."

"God. How terrifying."

"Yes, it was. It was a very strange experience. Have you ever had that, been hit out of the blue? I mean, without anticipating it, or seeing it coming?"

"No." Meri shook her head, and her limp hair swayed.

"This was quite . . . bizarre." Delia shivered, recalling it. "It was as though the world had suddenly blown up. I couldn't imagine for about three seconds, probably, what had happened. Three *long* seconds. This horrible loud noise, and the car flying through the air, sideways—I simply didn't *know* anything for a moment. I barely knew who I was."

"But you weren't hurt."

"No, and neither was the poor woman who hit me. The *car,* on the other hand . . ." She raised her eyebrows.

"But you can drive it." Her face made it a question.

"Oh yes, I *have* been. I'll have to get it fixed at some point. But first I have to get the insurance man to come and look it over. I just"—her hand waved—"I haven't got around to it yet."

"It'll take a little while, I would think. Fixing it." Meri was looking out the window again.

In profile, Delia thought, she looked very young. The fatigue just vanished. "Yes, I'll have to time for it when I won't need it for at least a few days."

"Well, you can always borrow ours for errands and the like."

"Thank you, dear. That's kind of you, but I don't want to impose."

"It wouldn't be, imposing."

"So you say. But I'll manage. I thank you, but I'll manage. I feel I've imposed on you enough, asking you to take on this sitting for Tom."

"No, Delia. No." She said this firmly, looking right at Delia. "No, I looked forward to this all day. To be in someone else's house—a place where there are no . . . chores left undone. No messes that are my responsibility." She smiled. "Messes. Yes indeed. Do you know, I dropped a bottle of olive oil on the floor in the pantry this morning, and I still haven't wiped it all up? There are footprints all over the first floor now. It looks like . . . a ghost has been walking around." She smiled sadly. "That ghost would be me."

Delia didn't know quite what to say. She was aware of feeling that Meri was asking something of her, and she was aware of her own resistance to that.

Meri was swaying her body slightly back and forth, patting the baby's back. "No, I loved sitting here in the quiet," she said.

Delia was relieved that the subject seemed to have changed, that they'd moved on.

"And the driver does everything anyway, just as you said he would. He gets him into his room, gets his shoes off. He's very kind. I can hear him talking to Tom."

"He does seem lovely, doesn't he?"

"Well, maybe not exactly *lovely*." Meri made a face.

"Oh, I know, I know," Delia said. "He *does* have that wretched pompadour. A man with a pompadour is a man who thinks too much about himself."

Meri smiled at her and moved to get more comfortable in her chair.

"Well, I'm glad then," Delia said. "I'm glad if being here is actually a momentary haven." She looked at her own hands on the table, the ridges of greenish veins running across them. "I remember when the children were small, I used to love taking them to the doctor's office because there were toys and other children and they'd play, and I'd be able to sit there utterly idle for five or ten or even fifteen minutes. No chores to be done. Sometimes I'd actually have time to read some ridiculous article in a magazine, *Ladies' Home Journal* or something like that, and I'd think, 'Why, this is utter *bliss.*' "

Meri was looking intensely at Delia. "But you loved your children."

"Well, of course I loved them. I mean, there were moments with each of them when I didn't. Moments, you know." And Delia was suddenly remembering them, those moments. Remembering how it had felt, the rage at something your child was doing or saying in pub-lic—doing or saying with what must be a kind of instinctive canni-ness regarding the upper hand he held, an inborn sense of how deeply embarrassing his behavior would be to you. The shrieks at the checkout line in the grocery store over the candy and gum they per-versely stacked by the cash registers. The wails, the collapse on the ground when she would announce it was time to leave the park. She remembered turning to one or another of her children when she had them alone finally, in the car or at home, turning to them and *paying them back* with her own real anger, her rage.

She said, "But everyone has those moments." She waved her hand. "You have to forgive yourself for those moments. You need to, or you can't go on. Forgiveness is essential. Forgiveness of yourself, first. Then it's easier to forgive others."

Meri's mouth made an odd shape. "Neither is a great gift of mine, I'm afraid."

"I find as I get older that they are, of mine. Interesting, isn't it?" And Delia felt it suddenly as a point of pride, an accomplishment. She felt, she realized, that having Tom here now was connected to her having forgiven him all those years ago. Having let go of so much. It was like a reward for that, for that generosity. She smiled. "Maybe I *am* trying for sainthood, as my daughter suggested."

"Did she?"

"She did, but she was mad at me at the moment. It wasn't meant kindly."

The baby made a little noise and Meri began again to sway her upper body from side to side. She said, "I think I remember Tom describing her as formidable, didn't he?"

"When was this?" Delia asked. She was surprised by this, by Meri's calling up of Tom, whole. How would she know?

"When we came over just before last Christmas. When he was visiting. When your son came."

"Oh, yes!" Delia said. She'd forgotten that Meri had met Tom then. Now she thought back to that evening. She remembered it clearly. Most of all, Tom's presence then. His elegant presence—she could recall even the color of the shirt he was wearing, a pale gray. She remembered too the night before, which was the last time they'd made love before the stroke. "That seems another universe, doesn't it? It *was* another universe." They sat for a moment. "Well, *formidable* Nancy is," she said.

Meri sighed. "It's so hard to imagine, having grown children who actually have *characteristics*. Who are people, people you've helped to make." She shook her head. "Part of what's difficult for me now is that I can't really believe anything I do with Asa has anything to do with him as a person. I mean, I feel I'm just doing chores when I care for him."

"You are a very conscientious mother, dear," Delia said.

"Well, of course I'm conscientious. He's my *job*. I always do a good *job*." Her eyes seemed to be glittering. She looked down at the table.

Delia waited.

After a few seconds Meri said, "It's just that I feel so . . . well, brain-dead, I suppose. So much that I'm just this, animal. This . . . body." She gestured down her side with her free hand.

She started to speak, and stopped. Then she said, "Did you feel that? when your children were babies?"

"Of course. It's one of those times, isn't it? when you're reminded of your animal nature—labor, and then the kind of fog you live in for a while after the baby comes—one of those times when you're so *aware* that you live in your body. We get to forget it most of the time. But we *are* our bodies after all. We may feel full of lofty concerns most of the time, but it all comes down to that in the end. We live in our bodies, and we get reminded of that from time to time."

"God, don't tell me there are times when I'm going to feel this way again. I don't want to know it."

"Ah, but there are, of course," Delia answered. "In old age, for example, when the body begins to go wrong, to fail in any of a variety of interesting and depressing ways." She snorted lightly. "You wake up every morning, I assure you, very much in your body. Very aware of it. And in illness, with something like what's happened to Tom. It forces you to understand how provisional it all is—the body's working correctly."

Meri's lips tightened. Her head moved, bowed almost, in what seemed a kind of apology, or concession. *Okay.*

"Yours, now," Delia said. "The feeling you have of . . . *bodiliness,* of being overwhelmed by it—yours is actually the kindest version of that, I would think." She smiled. "Because it's just that your body is working so hard. But it's working *well*—it *is* working correctly—and that's something to be grateful for." She was aware that part of what she was telling Meri was that she shouldn't complain, that she should be braver than she was; and she was aware that she felt some unkindness toward the younger woman as she did this. But she couldn't help it. Life was hard, hard for everyone. One never stopped having to work at it. Meri was of an age when she ought to know that.

Meri looked as though she was beginning to say something, but then there was a noise, a cry from Tom in the dining room. "Dheee!" Delia.

Delia smiled at Meri. "Ah, *my* baby," she said. She stood up.

Meri stood up too, more slowly, adjusting the baby on her shoulder. Delia walked with her to the living room, where Meri carefully lowered Asa into his bassinet, trying not to wake him. They stood together over the basket and watched him as he unfurled himself spasmodically. His eyes opened, he seemed to gasp, as though surprised by what he saw. Then they closed again, he curled slightly to his left, and his little fist rose to his mouth.

Meri sighed in relief. She picked the basket up by its handles, and Delia followed her down the hallway to the front door.

"Well, thanks for the tea, Delia." There was a pregnant pause, as though she wasn't sure what to say next. "And for the company."

"Oh, please, not at all." Even though she felt an itchy impatience,

Delia was trying to keep her voice gracious and unrushed. "And thank *you*, again, for staying with Tom," she said.

She waited, smiling, until Meri had stepped outside, had moved away on the front porch. She waved then, and shut the door.

She turned back down the hall, feeling an almost giddy sense of release, of escape. Eagerly, quickly, she crossed to the dining room door.

CHAPTER SIXTEEN

Meri, July 7, 1994

ON THURSDAY, Meri's fourth time at Delia's house, she was once more sitting in the living room while Tom napped. This time too she'd barely spoken to him. The driver, Len, had helped him up the steps as he always did, had walked him in, waited for him outside the lavatory, and then taken him in to lie down on his bed in the dining room.

Len liked Meri. He often stopped for a few minutes to chat with her. He liked Tom too. Today after he'd shut the dining room door, he'd come and stood leaning against the frame of the living room doorway in his black suit to talk about him. "He's a good guy," he said. "A good guy. Sharp. It's a shame." He shook his head. "If that a happeneda me . . ." His lips pressed tight together to end his sentence, leaving Meri to fill in the blank for herself. *I'd be sad? I'd kill myself?*

He pushed away from the frame and tapped it with his palm. "See ya Tuesday, right?"

"Right," Meri said, and mirrored his pointing index finger.

"Hah!" he said.

After Len left, she simply sat for a while in the pretty living room—prettiest at this time of day, she thought—looking down from time to time at Asa when he made the startled noises and movements that punctuated his sleeping life. She was thinking about nothing. Well, lots of things, actually—images: Nathan, getting out of bed this morning, his body gleaming white in the bright sunlight.

Delia's face when she was talking to her the other day, suddenly so seemingly cold. The almost-empty refrigerator. What she needed to buy. But nothing like a thought.

She sighed. The *New York Times* was lying in front of her on Delia's coffee table. She leaned forward and started to read. She went through the beginnings of a couple of articles on the front page. She'd just gotten engrossed in one about the national health plan, about whether abortion services would be included in it, when she heard the door to the dining room open. She looked up. Tom Naughton was starting across the hall toward her, using his metal cane, swinging his leg with each step.

She stood and began to move to him, to help, but he held up a hand. "Hokay." Okay. It's okay.

She sat back down then and waited, trying not to watch his hitching progress. As he came into the room, he stopped at the bassinet, looking down. "Ace," he said softly, smiling a little, gesturing at the sleeping baby.

Meri was pleased to have him remember Asa's name, to have him speak it. Delia had told her that he'd been charmed by the baby, that the night the two of them had babysat, he'd held him for a while. It argued for Tom, in her mind.

He moved to the sofa opposite her. He stood above it for a moment, and then more or less collapsed into it, a noise like a groan emerging from him.

Meri felt awkward, suddenly, in his presence. He was supposed to sleep when she was here. But perhaps this was a good sign, a sign of recovery—that he was less exhausted by his rehabilitation sessions than he'd been earlier.

Still, was she in charge of him now? Was she supposed to figure out what he wanted, or needed? "Would you like something to eat?" she asked. "Or drink?"

He shook his head.

They sat for a minute more. "I was reading," Meri said. "The *Times*." She gestured at the paper lying on the table in front of her. She kept her voice low. "There's an interesting article on the Clintons' health plan. On abortion and the Clintons' health plan. Would you like me to read it to you?"

"Yeh," he said, with a pronunciation that sounded only mildly interested. And then he nodded and said it again, more clearly, more decidedly. "Yhes."

Meri picked up the paper, rattled it flat, and started to read aloud. When she had to search through to a back page for the continuation, he waited patiently. She could tell he was listening—every time she looked up at him, he was frowning in concentration.

She came to the end of the article and there was another long silence.

Asa smacked his lips, nursing in his sleep.

She said, "There's a piece here on Breyer too. On the Supreme Court hearings. Shall I read that one?"

"Mmmm," he said, nodding. She flipped back to the first page and started again.

This time, partway through the article, Asa stirred and shook himself—she could see him in her peripheral vision. He began to whimper.

On schedule: it was about the time he'd been nursing for the last few days. She tried to ignore him. She read on. But when she folded the paper back to the end of the story, the noise seemed to wake him fully. He started to move his arms and legs, and then to squawk.

"Oh, excuse me, I'm so sorry," she said to Tom. She set the paper down, and bent to pick up the baby. She lifted him to her shoulder. She patted him gently for a few minutes, but his noises only became more frantic. And then he was really crying, fighting with her, pushing his body against her to get to her breast.

"Hong," Tom said.

"*You're* hungry?!" Meri asked, jiggling Asa harder. What next?

He shook his head. "*Ace,* hong."

"Oh, yes. Yes," she said, and smiled helplessly. "I'm afraid he is."

"Feeuhmm."

"Feed him?"

He nodded. "Feeuhmm. Sokay."

"You don't mind?" she said, realizing, even as she spoke the words, that she *did* mind. She did, of course she did, or she would have done it on her own, fed Asa without being given permission. She hadn't fed him in front of a stranger since the time the old woman in the lunch place had turned from her in revulsion. She'd even tried to avoid nursing him in front of Nathan, though that wasn't always possible.

He shook his head.

What she wanted was for him to go away, go back into his room—but she didn't feel she could say this to him. It would be too rude. It would be unkind. She lowered Asa and rested him along her arm. As he stopped crying and began his noisy snuffling toward her, she lifted her T-shirt on that side.

But she did it awkwardly because she was trying not to expose her breast to Tom, and Asa was left rooting and snuffling at the fabric of her shirt. By the time she tilted her body back to pull him away from her and put her hand under her breast to lift the nipple to him, milk was spurting out. It landed all over Asa's face. His body started, and he swung his head quickly back and forth in recoil. He made a funny spitting noise with his mouth and tongue, a kind of infant Bronx cheer. And when he came forward again, she saw that there was milk on the lids of his eyes and in his ears.

As Asa attached himself, she heard Tom make a noise and looked over at him. He was laughing, his head thrown back. She remembered that laugh from the evening at Delia's house at Christmas, his light hoarse laugh and the way he gave himself over to it. It had made her smile then, and she smiled now too.

She watched him as he subsided. Their eyes met. There must have been something quizzical in her smile now, because he shut his eyes, turning his head as Asa had, making Asa's noise. He was *explaining* himself in pantomime, she realized—explaining the joke. His hand waved in front of his own face imitating the milk, her spurting milk as it landed on Asa.

Meri laughed. It *was* funny. *Asa* had been funny, in his piggy, grunting gluttony, with the little raspberry noise he had made, his tongue sticking out. She looked down at him now. She lifted her hand to wipe the whitish liquid from the intricate whorls of his tiny ears.

By the time Delia's car pulled into the driveway, Asa had finished on the first side and Meri had him on her shoulder, burping him.

"Dhelia," said Tom. His voice was warm—excited, Meri would have said.

"Yup," Meri said. "She's home." She smiled at him and he smiled back, the small, self-mocking smile that he'd had when he was whole. His hand rose to his face, to his mouth, and he lifted his finger to his lips. *Shh.*

But then the hand kept moving, up to his eyes. He rubbed them briefly, as though he was fatigued. Meri wasn't sure, she couldn't have sworn that he intended the gesture she thought she'd seen him make along the way.

CHAPTER SEVENTEEN

Delia, July 9, 1994

EVAN WAS COMING TO VISIT, arriving any moment. He was coming because Nancy had asked him to. She couldn't take the time off from work to come east again herself, she told Delia, so she wanted him to "check on things."

Delia was waiting at the train station. It was hot. She was standing in the shadow of the building on the platform.

She and Evan were to have lunch together on the way home, and then he'd stay overnight, casting a critical eye on her arrangements, his assigned task. She'd asked Matt to come over to be with Tom today until they got home. She'd promised him time and a half—it was, after all, a Saturday.

Evan dropped down off the train in a single graceful motion. He was carrying only a small case. His face opened to see her, and she was startled by the strength, the power of his embrace.

"You are almost unbearably handsome," she said, stepping back from him, looking up into his pale, amused eyes behind the horn-rimmed glasses. "You must be utterly impossible to live with."

"I am," he assured her, grinning.

And perhaps this was true. He'd had a messy divorce from his first wife, the mother of his kids, in part because he'd begun a relationship with his second wife before the marriage ended. Delia thought she'd gotten the sense of a tremor or two now in the second marriage, but she wasn't sure.

When Evan saw the damaged car, he asked what had happened to it. She didn't want to tell him the truth. She said the other driver had run the light. They commiserated.

As they drove, he told her he'd mostly come to see her, but also because, as he put it, "I want to get Nancy off everyone's back." They talked about Nancy, about how angry she was over all this.

"Well, she has a right to be, I suppose," Delia said. "I did pretty much lie to her about it."

"I bet Nan's the kind of person a lot of people pretty much lie to, just to make their lives easier," he said.

"Poor Nan," Delia said. "I'm sure you're right." They were quiet a moment. She said, "Well, at least I don't lie to myself."

"No?" he said.

She looked over at him. He was smiling at her, fondly, she thought.

They talked about the heat. It was much worse in New York, he told her. "The whole city has that overriding stench of things rotting that it gets when it's this hot."

They stopped for lunch at the restaurant in the old mill just outside of town. It was dark as you entered it, but the back was full of light. It had been opened up and glassed in. It looked out across the dam and the water rushing over it—this was why people came.

There was no air-conditioning, but all the windows were open back here, and there was a breeze off the spilling water, a breeze with a fresh, slightly algal smell to it. As they sat down, Delia noticed that there were kids far below them, boys in wet blue jeans, barefoot and bare-chested, climbing on the rocks at the bottom of the falls where the water crashed with a smoky foam. She pointed them out to Evan.

A young waiter came over and Evan ordered a martini. "Do you want a drink, Mother?"

"I'll have wine," Delia said. She looked up at the waiter. "A sauvignon blanc if you have it."

They sat back. The sound of the water was a steady noise around them. Delia asked about Evan's work. The drinks came. They talked about his kids, about his wife, about how busy she was at the moment. She did set design, and she had two shows opening in the fall.

Over lunch, their conversation became more desultory, both of them falling silent every now and then to look at the water, at the young men diving in the pool at the bottom of the falls. Delia thought of the boys Mrs. Davidson had told her about at the rehab place in Putnam, the daring young men who'd fallen, or crashed, or leapt from something they shouldn't have into something they shouldn't have. She thought about Evan when he was younger—Evan, who so much more than Brad had beckoned danger. She'd actually been relieved when he entered the Peace Corps, where it would be the government's job—no longer hers—to keep him from harm.

They'd almost finished when Evan asked more specifically about Tom, about how much improvement there'd been since he saw him in Washington.

Delia described him, and then the arrangements she'd made. She talked about the way their days went. "It's very companionable, really. It makes me realize how solitary I'd become."

"So this is what you want. For the foreseeable future."

"Yes. It is."

"And Paris?"

"Ah." She shrugged. "Well. Maybe *you*'ll use it more." She smiled at him. "It's true. It means I'll go less. But that was bound to happen eventually."

"And you won't miss it."

"Of course I'll miss it! But I will go from time to time. Just not for as long a time. I will not feel deprived, dear."

"No. You do sound happy, in fact."

"I am."

"Do you think you're . . . falling in love again? As it were." And now he sang the song, in Marlene Dietrich's German accent. "Fawleen in luff a gayn, whaat am I too doo . . ."

Delia laughed. Then, looking down, fussing with her napkin, she said, "Oh, I've always been in love. As you no doubt know."

"Well, but it was on hold for a long time." He said this carelessly, his hand made a quick airy gesture. "Or on the back burner, or something."

Delia felt a prick of irritation at him, at his easy assumptions about her life, and Tom's. "It was never on hold," she said.

"I just meant, you know, you didn't act on it," he said, apology in his voice.

"It was never on hold," she said. "It was never on the back burner, as you put it. We acted on it."

"You acted on it."

"Yes." Delia sat back and looked levelly across the table at him.

"What are you saying, Mom? That you and Dad were lovers all these years?"

She let a few seconds pass. "Yes."

His mouth opened, his eyebrows lifted. He looked away from her, over the water, down to the boys below. Then he looked back at her, smiling broadly. "Well!" he said.

She smiled back. "Yes. Well." She pushed back her chair. "Shall we go now, and see your father?"

As they stepped into the kitchen, Delia could feel it—the cool air. "Ah, the air conditioner!" she said. "Isn't it lovely?"

He nodded.

"It's been sitting in the basement for lo! these many years. I wasn't even sure it worked anymore. So you see, having Tom here has helped me too, in fact. Matt put it in, just today. I didn't know if he'd have time or not."

"And Matt is . . . ?"

"He's the student, the one I told you about. He's my Tom-sitter, and jack-of-all-trades. Come, meet him."

Evan followed Delia to the living room. Matt was sitting on the couch, a book on his lap, pen in his hand, his bare feet propped against the coffee table. He hadn't heard them because of the noise of the air conditioner. It *was* noisy, the result, no doubt, of its age and its sitting unused for so long downstairs in the damp.

Matt scrambled up. He danced around, blushing, sliding his feet into his sandals and greeting them. He shook Evan's hand. They were almost the same height, but Evan looked slender and graceful next to Matt's childish bulk.

Matt told Delia that Tom was napping after a long walk outside. "We made it almost to the corner," he said as he gathered his work together. "He's awesomely tough."

"You know, those are the very words I would have chosen for Dad," Evan said, smiling at Delia.

BUT WHEN TOM limped into the kitchen late in the afternoon and offered Evan his version of a greeting, Delia could see that Evan was appalled by his state, maybe even repulsed.

Over the course of the evening, though, as she cooked dinner, as they ate, as they sat around the kitchen table talking, she could watch Evan *getting it,* figuring out the rules for how Tom talked now. She could tell that he felt, just as she did, the presence of the person Tom had always been.

She watched Evan, his beautiful face lifting in response to Tom, smiling, talking. How much he had changed over the years!—that idealistic, romantic young man become a *money guy,* as he called himself, wearing his expensive clothes, living in his expensive loft in the city, having his children over once every few weeks. And yet the love she felt for him was unchanged, was based on who he'd been and who he still was to her. This is how it is with your children, she thought. You hold all the versions of them there ever were simultaneously in your heart.

ON THE WAY back to the train station the next day, he asked questions about the prognosis, and Delia answered honestly. More progress was always possible, and Tom wanted it, so he worked hard. "I think happiness counts too," she said. "I'm sure it does, in fact. And he is happy here. With me." She heard the pride in her own voice and was embarrassed, suddenly. "But there are limits," she said. "I don't deceive myself. He won't work again. That's clear."

Evan made a noise of agreement. After a moment he said, "We should think about closing down the Washington house, too, I suppose. Selling it."

"Oh!" she said. She looked over at him. "Do you think so, at this point?"

"What do you mean, 'at this point'?"

"Well, in case he recovers enough to want to go back."

"And live alone?"

She could hear the incredulity in his voice. She didn't say anything.

"Mom."

She looked at him again. Evan—so self-contained, so handsome.

His eyes were steady on her behind his glasses. His voice was gentle. "He won't live alone again. Don't you know that?"

She looked back to the road.

"And if he does, it'll have to be in some kind of assisted living place." When she didn't answer in a minute, he said again, "Mom?"

"I suppose you're right. It's just . . ." She was silent for a long moment, driving, and then she said, "But I'd rather not do anything like that until he and I have talked. Until we know that's something he wants. Or that it's all right with him, in any case."

"That's fine. We'll wait then." After a minute he said, "I'm sorry. I didn't mean to rush you. To make you go any faster than you want with this."

She nodded.

He wouldn't allow her to come into the station to wait for the train with him. He leaned in the open passenger window after he'd gotten out. "I've gotta say, Mom, you're full of surprises." He was grinning. "Secrets and surprises."

She rolled her eyes.

He laughed and touched the door in farewell before he turned away.

Delia drove home slowly, the fender rattling. She had known it, hadn't she? That Tom wouldn't be able to go home, that he would have to stay with her. She had held out the hope—for his sake, of course—that he would get better, but she'd known almost right away, she realized now, that he wasn't likely to get better *enough*. That she would keep him. He would be hers.

Hadn't she even wanted that, some part of her? Wanted him to have to stay with her?

She tried to think that through. She didn't think so. She really didn't. Even in her joy at having him, those early days, she had always been working for what was best for him, she had always wanted that. She was sure of it.

CHAPTER EIGHTEEN

Meri, July 9–15, 1994

OVER THE LONG, hot weekend, Meri thought of Tom from time to time, his eyes on her as she had nursed. She had felt attractive then, she realized afterward. She had thought, maybe for the first time since Asa was born, that she could be his mother and still be herself, whole. Meri.

She thought too of Tom's gesture, that gesture of secrecy—if that's what it had been. Had it? Was that what he had meant? Or was it just an accident, as he lifted his hand to his eyes? She couldn't be certain either way.

Tuesday the temperature was supposed to reach ninety. Meri kept Asa in just his Pampers all day. Even so he was fussy, and when she nursed him, the heat of his flesh made her wet with perspiration where they touched. She had to unstick him when he was through.

It was cool at Delia's, Meri felt it as soon as she let herself in. Heaven. She could hear the rickety hum of an air conditioner as she came into the living room. Ah, there it was, an older model, set in one of the windows on the fireplace wall. Thank you, Delia. She set the bassinet on the floor, put a little cotton blanket over Asa, and sat down to wait.

When Len came in with Tom, Meri went out to the hall to ask him to keep his voice down. They chatted in whispers while Tom was in the lavatory. When he came out, Len turned to him. "You tired? Wanna rest?"

Tom shook his head. "Leeh rhoom," he said.

Len took his elbow, but Tom shook him off. "Okay," he said clearly. "S'okay."

Len backed up dramatically, holding both hands in the air. "The guy wants to do it on his own," he said, with a rising intonation, "*let the guy do it on his own.* That's what we call progress, my friends."

By the time Meri said good-bye to Len and came back into the room, Tom had settled himself on the couch again. Meri asked him if he wanted anything to eat or drink. He shook his head no. She asked if he wanted her to read to him. He nodded, smiling. With a sense almost of ritual, Meri opened the paper, found an article, and began. She was aware of Tom's alertness, of a tension in him, until Asa stirred.

She set the paper down on the table. She picked Asa up and lifted her shirt. She was intensely conscious of Tom, and conscious again of feeling attractive to him, of feeling sexual.

When she saw Delia's car swing into the driveway, she shifted Asa to her shoulder and pulled her shirt down. "Delia's here," she said.

Tom stood up laboriously, and started across the room, toward the hall. As he passed Meri's chair, he touched her shoulder. She looked up. He inclined his head slightly, and raised one hand and put it flat on his chest in a motion that looked to Meri like one of gratitude. *Thank you.* He was smiling, his eyes were full of a gentle amusement.

The next Thursday was the same. When she came into the living room after closing the door behind Len, his face was open in amused anticipation. "Tom," she said.

"Mehr," he answered.

She made a funny curtsy, and sat down. "Shall I read for a while?" she asked.

He nodded, and she leaned forward over the paper.

When Asa started to fuss, she looked at Tom. He was sitting back, waiting. She'd deliberately chosen a blouse today with buttons down the front, and she let it fall open while Asa nursed.

Every time she looked up, Tom's eyes were on her—moving from her breasts to her face, and back. Each of them smiled at the other when their eyes met.

She felt lovely.

It was a *game,* she thought, one they'd invented, one they'd worked out the rules to, one they each had a stake in. For her, it had to do with sex, with somehow restoring her sense of being sexual. And she could feel that that was happening—feel it in her breasts, in her womb.

For Tom? Well, maybe he had some parallel need. He'd been a man used to moving around among women after all, making flirtatious overtures, sexual overtures. This was perhaps a reminder of all that, of everything he'd lost. A healing reminder.

They were *mending,* she thought. They were mending themselves, and each other. Whom did it hurt? Not Asa. She stroked his head as his busy cheeks and throat worked. Not Nathan either.

When she burped Asa, when she switched him to her other breast, she was careless about covering herself, she let Tom see her.

Asa was still nursing when she saw Delia's car pull into the driveway, dented, disreputable-looking, the left rear fender crazily pointing skyward. She lifted Asa away from herself quickly and laid him across her lap as she buttoned her shirt. Tom's eyes were steady on her.

Delia came in the back way, she was walking down the hall from the kitchen. "How deliciously cool!" she cried, entering the living room. "I'm so glad you're all enjoying it."

OVER THE NEXT few days Meri thought often about these afternoons with Tom, she examined her part in them from now one angle, now another. She knew that she was the kind of person capable of acting on feelings of slight, of anger. And she knew that she had felt slighted, and angry too, at Delia, for being inaccessible to her—and maybe, Meri thought, not even entirely accessible to herself. And of course earlier she had been angry at Nathan, because he had been so turned away from her, but she didn't feel that anymore.

And that wasn't how these times with Tom felt to her anyway— angry, or vengeful. No, the way they seemed to her was as if they existed almost in another dimension from the rest of her life. When she was with him, it was as if she dropped out of time, out of its press and obligation, out of its failings. Her failings.

Some of this was perhaps due to the feeling she had whenever she entered Delia's house—that oddly transformed version of her own—the feeling of being *away*, in another place. Some of it might even have been the white noise provided by the air conditioner, the way it blocked out the world and closed around them. But mostly it was her sense of being alive under Tom's gaze, of his returning her to who she was. Who she'd been. Herself.

If someone had asked her about the nature of what happened between them, of course she would have had to acknowledge its eroticism, its sexuality. But it was more than that. It was a charge between them. Or a *recharge,* she thought.

Yes, they were like batteries that had run down, and down, and then had stopped working. And now they were sparking, humming. After each of her afternoons with Tom, she had been aware of feeling easier, lighter in her life with Asa—and with Nathan too.

In fact on Friday, full of the sense of herself as strong, as attractive, she went out to the front porch with Asa and sat on the steps to wait for Nathan's return home. She had washed her face and put makeup on. She was wearing a dress that had just begun to fit her again, a sundress she'd worn often the summer she met Nathan. She laid the baby on his back along her thighs so he could look up at the trees, the sunlight flickering through them.

Nathan appeared on his bicycle on the street. She watched him see her, watched his expression change as she smiled at him and held Asa up quickly by way of greeting.

He rode up the driveway and swung his leg off the bike, graceful as a dancer. He walked across the lawn and up the steps to her, grinning. He bent and kissed her, one of his chlorinated kisses. He squatted and kissed the top of Asa's head.

He sat down next to her. "To what do I owe this great, great pleasure?" he asked.

Her mouth opened, her breath drew in, and then she just smiled.

CHAPTER NINETEEN

Delia, July 19, 1994

THE MAN FROM Bodyworks drove Delia back into town on Tuesday and dropped her off at the Apthorp house. She was early, because they had wanted the car by eight. She went around to the back of the house and sat at one of the picnic tables. It was supposed to be hot again today—the heat wave might break records for length, she'd heard on the radio. For now, though, it was only in the low seventies—it had cooled off in the night. Birds were calling from high in the trees—a warbler's sweet-sweet-sweet song, and the bossy squawk of the jays in reply. The breeze stirred through the leaves from time to time. The orange daylilies were out, and the sky-blue balls of hydrangea.

Delia sat. She hadn't brought a book or notepaper or anything to pass the time, but she didn't need it. Her thoughts rushed by, turning her from one thing to another. She thought how her life seemed to have been enlarged suddenly—peopled, complicated, full of duties and chores and obligations. And pleasures. Exactly the things, she thought, that keep you alive. She thought of her own mother at her age, how old and resigned she had seemed, and of how different from that she felt. She went over the day's routines, the ones she'd set up so carefully. Tom off at nine to Putnam with the driver. Her long day here, which would likely be moderately busy. She'd have to walk home, of course, today and tomorrow too, but she didn't mind doing that. She'd been driving lately only on account of the increased number of errands she always had to run, and because she was always rushing to get back to relieve Meri or Matt.

She thought of Meri, with that slightly evasive, sly quality she had, a quality she'd lost for a while after the baby was born. Perhaps even earlier—during the pregnancy. It was coming back, Delia was happy to see. She seemed less desperate, less lost somehow. Less in *need,* Delia thought. It was easier to be around her. And she was beginning to look better again, tomboyish and sexual. It would all be fine, Delia thought, once that baby came a little more into his own.

She tried to remember if she'd been as overwhelmed the first time around, with Nancy. She doubted it. For one thing, she'd been surrounded by other women and their children. They were all stuck at home and would be at home for years, stuck, making the most of it together.

Meri's life was utterly different. Of course it was good that she would go back to work. But it meant that she'd never settle in, as Delia had, to the rhythm of day after day at home, to the idle pleasure of it, the easy boredom. The awareness of the tiny shifts in your children's behavior that marked their growing up, their developing personalities.

What had she done all that time? She really couldn't account for it. The days and days, years and years, of meals, of laundry, of shopping, of sewing, of setting up projects for the kids, helping them with homework. Later their games and plays and recitals and shows. Later than that, the nights of waiting up for kids who'd missed their curfews, who were driving for the first time, who'd gone off somewhere with a dangerous older crowd.

She had subsided into all that, happily enough, she would have said. Into that, and later the coordination of their double life in Washington and in Williston—into the campaigns, the good works required of her, all the socializing, all the arrangements to be made. It wasn't really so surprising, she supposed, that Tom had looked for a kind of excitement in sex elsewhere—for year after year she could hardly have provided it; though his arrival home at the end of the day, at the end of a week, had always made her heart feel lighter. As it did now, she thought.

When Adele arrived, Delia went inside with her. It was cooler in the dark rooms of the old house, but musty. She and Adele decided they would open the windows for an hour or so anyway to let the fresh air in. They moved separately through the rooms, turning the old latches, sliding the sashes up, propping them open. Delia had the sense, which she only fleetingly got, of what life might have been like—what a *moment,* anyway, of life might have been like—for Anne Apthorp, moving through these rooms on a warm summer day in the nineteenth century.

Life doesn't change in its fundamentals, she thought. The same small things bring pleasure, and always will.

CHAPTER TWENTY

Meri, July 19, 1994

At six it was already bright and hot in their bedroom. They all woke early—Asa first, then Meri, then Nathan. Nathan got up and went to the bathroom. Meri could hear him in the shower.

She changed Asa and nursed him in bed. Then she carried him downstairs. Nathan was already down there, padding around in his bare feet, fixing coffee, getting breakfast things out of the pantry.

The kitchen was cooler and darker than the rest of the house. Meri set Asa in his tilting chair up on the counter, and as their faces moved past him coming and going, he waved his arms and legs in excitement. The radio was on, turned low, but when the weather forecast came on, Meri turned it up. Another day in the mid-nineties.

"Christ!" Nathan said. "This has got to end soon."

"Well, at least Asa and I will be comfortable at Delia's," Meri said. She thought of Tom suddenly, and her face warmed.

"We should probably get an AC too," Nathan said after a minute.

"Oh, yes, Nathan. Let's. For the bedroom anyway."

"Then maybe we can try making love again sometime in the near future."

She turned to look at him. He was pouring milk on his cereal. As he set the carton down, he looked directly at her from under his thatch of hair, an unsettling gaze that seemed to her so freighted with desire, but also with the memory of their difficulties, that her throat tightened and she had to look away.

MAYBE PARTLY BECAUSE of the heat, Asa was fussy earlier than usual, scrambling desperately at her an hour or so before she was to go over to Delia's and wait for Tom. She nursed him at home, feeling a little sorry that she and Tom wouldn't have their game.

But he was also unusually alert through most of the feeding, his eyes focused on her face. "Do you see me?" Meri asked. "Do you see me?" With her free hand, she stroked the pale golden down that covered his head now.

"Our *own* game," Meri whispered to him. He stopped sucking for a moment, looking up at her, and his lips curved in what seemed a rehearsal for a smile.

Meri smiled back. "You're funny," she said. "You're quite the funny little person."

He fell asleep as he was finishing, so when Meri crossed the porch to Delia's, she was carrying him once again in the bassinet.

The coolness of the house was a welcome relief, and Meri went straight to the living room. She set Asa down, covered him, and went back into the hall to pick up the mail lying on the floor. After she'd put it on the telephone stand, she stood with her back resting against the wall, looking out at the porch and the sun-bleached yard. It all seemed far away, closed up as she was in the humming silence.

While she was standing there, the black town car swung up into the driveway. When it stopped, Len got out and came around to Tom's door. He opened it and reached down to help Tom stand, he moved slowly next to Tom across the bumpy walk. Meri could see that he was talking away as usual, she could hear the faint rise and fall of his voice. He helped Tom up the steps. She opened the door for them, her finger to her lips.

"Baby's sleeping?" Len said softly.

"Yes. Sound asleep," she said.

On his own, Tom went to the lavatory. When he came out, Len, who'd been talking to Meri about someone who'd almost cut him off on the ride home, turned to him. "How 'bout you? You gonna nap?"

Tom shook his head. "No nap. Leehven rhumm." And he started on his way, shaking off Len's hand at his elbow.

"Be quiet in there," Meri said. "Mum's the word."

Tom turned. "You, mum."

"Very funny guy," Len said, grinning. "A regular Groucho."

"See you next week, Len," she said softly, hoping to get him to lower his voice, to leave. But Len wanted to talk. He wanted to describe to her the summers in Queens when he was growing up, the melting tar in the streets, the shimmer of heat above it. It was much, much worse than this, he told her. It was for this reason that he believed none of this global-warming bullshit.

When he'd finally gone, Meri came in and sat down in the chair opposite Tom. "Shall I read?" she asked.

Tom nodded, and she went through several articles from the paper, keeping her voice low. She could sense the impatience in him. She was flipping back to the front page again, looking for another story he might be interested in, when he spoke.

"Fee Ace?" he said. Feed Asa. His fingers moved in pantomime at the buttons of his own shirt.

"Ahh." She made a face and raised her hands, helpless. "He nursed earlier. He'll just sleep now—it's his sleepiest time of the day." She looked down at her son, splayed, utterly relaxed in his bassinet. "He'll be out till early evening."

Tom nodded, his lips pressed together. Then he lifted his hands too, imitating her gesture of regret.

They sat for a moment. She asked him if he'd like her to read again, and he shook his head, *no*.

It was almost embarrassing, the silence. She didn't know what to do. To escape it, she leaned forward and started to read to herself—an article about the FBI's having spied on Leonard Bernstein for years on end.

A minute later, he said, clearly, "For me?"

She looked over at him. He'd lifted one of his hands so it rested, open, turned up—a beggar's gesture—against his chest.

She was still unsure what he meant, and then he made again the motion of unbuttoning his shirt.

"Oh!" Meri said, and sat up. This would change the rules.

Her first instinct was to say no. She was looking across at him, and his eyes held hers.

He *was* behind his eyes, as Delia had once said to her. She could see how much he wanted this—their game, their way of being together.

And in response she felt a pull of interest. She wanted it too. Why? Perhaps, she thought, to feel again the way Tom's gaze made her feel—beautiful, erotic. She was aware suddenly of the weight in her lower abdomen, in her crotch, that signaled sexual readiness to her. So it was that. Of course it was.

But it was also a desire for something they had made together, something that had happened because he was exactly who he was, and because she was in some way *like* him, she thought. Hungry. Greedy.

She sat very straight and smiled at him. She raised her hands to unbutton her blouse.

And with that light touch, her breasts were suddenly as full, as heavy and swollen, as when she was about to nurse. As she finished with the buttons, her blouse fell open and she moved her hands under her breasts. She cupped them, she held them gently.

She was watching Tom's face. His eyes moved over her. The air was cool on her flesh and her nipples shriveled tight. She looked down and saw that drops of milk were beading on their tips. When she slid her hands slowly over them, it spurted out, it wet her hands, it slipped through her moving fingers and down her arms. Tom never stopped watching.

CHAPTER TWENTY-ONE

Delia, Late Afternoon, July 19, 1994

DELIA STOPPED IN town to pick up a bottle of wine and a roast chicken. They'd have a salad too, a cucumber salad with yogurt and garlic and mint, but she had those ingredients at home. She hooked her bag over her shoulder and walked slowly up Main Street in the blistering heat. The secret of this weather was to go slowly, never to rush.

She stopped just before the turn onto Dumbarton to talk to Peggy Williams, her old neighbor, widowed now, who had just put her house on the market. They spoke of the revival of the real estate boom, how helpful it would be to them and how hard on the younger generation. Peggy would move away once the house sold. She was going to live in what was called an *active-adult community* near her son in northern California.

She asked about Tom, and Delia offered the quick version.

"Well, no matter what," Peggy said, "he's alive. That's the important thing."

"For all of us, I would think," Delia said, and they smiled and walked off in their separate directions, Peggy toward town, Delia home.

She was grateful for the deep shade on Dumbarton. She walked slowly, lifting her head to greet the slightly cooler air under the trees. She passed the house that had belonged to the Bowers, the one the

Donahues used to own. Little children were playing in a plastic pool in the driveway, shrieking and splashing.

She turned into her own driveway and went up it. She would pick some mint for the cucumber salad now, she thought. Then once she was in, she could stay in, with Tom, where it was cool.

She set her striped bag down on the back steps and broke off four or five stems of the mint. It had taken over the whole bed on this side of the back door. She should get Matt to pull some of it out. She bent her face to smell it, its fresh scent, before she put her sprigs in her bag and mounted the steps.

The house was cool and utterly still but for the noise of the air conditioner. Perhaps Tom was napping. Perhaps even Meri and the baby had dropped off in the living room. She wouldn't be surprised, in this heat.

She shut the door slowly behind her, hearing the latch click metallically in place with a wince. She set her bag and her keys down carefully on the kitchen table. Her hands still smelled of the mint. She raised them to her face for a moment and inhaled. *Mint,* she thought, *is the smell of happiness.*

She would tell Tom this. She would put her hands to his face and tell him. She walked across the kitchen and into the hallway. How lovely and cool it was in here! She'd have to remember to thank Matt again for the air conditioner when she saw him next.

She moved as quietly as she could in its steady, reassuring hum down the hallway to the living room.

CHAPTER TWENTY-TWO

Meri, February 2007

MERI IS SITTING in the bleacher seats that rise above the indoor pool at Williston High School, waiting for Asa's event to start. She and Henry have barely made it here in time—she was late leaving work, and he dawdled, as usual, leaving preschool. He had to say good-bye to two friends. One, David—his beloved David ("What does he see in the guy?" Meri had asked Nathan not long ago, and they had discussed the improbability of most childhood romances); and Jeff. Jeff, because he was too shy, Henry explained in the car.

"Wait, I didn't know this," Meri said. "So *you're* in charge of the kids who are too shy?"

"No!" he shouted, grinning in delight. He's the only one who still believes in her great wit. Then he sobered. "But *I* am not shy."

Henry is her angel, the last child she will have. She looks over at him. He's large for a three-year-old, sturdy and blond, unlike the older two boys. An enthusiast, unlike them too.

"Yes," she said. "I know that."

It was twenty-one degrees outside, and the heater in the car had only just started to blow tepid air over them when she parked and she and Henry made their dash from the sidewalk into the gym.

In here the air is heavy and warm, the bleachy, clean odor engulfs you, the tiled walls make every noise reverberate. They're calling out the times of the previous race, while those boys, their hair wet, their noses pinked, stand around with towels draped over their shoulders.

But these races don't really count: Asa is a freshman, on the freshman team. The important competitions of the day are over—at this point in the meet, the bleachers are only about a third full. Meri feels that this makes it especially important that some members of the family be there to watch Asa. She and Henry are the only ones today— Nathan has an afternoon class, and Martin, her eleven-year-old, is at his clarinet lesson.

She spots Asa down among the other freshmen, wearing a tiny red Speedo. This is the closest to naked she gets to see him now—he was swamped by modesty at about age twelve. With his own money, he's actually bought a hook and eye for the inside of his door so the younger boys can't barge in on him.

She watches him. He's very tall for his age, like all of their children, and his body is just beginning to widen out a bit after his last spurt of growth, helped by the muscles he's developed swimming. He's fourteen. His voice has changed within the last year, without awkwardness—just slipping lower and lower—and his face is changing too. His jaw is suddenly strong, like Nathan's, and his eyebrows have come in full and dark.

He looks up at the stands and she catches his eye and waves, points to Henry next to her. Asa nods almost imperceptibly, and his eyes shift quickly elsewhere.

Henry has been describing a game to her, describing it at length and in great detail. It's a game he and David invented at preschool. First they were robbers in the game, and then they became super-heroes trapping the robbers—but not like the superheroes he has dolls for, he says, and he lists them and all their superpowers. He and David were a different, a *better* kind of superhero.

"Hold that thought and pay attention," she says. "They're going to start. See?" She turns Henry's head in Asa's direction and points. The gangly boys are lining up, getting ready, shifting their weight from foot to foot and shaking out their hands. Now they hunch over on their starting blocks, and then there's a *pop!* and the noise of their hitting the water, all at once. Yelling fills the room.

She and Henry yell too. It's one of his favorite things to do.

Asa does the breaststroke, that wastefully extravagant way of moving through water. His head and shoulders come heaving up out of the pool with an astonishing circular lift of both his arms, and then the arms disappear underwater, pulling down and back, his body rushing forward. With all this dramatic upper-body motion, the action of the boys' lower bodies is regular, just a steady rocking of their buttocks in and out of the water, a motion that startled Meri when she first saw it, it was so like fucking. Even now she's unable not to take note of it. She wonders whether the boys even think about it, whether they sometimes joke about it with one another.

Asa turns underwater at the end of the pool and comes up again. He's ahead of everyone else, way ahead, which isn't surprising. He's the largest boy in the pool, and a fine swimmer. Nathan taught him. He's taught all the boys. Even Henry can do the crawl better than Meri, who didn't learn to swim until she was an adult.

"Ace! Ace! Beat *all* of the others, Ace!" Henry yells.

"Come on, baby," Meri calls out. "Go, go, go, go!"

Everyone is yelling, whistling, clapping. A girl on the bench directly below them is standing, stomping her feet frenziedly and squealing in what sounds like either pain or ecstasy. The din in the tiled space is overwhelming. Henry laughs in joy.

At the second-to-last lap, someone else on the Williston team starts to catch up to Asa. He actually makes the final turn only a second or two after him, but Asa pulls ahead easily at the close, and then suddenly he's hanging at the end of the pool, panting, grinning up at his coach and waiting to hear his time amid the screams of the crowd.

When the meet is over, Asa disappears with the other boys into the showers. Henry and Meri bundle up before they go out to the car and start home. Asa will come home on his bike.

In the car Henry says, "My throat is *burned* from my yelling."

"Mine too."

He's quiet a minute. Then he says, "Why do you call Asa your baby? He's not a baby."

She looks at him. He's frowning under his thatch of blond hair, hair she still trims herself, at home. "Who *is* a baby?" she asks. "Are you my baby?"

"No. You don't even *have* a baby."

"Ah, but you used to be my baby. Even Asa was my baby once upon a time."

"But that was too long ago."

"Well, you're right. I should just cut it out, shouldn't I?"

"Yes, you should," he says, sternly.

They drive along. Meri is thinking, as she does at least several times a week, of Asa as a baby, thinking of him with the usual pang of sorrow for how little she was able to give to him then, to do for him. Her love for the other two boys as newborns was instant and complete—she was ready to adore them even as they emerged, bloody and gummy, from her body. But she had to learn those feelings slowly and reluctantly with Asa, and she's never stopped feeling guilty for what he missed out on. When Nathan wanted to have a second child, Meri had at first resisted, out of that guilt, out of the sense that Asa should have all of her love forevermore because she was so incapable of loving him at the start, so frightened and closed in.

But Nathan had prevailed, and they'd had Martin, and then much later Henry—like Asa an accident: she was forty-eight at the time, careless about contraception because she thought those days were over for her. And each of the younger boys had made Meri more generous, more profligate with her love, just as Nathan had predicted. Each of them had made her love Asa more, and then more again.

But not just Asa. She had also felt, in the universe she and Nathan made with the boys, that she was somehow revising her own childhood too, giving herself retroactively a sense of safety, of encirclement she'd never had then.

She pulls into the driveway. Nathan's bike, and Martin's too, are leaned against the side of the house. The windows on the first floor blaze with light. When she and Henry come into the living room, she can hear Nathan's voice in the kitchen. They leave their coats on the hooks Nathan installed by the front door. She helps Henry off with his boots, and they head down the hall.

Nathan has already started supper. He greets them both, a kiss for Meri, a high five for Henry. "Did Asa win?" he asks, turning back to her.

"He did."

"Asa won?" Martin says, looking up from a book he's reading at the kitchen table. He wears glasses and looks geekier than either of the other boys. He *is* kind of a geek—but oddly, given this, he's enormously popular. When the phone rings, none of the rest of them bothers to answer it if Martin's around, it's always so likely to be for him.

"Easily," she says.

"What was his time?" Nathan asks.

"That I couldn't tell you. You'll have to wait and ask him when he gets home. What are we having for dinner?" She smells garlic and onions, and he has the big kettle on.

"Spaghetti," he says.

"Spaghetti!" Henry yells. "Spaghetti! Spaghetti!" He dances around the cooking area of the kitchen. "I. Love. Spaghetti!"

"Henry!" Nathan calls. "Hen! Henry, hold it down." He points to the party wall, the wall their neighbors, the Switalskis, live behind. Live behind *quietly,* as Meri and Nathan often point out. They have two little girls, six-year-old twins who seem to be completely orderly children, acoustically barely there.

Meri leans over Nathan's shoulder as he stirs some sausage meat into the sizzling onions, breaking it up with the wooden spoon. She asks him about his day. She tells him about hers.

Nathan says, "I bought a *Times,* and the *Register*"—the local paper. "This'll take me at least a half an hour, if you want to sit down and read for a while."

"I will, I think. I haven't stopped since this morning." She goes into their living room. She sits down and looks quickly at the front page of the *Times*. More horror stories from Iraq. She can't bear to read them.

In the kitchen she can hear Henry's voice going up and down, dramatic endings on every sentence. Nathan only has to murmur something occasionally to keep him going.

She skims through the Arts section, finds a pen, and does the crossword puzzle. It's easy today, a Tuesday. By Friday it's hard for her, and she hardly ever even tries Saturday. Then she opens the *Register* and flips quickly through it, skimming a few articles. When she comes to the obituaries, her hands stop and she makes a little noise.

It's Delia, her face smiling back at Meri.

It's a photograph taken perhaps in her early middle age, but it's unmistakably Delia. The headline is "Senator's Wife Dies at 89."

Meri feels the deep pounding of her heart. She reads through the obituary once, almost breathless, barely taking in the facts presented. Then she forces herself to read it again, more slowly. But even this second time, trying to understand the details, what she's mostly thinking of is the last time she saw Delia, the awful scene that ended everything.

TOM'S FACE, which had been heavy-lidded and rapt watching her, had suddenly changed, his eyes shifting past her, widening. Meri turned, her hands still on her breasts, and saw Delia. Delia, frozen, her mouth dropped open, her eyes wild.

Meri isn't sure what she did first—maybe she tried to pull her blouse closed, maybe she started to get up. She remembers that across the room, Tom was struggling to stand too. When she looked around at Delia again, the old woman had backed up a few steps, her face terrible to see—and then she turned and vanished down the hall.

Meri got back to the kitchen within seconds. Delia already had her purse, her keys, and she was at the opened door. Meri started to speak, to say something, but she was aware at the same moment of Tom's voice in the house behind her, his strange noise, his cry: "Dheee!"

What Delia said to Meri was "No words. Not one word." Her face was ravaged, but fierce. Her hand was up, her fingers spread: *stop.* And then she was gone.

Meri stood stupidly, not moving for a moment. Then she followed, out into the bright, hot sunlight. She caught up to Delia, saying . . . what? She can't remember. *Delia, this isn't what you think. Delia, please come back.* It didn't matter what. It was just *words,* as Delia said.

They reached the end of the driveway. Delia had said nothing to her, hadn't even looked at her, but her mouth was open and moving. She was breathing noisily and irregularly, a kind of *hysterical breathing*, Meri would have said, if she'd ever spoken of this moment to anyone. Meri touched Delia's arm and the old woman jerked herself away, spinning to face her.

"*Get back there,*" she said. She pointed, and Meri looked back and saw Tom just starting toward them down the sunstruck driveway— no walker, no cane, just his slow, perilously uneven lurch. "It's your mess now," Delia said. Her voice was shrill. "Get back there and see if you can fix it, fix what you've done."

She turned and walked quickly down Dumbarton toward Main Street.

Meri had stopped, she couldn't go any farther. Asa was back there, alone in Delia's house, asleep. And behind her Tom cried out again, a long, deep wail—as Delia moved rapidly away far down the street, her figure seeming to bob under the dappled shade of the trees. Meri watched her for a moment.

Then she turned and went slowly back up the driveway to Tom.

SHE LIED TO NATHAN. She never thought for a moment of not lying, of telling the truth. She was lying to save herself, to save herself and Nathan together, to save Asa. She was lying for all of them. Tom, listening, said nothing to contradict her. What she told Nathan was that she had just finished nursing Asa, that Delia had arrived and misunderstood what was happening.

Nathan had believed her. He had sided with her, he had been sympathetic and supportive. Weeks later, when they were going over all of it again—as they did repeatedly during that time—he said, "So maybe to her way of thinking he wasn't maimed *enough*."

It was the first time either of them had spoken of it with anything approaching distance, much less levity, and Meri felt a simultaneous sense of gratitude to Nathan, and loss. Loss, because he'd moved that far away from it already, far enough away to make a joke—and she knew that she couldn't. That she wouldn't, ever.

She reads the obituary yet again, this time finally forcing herself to imagine it, the way the rest of Delia's life has played out.

The cause of death isn't given, but the obituary says that Delia died in an assisted-living home in Denver.

Near Nancy then. This saddens Meri. She'd met Nancy. She remembers Tom's word for her—*formidable*—and the little shudder of mock fear he'd given after he said it. She knows enough to surmise that it must have been hard for Delia to end her life in Nancy's care.

But the obituary says she'd been living in Paris until two years before her death; it tells of her love for all things French. It mentions the Apthorp house, and speaks of her part in making it a museum.

It says also that she grew up in the small town of Watkins, Maine, where her father was headmaster at a boys' school. That she went to Smith College. That she was married to Thomas Naughton in 1940. That he later was a member of the House of Representatives for two terms, and then a senator for two terms also. That in Washington Delia was known for her beauty and charm, her wit. That parties at the Naughtons' house were coveted invitations.

That she is survived by three children, seven grandchildren, and four great-grandchildren.

That she and the senator had lived separately after his second campaign for the Senate, though they never divorced. That he predeceased her, in 1998.

But Meri knew that. She and Nathan had been in bed, reading the paper, when Nathan came across that obituary. Wordlessly, he'd held it up in front of her. The photo of Tom's young, eager face had made Meri remember his expression in Delia's living room, watching her.

And then, as now, the other memories flooded her. His mostly silent dinner with them the night that Delia left, a meal during which they kept reassuring him that she would come back, that surely she'd call. He had seemed to seize on this, repeating it, as a child would. Meri had seized on it too, silently. Of course Delia would call. She'd forgiven Tom so much already. She loved him. This couldn't be the end of all that. It wasn't possible that Meri could have set such a thing in motion.

Nathan went over to help Tom get to bed, to spend the night. He slept on the living room couch—he told Meri he wouldn't have felt comfortable going upstairs, poking around up there to find a place to sleep. He'd gotten Tom up the next morning and brought him over for breakfast before Len came to pick him up. They were sure she'd call today, they told him.

But she didn't. And she wasn't there by that evening either, when Matt came over to say he had to get going.

Once again Tom stayed with them for dinner. Once again Nathan went over to help get him to bed. After he'd fallen asleep though, Nathan came home for a while to talk with Meri about what course of action they ought to take. They were sitting in the kitchen still trying to decide this when Nancy called. Meri answered the phone.

Nancy said her mother was with a friend in Washington. That she had decided—"*finally*," Nancy said, with heavy emphasis—that it was too much for her, that she couldn't manage Tom's needs by herself.

She said that for now she had arranged for Tom to go back to Putnam as a resident. The driver would take him there tomorrow. She was calling to ask if they would be willing to pack a few days' worth of clothes and toiletries to go with him. She'd be very grateful. She was already very grateful to them for stepping in with Tom over these last few days. She herself would come east over the weekend and do the rest of what needed to get done.

Yes, Meri said. No, no, it wasn't an imposition. No, they'd be happy to.

Nathan had done it, the packing. He'd gone back over that night to stay with Tom again, and in the morning, while he put the old man's things in a suitcase, he explained to Tom what was happening. Tom came over and had breakfast with them for the last time, and then Len arrived and led him out to the car.

Meri had already said good-bye, and she stayed in the house, watching their slow progress down the stairs and over to the driveway. At the last minute, though, she ran after them. "Tom," she called. They were at the car, Len had opened the door.

Tom turned to face her. He seemed more hunched over; he looked abruptly years older, years weaker.

She could feel her eyes fill with tears. Len was speaking to her cheerfully, but she paid no attention to him. "I wanted to say good-bye," she said to Tom.

He nodded. "Unh," he said.

She put her hand on his arm. It felt bony, the flesh felt loose. She couldn't remember ever having touched him before. "I'm sorry," she said. "I'm just *so* . . . so sorry."

He shook his head, and then he smiled—his amused, wry smile, that small pursed twist of his mouth. "Noo," he said. His hand rose to rest flat on his chest, and then he struck himself there. "*Mhea* culpa!" he said, clearly, still smiling at her.

"Ha! See?" Len said to Meri. "You can take the boy outta the church, but you can't take the church outta the boy." He helped Tom into the car.

Meri stood in the driveway and watched the sleek black car back down the driveway and make its turn. She watched until it moved out of sight.

Tom's obituary had said that he died in a hospice in Washington, of a long illness. It focused mostly on his career in government, his then-unpopular resistance to the forms the antipoverty movement took under Sargent Shriver. Delia was mentioned as surviving him, she was called the wife from whom he'd been separated for a long time.

Meri is sitting, looking at nothing, having set the paper down. She thinks again of Delia's face in the terrible moment of her discovery, and then of all that happened after she left. She remembers Nancy's arrival that weekend, grim, satisfied, packing her father's possessions up, and some of her mother's too. She remembers the slow emptying out of the house in the months that followed before it was put up for sale, the various visits by Brad and Evan, the rental van Brad drove, the moving trucks that came to take things to Evan, to Nancy.

She remembers going over there alone once that fall on a night when Nathan was off at a meeting. She remembers standing, weeping, in the emptied-out rooms. She remembers the way her cries echoed in the dark.

Henry comes out from the kitchen. "Sing to me, Momma," he says, as he climbs onto her lap.

"Shall I?" she says. She feels that he's calling her back, that she's still far, far away.

"Yeah."

"What shall I sing?"

"Sing 'Pay My Money.'"

This is a song from a Bruce Springsteen CD that Nathan brought home recently. Henry has fallen in love with it.

Meri starts, her voice soft and croaky at first. "Well I thought I heard the captain say, / 'Pay me my money down. / Pay me or go to jail . . .'"

Asa rescues her after a verse or two, coming in the front door, dropping his backpack on the floor. "Hey," he says. His face is red and chapped-looking. His eyes are teary and pink-rimmed from the cold. He takes his hat off, his mittens and coat.

Henry has sat up. "We seen you win, Ace," he says. "We yelled and yelled."

"Yeah, I heard you up there." He grins at Henry.

Henry slides off Meri's lap and goes to Asa. He drapes himself around one of Asa's legs—that's how much smaller, how much younger he is than his brother. "Ace is the winner!" he yells.

"You were great, honey," Meri says.

"Yeah, well, I'm *starving*," Asa says. He starts back toward the kitchen, pulling Henry along.

"I'm starving too!" Henry cries.

Feeling numb, distracted, Meri follows them. In the kitchen, she gets out a tablecloth and sails it open over the kitchen table. She gathers utensils from the drawer and moves around the table, setting them in place.

The boys leave to wash their hands. Meri thinks of telling Nathan about Delia now, but she doesn't. She doesn't because she knows he'll be sympathetic, sympathetic to *her*—he'll remember what he understood of her sorrow at the time, of her guilt, and he'll think of it as being compounded, being redoubled now, by Delia's death.

And it isn't. It just isn't, she doesn't know why.

She looks at him, grating cheese now, his big hands in motion, his hair swaying with each push. Nathan.

The boys come back, wiping their wet hands on their jeans, and they all sit down. Nathan serves the spaghetti, and they pass the pasta dishes around the table. He starts to sing: "Oh, *Muss*-olini was so proud, was-so-proud. / He *ate* spaghetti long and loud, long-and-loud. / He used to *wind* it round and *round* . . ."

The boys' braying drowns him out. They've heard it before—many times before. Almost every time they have spaghetti.

"Shh, shh, shh," Meri says. "Let's be quiet. Let's be elegant."

They start to eat. "But what *is* elegant?" Henry asks after a minute.

"Elegant is behaving terribly well. Is being polite. Is saying please and thank you."

"All the *time*?" Henry asks.

"Whenever appropriate," Nathan says.

Martin asks to have the Parmesan cheese passed to him.

"Please," Meri says.

"Please, please, please, please," Martin says, making his voice whiny.

"What is *appropriate*?" Henry asks.

Meri explains while Nathan asks Asa about the meet. They talk about that, about Asa's chances of getting on the varsity team next year. About Henry's burned throat from cheering him on.

Martin asks Meri if she'll go over his lines with him after dinner. He's in a play at the college—he has the only *kid* part in it—and he dreamed last night that he got onstage and couldn't remember anything. He couldn't even recognize his cues. "And in the dream everyone was trying to help me, whispering them so loud it was like screaming, but it didn't help. I still couldn't remember them."

"Everybody has those dreams, honey," Meri says. "It doesn't mean anything."

Nathan talks about a dream he once had in which he was giving a lecture with notes that turned out to be in some unrecognizable hieroglyphic language.

"What's hydroglippic?" Henry asks.

Asa explains. He gets up for some paper, and draws various glyphs he invents for Henry, in the end making a sentence with an eye, a heart, and a soccer ball, a sentence that Henry reads out loud with delight several times over.

After supper they clean up. In the living room, Meri goes over Martin's lines with him. Nathan has gone up to his study, and Asa is doing his homework on the dining room table. Henry sits across the living room, earplugs in, listening to songs only he can hear on his portable CD player. By himself—a matter of pride—he's changed into his pajamas, an old pair, almost worn out, that have come down from Martin, and before him from Asa. Meri can remember Asa in those pajamas, remember the ways in which he was exactly himself, even at Henry's age, completely different from the way Henry is now, and from Martin at that age too—grave and always anxious about being good, about pleasing her. Henry, unworried about any of that, occasionally sings a phrase out loud while he waits for Meri to put him to bed.

When Martin feels safe with his lines, Meri takes Henry upstairs and reads him two picture books. He leans more and more heavily against her. She turns off the light and lies beside him as his breathing slows and deepens. She's thinking, as she has on and off throughout the evening, of Delia, of Delia and Tom, and of herself, then. That Meri, the Meri who had known them, who had cared so much about what their story was, about their history, about what they thought about her—the Meri who had so carelessly wrecked their lives—that version of herself seems impossibly far away, her life is so absolutely *here,* so bound up with the boys and Nathan.

She can remember feeling then that she and Nathan would have no story in the sense that Delia and Tom did, no parallel deep currents of love between them. She had thought she knew already what their marriage was, what its limits were. She had thought they were *in* it. She didn't know they'd barely begun. She couldn't have imagined the long, slow processes that would change them, change what they felt for each other. She would never have guessed, either, the way the children would remake them and their love.

Once, recently, as she and Nathan collapsed into bed at the end of the day and then lay there next to each other, neutered by fatigue, waiting only for sleep, that *summum bonum,* she jokingly said to him, "Think we're a match made in heaven, Natey?"

He didn't answer for a moment, and she thought he'd dropped

off. But then he turned and touched her face. "I think we're a match made right here on earth, in this very house."

That feels right, and true to Meri—that it is the things she and Nathan have lived through here, with each other and the children, that have made them who they are, and who they are together.

BUT TOM AND DELIA were a part of that for her, she's thinking now. They changed her also, they had a role in fitting her for the life she has now.

She had, she knows, *wanted* Delia to change her. She had sought Delia out, she had thought she could learn from her. She had even thought she could learn from the private story of Delia's life, from the letters from Tom that she went through. Meri remembers Delia's face when she said that life teaches you you can endure anything, when she said you needed to forgive yourself. It always seemed to Meri that she was about to understand something large and important about how to *be* in the world from Delia.

But in the end she has come to think it was Tom who changed her more, who gave her something, something that she didn't know she needed. It's the memories of him that have stayed with her, that have come back to her most clearly, most often. Over and over in those few odd afternoons she shared with him, he seemed to be inviting her to smile, to laugh with him. She remembers it all—the humor in his eyes, the gentle comedy in the gestures he made to her. The day he thanked her with his hand on his chest, the day he raised his finger to his lips. She remembers. She remembers his acting out Asa's greed, his funny protest of the milk that had spurted from her all over him. She remembers laughing with Tom then, laughing at him. Laughing at Asa for the first time. Even—yes—laughing at herself. She remembers that Tom made her feel whole, happy. That he made her feel beautiful.

"Mea culpa," he had said after Delia left, and that was a great, generous gift to her. But he was smiling when he said it, and that was perhaps the greater gift.

Henry stirs beside her in the bed. "Blue," he says, or something like it. She looks down at his sleeping face, restored to near-infancy in its utter relaxation. Carefully she slides her body off the bed, slowly she gets up. She crosses the room, steps into the hall and closes Henry's door behind her. She stands in the hallway, listening. Martin is going over one of his lines again in his room, repeating it, trying different emphases. Asa has music on low downstairs. She can hear the dining room chair creak as he shifts his weight in it. Henry is in his bed, Nathan is in his study. She has the sense of her life surrounding her, of being held in it. Of belonging here.

She thinks of the photo of Delia again, and she remembers her desperation trying to talk to her, trying to explain herself. And of course, there was probably nothing she could have said that would have changed anything then. She had done what she had done.

But what she would have told Delia if she had had the words then for what she has come to feel over the years, what she would have said—and she would swear that this is true—is that she did what she did with Tom that day for love. Out of love.

B L O O M S B U R Y

Also available by Sue Miller

While I was Gone

An Oprah Book Club selection and a *New York Times* bestseller

Perhaps it's best to live with the possibility that around any corner, at any time, may come the person who reminds you of your own capacity to surprise yourself, to put at risk everything that's dear to you...

Thirty years ago Jo Becker's bohemian life ended when she found her best friend brutally murdered. Now Jo has everything: work she loves, a devoted husband, three grown daughters and a beautiful home. But when an old friend settles in her small town, the fabric of Jo's life begins to unravel, as she enters a relationship that returns her to the darkest moments of her past, imperilling all that she loves.

'A moving story of secrets and lies'
The Times

'An astonishing mix of the warm, complex and frightening ... the stuff of real life that is rarely conveyed in fiction'
Julie Myerson, *Mail on Sunday*

'Beautiful and frightening ... difficult to forget'
New York Times Book Review

ISBN: 978 0 7475 9926 5 / Paperback / £7.99

BLOOMSBURY

For Love

Lottie is relieved to have escaped to her mother's house for the summer
because her second marriage, barely begun, is in trouble. Also at home is
Cameron, Lottie's brother, who has been in love with their neighbour
Elizabeth since high school. Elizabeth is married with three children but
now, finally, Elizabeth and Cameron embark on a passionate affair.
But as Lottie, Cameron and Elizabeth are reunited, a senseless tragedy
befalls them, and Lottie is forced to examine the consequences of what
she has done for love.

'Absolutely flawless ... Extraordinary'
Anne Tyler

'A tour de force by any standards ... One reason for Miller's popularity is
that she earns her fans in a time-honoured way: she writes for readers'
Newsweek

'*For Love* may be the most honest twentieth-century
love story we've had in a while'
New York Times Book Review

ISBN: 978 0 7475 9504 5 / Paperback / £7.99

BLOOMSBURY

Lost in the Forest

One minute John is the cornerstone of Eva's world, rock to his two
teenage stepdaughters and his own son Theo, the next he is tossed
through the air in a traffic accident, and snapped like a twig. His sudden
death changes everything. Eva struggles with the terror and desolation
of loneliness, and finds herself drawn back to her untrustworthy
ex-husband; Emily, the eldest daughter, grapples with her new-found
independence and responsibility. Little Theo can only begin to fathom
the permanence of his father's death. But for Daisy, John's absence
opens up a whole world of confusion just at the onset of adolescence
and blossoming sexuality. And in steps a man only too willing to take
advantage.

'Sue Miller brings unusual skill in the exploration
of women's hopes and regrets'
Daily Telegraph

'Miller's novel may be firmly rooted in the domestic, but its dreamy,
mesmeric prose gives this tale of grief and loss the quality of a fable'
Daily Mail

'Meticulously observed and utterly gripping'
Marie Claire

ISBN: 978 0 7475 7898 7 / Paperback / £7.99

BLOOMSBURY

The World Below

Catherine Hubbard is at a crossroads in her life. Twice divorced, she has three children who are now grown up and scattered. Then news comes that she has inherited her grandmother Georgia's home in Vermont. There, Catherine finds not only the ghosts of her own past but those of Georgia as well, whose diaries reveal a deep secret and a tragic misunderstanding. This stunning novel captures a world of lost possibilities, exploring the hopes and regrets that lie buried in the hearts of women.

'Beautifully written ... full of insight and poignancy'
Daily Mirror

'A beautiful, wistful meditation on the concept of home'
Elle

'Masterful storytelling'
Good Housekeeping

ISBN: 978 0 7475 8462 9 / Paperback / £7.99

BLOOMSBURY

The Distinguished Guest

At the age of seventy-two, Lily Roberts became a national celebrity on writing her first book – a spiritual memoir. But her new-found fame was not well received by her son Alan and wayward daughter Clary, both profoundly disturbed by Lily's intimate revelations about her married life. Ten years on their resentment is still raw, and when Lily, now ill and frail, comes to live with Alan, the bitter legacy of their very different memories threatens to upset the precarious balance of their lives.

'Miller depicts her characters with grace and elegance, enriching their perceptions with strands of connecting images and intertwined history ... A very moving book'
New York Times Book Review

'Wonderful – rich, intelligent and moving'
Los Angeles Times

'Miller's skill at dissecting relationships is as well-honed here as ever'
Newsweek

ISBN: 978 0 7475 8464 3 / Paperback / £7.99

BLOOMSBURY

The Story of my Father

In the spring of 1986, Sue Miller found herself more and more deeply involved in caring for her father as he slipped into the grasp of Alzheimer's disease. *The Story of My Father* is a profound, deeply moving account of her father's final days and her own response to it. With care, restraint and consummate skill, Miller writes of her struggles to be fully with her father in his illness while confronting her own terror of abandonment, and eventually the long, hard work of grieving for him. And through this candid, painful record, she offers a rigorous, compassionate inventory of two lives, a powerful meditation on the variable nature of memory and the difficulty of weaving a truthful narrative from the threads of a dissolving life.

'Beautifully written and moving ... Every relative of an Alzheimer's patient feels this guilt, here painfully anatomised ... *The Story of My Father* is the best book of its genre I have ever read'
Sunday Telegraph

'Much more than a memoir, her book is an exploration of the nature of self and an extraordinary testament to an extraordinary love'
Independent

'Remarkable for its honesty and courage, and for the muted gallantry with which its subject met the loss of everything that made him human'
Daily Telegraph

ISBN: 978 0 7475 6522 2 / Paperback / £7.99